ANNABELLE

ANNIE WESTPHAL
228 Park Ave S
PMB 39750
New York, NY
10003

ISBN 978-1-7372680-1-7 (trade paperback)

All inquiries contact admin@anniewestphal.com

For more information visit www.anniewestphal.com

Cover Design by Kim Dingwall
Map created using Map Effects from mapeffects.co

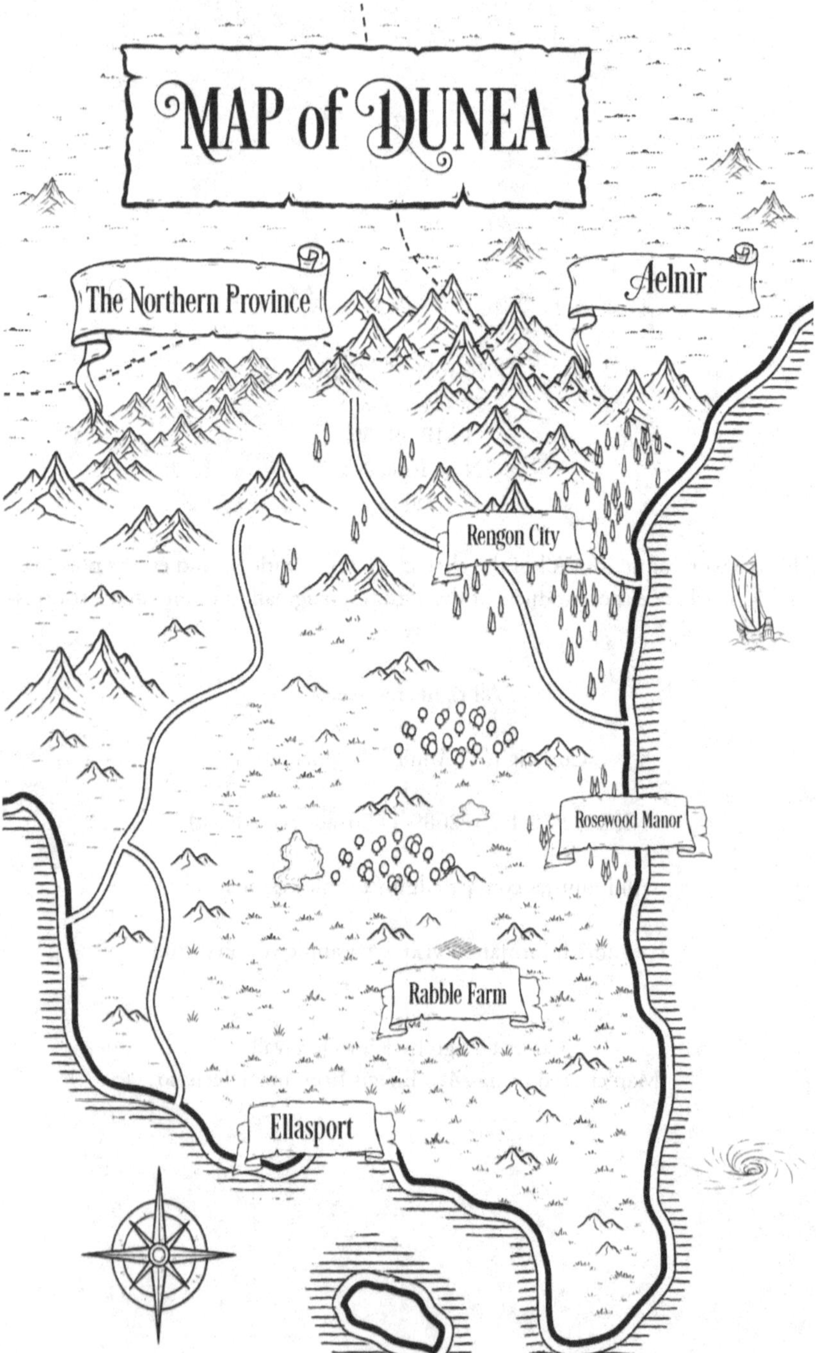

MAP of DUNEA

The Northern Province

Aelnìr

Rengon City

Rosewood Manor

Rabble Farm

Ellasport

For my mother,
who gave me the gift of stories

Chapter One

Another peal of thunder sounded, but it was far off by now. Annabelle watched as the wind blew the storm away across the churning slate-gray waters of the sea—the last in a string of storms that had battered the coast for days. The salt air that snaked through the gap in the shutters was soothingly cool as it kissed her cheeks. The unseasonable heat of early spring had at last broken, and now they might have some relief; relief from the heat and the raging storms, in any case.

Annabelle sighed and settled back in the chair she had dragged up beside the window so that she could watch the giant black clouds roll off into the distance. She loved storms. Having her own way, Annabelle would have been down on the cliffs while the wind and rain raged, arms spread wide, with her face turned up into the spray. Aunt Penelope always said that if she continued to dare the Gods, they might one day strike her down. Annabelle thought she would have liked to see them try.

But there was no standing on the cliffs, no rain-soaked skin, or wind tangled hair. Annabelle was safe and dry behind the walls of Rosewood Manor, as she had been for a long time. She had been only five years old: terrified and confused by her mother's sudden and tragic death. With its high stone walls covered with creeping ivy, the manor had seemed cold and strange to her fearful young eyes. But the baron and baroness had been kind and patient, and now, Rosewood Manor felt more like home than stories of a faraway palace.

A bolt of lightning forked down from the heavens, appearing to touch the horizon. Annabelle yawned, fatigue pawing at her. As the sound of the storm grew fainter and fainter, so too did the energy seep from her heavy and sorrowful body. It had been, to be perfectly fair, a very long day.

It had begun early, with the unannounced arrival of Annabelle's aunt at the manor. She was actually Annabelle's great-aunt. "The Duchess," as the entire kingdom knew and called the old woman, had been the old king's favorite sister. Not having been blessed with children of her own, she had decided to mother everyone else instead. The Duchess was the moral backbone of the Isren family and ensured everyone did their duty to the realm.

She had arrived in her stately carriage before breakfast, and the entire family had dragged themselves from bed to greet her—all save Lady Ellen. She was far too weak to leave her rooms. Nobody would find fault with Lady Ellen. Not now. Not after everything that had happened.

A sound in the corridor drew Annabelle's attention from the window. She rose from her seat as a maid entered her bedchamber. She was a slight girl and shorter than Annabelle by a full head, with soft brown eyes and mousy hair that poked out in wisps beneath her white cap.

Red-rimmed eyes roved the room and settled on Annabelle. The girl rushed forward.

Annabelle caught the maid in an embrace and held her tightly as she cried. "Oh, Emily," Annabelle sighed, rubbing her gently on the back. "Shh. It's alright."

Emily pulled away, wiping at her face and sniffing. "B-but it-it isn't alright," She hiccuped.

"No," Annabelle amended sadly. "I don't think it will be alright for a long time."

"How was it?" Emily asked when she'd gotten a hold of her composure.

"The funeral?" Annabelle hesitated. "It…was fine."

Emily raised a skeptical eyebrow. "That bad?"

Annabelle's face fell. "Oh, I'm sure you can imagine. Somber. Official. Appropriately tragic. He would have hated it."

"Yes," Emily agreed. "It sounds like he would have. The baron was a man of the open sky. They should have had the ceremony by the sea or in the forest."

"We've been over this already, Emily," Annabelle said patiently. "We all know it was what he wanted, but with the storms and…everything," She sighed. "It was decided that the temple would be more appropriate."

Emily's expression darkened, and she snorted derisively. "And I've told you already that I don't believe it. I think this was all about appearances and *some people* not wanting to get wet. Well, I don't care. If *some* people had a problem with getting wet, *some* people could have stayed home."

"Careful. You wouldn't want anyone to overhear you talking about your new lord and master that way," Annabelle warned, but she was grinning.

Emily scoffed, her little nose scrunched up in a way that made her look a bit like a piglet. "Like I care. Besides, he won't be my lord and master for long. I'd rather go back to the farm and spend my days chasing after chickens than bringing Gustav his supper."

"You hate chickens," Annabelle pointed out.

Emily shrugged. "I'd take chickens over him any day. At least you can kick chickens if they're rude to you."

Laughing, Annabelle lay a gentle hand on her friend's shoulder. "Sleep on it," she urged. "But I have to tell you now if you kick Gustav and I'm not there to see it, I will never forgive you."

Emily giggled and opened her mouth to say something in response, but a knock on the door interrupted her, and she rushed to answer it.

Franc, the butler, stood on the threshold, wringing his hands and looking harassed. "The Duchess has requested that you join her for tea," he said to Annabelle without preamble. "And I think you'd better hurry, Princess. It's nearly past the hour."

Annabelle groaned. After the tragic events of the day, tea with Aunt Penelope sounded about as pleasant as chewing on rocks. "Is she already in the library?" Annabelle asked Franc.

"She is," he replied with a sympathetic look.

"Of course she is," Annabelle muttered darkly.

"I'll escort you if you like," Franc offered, though he did not look delighted by the idea.

"No, that's alright, Franc," Annabelle said kindly. "You deal with the tea; I'll deal with my dear aunt."

And with one last lingering look out the window, Annabelle turned her back on the sea and sky, taking with her only the cool kiss of salt air that still tingled upon her cheeks.

)))●(((

The library was Annabelle's favorite room in the manor. Its tall mullioned windows always provided plenty of light for reading and looked out onto the garden and Lady Ellen's impressive rosebushes. The shelves were spaced at intervals that created little alcoves with overstuffed armchairs that provided plenty of privacy if one wanted to relax or hide.

The Duchess preferred to take her tea in this room rather than the formal parlor. This eccentricity greatly distressed the servants. Due to the unexpected nature of her visits, Lord Roger ordered Franc to have a table and chairs moved into a corner of the library permanently. This change significantly reduced the poor butler's anxiety.

In that corner, Annabelle found her aunt, Penelope Penberthy, Grand Duchess of Walthon Down.

The Duchess was a severe, forbidding woman who sat ramrod straight on her little chair. She wore her usual gown of black silk and laces, fastened at its high collar by a large emerald brooch, twin to the one that adorned the pommel of the cane she clutched in her gnarled hands. Her white hair was twisted into an elegant knot at the back of her head, not a single strand out of place. She regarded Annabelle frankly over spectacles perched at the end of her long straight nose.

"Hello, Aunt," Annabelle said, sliding onto her own chair.

"You look flushed," the Duchess said by way of greeting. "Are you ill?"

"I feel fine, Aunt," Annabelle replied.

The Duchess's eyes narrowed, taking in Annabelle's disheveled appearance. If she thought Annabelle looked like she had spent the last hour hanging out of an upstairs window like a piece of laundry on the line—which, admittedly, was true—she did not say. Thankfully, Emily appeared at that moment carrying the tea tray. Annabelle supposed Franc was still hiding in the kitchen.

Annabelle eyed the little plate of sandwiches hungrily. There had been nothing at all to eat since breakfast, and Annabelle was ravenous. When the tea had been poured and Emily had gone, Annabelle snatched up a sandwich. She munched it happily as the Duchess helped herself to cream.

The two women drank their tea in silence. Annabelle did not feel pressure to speak. This was always the way with her aunt: first tea, then talk.

"This has been a sad day," the Duchess said frankly when she finally placed her empty cup upon its saucer. "A terrible and sad day."

"Yes," Annabelle agreed.

"Damon mentioned to me in passing that you have been a great comfort to the family," the Duchess continued. "I was glad to hear it."

"As am I," Annabelle said, feeling a lump form in her throat.

Damon Wallace was the younger of Lord Roger's two sons and, though he was nearly eight years her senior, he and Annabelle had become close friends. When Damon earned his knighthood, the king sent him back to the manor to serve as Annabelle's personal guard. Still, it was Annabelle who felt more in service, and gratitude, to this family that had given her a safe place to live and to grow up.

"The Baron and Baroness have been so good to me," Annabelle continued. "I have tried my best not to give them a reason to regret it."

"They have sheltered you and raised you well," the Duchess agreed, nodding. "Lord Roger's passing must be as hard on you as it is for his own children."

Tears welled in Annabelle's eyes, and one rolled down her cheek. She swiped it away. "He was...I cared for him a great deal, yes."

It was as much of the truth as Annabelle could say aloud. In fact, Lord Roger had been the only father Annabelle had ever known. She barely remembered her true father, King Alexander, as she had not seen him once since her mother died. To Annabelle, he was simply the king—a symbol of the legacy that she was born to and expected to uphold. Lord Roger had taught Annabelle to ride a horse, wiped away her tears when she was sad or hurt, and filled her childhood memories with the sound of booming laughter.

He had always been present, not a fading memory or a fantasy in her mind. He had been real and strong and full of life, and now he was gone.

"It is a particular kind of tragedy when such a great man is felled so young," the Duchess went on. "I admit, my memory is not what it used to be, and I find I am still...confused about the events of that day. I would appreciate it if you could answer some of my questions."

Annabelle frowned. She did not believe the nonsense about her aunt's fading memory for one minute. The woman had the eyes of a hawk and a memory more air-tight than the legendary vaults of Pharos. She missed nothing, forgot nothing. There was a purpose behind her questions, and Annabelle was in no mood for her aunt's games, not today.

"Forgive me, Aunt. But is now really the time?" she asked. "Lord Roger's funeral was barely an hour ago. I don't want to revisit those memories. It's already too sad a day."

The look the Duchess gave her was stern with reproach. "Annabelle, we are royals," she said imperiously. "We do not have the luxury to lose our heads in times of distress or tragedy. This is your lesson for today."

A lesson. Today. Annabelle felt so foolish for not seeing it coming. The Duchess had a lesson for every day, every moment in life, no matter how painful or inconvenient.

"Yes, Annabelle, your lesson," the Duchess repeated, reading her thoughts, "and this one is perhaps the most important of them all. You are the crown princess of Dunea. One day, if the Gods will it, you will be queen, and you will bear that responsibility whether you face stormy waters or under clear skies."

"Is a queen not even allowed the privilege of grief?" Annabelle demanded, furious with her aunt now for shoving this subject down her throat when she was already raw with sorrow.

"Your heart may grieve," the Duchess said patiently, "but your mind must always remain clear. Your father, the king, understood this when he sent you away. Your mother was gone, and you had no one to care for you. You would have grown up alone in the castle surrounded by courtiers who would seek to use you for their own ends. Instead, he sent you here to have a childhood, to be free and loved. He did this because, though his grief over your mother's passing was fathomless, he had responsibilities. The rebellion in the north rages on, and he is where he ought to be—leading his kingdom, free from distraction."

Distraction. The word cut; Annabelle had been a distraction. Her mother had been warm and kind, and she loved Annabelle with all her being. Even when the queen was alive—where had her father been? Annabelle had grown up hearing this story, the sacrifice her father made to give her a better childhood. It was a lie. Annabelle chewed on her tongue, biting back the truths she longed to hurl at her aunt. She had heard the Duchess and Lord Roger whispering late at night. She had heard what he said to her.

"Your plan to bring the princess here, Duchess, was a good one."

Her idea. Her plan. Her protection.

But she must allow the Duchess to keep up the pretense. It was one fragile string that held the world together. Annabelle was terrified to find out what would happen if she pulled it loose.

"Can't I keep my grief this one last time?" she pleaded. "If it is as you say, one day I will be far away from this place, and my life will no longer be my own. Can't I have this one last day with my friends to grieve and live in peace, in memory of Lord Roger and everything he gave me?"

The Duchess's expression softened. "I have questions, Annabelle. And I would like for you to answer them. But after that…yes. You may have this day."

Annabelle wanted to argue, but she knew it was no use. The Duchess's offer was a fair one. "Very well," she sighed. "What would you like to know?"

Reliving the events of that horrible day was tiring and sad work. The Duchess wanted to know everything, and so Annabelle told her everything she could remember: what time the Wallace men left to go hunting that morning; the hour that they returned from hunting; who bore Lord Roger's body across his horse; the title of the book that Annabelle had been reading when she heard Lady Ellen's panicked cries. The poor thing was probably still there, Annabelle realized, lying open on the ground beside the rose bushes—sodden and useless now. Another casualty of a senseless tragedy.

"His heart gave out," Annabelle said when the Duchess requested that she describe the cause of the baron's death. "The healer tried to revive him, but by then, it was too late. Damon told me it was sudden. One moment he was laughing, kneeling to inspect some tracks in the mud...and he never got back up."

The Duchess sat in thoughtful silence for a long time after Annabelle finished answering her questions.

"Thank you, Annabelle," she said finally, sighing heavily. "It is strange. He was in such good health...but it appears that this was simply the will of the Gods—tragic and swift, but unavoidable."

Annabelle opened her mouth to ask what else it could have been, but the door to the library swung open, and Sir Damon Wallace strode into view.

He was a handsome man, strong and tall as his father had been, with the same warm eyes and broad smile. It broke Annabelle's heart to see him so deflated by the loss of his father. He looked so tired. She wished she could wrap him in a blanket and rock him to sleep like a child.

Damon's eyes widened when he spotted them, and he dropped into a hurried bow. "Duchess, forgive me. I forgot…" he gestured vaguely toward the tea tray on the table. "I am disturbing you. I will go."

"Nonsense, Damon," the Duchess said, rising from her seat. "The princess and I have finished our tea, and I will go up to rest before supper."

"Thank you for being here, Duchess," Damon said with another bow. "I know my mother is honored by your presence, and…father would have been pleased."

The Duchess patted him on the shoulder as she passed. "Not at all, young man. Has Lady Ellen retired to her bedchamber?"

Damon nodded, scrubbing a hand over the back of his neck. "She didn't have the strength to…after the funeral, I thought it best."

"She should rest," the Duchess agreed. "I will look in on her before I come down."

"She would consider it an honor, Duchess."

"I highly doubt your poor mother is capable of considering anything an honor at all," she said sadly. "All the same."

Damon bowed her from the library and then sagged into a nearby armchair. "What a day," he groaned, rubbing at his face.

"How are you?" Annabelle asked, settling into a chair beside him. She cringed inwardly at her foolish question and added, "Apart from the obvious."

His chuckle was devoid of its usual mirth. "Oh, I don't know. I suppose I'm fine, even though the Gods know everything is going to pieces."

"Don't say that." Annabelle protested, even though she knew exactly how he felt. Gustav was baron now. The world had shifted on its axis. The look Damon gave her said as much. She shrugged. "It may be true, but you saying it aloud isn't any help."

Damon laughed in earnest then; the sound was musical and deep. Annabelle could have cried.

"Gods, I'm glad you're here through all of this, Annabelle," Damon said, taking her hand in his big one and squeezing it. "With my mother a wreck, Gustav locked in my father's study day and night—*his* study now, I suppose—and with…" he trailed off for a moment, a faraway look glazing his eyes, then shrugged. "Well, you know. It's good not to be alone."

Annabelle felt suddenly uncomfortable. She knew what Damon had been about to say, and she was grateful to him for not saying it, despite the guilt that suddenly welled up to join the pain twisting in her gut. She wanted to tell him it was alright, that she didn't fault him for how he felt.

"I wouldn't be anywhere else," she said instead.

"Walk with me?" he asked, pushing up from the chair. "I need to get out of this house, and the garden will be beautiful after so much rain."

Ecstatic about finally having an excuse to go outside, Annabelle followed Damon out into the gold of the evening light.

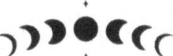

The temple was dark and quiet by the time Sam pushed open one of the heavy oak doors and stepped inside the cavernous chamber. All mourners had departed, and the family was nowhere to be seen. The priests had retreated to their cloisters. There was no soul to witness the man creeping toward the dais, just another silent shadow in the fading light.

Standing upon the stone platform, he gazed down upon the shrouded body of Lord Roger. His insides were cold. How many bodies had he seen during the past few years? How many shrouds? How many wailing widows and stoic sons? How many fathers?

Almost without conscious thought, his hand reached out and, grasping the edge of the shroud, lifted it back to expose the face. Sam had expected this moment to be different from the others. After all, this man had raised him as his own. Lord Roger was the closest thing to a father he would ever have. Surely that meant something would be different, that he would fall to his knees, pounding his fists on the ground, cursing the Gods as the other sons had done. Alone in the silent temple, Sam looked down upon that hollow face and waited.

But nothing happened. It did not feel real. It was difficult to recognize the man he had known in those sunken cheeks, the pallid skin and faded beard. Hard as he tried, Sam couldn't find the man he longed to see, to laugh with him, to comfort him.

He replaced the shroud, suddenly disgusted with himself. What was he doing? Lord Roger was gone. This body was just an empty shell. He had known it, but he supposed that knowing it hadn't been enough.

A tear slid down his long nose as he bowed his head, remembering. He could see sunlight, a broad hairy face, and the sound of booming laughter.

His knee hurt, and his cheeks were wet as he looked up at the big man, but the pain was nothing to the fear he felt. Lord Roger had told him not to climb that tree, that he would fall. But the scolding did not come. Instead, Lord Roger lifted him up and up into his big arms and smiled in his face, wiping his tears away.

"Well," the man said, eyes twinkling his amusement, "I suppose knowing and understanding are just two banks of the same river, eh?"

The sunlight of the memory faded, leaving Sam standing alone on the cold temple floor, feeling like that lost little boy.

"Goodbye, old man," he said, voice echoing slightly in the empty room.

The room did not answer, and so Sam turned on his heel and walked from the temple, comforted by the knowledge that Lord Roger would not lay in that cold dark room alone. Lord Roger was gone.

Sam took deep breaths in the courtyard outside the temple, chasing the stale perfumed air from his lungs. He knew the road to his next destination so well, he could have walked it on a moonless night without running into a single tree or falling in a ditch, but he couldn't bring himself to mount his horse. Instead, he patted her neck while she drank from a trough by the horse tie, biding his time, thinking of ways to avoid moving on.

Around him, the village appeared deserted. Shop windows were shuttered, and not a soul wandered the streets, even just to pass through. The entire region would be in mourning, he knew. No inn would open its doors, and no tavern would provide a safe haven tonight. So Sam stood in the middle of the road and waited for his courage to find him.

It had been the same in the north, fighting the endless trickle of rebels that plagued the border towns. Sam was not quick to attack, as his companions were. There was always something more to know— some other angle to see, an ambush ready to spring. And so Sam would wait, breathe, watch, and listen. Only when his gut felt settled did he move. Only when a voice in his head said *go* did he attack.

And so Sam waited. The storm that had pummeled his face while he rode had blown off across the sea, and the clouds were dissipating, revealing a sky alight with gold and pink. The warmth from the sun eased some of the tension from Sam's shoulders. He felt better, and so he mounted his horse.

Delaying would change nothing—not what had already happened and not what was to come.

The old house emerged from the trees, a rocky edifice, as much a part of the surroundings as any tree, leaf, or blade of grass. Despite the distance and the years, Sam still felt that familiar warmth of safety spread from his belly into his feet. Home will always do that to a man, he thought, no matter how far he travels.

Nobody awaited him on the front steps, for nobody knew he was coming, but that was how Sam had wanted it. He led the horse around to the stables himself.

Sam took his time, wandering through the gardens toward the back entrance of the manor. They were bursting with life, swollen and lush with the bounty of the rain. He had forgotten how beautiful they were, with their winding paths of rose bushes, tall trees, and fish pond. The earth in this place was alive, and Sam lost himself amidst it, finding comfort in tracing these pathways of his childhood.

Lost in memories, Sam did not hear the voices until he turned a corner. He simply let his feet guide him, and then, suddenly, there they were—two people he knew as well as his own self. The two people he longed most to see and was terrified to see, in equal measure.

"Sam!" Damon's shout of surprise dislodged several birds from their perches in a nearby tree. The big knight rushed forward and pulled Sam into a rib-cracking hug, laughing his delight. Sam grinned and stepped back to get a good look at his friend. Damon looked weary, his eyes dark and shoulders slumped with grief, but otherwise healthy and whole.

"It is good to see you, Sam," Damon said, tears shining in his eyes. "I thought you couldn't come."

"I couldn't," Sam said with a shrug. "And then I could."

Damon barked a laugh that was half amusement, half disbelief as he said, "We'll get the full story out of you later, Sammy. Won't we, Annabelle?"

The elation that Sam had felt at his reunion with Damon faltered as his gaze fell upon the woman standing before him. Five years had not changed her, and yet she was no longer the girl of fourteen she had been. Those emerald eyes regarded him cooly, and that monster of shame roiled in his belly.

"Hello Annabelle," he said with a shy smile, an invitation, a quiet plea for her forgiveness.

But Annabelle did not return his smile. Her eyes lit with fire and, without a word to Sam, she turned on her heel and strode away toward the manor.

"Ignore her," Damon said, slinging his arm around Sam's shoulder as they trailed after Annabelle. "Welcome home, Sam."

"It's good to be here," Sam replied. But as he watched Annabelle's retreating back, he felt that same sick, guilty twisting in his gut.

Welcome home, indeed.

Chapter Two

Supper that evening was a somber, subdued affair. Lady Ellen was still too weak with sorrow to rise from her bed. So Annabelle had taken the seat of the lady of the house at one end of the long table. The great chair at the other end loomed somehow larger due to the absence of its usual occupant.

This new seat gave Annabelle a good vantage point to observe the others, which was perhaps lucky considering she could not have eaten a thing if she tried. Grief, pain, and anger roiled like nausea in her gut, making even the thought of food impossible. Everything seemed impossible now: impossible that Lord Roger was gone; impossible that he could be gone, and they could all be sitting there pretending to want to eat; impossible that the world had not come to an end.

Damon was in better spirits since Sam's arrival that afternoon. He still looked sad and tired, but at least he was eating. Sam sat to his right, politely chewing at intervals, carefully looking anywhere but at Annabelle. She ignored him in equal measure. The Duchess watched them all over the rim of her wine goblet, her plate sitting empty, her plate untouched as Annabelle's own.

The only guest whose appetite appeared unaffected by the sadness and discomfort of the occasion was Lord Velton of the Golden Hills Province. He was the only friend of the Wallace family to travel to the village for the funeral. He sat next to the Duchess, and the contrast between the two nobles was stark.

Where the Duchess was poised, tall, and elegant, Velton slumped over his plate, wisps of white hair sticking out from either side of his head, the bald swath of skin between them shining in the candlelight. Annabelle suddenly had to overcome the urge to laugh, seeing her aunt's scandalized look as Velton slurped his wine between bites. She liked the old lord immensely.

Velton had been friendly with Lord Roger's father, Baron Edgar Wallace, and had been a kind of uncle and confidant to Roger after his father's passing. With grown sons of his own who saw to the running of his estate and province and a wife who had long since passed, Velton was a common fixture at Rosewood Manor. He could be a bit of a curmudgeon at times, but Annabelle liked it when he told stories about the city of Ellasport to the south and the great keep of Rengon Castle to the north.

Lord Velton was a good man—a member of the court who detested court life with its airs and political machinations—and a true friend. Rosewood was a small and remote barony with few resources and tenants. Most of the court, Annabelle was sure, would consider the Wallace family to be no better than ordinary people. The Wallace's were good, kind people, and they deserved more than an obscure existence. And Annabelle would always be grateful because it was for this reason that the Duchess had selected Rosewood Manor for her home.

The arrangement had been a simple one; the Baron and Baroness would take in the young Princess as their ward, raise her as their own, and keep her safe. The rebellion in the north continued, on and on. There was little gold to spare, but they would have what they needed to raise the Princess in comfort. The family would do this out of duty and honor. They would lead quiet lives and abandon ambitions for the betterment of their descendants. They would have nothing more but the promise that the future queen of Dunea might remember their generosity when she ascended the throne.

Lord Roger and Lady Ellen Wallace had agreed, not that they had a choice, and they never once made Annabelle feel that the request made of them was somehow wrong or her fault. Which, of course, meant that Annabelle felt both responsible and guilty, often and acutely. If she ever did ascend the throne, she would ensure that the Wallace family was lifted high and exalted above all others.

All, save for Gustav, Annabelle thought spitefully. The eldest of Lord Roger and Lady Ellen's two sons had always chafed against the smallness of life in Rosewood Province. He spent much of his time in the cities and abroad, funding his travels with business ventures and connections, which Annabelle doubted were legitimate or respectable. He had never shown the slightest interest in his own birthright, save for assuming his father's property and title at the time of his death—which he had now done.

Annabelle was confident that Lord Roger would have found a way to pass the barony to Damon had he lived long enough to see his duty to the crown accomplished. It was nearly impossible to alter the line of succession, but it would have been a just reward for ensuring the health and safety of the heir to the throne. Of course, that would never happen now. Annabelle wondered if Damon knew if that was a part of the loss he now bore.

If the gods do determine our fates, Annabelle thought, they have a wicked sense of humor.

Almost unconsciously, her eyes flicked to where Sam sat. His pale blue eyes lifted to hers a moment later, and she looked away, cursing inwardly, a fresh wave of rage making her feel momentarily sick. None of this was fair. She wanted to scream and cry and break things. Lord Roger was gone, Gustav was Baron, Sam was here—and he *should* be here! That was the bit of it that really burned. He should be here, and Annabelle should be revived by his presence. Annabelle and Sam should be like siblings reunited. Instead, there was nothing but horrible silence between them.

And whose fault is that, anyway? Annabelle thought mutinously, shoving back the more mature and reasonable argument that the blame fell in equal measure upon her own shoulders. They had been the best of friends, inseparable since childhood. They had bonded as misfits of the manor—he the lord's ward, and she, the Crown Princess; both from different worlds, both outsiders in another family's home. Their friendship had been the best thing that Annabelle had ever known, so how could it be her fault that it had fallen to pieces?

No. Sam was the one who left. He was the one who stayed away, with no word, for years. He was the one who turned up with no warning and had the nerve to greet Annabelle as if no time had passed. That she didn't launch herself across the table and throttle him where he sat was a miracle.

Annabelle shifted in her seat. Ruminating on old wrongs and unhealed wounds rendered the air in the hall suddenly stifling. She needed some air.

Annabelle made to rise from the table, good manners be damned, but the door to the dining hall swung open, and Baron Gustav Wallace strode into the room.

Nobody in the house had seen Gustav in days, save for one brief glimpse at the funeral ceremony that morning. He had been cloistered in his father's study, night and day, from the moment the healer had declared that Lord Roger was gone.

Annabelle noted Gustav's simple black jacket, bereft of any adornments, and the ink stains and smears of dust that marred the front of his white shirt. This disheveled appearance was all the more unusual because Gustav Wallace cared for his finery. His clothes were always clean and ornate, and he never had a hair out of place. Tonight Gustav's hair hung lank and greasy to his shoulders, swept back from his face in pieces by the relentless combing of restless hands.

Though Damon was the spitting image of his father, Gustav had inherited Lady Ellen's slim build and willowy grace. *Graceful like a snake coiled to strike*, Annabelle thought as he sauntered the length of the table and slumped into his father's chair.

Gustav seized his wine goblet at once and drank deeply. He really did look terrible. Annabelle wondered if it were possible that even the cruel and aloof Gustav Wallace was touched by his father's passing.

That may have been so, but there was an odd gleam in his eyes as he set his goblet down and surveyed his guests that made Annabelle uneasy.

When nobody spoke, Damon cleared his throat.

"It is good to see you, brother," he said, even though his tone suggested this was far from the truth.

Gustav leveled cold eyes at Damon but said nothing in response. Instead, Gustav's gaze passed from Damon to Sam, and his lips twisted in a sneer. "I see father's stray pup has found its way home at last," he drawled. "Come to beg for scraps from your new lord and master, pup?"

Damon's shoulders stiffened, but Sam did not seem concerned by this insult. He only met Gustav's gaze unflinchingly and said, "I am here to pay respects to Lord Roger and to comfort his family. I owe your late father a great deal."

Gustav's sneer widened, and this time his gaze landed on Annabelle. "Yes, well. There are quite a few strays who have benefitted from my father's…generosity." He chewed upon the last word as if it were something distasteful. "And now here you all are, like dutiful little children. Pathetic."

"Oh, now. There's no need to be cruel." Lord Velton's attention had been pulled from his dinner by Gustav's appearance, and now his mustache ruffled as he bristled at Gustav's words. "What would your father say if he heard you mistreat your own family so!"

"Respectfully, Lord Velton," Gustav hissed, "they are not my family. And my father is not here, is he? This is my home now. If you are displeased with the way I choose to behave, you may choose to leave it."

"To what do we owe the honor of your presence, Baron?" the Duchess cut in sternly before Velton could muster a response. "You have been occupied these past days."

That light—that horrible glimmer that set Annabelle's teeth on edge, returned to Gustav's eyes as he gave the Duchess a long predatory look, stroking the stem of his goblet, and said, "I am so glad you asked, Duchess."

Annabelle and Damon exchanged a look. They both knew that whatever was about to happen, it wasn't going to be good. Damon was a knight, a warrior, trained to ride a horse into combat and spar other men with fists and steel. Gustav's weapons were knowledge and manipulation. Whatever he had to say, he had planned it, had waited to reveal it. Together, they braced for what was to come.

Gustav drained his goblet, refilled it from a jug on the table, and took another sip. Unhurried—he knew he had a captive audience. "I have been familiarizing myself with my father's documents," he said, replacing his goblet upon the table. "His contracts, his records, and his secrets."

He paused for effect. The tension in the room was palpable. Annabelle couldn't help but notice Sam's expression as he watched Gustav. His face was smooth and unreadable, but his gaze was piercingly intent. At that moment, Sam looked just as dangerous as Gustav, and Annabelle wondered if the snake knew there was another predator in his midst. The thought sent a shiver down her spine.

"Most of what I discovered was the usual business—tenant agreements, ledgers, the like..." Gustav continued, waving a dismissive hand. "Nothing out of the ordinary. Though you all knew my father. I do not need to tell you how incurably boring he was."

Damon let out a sound that could have been a growl, but Gustav ignored him.

"There was one letter, however, that I found very interesting indeed," he said with a poisonous smile. "It was just sitting there on my father's desk—unsealed and unfolded. I thought it a pity he never had the chance to send it. So I perused its contents, thinking to forward it to its intended recipient."

Likely story, Annabelle thought. *You snooping, slimy crook.*

"To my distinct pleasure, I realized that it was addressed to you, Duchess." Gustav reached into a pocket of his jacket and produced a scroll of paper. "How lucky that you are here, and I can deliver it to you in person."

He extended the scroll to the Duchess, and, after only a moment's hesitation, her gray eyes searching his brown ones, she took it from him. "Thank you," she said, though her eyes were still narrow with suspicion. "I enjoyed my correspondence with Lord Roger and will be glad to have this as a remembrance of him."

Gustav nodded solemnly. "Of course, Duchess. You have always been a friend to our family. I am at your service."

Lord Velton smiled jovially. "A nice thing to do, Lord Baron. A *kind* thing."

But Annabelle was not fooled, and neither were Damon or Sam. They still looked wary. They, like she, knew that Gustav would never have gone through such a production to simply deliver a letter. The ax had yet to fall.

"Now that's done," Gustav said then, slapping his palms against the thick wooden arms of his chair, "I believe a toast is in order."

He stood, uncoiling with a burst of sudden energy that gave Annabelle a start, and lifted his goblet into the air, smiling down at the rest of them expectantly. Nobody moved. They all simply gaped at him.

"You cannot be serious," Damon protested angrily. "Father is dead, Gustav. Show some respect."

"Oh, but I do respect our father, little brother," Gustav retorted, his tone still light and pleasant, but his eyes flashed with anger. "And I know that he would not want us to be sad today. If there was some happy event on the horizon, he would want us to raise our glasses in celebration."

"What is this? What happy event?" Velton blustered, looking between Gustav and the Duchess. "Penny, what is he going on about?"

"I believe the Baron intends to tell us, Georg," the Duchess said. "Before we all die from suspense, no doubt."

The Duchess's expression had not changed, she still surveyed Gustav with tight-lipped disapproval, but Annabelle saw that her wrinkled face had paled. What was going on?

Gustav adopted an expression of feigned confusion. "But…surely you all know!" he said with disbelief etched all over his thin, snide face. It was masterfully done. Then, as Annabelle had predicted, Gustav finally lowered the ax.

Those horrible eyes found her own as Gustav proclaimed, "Our own Princess Annabelle has been engaged to Prince Mica of Eìrlan."

Annabelle froze, unable to breathe as the world around her went dim and fuzzy. *Engaged.* She could not think. *Engaged.* The word echoed in her ears. All eyes were upon her now, she could feel them probing her with their curiosity, but she could do nothing but stare at her plate. The room was silent.

"I had not informed anyone of this news just yet," the Duchess said after a long moment. "So, no," she added. "Nobody, save me and the late Baron knew of the engagement."

"Oh, I do feel foolish," Gustav said, his tone apologetic but his face alight with amusement as he settled back into his seat to watch the drama he had created unfold. "Forgive me for my misstep, Duchess."

"But, Eìrlan!" Lord Velton burst out, his mustache dancing as if in a great wind. "It's impossible! They would never forge an alliance with us. Our mutual enmity goes back hundreds of years. Surely the situation in the north cannot be as desperate as this!"

"Georg, *do* calm down," the Duchess sighed, looking tired and harassed. "I assure you, the match is genuine. In exchange for a royal bloodline tie to Dunea, the king of Eìrlan has agreed to provide us with ships to bring the conflict to a long-awaited end. Surely we can all put aside our prejudices for that happy outcome?"

Velton muttered under his breath in a way that seemed as if he very much doubted it, but the Duchess ignored him. Her eyes sought Annabelle, but Annabelle could not look at her, could not look at Damon or Sam, could not bear the weight of their gazes upon her. The walls of the dining hall were closing in, and it was becoming hard to breathe.

"Annabelle," a voice said. "Are you alright?"

The words were so kind, so softly spoken, that Annabelle was startled to look up into Sam's water-blue eyes. There was no pity there, only open and genuine concern. For one long moment, they were children again—bonded by their lack of belonging to anyone other than each other. And Annabelle knew that if she did not get out of there, did not run from his caring eyes, she would fall apart.

Rising from her seat with as much poise as she could muster, Annabelle Ilenna Alexandria Penelope Isren, crown Princess of Dunea, fled the dining hall.

Chapter Three

"You should have told me."

"That's enough, Annabelle."

"You let me walk into an ambush."

"Don't be melodramatic."

Annabelle glared at her aunt as their carriage trundled along the rocky passage to the Eastern Road.

It had been two days—two days since the catastrophic dinner that had sent Annabelle's world careening headfirst into chaos and confusion. She had slept fitfully that night, her precious few hours of rest plagued by visions of storms and the feeling of being chased through darkened hallways. The dreams sent her tumbling from sleep in the pre-dawn hours, trembling and covered with sweat.

Emily had been her only friend and confidant. Annabelle hadn't wished to burden Damon with her woes, she couldn't stand so much as to look at Sam, and she was too furious with her aunt to tolerate her presence, let alone any explanations. So Annabelle and Emily had hidden away in the princess's rooms, talking and packing.

For Annabelle was betrothed. It was time to return to the city of Ellasport, her birthplace, at last.

For her part, Annabelle was not exactly sad to leave the manor. Though she would miss the cliffs and the tall trees, she did not welcome the idea of being trapped under the same roof with Baron Gustav Wallace a moment longer than was entirely necessary. Rosewood Manor was not her home any longer. Lord Roger was dead, and Damon and Emily would accompany her to the city. Home was people. Without them, the manor was just a house.

At first, Annabelle had felt relief as the stone walls of Rosewood Manor faded into the distance. But then she and the Duchess were alone, sitting opposite each other in the Duchess's fine carriage, and fury began to rise in Annabelle's chest until she feared it might choke her.

"You should have told me!" she repeated when the Duchess continued to sit in stony silence, her lips pressed together in a thin line.

"Young lady, hush," her aunt snapped, pounding her cane upon the floor of the carriage for emphasis. "I will not be scolded by you any longer. What is done is done."

Annabelle wanted to let it go, knew she was dancing desperately close to some line, but the hurt and betrayal rotting in her heart urged her on.

"If you aren't even going to apologize—"

"A man was dead, Annabelle," the Duchess cut across Annabelle, her expression forbidding. "My friend, the man who raised you. I was already on my way to the manor to fetch you when I received the news."

She sighed heavily. "I knew you would be deeply saddened. So yes, I decided to wait to tell you the news of your engagement."

"I thought we were royals," Annabelle grumbled. "I thought we didn't have the luxury to grieve."

"We do not," the Duchess said, and Annabelle was shocked to see the sadness in her eyes as her face crumpled. "But…but you asked for a day, and I wanted to give you that one last day to grieve, to not be a princess. I intended to tell you first thing in the morning, but apparently, the Gods had other plans. I know my intentions cannot change the terrible way you found out, but I will not apologize for trying to give you one more day of peace."

Annabelle was finally quiet. She understood this, but she did not want to release her anger. The fury was keeping another feeling at bay, something immense and terrifying. Her eyes drifted to the carriage window and the seemingly endless expanse of forest that stretched out beyond it.

"You let me walk into that dining room without knowing the whole story," she said quietly without looking at her aunt. "You left me vulnerable to attack."

She did not mean to sound accusing. It was simply the truth.

"Annabelle, look at me, please."

Annabelle hesitated, breathing back the tears that threatened to escape at the corner of her eyes when she spoke such truths. Finally, she met her aunt's gaze. There was steely resolve in every line of her wrinkled face.

"I will not let anything happen to you," she said firmly.

Annabelle blinked. "I don't know what you…" but the Duchess held up a gnarled hand, and Annabelle fell silent once more.

"You are afraid, child." The old woman said. "Of course you are. By nightfall, we will reach the camp and join the retinue sent to escort you to the palace. From the moment that carriage door opens, you will no longer be Annabelle; you will be the Crown Princess of Dunea. You will be scrutinized, adored, criticized, manipulated, wooed, accused, flattered: all the things for which I have spent these last years preparing you. But you will not be alone."

Annabelle was having trouble breathing. Tears slid unbidden down her cheeks, and there was nothing she could do to stop them now.

"I will not let anything happen to you," the Duchess repeated, leaning forward in her seat. "I will surround you with people who love you, and we will keep you safe. Do you understand me?"

Annabelle sniffed and nodded, but then she frowned as something clicked into place.

"Sam," she said. "He's here because of you, isn't he?"

The Duchess watched her for a long moment, lips pursed as if considering her response.

"I meant what I said, Annabelle," she said at last. "Now get some rest while you can. Soon the real challenge begins."

Annabelle leaned back in her seat as best she could, but she could not have rested if her life depended on it. She was distracted by curiosity and fear—wondering about the city and the palace of legend, perched high on a cliff over the sea. She dreaded what awaited her there. Engaged to a prince of Eìrlan and bound for a future that she could not imagine if she tried.

Little was known about the small island country to the northeast. All Annabelle could remember from her history lessons was that Eìrlan was an old country but a new kingdom. The entire land had been divided between several tribes and groups scattered throughout its archipelago for centuries before the first king had united them. He had five sons; the eldest, Leo, had become Eìrlan's second king after his father's death ten years ago. That was all Annabelle knew—all anyone had found important enough to teach her.

Eìrlan's borders had remained closed since the Great War. Annabelle didn't know what to expect from her new life at court; she at least knew her own land—its history and its customs. Even if her betrothed had come from Petra or Aelnìr, she would have had a vague idea of what kind of man to expect. But this prince of Eìrlan was shrouded in mystery, and it was that complete unknowing that made her anxious.

So Annabelle watched the trees of Rosewood Province pass by the carriage window, and she prayed to the Gods that, no matter what sort of man he turned out to be, her future husband would be kind.

꙳ ꙳꙳ ● ꙳꙳ ꙳

Sam and Damon rode together at the head of the little caravan as they traversed the mountainous terrain of the eastern coast. It felt good to be back on the road and back in his friend's company. The events of the past few days had been horrible enough, and Sam still worried about Annabelle and how she was holding up since the revelation of her betrothal.

He had feared something like this might happen, though the Duchess had refused point-blank to tell him why she was ordering him away from his post in the north. He had assumed it was a gift to go home—thought that he was being rewarded for his service with the chance to see his family again. Now he knew better.

At least Damon was in better spirits now that they had left the manor and Gustav far behind them. They had spent most of the journey riding side by side, swapping stories of their time apart. Now, as they neared the eastern crossroads where their small winding track met with the Great Road that would take them south to Ellasport, Damon had begun regaling Sam with tales of his time there as a squire attending Lord Velton.

"...food everywhere, and all of it tastes like it came from the Gods' own table—even the pastries out of street carts and market stalls," he said, a dreamy, faraway look in his eyes. "And the *women*, Sam!" he exclaimed, a fuzzy grin splitting his handsome face. "I've never seen so many beauties in one place. It's enough to drive a man into madness."

"It sounds like a horrible place," Sam said with a wry smile, "It's a wonder you survived it."

He had meant the statement to be a joke but knew at once that he had said the wrong thing. Damon's smile remained, but his eyes had gone suddenly cold as he said, "Look, it isn't my fault that Velton hates court and would rather spend his time by the sea than holed up in a great cold place like Rengon City. I won't apologize for enjoying myself while you were freezing your ass off up north, Sam."

This outburst took Sam by surprise. "I don't expect you to apologize," he said. "I meant it as a joke, Damon. I'm happy you enjoyed the city, and I'm glad you'll have the opportunity to return."

Damon sighed heavily, scrubbing a hand across the back of his neck. "I know that. I don't know what came over me. It's just... it's so strange having you back. I keep forgetting you aren't the skinny little boy I knew who dreamed of becoming a knight." His smile returned, though somewhat diminished. "At least now we get to go south together, and I can introduce you to the wonders of Ellasport." He paused, then his smile returned in full force as he added, "And maybe a few of those ladies, eh?"

Sam returned the smile and nodded, "I look forward to it."

Damon knew the lie for what it was. He gave a kind of half-nod, half-shrug and then said, "The crossroads isn't far—just over this next hill. I should notify the Duchess."

Then he steered his horse around and was gone.

As Damon left, Sam could feel a crack form in the solid bond that once stood between them. But he shrugged it off. It meant nothing, only that they had spent too long apart. There would be time on the road to repair the years and distance, he told himself, and not just with Damon.

A few minutes passed as Sam considered what he might say or do to begin repairing some more old wounds that had been left to fester when there was a shout from behind him.

"Stop! Stop the carriage!"

The carriage slowed and stopped, as did the wagon that hauled their possessions. Confused, Sam watched as the carriage door opened and Annabelle emerged. To his shock, she stomped right up to the side of his horse, looking up at him with a defiant expression.

"I want to see it," she said. "The camp."

"I..." Sam did not know what to say to this. Annabelle had not so much as looked in his direction for days, and this request had him completely wrong-footed.

"I can take you, princess." Damon had rejoined them at the front. "Climb up behind me, and it's just a short—"

"I want Sam to take me," Annabelle cut across the knight. "And I want to walk."

Sam and Damon exchanged a look, and the latter shrugged as if to say, *Better you than me, friend.*

So Sam dismounted, handed the reins to Damon, and hastened after the princess, who was already climbing the hill.

Neither of them spoke for the duration of the climb. It was not far, nor was it steep, and so Sam and Annabelle soon stood at the top, gazing down into the valley below.

They had left the forest behind them, and the land sprawled out from the foot of the hill in a vast swath of rolling green and brown countryside. Cutting through the fields was a wide strip of dark earth that Sam knew was the Great Road, and where their snaking track intersected with it stood a small tent city.

A few larger tents were surrounded by many smaller tents, a paddock for animals, two long tents that Sam knew were a makeshift barracks and mess, and a training ring. He had seen the king's own camp once, and this one was small by comparison, but with standards flying—each bearing the rose and crown insignia of the royal family, even Sam had to admit that the effect was impressive.

"So that's where it will begin," Annabelle said so quietly that Sam almost missed it.

He turned to her, but she was staring at the tent village, a peculiar look on her face. Then she took a deep breath and turned to face him.

"We don't have time to do this properly," she said. "One day, we will have to, I think. There's been too much time and too many…things that have happened. We don't have time to really have it out now the way we need to, but I need to know something before we go down there and everything becomes...unpredictable."

"Anything," Sam said, curious about where this was going.

"Can I trust you?" Annabelle asked bluntly. "Even if things are still...still not alright between us. Can I still trust you to be on my side?"

"Yes," Sam said without hesitation. "You can always trust me."

Annabelle nodded and said, almost to herself, "Good. That's good to know."

"Annabelle, I—I have to tell you," Sam said, almost despite his best efforts to keep his mouth shut, "I am sorry for what happened with Gustav. If I had known about your engagement, I never would have given him the chance to tell you. I would have told you myself if I had to, and damn the consequences."

"The Duchess was the one who summoned you to the manor," Annabelle said, eyeing him. It was a question and not a question.

"She did," Sam admitted, "but I did not know why she summoned me, I promise you. I know it doesn't do any good now, but I am sorry that you found out in that way. You didn't deserve that."

"Thank you," Annabelle said and gave him a small smile.

Her thanks was simple but genuine. Sam felt the tension in his chest ease somewhat.

He and Annabelle returned to the caravan then, and for the first time in days, Sam felt like everything might turn out alright in the end. Annabelle was strong and kind, as she had always been—that much would never change—but there was a certainty Sam had now, a knowing that made all the difference: from now and to the end of his days, for every moment Annabelle needed a friend, he would be there.

Lord Ronan Barrick was unhappy. He preferred to see plans through himself and very much disliked to have a situation wrenched from his grasp by fools who thought they knew better.

The pieces had been set upon the board, and so far, the strategy had been executed to perfection. Ronan had made sure the king and his court were safely and happily settled in the southern palace, already celebrating the betrothal. He had carefully selected a group of representatives to accompany him to escort the princess to court. The company set out to the eastern crossroads before dawn four days ago, ensuring they would be awaiting the arrival of Princess Annabelle.

The plan had been well in hand.

Now Ronan forced his face into a smile as a big man with a salt and pepper beard, the bald dome of his head shining in the afternoon sun, dismounted his stallion and approached, offering a broad hand.

"Barrick," the man said as he clasped Ronan's hand, squeezing.

"Asby," Ronan endured the man's iron grip without flinching. "Truly a pleasure to meet you here, of all places."

"'Of all places...'" Asby raised a furry eyebrow. "If you ask me, at this time on this day, this is the only place in the world that is worth being."

"Indeed. I only thought you might have hastened to his majesty's side." It was a sloppy challenge, but right then, Ronan had no patience for subtlety.

Asby chuckled and clapped Ronan on the shoulder. Ronan fought not to cringe away. "Sorry to disappoint, Barrick. We are here to stay, I'm afraid."

"All of you?" Ronan glanced around the big man to where his company was already dismounting their horses and unloading wagons.

His men bore the smoke and gold insignia of Black Mountain—lines of gold and silver embroidery running up the base of a great mountain set against a steel-gray sky. Asby had come with quite a host, and it irritated Ronan like a grain of sand stuck underneath the skin, where its itch could not be reached or rightly dealt with.

Asby steered Ronan toward the great tent at the center of camp. "Come, my Lord Barrick," he said as they went. "Don't be such a grump. This is a happy occasion, no? Our sweet princess returned to her family's embrace at last."

"You know as well as I do," Ronan said, keeping his voice low, "that matters are not quite as…forthright as you make them out to be."

The big lord snorted. "Understatement of the age, my friend. Why else do you think I am here?"

They reached the great tent and ducked under the flap. Ronan crossed to a small table, set with goblets and a pitcher of wine. He poured two glasses and held one out to Asby, who accepted with a grateful nod.

"I make a habit not to assume motives," Ronan said as Asby drank deeply from his goblet. "So though I think I know why you are here, I do not *know* why you are here."

Asby eyed him seriously; all humor was gone from his expression. "I am here for the same reason you are, I expect: to make certain that the princess is welcomed home by friends."

"A task you did not think I could handle alone?"

"On the contrary. I have nothing but faith in you." Asby offered his goblet, and Ronan refilled it. He took a delicate sip before elaborating. "I trust that you care for the girl, as do I. And I trust that you have your reasons to befriend her, early and well, as do I. But I also trust that our motives are…different, if not opposed."

"I'm curious now," said Ronan. "What motives do you believe I have, beyond simply wanting to show my princess and future queen her due respect?"

"I have a few theories," Asby replied with a shrug, settling his large frame in a carved wooden chair with a grateful sigh. "The most promising theory has to do with chess."

"Chess?" Ronan lifted an eyebrow.

"Chess," Asby nodded. "You see, I think you fancy yourself master of the game—you see all the pieces on the board, and you know how to move them. The girl is an unknown. The way she moves, the way she thinks, is as yet unpredictable. You want the opportunity to observe her in action before you place her on the board."

"Interesting theory," Ronan took another sip of wine. "Say you're right. Why do you believe your motives, whatever they may be, are different from mine? Are we not all trying to be masters of our own game?"

"Perhaps. But the princess is still young, probably terrified, and we are about to throw her into the lion's den without a sword." He set his goblet down on the table with a clunk, meeting Ronan's gaze, the hard steely blue of his eyes alight. "I intend to put the girl through her paces before delivering her to the king—find out who she really is and what she is capable of."

The words ignited a fire in Ronan's heart, but he did not dare let his anger show. "You would interrogate your own princess?" he asked as casually as he could manage. "You are bold."

Asby held his gaze for a moment as if looking for something there, but he seemed not to find it. Sighing, he pushed himself from the chair and moved toward the exit. "By the Gods, Ronan," he said as he went, "one day I'll prove you've a heart that beats and bleeds, as we all have."

"I look forward to our next sparring match, friend," Ronan replied, and Asby was gone.

Alone in the tent, Ronan poured a fresh goblet of wine and sat in the chair that Asby had vacated. As he drank, he reached into his jacket and retrieved a folded letter from an inner pocket. Ronan did not open the letter—knowing that the words within had long ago faded from the surface of the paper. Instead, he ran a finger over the wax seal that still remained affixed to the front. The insignia impressed into the wax had been smoothed over the years, but he could still see a shadow of the crown and rose imprint. Soon, that too would be gone.

He shoved the letter back into his pocket and shoved down the sudden surge of emotion. It would not do to lose his composure, not at this critical juncture. That Asby thought him so callous suited Barrick just fine. And if Asby truly meant to protect the girl, well, that would hardly matter in the end. Let him have his noble mission, foolish though it was. Better to keep the lord distracted by his little theories and his honor. At least he would be out of the way.

Ronan moved to the entrance of the tent and peered out through the flap at the bustling activity of the camp—wagons being unloaded, tent spires rising into the sky, shouts of greeting, and shrieks of laughter. They were the sounds of celebration. And it will be a celebration, Ronan smiled to himself. But not yet. Still, Ronan felt the surge of anticipation rise in his chest. He was close now.

So close.

Chapter Four

The driver held the door open, patiently waiting to help the princess climb back into the carriage, but she could not take his offered hand. She could only stand there, staring into the dark interior, waiting for the buzzing inside her head to resolve into an identifiable thought or idea.

Seeing the camp—being able to watch the flags snap in the breeze and people running about making preparations, their excitement palpable even from a distance—had made that faint, intangible future come into sharper focus. Annabelle did not want to get back into the carriage, to be dragged before her fate blind and unknowing. There was a power in being able to see the road before her feet, and she would not give up a shred of that power; not when she would soon be in dire need of every last scrap of it, she could muster.

"Bring my horse," she said, at last, lifting her chin high and trying to mimic her aunt's commanding tone. "I want to ride into camp."

Nobody moved to grant her request. Henry, the driver, looked uncertainly towards the Duchess for his command. Annabelle met her aunt's gaze unflinchingly. *Please*, she prayed silently. *Please let me do this.*

"I don't know what you're doing standing around gawking," the Duchess said finally, raising a thin white brow. "Your princess gave an order."

Immediately people started moving, every guard and attendant rushing to fetch the princess's mount. As Annabelle turned from her aunt, she could have sworn she saw an approving smile tug at the corner of the wrinkled mouth.

Henry returned moments later from the back of the line holding the reins to a chestnut mare with mane and tail so flaxen they were almost white. The horse's name was Sparrow, and she had been one of Lord Roger's favorites. She had a gentle demeanor, and Annabelle rubbed one hand down her neck, murmuring a greeting to the horse, before allowing Damon to help her into the saddle.

Annabelle rode at the front, with Damon and Sam flanking her on either side. Even though nerves still fluttered in her stomach, she felt more confident sitting high atop Sparrow, the sun on her face, the world open before her. She would ride into camp with clear eyes, carried by the horse and her own free will, not dumped at their feet like a package waiting to be unwrapped.

The moment their small company crested the hill, the clear trumpeting of horns filled the air, and Annabelle could see the standards raised to announce their arrival—the sigils of Walthon Down, the Isren rose, and the golden crown of the monarchy. Annabelle's stomach leaped into her throat at the sight of it, and she sat more upright in her saddle, trying to look worthy of that crown and the legacy it represented.

The trumpeting of the horns died away as they rode into the royal camp. All bustle and flurry of activity had quieted. Annabelle couldn't help it as her eyes darted from tent to tent, expecting to see bodies and faces peering back at her, but the camp appeared deserted. The unexpected emptiness was disconcerting, and Sparrow snorted her objection as Annabelle gripped the reigns more tightly.

As they pulled to a stop before the central tent, the largest tent in the camp, Annabelle had to hold in a gasp. Every person in the camp—every guard, groom, maid, and squire—had gathered together, standing at attention, to greet their princess as one.

Annabelle's mouth went dry to see them all standing there, straight and tall. The first thing that struck her was how beautiful they looked. The white of the maids' caps shone in the afternoon sun, and the deep burgundy of the squires' jackets was brushed and crisp. The guards stood with their chests puffed out, polished and impressive, the gleam of their armor dazzling, the golden crown and rose insignia winking at her from all directions.

They watched her, waiting, and Annabelle realized in a moment of icy panic that she had no idea what to do now. *Oh no*, she thought, losing a grip on her fear. *Oh no, oh no, oh no, oh no...*

Before Annabelle could lose her senses entirely, Sam leaned in and murmured "Stay here" before dismounting and striding confidently up the aisle toward the great tent. She didn't need his urging. Her legs felt like jelly in the stirrups.

Annabelle looked on nervously as two men who stood nearest the tent entrance stepped forward to meet Sam.

The first man was large, tall as Lord Roger and just as broad, with a massive bald dome of a head that shone above an impressive beard long enough to graze his broad chest. He wore a blue jacket embellished with gold brocade, brown pants and boots, and a chain around his neck that glittered with sapphires. His size and resplendence would have been terrifying to behold, but Annabelle saw warmth and kindness in the rosy apples of his cheeks and twinkling in his eyes.

The other man was shorter and slim as a reed. He wore his long golden hair tied back in a horsetail, which threw the angles of his face into sharper relief, and his ice-blue eyes were piercingly intent. He was dressed in black from head to toe, and somehow, though his clothes were unadorned, the effect made him look more regal and dignified than his bejeweled companion.

The quiet aura of power about this man gave Annabelle pause, and she wondered if he could be the famed Lord Ronan Barrick of Ayleswood: the king's closest friend and most trusted advisor. If she was right, this man was the most powerful noble in the kingdom. Even the Duchess did not hold such sway over the king.

Sam stopped several feet before the two men and bowed deeply. "My Lords," he said loudly and clearly so that his voice carried over the assembled crowd. "My name is Sir Sam Fisher, Knight of the Realm, servant of the king. It is my honor to present Her Royal Highness, Annabelle Ilenna Alexandria Penelope Isren, Princess and heir to the throne of Dunea."

As one, the assembled crowd sank to one knee, heads bowed. Annabelle could not breathe, her back seizing up with panic as she stared down at them all. She could not do this. *She could not do this.*

"Psst."

Annabelle glanced over her shoulder to see Emily perched atop one of the wagons behind the carriage. Her friend raised an eyebrow and gave a little jerk of her chin as if to say, *Pull yourself together, Annabelle.* Annabelle nodded, feeling a swell of gratitude that Emily was there, that all of her friends were there. *I will surround you with people who love you, and we will keep you safe.* Her aunt's words echoed in her mind as Annabelle took a big steadying breath and finally signaled for Damon to help her down from Sparrow's saddle.

With Emily and Damon watching from behind and Sam waiting before her, smiling proudly, Annabelle, at last, took one step forward and then another.

Behind her, the carriage door opened, and Annabelle and knew that the Duchess was following in her uncertain footsteps. She attempted to carry herself a bit straighter, feeling the heat of her aunt's gaze upon her back, trying to remember the years of lessons and coming up strangely blank.

When Annabelle reached the place where Sam waited, he stepped to the side. He nodded his encouragement as Annabelle passed him. She would take the final steps on her own, but she would never really be alone, not when she had him by her side. The thought made her feel stronger.

When she, at last, stood before the two lords, the larger man stepped forward and bowed low.

"Your Highness," he said in a voice that was deep and sonorous, "it is an honor to greet you, after all this time. I am Lord Richard Asby of Black Mountain. My companion is Lord Ronan Barrick of Ayleswood."

Lord Barrick bowed when he was introduced, though his eyes never left her face. There was a strangeness to his gaze that Annabelle could not put her finger on, an emotion that she could not name.

"Princess," Barrick said in a hushed voice. "An honor."

Annabelle's cheeks flushed. "Thank you, Lord Barrick, Lord Asby," she said

Barrick smiled kindly. "You will not remember us," he said. "You were so young the last time we saw you. But I must tell you now that to know you as a child was truly one of the gifts of my life. Was she not every bit as lovely as she is now, Asby?"

Barrick turned to his companion, who chuckled, his mustache fluttering. "I daresay she was, though mischievous in the extreme if memory serves." He gave Annabelle a hearty wink.

She knew they meant to put her at ease, to let her know she was among friends, but the revelation that Annabelle was surrounded by people who had known her and of whom she had no recollection, made her feel even more uncomfortable. What did they expect her to say? The enormity of what had been taken from her—not just her home, but friends as well—settled upon Annabelle's shoulders, and she was suddenly painfully aware that there were some fifty-odd onlookers to witness her embarrassment.

Thankfully, the Duchess chose that moment to chime in. "You two are turning into sentimental old men," she quipped, coming to stand beside Lord Asby. "Come. Let's go inside. We have been traveling for a week. There will be plenty of time for days gone by once we've all had a meal, a rest, and a wash."

Without another word, Lord Asby offered the Duchess his arm, and together they led Lord Barrick, Sam, Damon, and Annabelle into the tent, away from the curious stares that she could feel undressing her from head to toe as she went.

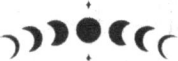

The interior of the tent was massive and finely appointed. A large bed stood in the far corner, set with ivory linens, fur blankets, and piled with overstuffed pillows. Annabelle longed for nightfall so she might lose herself amongst such comfort. A massive square table dominated the center of the space, set with copper bowls of food—fat juicy berries, dried spiced meats, bricks of cheese, and bread with honey and jam. Underneath it all, vast ornate rugs were spread to spare their feet from the indignity of the ground.

Altogether the effect was stunning, and Annabelle could do nothing more than stand gaping as Sam moved to a sideboard and retrieved a goblet of wine. He lifted her left hand and closed it around the goblet.

"Drink," he ordered her quietly, "and sit down."

Giving him a grateful smile, Annabelle settled in one of the canvas chairs that stood around the edge of the table, relishing the sweetness of the wine and sighing heavily as her cramped muscles began to relax at last. Feeling content, she reached across and plucked a raspberry from its bowl and popped it into her mouth.

As she ate, the others took places around the table as well. Only Lord Asby approached the table but did not sit.

Instead, he raised his wine goblet high and proclaimed, "Her Royal Highness, Princess Annabelle."

"Princess Annabelle," the others echoed, and they all drank deeply while Annabelle attempted to look appropriately modest, appreciative, flattered, and unsurprised—all at the same time.

"Outstanding wine," Asby said appreciatively as he settled his large frame into the small chair, which groaned in protest. "Gods above it is good to have you here, at last, Princess."

"Thank you, Lord Asby," Annabelle replied with a shy smile, "it is good to be here."

They all helped themselves to the food. Asby, Barrick and the Duchess fell into comfortable conversation about the journey, the state of the roads, and whether the rumors were true that bandits had been spotted as far south as the Golden Hills. Annabelle was thankfully left out of the conversation for the time being, but she refused to fully relax as she ate, careful to remain poised despite her ravenous hunger. She was no fool. The inspection of Princess Annabelle had only just begun.

Her suspicions proved correct when Lord Asby turned his next question to her.

"Are you looking forward to returning to Ellasport, Princess?" he asked.

"Yes, of course, Lord Asby," she replied. It was the truth. Annabelle had only faint, vague memories of her birthplace that was rumored to be the most beautiful city in the kingdom. She longed to see the place again so she could make up her own mind about its splendor.

"Your father the King anxiously awaits your arrival," Asby said with an approving smile. "We will leave tomorrow first thing and should arrive at the palace within a week."

Annabelle nodded, unsure of what she was supposed to say. Of course, she knew this already but did not think pointing out such a thing would ingratiate her to such a powerful Lord.

This gesture seemed sufficient, however, as Lord Asby continued, "The King and court have taken up residence at the palace for the time being to play host to the delegation from Eìrlan, which is set to arrive not long after your Royal Highness. The Gods willing, negotiations will go smoothly, and you will be wed to his Highness Prince Mica of Eìrlan before the month is out."

Annabelle fought the urge to fidget. She *knew* all of this already. Did he think that she was foolish and ignorant? If so, she had hoped that the Duchess might intervene on her behalf, but her aunt only observed Asby, her eyes narrowed to slits.

It was Lord Barrick who came to her rescue.

"I'm sure the princess understands what awaits her in Ellasport, Asby," he said. His tone was casual, but his eyes flashed dangerously as he regarded Asby over the rim of his goblet.

"Of course she does," Asby agreed calmly. "But it never hurts to review details to make certain there are no surprises. To ensure that the princess is prepared."

Barrick opened his mouth, but Annabelle cut across him, "Lord Asby, you may ask me whatever you wish."

Asby inclined his head respectfully, then asked, "Do you know what the king's cabinet is, Your Highness?"

The question took Annabelle aback with its simplicity, but she answered all the same, "I do. They are the king's closest advisors, each appointed to oversee a certain aspect of the realm and its governance."

Asby smiled widely at her response. "Excellent, Highness," he said, the condescension in his tone making Annabelle's jaw clench. "And do you know the members of your father's cabinet, as well as the positions they hold?"

White-hot irritation rose in Annabelle's throat like bile. She sat up straight and looked Asby dead in the eyes as she said, all intentions to please and flatter this man gone. "You are my father's Minister of War. Lord Raymond is the Minister of Finance. Lord Salis is the Minister of Foreign Diplomacy. Brother Eggles is the High Priest, and Lord Barrick is...well...he's anything and everything the king needs him to be." Annabelle spared Barrick a small smile. After all, he wasn't the one treating her like a misbehaving child. He did not return the smile as he was still looking daggers at Asby, and Annabelle was concerned to see that Damon was also glaring across the table at Lord Asby.

"And her Grace the Duchess?" Asby continued to probe her, paying no attention to the others.

Annabelle did not bat an eye as she shrugged and said, "You evidently mean to trick me, Lord Asby. My aunt holds no formal position in the king's cabinet, though I daresay if the rumors are to be believed, she may just outrank you all—even you Lord Asby."

Damon let out a guffaw which he quickly attempted to pass off as a coughing fit, and Sam was smirking. Even Lord Asby smiled as he asked, "Do you think this is a joke, Princess?"

An icy silence fell within the tent as a wave of tension passed around the table.

"Watch yourself, Asby," Lord Barrick hissed, his tone dangerous. Damon looked like he was weighing the pleasure it would give him to strike Lord Asby across the face against the punishment that would come from attacking a great Lord of the realm. Sam's face had become an unreadable mask, and the Duchess's knuckles were white as she gripped the edge of the table. Asby ignored them all, watching Annabelle intently, waiting for her reply.

She had no idea what it was exactly that he wanted her to say or do, but his words had set her veins burning with icy rage. Without looking away from her quarry, she said, "Sam, please take Damon outside before he breaks something. My new…" she paused, "friends and I need to have a little chat."

Damon opened his mouth to protest, but Sam was already on his feet. He rounded the table and seized his friend by the upper arm, leaning over to whisper something into Damon's ear. The knight closed his mouth and nodded, albeit a bit sulkily, and followed Sam out of the tent.

"We'll be right outside if you need us, Your Highness," he said as he ducked through the flap, casting Lord Asby a mutinous look before he went.

"Princess…" Asby began to say as the tent flap closed behind Damon, but Annabelle held up a hand, and he fell silent at once.

"No," she said, pinching the bridge of her nose to ward off a headache. "No, you have had time to speak. Despite my desperate need for a meal, a bath, and a good night's sleep, I let you do so because I understand my position. A Princess does not have the luxury of owning her own time, and so I let you speak, but now it is my turn."

She waited to see if he would respect her wishes. Nobody so much as moved or even breathed, and so she continued.

"I asked my friends to leave to prove a point. We grew up together at the manor, you see. Though they are both much older than I am, we managed to become friends. I consider them my brothers. It was not easy to do. Even as a small child, I knew who I was. *Princess*. I would one day be Queen, and I would have the power to change their lives forever."

Asby stirred then as if he would speak, but Annabelle did not give him a chance.

"At the age of ten, I realized that it was not only over my brothers that I might someday hold dominion. I realized that I was more powerful as a child than every person I had ever known—even the late Lord Roger, my caretaker. And yet, we became a family. No contracts protect our bond, only trust—trust that we built over years."

Annabelle felt every word she uttered as if she was spitting them out to roll across the table.

"I spend every day aware of the chasm between me and everyone in the world whom I love because I have never forgotten who I am and what that means. And you have the nerve to sit there and ask me if I think all of this is a joke as if you have earned the right to speak to me however you wish."

She paused again, smiling to herself. Knowing what she would say next and refusing to rush the pleasure of it.

"The only friends I have just walked out that door. You may outrank them in the eyes of the realm, but they have earned privileges with me that you have not." Annabelle leveled a glare at Asby and was pleased to see his face pale slightly, "Now get out of my tent."

Asby and Ronan walked together out of the tent and headed toward their own lodgings around the corner. Sir Damon and Sir Sam watched them go, their eyes boring holes into Ronan's back.

When they were finally out of earshot, Ronan chuckled and said, "Well, I hope you think twice the next time you mean to go toe to toe with our princess." Pride swelled in his chest to think of how she had looked—regal, beautiful, so like her mother that it had left him staring in awe.

Asby stopped walking and lifted a quizzical eyebrow. "What in the Gods' earth are you talking about, Barrick?"

"I'm talking about how the princess just undressed you better than the Countess of Greenham could have done." Ronan elaborated, smirking. "And with far fewer references to the size and functionality of your manhood, now that I think of it."

To his surprise, Asby actually laughed aloud. "My dear Lord Barrick," he chuckled. "Do you honestly believe that what happened in there was an accident?"

Ronan's smile faltered. "You told me you had concerns about her, about her preparedness for court...."

"Indeed I did," Asby agreed, still looking amused, "but not about whether she could name the members of the cabinet. Hang the bloody cabinet! I meant to discover the kind of girl she is, and I think I did rather well."

Ronan scowled, no longer enjoying himself as much as he had been moments ago. "You tricked her," he said flatly.

"Oh, don't go getting all honorable with me now, Ronan," Asby clapped him on the back. "Our fun is just beginning, and if the show our Annabelle just put on is any indication, we are going to have a lot of it!"

And with that, he turned and strode off in the direction of his tent whistling a merry tune.

Ronan simply stood there, cold fury rooting him to the spot. Asby could be intolerable at times, but these *games*. They were the foolish games of a bored and powerful man, and Ronan had no patience for them. Not now. Not with so much at stake.

He had enjoyed watching the princess tear into Asby—though he might have cautioned her to be careful divulging so many personal details. Just like her mother, he thought. Ilenna hadn't been afraid to let others see her heart. It had been what made her so loved by her people. The thought should have comforted him, but it did not. Instead, it made him anxious.

He was too close to this one, he knew. For years he had carried on, unassailable, without a blind spot or a weak point. This had always been a possibility, of course. He had feared as much, yet the reality of his affection for the princess was far more disconcerting than the possibility had ever been. For the first time in many years, Ronan Barrick felt at a disadvantage. He needed help, he needed eyes and ears and information, he needed…

His eyes fell upon the young knight, Sam Fisher, speaking with one of the guards. Though he had not met the knight personally, Ronan had been watching Sam's steady climb through the ranks of the king's knights for a while now. And if the princess was to be believed, he was a member of her inner circle, trusted above all others.

Ronan smiled to himself. Yes, Sir Sam Fisher would do nicely. But he would have to be careful this time. His princess needed him, and he would not fail her again.

Chapter Five

The royal entourage moved south the following morning. Annabelle was so exhausted from the previous journey and from the excitement following her arrival at the camp, she hardly remembered getting out of bed. With Emily's help, she managed to dress and walk the short distance from the tent to the carriage without falling over and making a fool of herself. By the time the carriage pulled into motion, Annabelle was dead asleep once more.

The great road was wide and smooth, and so Annabelle slept most of the first day, waking stiff and hungry when they stopped to set up camp again by the river. That evening she once again dined in the company of the Duchess and the Lords Asby and Barrick.

Thankfully this meal did not share the theatrics of their last one. Both Asby and Barrick were respectful and jovial dinner companions. They did not mention Annabelle's outburst, and they no longer seemed interested in quizzing her knowledge of the court or her duties. Instead, they talked about Ellasport and the palace, people they knew, people they wanted Annabelle to meet, and best of all: they told stories about Annabelle's mother.

Before long, Annabelle actually began to relax and enjoy herself. Her only regret was that Sam and Damon did not join them. Annabelle knew she shouldn't be surprised or upset. They were her personal guard, and though she trusted them above all others, she knew they were not considered her equals. It was the first of many differences that made Annabelle long for the quiet halls of Rosewood Manor.

The following days were much the same as the first: Annabelle was roused before dawn and stuffed into the carriage, where she would try to sleep away the tedious hours on the road before the caravan stopped to once again make camp in some flat, grassy place. In the evenings, she dined with her aunt and the lords. At night she sat with Emily in hushed conversation, swapping stories of life on the road.

At the beginning of the week, Annabelle had felt that time was dragging on interminably. Then, in the blink of an eye, it was the day before they would reach Ellasport. *Too fast*, Annabelle thought. This was all happening too fast. Two weeks ago, she hadn't even known of her betrothal. Two weeks ago, her entire life had been different—her future was a mystery, and yet at the same time, it was filled to bursting with friends and family and sunlight.

Now? Now Annabelle knew what her future held: a marriage, probably children, and one day the throne of Dunea. So why did it suddenly feel so empty?

"You know what I keep wondering?" Annabelle asked Emily as her friend helped her dress that morning.

"What?" Emily said around a mouthful of pins as she fussed with Annabelle's hair.

"I've had years of preparation—all the lessons with my aunt, my studies with the Baron…and the closer I come to actually using any of that information, the more I wonder if I'm meant to actually *do* anything at all."

Emily's busy fingers paused. "What do you mean?"

"I mean…" Annabelle sighed. "I know that the Duchess has always told me that one day I would be Queen, and so I need to know all of these things, but nobody has fully explained to me what I'm expected to do—beyond marrying this prince Mica. It makes me wonder if a Queen is expected to do anything, or if it's more about *being*…I don't know. I don't know if that makes any sense at all."

"I can't say that I know how you feel," Emily replied kindly. "I haven't ever really worried about what I'm *supposed* to do, mostly because I always knew what I *had* to do. I don't think the two are the same thing."

"No, of course, they aren't." Annabelle felt a stab of guilt at Emily's words. "I'm sorry. I know I shouldn't be complaining."

"You aren't complaining exactly," Emily pointed out. She paused for a moment, chewing her lip. "Do you mind if I speak plainly?"

Annabelle smiled broadly. "I wish you would. Always."

Emily nodded. "I think you're scared—and of course you are. Anyone would be frightened to walk into a new world for the first time, with all those expectations. But…but I think being on the road has given you too much time to think, with too little distraction. You've begun worrying about things that there is no use worrying over. There's nothing to be done about them now, not until we finally get you to Ellasport, and you can begin figuring it all out."

"I think you're right," Annabelle sighed. "I'm being silly."

"You aren't being silly." Emily lay a hand on Annabelle's shoulder and squeezed gently. "You have every right to feel how you feel. I suppose my only suggestion is to put aside the things you cannot change and figure out if there is something you *can* do right now to help yourself feel better."

Something she could do? Well, Annabelle didn't have to think about that for long. There was still one thing she could do, one person she had yet to face. She did not know if it would help her concerns about her uncertain future, but they would arrive at the palace the next day. Time was running out.

She needed to talk to Sam, to have that fight, and then put the past behind her—all of it.

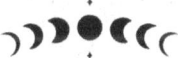

The afternoon was sunny and warm, not a cloud in the sky, and a cool breeze blew in from the east as Sam dismounted his horse and handed off the reins to one of the pages. Stretching lazily, he looked around. It was a pleasant enough place to make camp—flat and grassy as much of the land beside the road had been for the duration of their journey, once the caravan passed beyond the rolling hills and closer to the southern coast.

They had made camp earlier in the day, wanting to give everyone time to rest before the final stretch the following morning. As Sam walked through the camp, he witnessed guards polishing shields and blades, squires mending standards, and grooms brushing horses' coats to a gleaming shine. Grand arrivals, awe-inspiring in their effortless beauty, took a significant amount of preparation.

"Sam!"

Sam turned to see Damon crossing the field toward him, wearing a wide grin and carrying his sheathed sword in one big hand.

"Fancy a bit of friendly competition?" he asked, indicating the weapon he held.

Sam hesitated, eyeing the sword. In truth, he could use a bit of exercise. The days of riding hours on end had made him stiff and bored. But he didn't want to spar with Damon.

"I'm sorry, Damon, but not today," Sam said. "I'm so stiff from the saddle I think I might shatter if you beat me up with a sword."

"Oh, come on, Sammy," Damon urged. "You're as bored as I am, and it has been years since we've had a proper sparring match. I know you're dying to get me back for all those times I spanked you black and blue."

It was tempting, but there was something steely in Damon's eyes that worried Sam. He thought it far more likely that Damon wanted to remind Sam he could *still* spank him but kept that thought to himself.

"Alright," he agreed grudgingly. "One round. The first contact wins."

"If you insist," Damon said, rolling his eyes.

They chose a flat bit of earth just outside of camp for their match. Damon was already chomping at the bit, anxious to get started, but Sam insisted they stretch first. He hadn't been lying; he *was* stiff.

When Sam was satisfied that they were both adequately limber, he and Damon faced each other, weapons at the ready. They began to circle each other, each taking stock of the other's movements, each man waiting for the other to make the first move.

"Gods save me," Damon said after a few moments passed. "Have you actually learned patience, Sam?"

The comment rankled, but Sam kept his face an impassive mask. He had learned quite a bit more than patience.

"I'm just waiting for you to work up the courage to attack me," he said casually. "Are you afraid I'll beat you after all?"

"Afraid?" Damon scoffed. "Never."

But something tensed in his body as he said it, the subtle tell that he was about to strike. Sam shifted on his feet, readying for the impact.

And Damon did strike, fast and hard. Sam met each of his blows, relishing the way the impact reverberated down his arm and into his feet. The blade was a part of his body, and they moved as one with each strike and parry. With every breath, with every movement, Sam felt himself come alive. This was where he felt most himself, most in control. Before long, both men were grinning and sweating buckets.

Damon had always been good with a sword. He had been Sam's earliest teacher, challenging him to duels with sticks and wooden blades, doling out regular lessons in defeat. But Sam had idolized Damon, and he had a deep abiding desire to prove himself, so he met his beatings eagerly.

Not that Damon was ever cruel. He had known from early childhood that it was his destiny to become a knight. As the younger son of a country lord, it was the best future Sam could hope for. Damon took his own training seriously and, as he explained to Sam every time they sparred, falling in the dirt was how you learn.

Sam had wanted everything that Damon wanted but had known that he would always have to work harder, not just to become a great swordsman, but for every other opportunity that Damon took for granted. The determination to prove himself drove him to become an expert, not only with a sword but in all areas of combat. That same determination made him follow Damon to the capital to find a future and claim a name that had never been promised him.

By that time, Damon was squiring for Lord Velton, and before long, his master took him south to Ellasport, while Sam remained behind in Rengon City. Damon had enjoyed the pleasures of the south, finally winning his knighthood and returning home to act as a guard to the princess, while Sam was sent farther north to prove his mettle on the battlefield.

Damon's life had always been easier than Sam's, and Sam feared that Damon would never forgive him for it.

Lost in reminiscing about the past, Sam missed his footing and stumbled, giving Damon the opening he needed. Deftly, he smacked Sam's side with the flat of his sword, grinning from ear to ear.

"That's victory to me," he announced, panting from exertion.

They were both exhausted and drenched in sweat. Damon's shirt was soaked through, clinging to his torso, and Sam could see every sculpted muscle of his chest and abdomen through the thin fabric. Something deep and unpleasant tightened in his stomach. He looked away.

"Good one," he said as he forced a smile and bent to retrieve his belt and scabbard from the ground.

Damon, who did not appear to have noticed anything amiss, was chuckling to himself. "Don't feel too bad, Sammy. You'll beat me one day."

Sam felt his cheeks redden with anger, but he shoved it aside. "Maybe one day," he said with a shrug.

"Is it over already?"

Sam turned to see Annabelle sitting cross-legged on the ground several feet away, her full skirts billowing around her, expression dark with disappointment.

"I am sorry, Your Highness," Damon said with a wicked grin and a mocking bow. "You'll have to swoon over me another day. I think young Sam is spent."

"Is that true?" Annabelle asked, eyeing Sam suspiciously. "Is one of the knights who must defend my honor truly exhausted from one sparring match?"

"Don't fret, Princess," Damon said with a wink. "I think your honor is safe enough in my hands for the time being."

Sam turned away to fetch his belt and scabbard from where he had set them on the ground, not feeling up for this particular kind of banter. He made a meal of cleaning and sheathing his sword. Damon was gone when he was finished, but Annabelle was still seated on the ground, watching him.

"You shouldn't let him treat you like that," she said sternly.

He folded his arms across his chest. "Like what, exactly?"

She pushed to her feet, brushing grass from her dress. "Like you're still fourteen. You are a man now, Sam. And a knight worthy of the title. He should treat you with respect."

Sam gritted his teeth. He was not in the mood to be scolded.

"Was there something you wanted, Princess?" He asked, cringing inwardly when the words came out somewhat harsher than he had meant.

Annabelle's face hardened at his tone, but she did not balk or run away. She faced him, hands on hips, and said, "Okay then. We are doing this. Now."

)))●(((

"What is it that we are doing?"

"Fighting," Annabelle answered simply.

It needed to be done. Annabelle had known it from the minute she laid eyes on him in the gardens at Rosewood Manor. She hadn't known exactly when she had been ready to face her own anger and heartbreak. But the conversation with Emily had stoked that quietly smoldering ember into a flame. She hadn't been ready, not before, but she was ready now.

It was time to find out if their friendship was salvageable or if it was lost forever. Either way, they needed to move forward.

"I'm not really in the mood, Annabelle," Sam grumbled.

"Good," she retorted. "I want you tired and irritable. It will make you honest."

He would not get out of this one.

"Fine," he said with a sigh, rubbing his forehead as if to stave off a headache. "I suppose we're doing this."

"We are."

"I don't suppose you have an idea of where you'd like to begin?" he said, tone lazy with disinterest.

And like that—just like that, Annabelle was furious.

"How about we start with the fact that you *left*, Sam?" she shouted, unable to contain her feelings for one more second. "You left me alone at the manor without a word, just vanished without saying goodbye, and then stayed away for *years*."

"I was fighting in the north," he countered. "I couldn't exactly have popped home for a quick visit, could I?"

But Annabelle was ready for him. She had imagined this fight for years, had prepared for his every argument. "You could have written," she snapped. "You could have let me know that you were alright."

"You knew I was alright," Sam pointed out reasonably. "I wrote to Lord Roger. I know he shared my letters with the family."

He was still too calm, and it was painful. Annabelle needed him angry, needed something to rage against.

"Oh, so I'm supposed to be grateful that I received your news through Lord Roger, like some…some acquaintance. You were my best friend, Sam! And you didn't have anything to say to me?"

"What was I supposed to say?" Sam's face was red now, his temper rising.

Good, Annabelle thought.

"You made it perfectly clear how you felt about my leaving. *You* said you didn't want to speak to me again. I was respecting your wishes."

"Is that what you tell yourself to help you sleep at night?" Annabelle laughed mirthlessly. "Spare me, Sam. You didn't write me because you were scared to face what you'd done to—"

"What *I'd* done?!" Sam exploded. He was well and truly furious now, but Annabelle had already built up steam.

"You were the closest thing I had to a brother. I *loved* you." Tears were rolling down her cheeks as she finally gave voice to the deepest wounds of her heart. "But I was never enough, was I? You had to run after Damon to play soldier. I begged you not to go. I knew you would go, but I was going to miss you so much, and so I begged you not to anyway."

"You shouldn't have asked me."

His voice was so quiet, so filled with feeling that Annabelle's endless stream of rebuttals died on her tongue. She just stared at him, and he looked so young just then—as if they were both children once more.

"Even if you knew I would go anyway, you still shouldn't have asked me," he continued. "Becoming a knight was about more than following in Damon's footsteps. It meant I would have a name and a purpose. It *killed* me to leave you, Annabelle, but I didn't have a choice. Then you were begging me to stay, and I knew if I had to hear you beg one more time, I wouldn't go. So I left without saying goodbye. It was wrong, but I did it anyway because you put me in an impossible position."

Annabelle was crying in earnest now, the anger giving way to shame.

"Damn it!" she cursed, stamping her foot against the ground. "Damn it, Sam. I'm so careful. I'm always *so* careful, and it still wasn't enough. I still managed to hurt you."

Her whole life, she had tread so lightly with her few and precious friends, conscious of the differences between them and wary of how she might do harm with her carelessness. But Sam had announced his intention to follow Damon and…, and she had snapped. She would have done anything to make him stay, and she had only driven him farther away. So many years of anger and hurt, and she had been just as culpable.

"Look…" Sam said slowly. "Whatever you said to me, however, I felt about it, I should have talked to you. I shouldn't have just left, and I should have written to you. Just because I have my own side to the story doesn't mean that yours is wrong, Annabelle."

"I know that. Even so…"

She paused, unsure of what to say next, so she just looked at him. Now that she had said the things that needed saying, it was like seeing him for the first time. Without anger there to drown out everything else, she felt the things she should have felt when he walked back into her life: relief that he was alive, awe at the man he had become, and joy—a heart-aching, breathless joy that he had returned.

A little sob escaped her then, and she ran at him. He caught her up in his arms and held on tight as Annabelle cried into his shirtfront.

"I'm s—sorry," She sobbed against his chest as he held her. "I m—missed you so m—much. It made me s—so angry."

"I'm sorry too," Sam murmured, stroking her hair. "I shouldn't have left you there alone without knowing that I would always come back for you."

Annabelle had calmed down enough to pull away, and she smiled up at him, wiping tears from her cheeks. "You did come back for me, though."

"I did," he grinned. "And as long as the Duchess wants me at your side, I'll never have to leave again."

"She is a meddler," Annabelle said, scowling.

"That she may be, but I think this time it was for the best."

"As do I."

Annabelle flung her arms around his waist again, startling him into a laugh.

"Give me a few more moments," she said, her voice muffled by his shirt.

Sam snaked his arms around her shoulders and rested his chin gently atop her head. "Take all the time you need."

Annabelle sighed deeply, feeling the weight of years lift from her shoulders. Sam, her person, her best friend in the entire world, was home.

Chapter Six

"Absolutely *not*."

Annabelle gaped in horror at the monstrosity that Lady Malisa brandished before her, hoisted in the air so that she could see every horrible inch of it cascading down to the floor.

The trunks packed with gowns and jewels had arrived the previous night and with them Annabelle's new ladies in waiting—Lady Malisa Asby, the younger of Lord Asby's daughters, and Lady Rose Greenwood.

Lady Malisa was tall, blonde and willowy, and frequently wore an expression of distaste as if there were an unpleasant odor that only she could smell. Lady Rose was, if possible, the opposite of Lady Malisa. She was petite and bubbly with a pretty smile and warm brown eyes. Annabelle liked them both fine but was wary in their presence. These were court women, and she did not take for granted where their loyalties lay.

Malisa frowned, and she inspected the gown as if trying to ascertain what could possibly be the problem. "Is it the rubies?" she asked. "I know they're a bit understated, but with the right jewelry…."

"Ouch!" Annabelle jumped in her seat as one of the pins that Lady Rose was using to arrange her hair jabbed at the base of her skull.

"I'm so sorry, Your Highness," Rose said, "it's just this scar behind your ear. I can't seem to arrange your hair in a way that it is completely hidden."

"Don't worry about the scar, Rose," Annabelle said. "Just do your best."

"However did you get such a ghastly thing?"

Annabelle thought that "ghastly" was a dramatic way to refer to the thin slice that cut across her hairline, just behind her ear.

"I fell out of a tree when I was eleven," she said, fingering the scar. She smiled, remembering that day. Sam was climbing one of the tall evergreens by the manor. She always wanted to do anything he did, only she had been too small to reach some of the branches. It was fortunate that the stone had not pierced any deeper, or the healer said she could have died.

"Just do the best you can, Rose…" Annabelle said, turning back to Malisa and the nightmare of a gown. "It's not the rubies," she lied. "I was just hoping for something a bit…simpler?"

Malisa's expression was scandalized, but Rose abandoned her attempts to brutalize Annabelle's scalp and bustled forward.

"Malisa, really," she chided as she descended upon the trunks spilling over with Annabelle's worst fear of what gowns could be. "The Princess can't wear *that*. The color is all wrong, for one thing…" She trailed off, muttering to herself as she rummaged. In the meantime,

Emily stepped forward from her position in the corner to take up the task of doing Annabelle's hair. Annabelle could have kissed her for it.

When Rose at last surfaced from the depths of the trunks, she bore in her arms a dress that struck Annabelle dumb with its beauty.

It was a vision of emerald silk with a scooped neckline, fitted sleeves, and a full skirt that rustled pleasantly as Rose held it aloft. But the true masterpiece was the bodice. A great cresting wave was rendered in delicate silver embroidery, beginning at the left hip and ending in a whorl at her sternum.

"It's perfect," Emily breathed, drawing a sharp look from Malisa for speaking out of turn, but the maid paid the lady no mind.

"It is," Annabelle murmured in agreement, impressed despite herself. Malisa looked sour, but Rose glowed with pride.

They helped her into the exquisite dress, which fit Annabelle as if it had been made just for her. Which, she realized, it probably had been. Her corset was pulled so tight that she could hardly breathe. Still, Annabelle found that she barely cared as she stared at her reflection in the floor-length glass, fingering the delicate stitching across her torso in awe as Emily arranged her hair into a cascade of curls down her back that mimicked the embroidery on her gown. Rose added delicate color to her cheeks and the swell of her lips but otherwise left her face untouched.

Their work complete, they left Annabelle to stare at her own reflection in the looking-glass.

The woman in the emerald dress who stared back was tall, beautiful, and—*regal*. Annabelle's eyes sought Emily's as she whispered, "I look like a princess."

Emily giggled, but tears were shining in her eyes as she said, "It's about time you noticed."

Just then, the tent flap pulled back, and Sam stuck his shaggy head inside. "It's time," he announced. "Is she ready?"

Lady Rose giggled and moved aside to give him a better view. His gaze settled upon Annabelle and his eyes popped wide. Stepping into the tent, he crossed the room toward Annabelle and sank to his knee.

"My Queen," he murmured with a broad smile.

Annabelle shifted, uncomfortable. "Would you stop that? And get up. It's just me. And I'm not your Queen—not yet, anyway."

He gave her a quizzical look, and his face lit in mock recognition. "Oh, it *is* you. I thought you must be some great queen from a faraway land because *my* Annabelle would rather die screaming than be stuffed into such a magnificent pile of petticoats."

Annabelle punched him on the arm as hard as she could, her movement slightly encumbered by the stiff silk of her sleeves.

"Watch it," she warned as he pulled away, laughing and rubbing his arm. "I will be your queen one day, and I will remember you teasing me."

But his unwillingness to take her seriously had made her feel better. Nerves were already beginning to play jump rope with her insides. The dress and all the fuss had started to feel a bit overwhelming. For a moment, though, they were teasing each other, and everything was normal.

"Are you ready?" Sam asked her then, and that fast it all came crashing back.

Ready. Ready to leave. Ready to make the short trip to the city of Ellasport and the Golden Palace, to meet her father again for the first time in years and at last take up her rightful place as Princess and heir to the throne of Dunea. How could anyone ever be ready for all of that?

Fearing that she would vomit if she opened her mouth, Annabelle nodded. But Sam seemed to see the truth in her eyes because he gave her shoulder a gentle squeeze before holding the tent flap aside so she could pass through.

The scene that met Annabelle's eyes was exactly as it had been when she arrived at the camp days ago: guards, soldiers, squires, servants, all assembled to form a straight path from tent to the carriage that waited to bear her home—except that this carriage was resplendent with golden ornamentation and a large insignia bearing the royal coat of arms was rendered on the door and carved into the wheels. The time to hide, it seemed, had ended.

Damon, the Duchess, and Lord Asby waited beside the carriage, but Annabelle heard the sound of a throat clearing and turned to see that Lord Barrick stood to her right. He moved to her then and took her hands in his own. "Are you ready?" he asked.

Annabelle smiled wryly. "People keep asking me that. Does it matter if I am?"

He returned her smile, his eyes kind, and understanding. "I suppose it doesn't matter. And yet we care all the same."

A squire moved forward, bearing a wooden box inlaid with silver ornamentation across the lid. Barrick lifted the delicate latch, opening the box to reveal a tiara nestled in the soft velvet cloth within. The tiara was simply but beautifully wrought in pure silver branches that held a shining emerald the size of a robin's egg aloft. Annabelle gasped when she beheld it. It was the most beautiful thing she had ever seen.

Barrick lifted the glorious crown from the box and raised it high in the air before approaching Annabelle and settling it gently upon her head. It was heavier than she had expected, and Annabelle was slightly nervous that if she moved her head, it would tumble off into the dirt, but the fit was perfect.

Barrick smiled down into her eyes and so quietly that only she could hear him, he said, "You are as beautiful as your mother, Princess. To see you wear her crown so well is a balm to those of us who knew and loved her, and miss her still."

His kind words brought tears to Annabelle's eyes, and she beamed up at him. "Thank you, Lord Barrick."

"Ronan," he said firmly. "Please."

She raised an eyebrow. "I will call you Ronan if you will call me Annabelle."

Barrick said nothing to this, only smirked in that way that Annabelle knew meant he would be ignoring this particular request. Without another word, he stepped wide. Keeping a grip on one of her hands, he raised their arms high together and declared to the onlookers in a clear and strong voice, "Her Royal Highness, Princess Annabelle Ilenna Alexandria Penelope Isren. Your future Queen!"

The crowd erupted—everyone jumping and clapping and shouting in celebration. Annabelle's eyes sought her friends. Emily was standing on top of a nearby wagon, tears streaming down her face, hands clapping together above her head. Beside the carriage, Damon was grinning from ear to ear and gave an ear-splitting whistle, causing several horses to balk. Sam and the Duchess stood together, faces bright with pride. Annabelle met her aunt's gaze, and the woman gave a single nod of approval.

Looking out over them all, her friends, her family, and her *people*, Annabelle felt a warmth spread through her entire body, chasing away the fear. She beamed, standing tall in her mother's crown, feeling for the first time in her life one day she really could be Queen.

>>●((

The journey to Ellasport took the better part of the morning, though the anticipation made time move so slowly that Annabelle could have sworn they traveled for days—weeks, even. She sat beside the Duchess in the carriage, and her ladies sat opposite them. Not one of them spoke for the duration, and by the time she heard the horns sounding in the distance, Annabelle thought she might scream from either nerves or boredom; she couldn't decide which.

The first trumpet's blast had her launching herself at the carriage window, dragging aside the thin shade despite her aunt's protestations. Craning her neck, Annabelle managed to catch a glimpse of the palace, shining from its perch atop the cliff, so close now, before the carriage turned and it vanished from sight behind the high city walls.

Annabelle didn't care. There were people on the road—soldiers on horses, farmers driving carts loaded with goods, travelers on foot—and they all stopped to watch in awe as the carriage drove past. Feeling suddenly self-conscious at the close proximity of so many curious stares, Annabelle sat back from the window, but a few minutes later, she was lurching forward in her seat again.

They were passing through the massive city gates, and now Annabelle could see houses, shops, markets, merchant's stalls, taverns, all rolling past the window, their awnings, and signs fresh and colorful in the afternoon light. The buildings were crowded together on either side of the narrow cobbled street, and they were built of the same pale limestone that made the city shine in the bright sunlight. Annabelle couldn't take her eyes off of it.

Too soon, they made a turn onto a wider avenue and away from the noise of the city. Up a hill, they trundled past lavish residences with ornate facades and gardens that could only just be glimpsed from over the top of high walls. Annabelle thought she spied a temple down a side street, but then they made another turn, and everything vanished from view as they climbed higher still. Annabelle bade Malisa open the other curtain so she could look out across the city, sprawling down the slope of the cliff to the sea, where she could just make out the masts of ships in the harbor below.

"Princess," the Duchess's voice sounded from somewhere far away.

"Hm?" Annabelle said distractedly, still craning her neck to get a better view of the ocean.

"We have arrived," the Duchess said.

Annabelle turned and gasped. There it was. The palace stretched out before her eyes, golden and shining. It was a breathtaking sight that brought tears to Annabelle's eyes and sent her heart fluttering. This place was so magnificent, it seemed impossible that it could be *home*.

Damon opened the door to the carriage, and Barrick stepped forward to take her hand as she descended the steps, eyes still wide and staring.

"Come," he said as she took his offered arm, smiling slightly at her expression of amazement. "It's time to see the king."

Father. Annabelle was suddenly glad for the support of his arm; otherwise, she feared she might fall over. Why, oh, why hadn't she eaten more at breakfast? Too late for regrets, she let Barrick lead her past the lines of guards standing at attention, up the grand front steps, and into the palace.

If the palace's exterior had been breathtaking, it did not hold a candle to what awaited inside.

The entrance hall was immense, and Annabelle's footsteps echoed as her shoes clicked on the marble floor. Everywhere she looked was gold leaf and mirrors that made the light in the hall seem to come alive. Delicate paintings wound their way up columns and across the ceiling. Annabelle feared she must look like a bird the way her head kept turning this way and that.

An impressive marble staircase with a sculpted banister stood at the end of the hall, winding away to the upper floors, but Barrick led Annabelle toward a door set along the right wall. A guard stood at attention beside this door, his livery gleaming, but he did not so much as twitch a single muscle as they passed.

They stepped through into a long gallery lined with portraits on the right and great windows on the left that looked out into what must be only a corner of the legendary palace gardens. Annabelle itched to explore them but allowed herself to be dragged away down the gallery toward a set of massive doors with two guards stationed on either side, where a thin man paced the floor, wringing his hands.

When they drew near, the man stooped low into a bow.

"Your Highness," he said, "My Lord Barrick."

"Your Highness," Barrick said, presenting the nervous man to Annabelle, "Meet Mr. Elfreth, his Majesty's herald."

No sooner had Mr. Elfreth straightened, but he was stooping low again as the Duchess, Damon, and Sam joined them.

"Y-your Grace, Sirs," he stammered. "Is this everyone, my Lord?" He looked to Barrick, who nodded once. "Very good, very good."

Barrick extricated his arm from Annabelle's suddenly viselike grip and kissed the back of her hand before stepping away. She wanted to argue, to order him to escort her. Instead, she forced herself to stand tall and to look straight ahead, even though every inch of her skin was on fire and a voice in her head was screaming *RUN!*

As if from a great distance, she watched the guards pull the doors wide and heard Mr. Elfreth clear his throat and proclaim her title and those of her companions to the chamber beyond.

Now or never, Annabelle thought and, steeling herself, stepped into the throne room.

Chapter Seven

The rumble of muttered conversation ceased at once as Annabelle entered the throne room. As one, the crowd of assembled courtiers turned in her direction. Sunlight from the floor to ceiling windows that stretched along the south wall of the room danced in the facets of a thousand jewels, sending a glittering wave across the room that was dazzling.

Annabelle had not expected to see quite so many people. She supposed that every landed noble must be in attendance, from the great lords of sweeping shires to the most humble baron. Dunea had assembled to view its princess, and the weight of their collective gaze set Annabelle's teeth on edge.

Whispering, soft and subtle like the slithering of snakes over earth, began at the edges of the room as she made her slow progress. One noblewoman in a shocking pink gown leaned in to mutter something in her friend's ear. The other lady giggled and shot Annabelle a look that made her feel utterly undressed. She trained her eyes forward, determined not to be distracted into making a foolish mistake. She did not pay the gossips any mind but looked ahead toward the dais.

The dais, and the great golden chair in which a man sat upright and alert, staring. Suddenly the rest of the room fell away as Annabelle's gaze rested upon her father's face for the first time in since she was a child.

He looked different than she remembered him…thinner, perhaps. Annabelle supposed that age and the pressures of war had altered him from the man she had known as a young child—strong, tall, and full of laughter. Still, the raven's wing hair was the same. The angles of his face were the same. Those emerald eyes, the same as her eyes, gazed down upon her as she approached the foot of the dais, full of an emotion that she could not name. This man, this stranger, was nevertheless known to her heart. *Father*, it whispered.

Annabelle sank into a curtsy at the foot of the dais. "My King," she murmured to the floor. And waited.

Nothing happened for a long moment as Annabelle's heart thundered against her ribcage, desperately seeking an escape. But then, mercifully, King Alexander rose from his great throne and descended the three steps to stand before her. He placed his two big, warm hands on her shoulders and pulled her upright. She looked up into his face to see that he was smiling. The sight of him looking at her like that—like she was something precious and deeply loved—made her chest cave in.

"Daughter," his voice was a cracked whisper, and his eyes glistened as he said. "Welcome home."

Annabelle met his wet smile with one of her own, and then he pulled her close in an embrace. Despite the richness of his clothes and the thick fur cloak he wore, she could feel how thin he was. But the smell of him was the same: spiced meat, fir trees, and the sharp, clean scent of snow.

Annabelle had spent her first few years being raised by her mother, a woman of sun and sea. Her father had been born in the north. It clung to him like dew. She had to gulp down lungfuls of air to keep from falling to pieces as he pulled away and held their joined hands aloft to the court.

"My daughter has returned!" He shouted aloud, his deep voice echoing down the chamber.

There was no uproar of celebration as there had been at the camp. The court of King Alexander sank to their knees and bowed their heads as they murmured together, "Princess Annabelle, may the Gods save her."

Annabelle was unnerved by this display, but the King looked pleased as he turned back toward the dais. He escorted Annabelle to a chair that stood to the left of his own. Next to the glory of the King's seat, her own was small and simple. However, it was still the most delicate piece of furniture Annabelle had ever been allowed to touch, and she lowered herself onto its cushioned seat as slowly and carefully as she could manage.

The King sank back into his throne with a contented sigh and then motioned forward with two ring-clad fingers.

Lord Barrick was already stepping forward to the foot of the dais. He bowed low, first to the King and then to Annabelle. "Your Royal Majesty," he said, "Your Royal Highness. Please accept this token of my faith, love, and loyalty." He motioned, and another man rushed forward, nearly falling onto his face as he sank to the floor. "This is Mr.

Wright, my favorite tailor," Barrick continued. "I offer his services to your Royal Highness. He will fashion a wardrobe that will be…acceptable to our princess." He shot Annabelle the ghost of a wink, and she flushed with gratitude, thinking of her ladies in waiting and the trunks of frightful gowns they might yet foist upon her.

"I accept your gift, my Lord Barrick," she said. "Along with your faith, love, and loyalty."

Barrick bowed again before retreating with Mr. Wright.

And just like that, the ceremony of the gifts began.

꙳)꙳꙳●(((

Sam's eyes roved the throne room, using the distraction of the gifting ceremony to take stock of his surroundings. With the King, the Princess, and the entire court in residence, the golden palace had to be the most well-guarded building in the kingdom. But it was not the enemies outside the city walls with whom Sam was concerned. In all likelihood, his princess's greatest threat currently stood within the four walls of the throne room.

He had elected to linger near the back, slightly off to one side so that he would have the best view of the room and its occupants. It was every bit as impressive as the entrance hall and the gallery—twice as long as it was wide, with a massive hearth set at the center of the north wall and a line of towering glass doors set into the south.

Just like the windows in the gallery, these doors looked out onto the palace gardens. Through them, he could see the setting sun casting a burnished gold across the cacophony of greenery beyond.

Sam had never been to court before, and so he did not know many of the courtiers assembled, though a few he recognized by reputation alone. Lord Barrick, Lord Asby, and the other members of the king's cabinet gathered close to the dais—the most powerful men in the kingdom, and therefore the first to present their gifts and swear their fealty to the princess.

Annabelle's ladies, Malisa and Rose, stood with a gaggle of court ladies who whispered among themselves as they inspected some of the younger and more attractive lords who waited behind the cabinet to present their gifts.

Only one man seemed disinterested in the proceedings, choosing to remain near the end of the line. Sam could only see the back of his head, but those tufts of white hair sticking out at odd angles, he would know anywhere. Lord Velton had come to court. The gesture, Sam knew, would mean the world to Annabelle. It was a good thing for Velton to do.

As he continued his observation of the room, Sam's gaze fell upon a man who stood in the opposite corner of the room.

The man was tall, taller even than Sam, and heavily muscled. He leaned against the far wall, watching the proceedings with an expression of vague interest. Sam was not fooled. There was something too intent in his gaze. Whoever he was, Sam didn't like how the strange man was watching the princess or the small smile that played around his soft mouth.

As Sam watched, the man reached out a hand and pushed at the closest door. It slid open soundlessly. The man slid through the gap with a feline grace that was impressive due to his sheer size. Closing the door silently behind him, he vanished into the garden without drawing even a glance from the guards.

Sam was already moving. He reached the door in seconds and passed through it just as quietly. Then he paused, listening. There was movement on the path ahead. Breathing soft and slow, keeping his back to one of the tall hedges, Sam rushed down the path, turned left, then right, then down another path, tracking the footsteps of his quarry.

Another turn and Sam stopped dead in his tracks. He had reached the edge of the gardens. Nothing lay before him except a low stone wall and the open air; the sea stretched out beyond, glittering in the evening sunset. The only sounds that met his ears were the cries of gulls and the wind blowing through the trees at his back.

"Hello there."

Cursing inwardly, Sam turned. The man sat beside a fountain that gurgled at Sam's back, lounging on a stone bench. The length of his legs stretched out before him. He flashed a bright smile. "Good of you to catch up."

Sam fought against his irritation, mirroring the stranger's casual air. Though the man carried no weapons that Sam could detect, he let his hand drift to rest upon the hilt of the sword he wore belted to his waist. The man's shrewd eyes noted the movement, and his smile widened.

"I don't believe I've had the pleasure," Sam said.

"No," said the stranger, winking suggestively. "I daresay you have not." He held out a big hand. "Raphael Kane, at your service."

Sam did not take the offered hand.

"What is your business at the palace, Mr. Kane?" He asked, unamused by Kane's whimsical manner.

Kane raised an eyebrow. "Business? No, only pleasure for this lad. Taking in the general splendor." He made a sweeping gesture that encompassed the gardens and the vast, unbroken expanse of ocean beyond.

Sam ignored this. He was watching the man closely. Everything from his clothing to the strange way his accent lilted when he spoke was unfamiliar.

"You're one of them, aren't you," Sam asked, eyes narrowing.

The man frowned, expression quizzical. "One of whom? One of the sneakiest bastards you've ever met? One of the only people to sneak up on *you* for a change, I reckon. No? One of the most dashingly handsome men you've ever laid eyes on?" He winked. "You'll need to be more specific."

"It makes sense," Sam continued without acknowledging that Kane had spoken. "It's what I would do: send you in first to get the lay of the land while the ships wait..." he considered for a moment, "in Jewel Bay, or the Strand. Far enough from the city not to be spotted but close enough that it wouldn't take long to deliver your report."

Kane laughed and smacked a hand across his own knee. "Well *done*, lad. I say, my commander could use a few more like you in our clan. Ever consider defecting?" He asked, his eyes twinkling. "The pay is shite, but boy," he let out a low whistle, "the toys we get to play with are lovely and sharp."

"I'm fine where I am, thanks," Sam drawled, unamused.

"Suit yourself," Kane shrugged and lurched up from the bench, stretching lazily. "Right then. I've met you, which has been...well." He looked Sam up and down, "A pleasure, I'm sure. But I do have to be going."

He made to retreat down the path, but Sam blocked his way.

"Not until you tell me how you got into the palace," Sam said, crossing his arms across his chest.

"Oh, now. Don't go asking me something like that," Raphael said, scowling. "I wouldn't be very good at my job if I told you, would I?"

"And I wouldn't be very good at *my* job if I let you go without discovering how you infiltrated the king's court." Sam looked up at him, actually impressed despite himself that a man of his size could have made it so far without drawing attention to himself. Even the ladies of the court would remember seeing such a man. One wink from him would have been enough to set them falling all over themselves.

"You aren't bad at your job, lad," Raphael said, leaning down so that his face was mere inches from Sam's nose. He was so close that Sam could feel his breath on his cheek as he said, "I just can't tell you because then I'd have to kill you, and I'd hate to ruin something so beautiful."

And then he was gone. By the time Sam came to his senses enough to give chase, there wasn't even a trail for him to follow. He stood alone in the middle of the spectacular, breathtaking gardens.

I hope I do get to meet his commander, Sam thought to himself as he made his way back to the throne room. *I'd like to have words with him about his subordinates.*

Behind the frustration at being bested and the smarting of his wounded pride, fear boiled in Sam's gut. More than he wished he could have beat the man to a bloody pulp, more than he wanted to discover how such a man had broken into the palace in the first place, Sam hoped that he never saw Raphael Kane again.

The Duchess had explained the gifting ceremony on their journey to the city.

"The ceremony is for you," she had said as they bumped across the country in her carriage, "but the lords have begun to see it as an opportunity to show off to one another. Let them fight it out among themselves, but do not get involved. The gifting ceremony is long and arduous enough as it is without finding yourself in between Lord Something and Lord Whomever as they bicker over whose gemstones are largest."

Annabelle had chortled at the image, but just now—with every eye in the room trained upon her, watching, evaluating—she was grateful that her role was so easy to execute and was not at all tempted to veer even the slightest degree from the script.

As lord after lord moved forward to shower her with gifts, all of which were quickly whisked away by squires clad in the emerald tunic of the royal household, Annabelle repeated those words: "I accept your faith, love, and loyalty."

The ceremony was an impressive dance; each time a lord stepped away, bowing, another was stepping forward to take his place. A cursory inspection of the hall was enough for Annabelle to know that Gustav was not here, and she felt a grim sense of justice that he had not yet received an invitation to court. Serve him right for being such a pig's ass. But there was one familiar face that brought a smile to her lips as he limped forward to stand before the dais.

"Your Royal Majesty, your Royal Highness," said old Lord Velton in his wheezy voice. "I present you this gift as a symbol of my undying faith, love, and loyalty."

"*Thank you,*" Annabelle mouthed, touched that her dear friend would brave the court. Velton *hated* court. The significance of his gesture was not lost on her, confirmed when he returned her smile with a grimace as a squire moved forward to present his gift.

The squire lifted the lid to the simple wooden box upon Velton's command, and Annabelle gasped aloud. Nestled upon the velvet cloth within was a necklace—wrought in five tiers of pure white gold and set with a cascade of glittering diamonds. Despite the necklace's breathtaking beauty, Annabelle felt apprehensive of the prospect of wearing it. It looked *heavy*.

"Thank you, Lord Velton," Annabelle breathed, hardly remembering the next words she was meant to say, "I accept your gift as well as your faith, love, and loyalty."

Lord Velton bowed again, and a royal squire moved forward to whisk this box away with the others, but just then, the king lurched to his feet, hand held high.

"Wait," he commanded, descending the dais.

Both Lord Velton and the squire kept their eyes trained on the floor as the king lifted the necklace from the box and held it aloft. Some of the ladies gasped when they saw such a magnificent work of art, and there was a great deal of muttering as the king turned and approached Annabelle.

"Stand," he said, brandishing the necklace.

Annabelle obeyed, her heart sinking as her father fastened it around her neck and stood back to admire the effect. *Gods, it was so heavy*— even heavier than Annabelle had imagined. Her cheeks flushed under the collective gaze of a hundred courtiers. She could almost feel the envy of the ladies sliding like talons down her cheek, but it was to her father that she directed her eyes. What she saw reflected in his own made her blood run cold.

Those eyes, those glowing emerald eyes that were so much like her own, had changed alarmingly. Where they had been clear and warm before, they were now wide, red-rimmed, and wild. Icy fear rose like bile at the back of Annabelle's throat as her father looked her up and down, expression deranged.

"Take your hair down," he barked, his voice cold and harsh.

Annabelle blinked, surprised by this sudden request. Unsure of whether or not to comply, her eyes wandered from her father's face and found the Duchess in the crowd. Her aunt's expression of horror was not a comfort. Annabelle's knees began to tremble.

"Take your hair down," the king repeated, still speaking with that horrible, strangled voice. "*Now.*"

Hands shaking, painfully, excruciatingly aware of the rapt attention of the court, Annabelle reached up and began to pull pins from her head where Lady Rose had placed them so painstakingly hours before.

Annabelle had never been one to covet fashions, and the Gods knew she never cared much how she looked—hair or otherwise. Still, it broke her heart to undo the piece of art that her new lady in waiting had wrought upon her head. One by one, tendrils of black hair tumbled down, freed from their confines. Annabelle simply let the pins fall to the floor, each of them pinging loudly in the silence as they hit the cold marble. Finally, her hands dropped to her sides, her hair hanging free down her back, and she dared to look up at her father.

He just stared at her for a long moment. Something in his expression softened, and he reached out a hand as if to touch her cheek. Annabelle fought the urge to pull away. She blinked back the tears of shame that threatened at the corners of her eyes. For she knew at that moment that her father, the man who had embraced her and claimed her as his daughter, was far away. Whoever he saw, whatever face he reached now to touch, it was not hers.

An instant later, the king blinked, and the savage gleam in his eyes vanished. He pulled back his hand from her cheek as if it burned and stumbled away. Annabelle did not know where he had come from, but Barrick was suddenly there, taking the king by the elbow.

"Come, your Majesty," he murmured. "You are tired. Perhaps you should lie down."

But the king shook Barrick off. He gave Annabelle another look—was that fear burning behind those eyes?—before storming from the throne room through a small door at the back of the dais, which he slammed shut behind him with a resounding *boom*.

Annabelle couldn't move; she couldn't *breathe*. The entire world was frozen, and time slowed to a trickle as she reeled in the wake of her father's departure. What had happened? What *was* that? *Who* was that? Questions, one after the other, swirled and fought for dominance in her mind. At the same time, some far-off part of herself remained conscious and coherent. It was this part of her that shoved the questions aside and said in a clear voice: *They are waiting for you to do something, Annabelle. Pull yourself together.*

She looked out across the throne room at the skeptical faces of the court, her father's court—*her* court. Without hesitating, without thinking, without wondering whether or not it was the right thing to do, Annabelle lifted her chin high and returned to her seat.

She sank back onto the cushion with as much dignity and poise as she could muster. Lifting her right hand, she mimicked the king's gesture at the beginning of the ceremony. There was a moment of silence, but only a moment, before another lord hurried forward to present his gift.

Annabelle accepted the remaining gifts and vows of fealty and, when the ceremony had finally concluded, she stood and walked from the throne room—tall and straight—leaving a sea of pins scattered across the floor like the shattered pieces of her pride.

The Duchess, Damon, and Sam were waiting for her, and they fell into pace behind her as she passed. She did not look at her friends; she couldn't bring herself to face the concern and pity in their eyes. Instead, she simply walked forward—to where she did not know. Thankfully she was saved from the crisis of having to decide.

As she strode up the gallery, she heard the Duchess say from somewhere behind, "Mr. Elfreth, the princess is tired. She would like to retire to her chambers for some rest before supper."

"Of course, your Grace. Right this way." And the helpful herald bustled to the front, leading the way. With every echoing step Annabelle took down the cavernous corridors of the palace, Annabelle heard a single word, repeated over and over, mocking her as she fled the scene of her humiliation.

Princess, princess, princess.

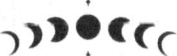

Annabelle's rooms were located in the west wing of the palace. Mr. Elfreth bowed her inside, opening the door to a beautiful sitting room complete with its own wiring desk, marble fireplace, soft upholstered armchairs, sofa, and a chaise set before a beautiful picture window.

Annabelle took in none of the splendor moving straight through the room to the door on the opposite side, which she assumed must lead to her bedchamber. She paused with her hand on the knob and turned. Her eyes sought Sam.

He stood behind the others, lingering near the hearth, eyes wide with concern.

"Keep them out," she said to him.

He nodded his understanding, and she knew he would do as she asked. So she entered her bedchamber and closed the heavy door upon the very people she knew loved her, who only wanted to help.

Alone, at last, Annabelle sank to her knees, breathing hard. Her hands went to the rich carpet that covered the cold floor and spread her fingers out wide. They looked so thin and pale against the deep crimson of the carpet. Were they the same hands they had been before? They could not possibly be.

How could she be changed so completely? What had happened to the girl she had been only hours ago? Gone. Stolen by a delusional man and his court of ghosts—faceless, nameless wraiths whose only role was to bear witness to her shame.

Fury and pain warred for dominance within her, and she lurched to her feet, the air of the chamber suddenly suffocating. Annabelle crossed the room and wrenched open the double doors that let out to a private balcony. She gulped down fresh air, hardly noticing that she was now standing with a view of the spectacular gardens. It did no good. She couldn't breathe with the damned necklace still hanging around her neck, choking her.

In one movement, she reached up and ripped it off. Pieces of it broke and scattered, pinging off of the stone railing. Disgusted, Annabelle threw the necklace as far as she could from the balcony and into the greenery below. It landed with a satisfyingly loud crash, and Annabelle only felt the tiniest pang of regret on behalf of Lord Velton. She would have to apologize to him for ruining his gift.

Shame rose once again in her chest, and she let out a strangled sob. It was so unfair. She had needed this one day to go perfectly, and it really had been perfect. And then? What had happened? What had she done? Had it just been the necklace, or was it something else? Her father had seemed thin. She had thought it was due to the natural course of time stealing his youth and vitality, but had it been something more? Was he ill? Why hadn't someone said something to her about it? Had they known?

A roar of frustration escaped Annabelle's lips, and she walked back into the bedchamber, pacing that lush, ornate carpet with restless feet.

In all of her hours of lessons, those long mornings and afternoons spent with her aunt or Lord Roger learning to be a princess, she had learned so many things. Yet nothing could have prepared her for this. *Hold your head high, Annabelle. Say the right words, Annabelle. Follow the customs, Annabelle. Don't embarrass the King, Annabelle.* But what about if the king embarrassed her? What if the king broke every rule she had ever been taught, abandoning his daughter to fend for herself before a sea of strangers? What *then*?

And was that what it was to be king? Did you simply have the liberty to behave however you wanted, regardless of how your actions impacted those around you? It seemed a nice thing to be king, then. Would she have the same freedoms when she became queen? Somehow Annabelle doubted it. After all, she had heard endless stories about how her mother had been common, wild, and improper. Not once had anyone ever thought to mention that her father was *insane*.

Annabelle fumbled at her back, trying to free herself from the prison of her dress. When she had first donned the exquisite garment, it had felt like a gift—something that she was lucky to wear. Nature captured in art. Now it chafed against her skin, and she wanted it off. But despite her best efforts, she could not reach the laces that fastened the back.

"Damn it!" Annabelle cursed as she spun on the spot, straining so hard she feared she might pull her shoulder out of its joint.

"Annabelle?"

She stopped fighting with her dress and looked up to see Emily peering around the edge of a door. No, not a door. A panel that had moments before seemed a solid wall had swung forward, and there Emily stood, looking concerned.

"Could you help me?" Annabelle asked, tears springing to her eyes at the sight of her friend. "Please?"

Emily rushed forward to unlace the dress as Annabelle clung, sobbing, to one of the bedposts. When the dress finally fell to the floor, Annabelle stepped out of it and into Emily's arms. They sank to the floor together, and Emily stroked Annabelle's hair as the whole story poured out into the maid's skirts.

"I'm so sorry," Emily breathed when Annabelle had finished. "That sounds terrible. I wish I could have been there."

Annabelle snorted wetly. "I doubt it will matter. People will be talking about it for years to come, I'm sure."

"You know that isn't what I meant."

"I know."

"Can I do anything for you now?"

Annabelle pushed herself up to sit, wiping at her eyes. "You're already doing it. And in any case, I don't know what else there is to do. I'll just have to figure out some way to...figure it out."

"On the bright side," Emily said hesitantly, "at least the worst is behind you."

Annabelle gaped at her. "*How?* I still have an arranged marriage to an absolute stranger to look forward to."

"True," Emily amended with a little nod, "but you always knew that would be an unknown. This was...this was seeing your father again. I know you always said you didn't expect anything from him, but he's your *family*. You can't have helped but have some expectation."

"He isn't my family," Annabelle said darkly. "Lord Roger was my family."

"Even so..."

"No, you're right." Annabelle sighed. "The worst part was that I did think I'd gotten the best I could have hoped for...and then... it just changed. Before, I was afraid of seeing him again. Now I'm afraid of *him*."

Emily looked so much like she wanted to say something that would make everything better, and Annabelle loved her for it, but there was nothing to say, nothing to do, nothing except stand up again and face whatever was to come, she supposed.

There was a soft knock at the door before it opened, and Sam poked his head around the corner. "May I come in?" He asked.

Annabelle nodded. "Please. There's plenty of rug for everyone."

"As comfortable as that sounds," he said, smirking. "I was hoping you would come out to the gardens with me. There's something I wanted to show you."

Annabelle and Emily exchanged a look. "Do I have to?" Annabelle asked.

"Of course not," Sam replied, "though if you do, I promise it will be worth it."

"You can use the maid's passageways," Emily offered. "If you don't want to see anyone."

The two of them managed to coax Annabelle back into a dress—one of the softer cotton dresses that Annabelle preferred—and through the winding passageways used by the palace servants. They let out into a back corner of the gardens, hidden from the rest of the palace. Sam led Annabelle and Emily down the winding paths, past fountains, grottos, and countless trees and flowers for which Annabelle had no name.

When they finally broke free of the foliage, Annabelle grinned broadly and inhaled the salty sea air deep into her lungs. She turned to Sam.

"I needed this," she said. "Thank you."

He smirked down at her. "Look again, Princess." And he gestured out to the bay below.

Annabelle walked up to the stone wall that kept her from falling off the edge of the world, eyes wide. Five ships, all under full sail, glided smoothly into the bay. They were unlike anything Annabelle had ever seen—sleek and low to the water, with enormous white sails, rising up, up, up into the sky.

"*Beautiful*," Annabelle breathed.

"Wow!" Emily exclaimed, bouncing up and down on the balls of her feet with excitement. "Sam, is it *them?*"

He chuckled at her enthusiasm. "Yes, madam, it most certainly is."

Annabelle felt a thrill as she realized what they were talking about.

She gazed down at the ships, terrified and excited and breathless.

The delegation from Eìrlan had arrived.

Chapter Eight

Prince Mica stood at the bow of his ship staring up at the palace upon the cliff and felt a sick sense of gloom take up residence in his gut. He had grown up hearing stories of the legendary Golden Palace, with its gilded walls and massive gardens, set high above a city that shone white in the sun; it was a place of myth and awe among the children of Eìrlan, despite the disapproval their rapture drew from the Elders. To Mica, those glittering walls looked like a glorious instrument of torture—close enough to offer a view of the horizon but far away enough that it couldn't be touched.

Their small contingent of five ships was anchored in the middle of the bay. It made him feel better, stronger, to stand firmly upon the boards of the deck, each one laid by deft Eìrlani hands, and know that whatever these Dunean nobles thought of him or his homeland—

he commanded the greatest sailors in the known world, the elite of his brother's armada.

But no longer, Mica realized. He had a new assignment. Charm the Princess. Gain an ally. Open the borders of his great kingdom, his home and bring the Eìrlani people out of obscurity and onto the world's stage. All he had to do was get married. *Such a simple way to die*, he thought.

"Don't tell me," a voice sang out from behind him, and he turned to see Raphael sauntering up the deck. "You were just worrying over the fate of your favorite cousin." He sketched a bow and grinned. "Well, never fear my Prince, I have returned unharmed."

Mica scoffed and rolled his eyes. "As if I need to worry about you, Raph."

"Hmm…no?" Raphael considered him for a moment. "Brooding again, is it?"

Ignoring his cousin, Mica turned and leaned on the rail, looking out across the bay to where the other four ships were in various stages of dropping anchor and sails, preparations to stay put for too long.

"Don't you wish to hear my report?" Raphael came to lounge beside him, his back to the water. He produced a green apple from his pocket and bit into it. The flesh crunched loudly. The big man pulled a face of disgust and lobbed the apple over his shoulder into the sea below. "The apples here are no good, word from the wise."

"They aren't in season yet," Mica drawled. "That was supposed to be red."

Raphael raised an eyebrow. "Don't change the subject, Mica."

Mica grimaced. "Can't you give your report to Raza and leave me in peace for once?"

"Now, what fun would that be? Besides, someone has to be responsible for saving you from yourself. Unlucky for you, that has been my number one reason to exist since you were born. How could I face my mother—or yours for that matter—if I were to fail in my quest to make you smile?"

"You'd survive."

"I beg your pardon!" Raphael gasped. "Those women are terrifying. Tsk, tsk cousin. Being so cavalier with my life. I should resolve never to speak to you again."

"Promises, promises," Mica muttered under his breath. "Very well, get it over with if it will finally get rid of you."

Raphael grinned widely. "Now that's the spirit! Well, as far as the palace and city are concerned, everything is more locked down than a Demosi prison. We won't have anything to fear from enemies without, but…."

"We'd be trapped if they decide to turn on us during negotiations."

"That's the long and short of it, yes."

Mica groaned. He had expected as much. There was a reason that Ellasport had never once been conquered in known history. Great walls to the north, an open sea to the south, and harsh cliffs to the east and west made the city nigh unassailable and inescapable. Any vessel attempting to flee across the ocean would be intercepted before it managed to escape the great expanse of the bay—any vessels except their ships, of course.

"Very well. Have all non-essential soldiers and members of the delegation sleep on board. I'll be sure to have boats ready to ferry them back and forth every hour of the day if needs be. I don't want there to be a single second when the escape of even one ship is impossible."

"Understood," Raphael said. "And agreed."

They stood in silence for a moment before Mica asked quietly, "Did you see her?"

Raphael observed Mica's expression as he said, "I did."

"And?"

Raphael let out a slow breath. "I only saw her from a distance, but I could tell that she was lovely, and her kindness seemed genuine. Other than that, it's hard to say. Still," he punched Mica lightly on the shoulder. "It could be worse, eh?"

Mica supposed he had a point.

"Anything else?" He hardly dared ask.

Raphael hesitated, "Like I said, I didn't get a good look at her, but...."

"About the *palace*, Raphael."

"Oh." His cousin shrugged. "Cosmetic observations only. We already addressed the piss-poor excuse for apples. The palace is quite impressive if you like that sort of thing—oh!" His face brightened. "I met the most interesting young knight while I was there."

Mica rounded on Raphael. "You did not."

"Oh yes, I did." Raphael waggled his eyebrows, and Mica had to bite back on his anger.

"Raphael."

"Yes?"

"You must behave yourself while we're here, do you understand? These people...this place; it isn't like it is at home. We all have to be careful, but you especially. Promise me you'll leave the poor man alone."

Raphael considered his request. "I promise I will let him be if you also make *him* promise to leave *me* alone, and in all honesty, I just don't see that happen—"

"Raphael!"

"Fine!" He held up his hands in mock surrender. "I promise to leave the *gorgeous* knight alone. Happy?"

"Not remotely," Mica sighed.

Raphael winked and pulled another green apple from his jacket pocket. Before he could take a bite, Mica plucked the apple from his hand and threw it overboard as far as he could.

"Steady on!" Raphael protested, watching the wide arc the apple made as it plopped down into the water.

"It's not ripe, Raphael!" Mica shouted and stormed off. He loved his cousin; he would not drown his cousin in foreign waters.

He did love Raphael, more than his own brothers at times, but he also had a habit of causing trouble just because he could. It was one thing to have to reprimand him for burning a wide path of debauchery through the tavern district of Danaa, but this was Dunea. One slip up here could mean death for Raphael, or worse. Mica didn't even want to think about what it would mean for the rest of them.

As he and the rest of the delegation boarded the longboats to head ashore, he watched Raphael—his face turned up toward the gardens atop the cliff, eyes far away—and prayed to the Goddess to protect his cousin, his best friend, his brother in arms. *Goddess protect us all.*

Word that the ships from Eìrlan had arrived spread quickly through the palace so that, in the short time it took Annabelle and Emily to retrace their path back to her chambers, Ladies Malisa and Rose were already waiting, the latter in a state of great distress.

"Your Highness! Where on the Gods' earth have you *been*?" She gasped as they emerged through the secret panel in the wall of Annabelle's bedchamber. "The whole palace is talking about it. The delegation is—"

"They're here," Annabelle cut her off, wearily throwing her exhausted body across the bed. "I know, Rose."

Rose mouthed wordlessly, looking desperately to Malisa, who was inspecting her nails, oozing boredom. "We—you—" Rose stammered, "you have to get dressed!"

"I *am* dressed," Annabelle objected grumpily. Emily had dug the most comfortable dress she could find from the bottom of one of the trunks—it was sky blue cotton and so soft, with golden roses stitched into the hem. The delicate garment looked odd set against the dark of Annabelle's hair and the decidedly un-delicate curves of her body. It would have looked much better on a willowy blonde like Malisa. Still, Annabelle felt at ease for the first time in hours, and she dreaded having to take it off.

"All due respect, your Highness," Rose continued in an apologetic tone. "That is not an appropriate garment to greet…well…anyone." When Annabelle continued to look surly, the Lady rounded on Malisa. "Would you help me, please?"

Malisa let out a bored sigh. "She's right, Your Highness. You can't wear that to meet the prince. Not every member of the court has made up their mind about you, but if you appear in that dress, you will have lost them."

Annabelle blinked at her. "Why?" She asked.

Malisa shrugged. "It is the way it is."

Desperate for someone to stand on her side of this particular argument, Annabelle gave Emily an imploring look, but her friend only sighed her exasperation and said, "For the Gods' sake, Highness. It's just a dress."

Outvoted and miserable, Annabelle allowed her ladies and maid to strip off the lovely blue dress and strap her into another heavy silken monstrosity—this one a dark silver with onyx beads stitched into the hem and square neckline. It was dreadfully tight in the waist, but even Annabelle had to admit that the overall effect was striking.

She only put her foot down when it was time to do her hair. Malisa approached her, brandishing a bowl of pins, but Annabelle held up a hand.

"No," she said. "If my father wishes me to wear my hair down, then I shall."

Annabelle also rejected her mother's tiara, selecting a simple silver circlet instead from the vast assortment of adornments provided to her. She nodded approvingly at her reflection. There were no swirls or frills, no soft lines to be found. Everything about Annabelle was sharp and dark and unapologetically wild. *Just like my mother*, she thought proudly.

Rose attempted to coax a silver lace veil onto Annabelle's head, but she waved her off, striding to the door without a backward glance. She would not be hidden or covered.

The banquet hall was a riot of color and light. Candles seemed to drip from the very walls, arranged in cascading braziers and sconces along the hall at regular intervals. They flickered amongst garlands and strings of fat blooms, interwoven with twining greenery.

As she entered the hall, Annabelle felt like she was walking in a garden of starlight—the illusion made complete by the fact that the high doors set into the wall to her right stood open, a cool evening breeze spilling in across the terrace and gardens beyond.

Indeed, despite the decoration and the long tables standing against the walls and upon the dais, this room was a mirror of the throne room. The two were set on opposite sides of the entrance hall and that great staircase, and together they spanned the full width of the first floor, their terraces overlooking those expansive, lush gardens and the sea beyond.

Most of the court was present in the banquet hall already, glittering with even more jewels—their richly made garments creating a living tapestry as they moved among each other, chatting excitedly about what was to come.

As Annabelle passed, each noble bowed low, hungry eyes roving over her appearance, the ladies' stares pausing on the simple crown, the tumbling length of her hair, the lords' gazes sliding over the curves of her body. Annabelle fought off a shudder of disgust as she felt their pawing glances and, keeping her head held high, approached the long table that was set upon the dais.

Her father was not there. Instead, it was Lord Barrick who smiled down at her from the position of honor and rose to his feet, bowing as he helped her into her chair.

"You look magnificent," he murmured as he resumed his seat. "I swear to the Gods I had to pinch myself when you walked in—you are so like your mother."

Annabelle tried to return his smile but only managed a grimace as she said. "Thank you, Lord Barrick. Um…" Her eyes roved around the hall, searching. "Is his Majesty…unwell?"

"Ah," Barrick's smile faltered, but only for a moment. "The king's health has been…inconstant as of late. But don't worry, Princess. This afternoon…seeing you again after so much time, looking so grown up and so much like…well," his smile was apologetic as he said, "after some rest, he'll be back to his old self in no time."

Annabelle nodded mutely. She didn't know how she felt to hear this. It made sense, and a small piece of her heart broke for her father. How lonely he must have felt, to lose first his Queen and then to send away his only child, his only piece of what he had lost. But did it excuse his behavior? She did not know.

Barrick must have mistaken the look on her face for one of concern because he smiled more widely and said, "Please don't worry, your Highness. Leave that to me. Tonight think only of your future."

Though she hadn't been remotely concerned for her father's welfare, Barricks's words, his smile, his earnest eyes—Annabelle felt a bit better. She was glad that it was he sitting to her right as the doors to the banquet hall swung wide, and Mr. Elfreth stepped inside, clearing his throat importantly.

"Your Royal Highness, my Lords, and Ladies of the court. The honorable delegation from Eìrlan."

Annabelle's heart stopped beating. The banquet hall went deathly quiet, and the light from the candles seemed to flare slightly as the Eìrlani delegation entered the room.

There were five of them in all—three men and two women—and Annabelle gaped in awe as they approached the dais and bowed as one. Their garments were simple, the lines of their jackets and trousers clean and straight, but the fabric was fine. The silver and gold embroidery that shone on their lapels and cuffs, strange swirling symbols that Annabelle did not recognize, glowed in the candlelight.

But it was not their clothes that made these people stand out like stars in the inky night sky. There was a strength and vitality that shone in their faces, that rippled down the lines of their muscled bodies. These were the warriors of legend, Annabelle realized, and their power made all the finery surrounding them pale and fade away like the shadows of night do before the rising sun.

A silver-haired man stepped forward and bowed low before the dais. "Your Majesty, I—" he began, but then a voice boomed out from behind Annabelle.

"I am the king."

Annabelle whipped around to see that Barrick had vanished from his chair, and her heart sank as the king stepped forward to claim his place at the long table. He looked dreadful, she noted, his salt and pepper hair in disarray beneath his crown, and his eyes still burned, red-rimmed as he glanced in her direction.

"Daughter," he rasped, and she smelled wine on his breath. Was he drunk? She fought the urge to recoil from him in revulsion.

"My King," she replied, keeping her face a serene mask.

Hurt and fury flashed in his eyes before he turned them to the poor silver-haired man who still stood stooped before the dais.

"Forgive my lateness," the king growled. "You may proceed with your introductions, my Lord…."

"Cerre, your Majesty." The silver-haired man said. "Ambassador to the great kingdom of Dunea from his Majesty, King Leo of Eìrlan."

Lord Cerre began his speech, praising the great house of Isren and its descendants, passing on a message of peace and allegiance from King Leo, but Annabelle was not listening. Her eyes roved over the members of the delegation, curious. She was not the only one.

The two women, in particular, drew most of the eyes in the room. One of the women stood tall as any man in the room. Her auburn curls were streaked through with silver and were woven into a thick braid that fell down her back to her waist, where the hilt of a silver dagger gleamed. Her brown eyes were trained upon the king, her face a stony mask, seemingly unknowing or merely unconcerned about the stares and mutters of the court.

If this woman was stone and earth, her companion was pure fire. Hazel eyes rimmed with gold burned in her thin face, and a mane of red curls surrounded her head in a wreath of flame, held back by one single braid that ran from one temple to the other. She sat in one hip, her lithe frame the picture of feline grace and elegance as a smirk played on her rosy lips. Her dragon's eyes took in their surroundings, lingering on the faces of ladies and lords who gaped in open astonishment, expressions scandalized.

Both women were clad in the same trousers and short jackets as their male counterparts, and Annabelle saw one lady point and whisper something wicked to a friend who stood beside her. They both barely tried to stifle their snickering. Annabelle watched as that fiery, dangerous gaze fell upon the ladies, that smirk widening into a poisonous grin. A shiver ran up Annabelle's spine as she noted that this woman wore no blade, no weapons of any kind. *She* was the weapon, Annabelle knew instinctively; the way she knew the cry of a falcon in a dive meant death on the wind.

The man who stood beside the red-haired woman leaned down to whisper something, and she rolled her eyes, shrugging him off. Annabelle's eyes slid over him, widening slightly as she beheld his height, his broad shoulders, the muscles that strained against the fabric of his jacket. This man was a warrior; it was obvious from the way he held his body, the way his weight balanced evenly on his boot-clad feet. She had seen that stance, that set of the shoulders before. It conjured images of Lord Roger mounting his horse, of Damon and Sam locked in furious combat.

Yet she did not shrink from him as she had from the lethal woman who stood by his side. There was something warm in his face, in the twinkling of his dark eyes as he winked at a nearby noblewoman who eyed those bulging arms. The woman blushed furiously and looked away, and the big man chuckled low in his chest, his smile light and amused, his stance casual as he swept a big hand through his dark hair. Annabelle found that she liked him and prayed to the Gods that she wasn't mistaken.

And…that must be him, she realized as her gaze fell upon the man now stepping forward to join the ambassador before the dais. Her world was silent as she beheld the prince, her betrothed, for the first time. There was no marking upon him, no distinguishing ornament or insignia to suggest who he was, and yet Annabelle knew before Lord Cerre opened his mouth that this man was Prince Mica of Eìrlan.

When he was introduced, the prince bowed low, his long dark hair falling in front of his face. He straightened, and his gaze met her own, his eyes a piercing sapphire blue. He was so handsome, though his was not the build of a warrior, but of a sailor. She spied long, thin scars decorating his hands. Rope burns, she realized. He had high cheekbones, and an angular jaw dusted with dark hair that gave him a roguish appearance. His long slanting brows arched slightly as he said, "It is an honor, Princess."

All eyes turned once more to Annabelle as she heard herself say, as if from a great distance, "The honor is mine, Prince Mica."

Lord Cerre was speaking again, and the prince looked away, releasing Annabelle from whatever spell he had wrought. She sagged back in her chair slightly, a breath whooshing from her as she felt a wave of relief.

"…the other members of our delegation. Raza of clan Eloithe and Phoebe of clan Eloithe, distinguished members of the High Council of Eìrlan." Cerre stepped aside as first the tall woman, Raza, and the red-haired woman, Phoebe, sketched bows to the dais. "And Raphael of clan Kane, cousin to King Leo and commander of the Branai order of warriors." The big man bowed with a flourish.

"You are all welcome in my court and my home," the king said, his voice emotionless. "Tomorrow, we will begin our work toward a new friendship and alliance between our two kingdoms. Tonight, we feast in celebration of your arrival. Eat, drink, and enjoy the festivities."

The delegation bowed once more, and the hall erupted with sound as the musicians began to play. The king turned his back on Annabelle, engaging Lord Barrick in hushed conversation. Grumpy, Annabelle seized her wine goblet and drank deeply, eyeing the spectacular feast set upon the table before her—glazed duck, meat pies, roast vegetables of every color—and felt no hunger for any of it.

"May I sit, Princess?"

She turned to see the prince standing at her left elbow, his hand upon the back of the chair beside her. "Of course, Prince Mica," she said, her heart hammering as he slid into his seat. He didn't say anything more, only began to help himself to some duck and potatoes. Annabelle steeled herself. This was her first moment to get to know this man who was to be her husband. The thought was enough to set her hands shaking. She took another sip of wine to steady her nerves.

"How are you finding Ellasport?" she asked, cringing inwardly at her pathetic question. But what was she supposed to say? How did she begin engaging her betrothed in conversation when he was both her intended and a stranger.

He set down his fork and knife. "It is…very beautiful from afar," he said thoughtfully. "I admit I haven't had the opportunity to explore the city yet."

"Nor I," Annabelle said. "Though I would dearly love to. I hear it is a glorious place."

His expression turned skeptical, but he said nothing, and Annabelle felt a surge of defensiveness for her birthplace, her onetime home.

She bit back her irritation as she tried again. "And how was your journey? Pleasant, I hope."

The prince shrugged, taking up his fork and knife once more as he said, "Uneventful. Only one minor squall, but nothing that would threaten *my* ships."

His ships. Her bride price. Annabelle scowled as he began to eat, his face inscrutable as he chewed, his eyes on his plate. She realized what this was, why he had taken his seat beside her. Duty. Responsibility. He had no interest in speaking to her, in getting to know her at all.

"Well, that *is* a relief," she said, perhaps a bit more loudly than she had intended. But she didn't care. There was something in the way he had said, "*My* ships," that set her blood boiling. "If your ships had sunk to the bottom of the sea, there would be no reason for us to meet, and that would be a tragedy indeed."

The prince had stopped eating again and was now looking at Annabelle in open alarm. "I…I'm sorry, have I offended you?"

"Of course not," Annabelle chirped, helping herself to more wine. "We were only speaking about the weather."

Annabelle turned to her right, thinking that she might try to engage with her father—to heal that rift that had yawned so wide between them in such a short time—to find that he had once again vanished from the banquet hall. Barrick gave her a sad, pitying look across his empty chair. *I'm sorry*, his eyes said. She couldn't bear to look at him but drained the contents of her goblet in one long gulp.

〉〉〉●《《《

The celebration raged in full force around Sam as he sat at the long table that ran the length of the hall. He ate and drank only what was necessary to remain inconspicuous but tasted nothing. The merriment surrounding him was a beautiful, simpering mask, and his attention roved, searching for the cracks.

His eyes fell upon Annabelle, sitting up at the high table, looking miserable. The king had gone, and the Prince took his meal in silence beside her. She met his eyes then, and he gave her a little smile. *Courage, friend*, he thought as he tried to send her strength and support. She only returned his smile with a grimace as she held out her goblet for a squire to refill and drank deeply.

He frowned. She ought not to drink too much. They could not risk letting their guard down for a second. The king's erratic behavior was enough to cause concern, and he did not trust these Eìrlani. Something was wrong. He could feel the unease slithering beneath his skin as his instincts barked with alarm. There was something sinister afoot, something that he could not yet see. She needed protection, or he feared she would break. Perhaps she was already breaking.

Annabelle had never fared well in captivity, had sought her freedom as often and recklessly as she could at the manor. But this was not Rosewood. They had to be careful. And where was the Duchess? Why did she not intervene on her niece's behalf? He found her, seated farther down the table, exchanging words with Lord Asby, unable to see that Annabelle needed her help. Sam hoped to get the Duchess's attention, to warn her that the princess was about to combust, but he was distracted by a burst of sound to his right.

He swiveled to face the end of the table, where the Eìrlani commander was surrounded by a cloud of giggling silks and perfume. Raphael Kane. The man who had slipped through the palace defenses and Sam's grasp. The rogue. The liar. "My commander could use a few more like you," indeed. Sam scowled down the table as Kane took a swig of ale before continuing his story.

"And then, if you'd believe it, the great idiot turns to me and says 'Raph! Thank the Gods you're here. Some rascal has been sleeping with my wife!' And of course, me being the obliging friend that I am, I said, 'That won't do, Perkins. Let me chase him down myself.' And just like that, I walked right through his front door, and he was never the wiser."

The ladies fell all over themselves in fits of giggles, and Kane grinned his self-satisfaction, every bit a puffed-up peacock. Sam snorted his disgust and incredulity. Slowly, the commander's gaze slid to his face, and Sam met his stare unflinchingly.

"You doubt my tale, lad?" Raphael called down the table, his tone light and amused.

"Not at all," Sam shrugged. "I only marvel that you would brag of such an exploit. From where I am sitting, you appear to be the villain of that story."

Kane's eyes popped wide, and he adopted a tone of shock and dismay as he intoned, "Not so! Why, I consider it a crime against the very laws of nature that any man should leave his wife unsatisfied. In fact, it is my duty, nay, my honor, to set such a terrible wrong to rights." He flashed a roguish wink at one of the ladies, who flushed crimson and fluttered her eyelashes up at him.

Sam cocked his head, unamused. "I doubt your *friend* would see it quite that way," he said.

That wide, mischievous grin never faltered, but something flashed in the commander's eyes—something hard and fierce that was gone as quickly as it had come. "Don't mind the knight," he said to the ladies, those teeth flashing. "Some people lack the proper imagination when it comes to matters of the flesh."

Sam took another swig of ale and pushed away from the table, turning his back on the warrior and his fawning crowd of admirers. Vultures in petticoats, the lot of them. They would enjoy his stories and smiles, maybe a few of them would bed him in the dark solitude of their chambers, but Sam knew that not a single respectable lady of the court would be caught dead with an Eìrlani savage on her arm. Sam wondered if he knew if this was all a game, if Kane, like Damon, simply sought to bask in the glory of all that Ellasport had to offer with no concern or care for himself.

Something caught Sam's attention, ripping it away from the irritating warrior. He froze, a hot poker of panic sliding down his throat and burning a hole in his gut as he stared up at the high table. Three chairs were now empty, where before it had only been the king's seat that had stood unoccupied. His eyes scanned the room, searching desperately but in vain.

Annabelle and Prince Mica were gone.

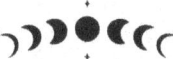

Annabelle was drunk; she knew it but didn't care. The night air was cool on her face, and she sighed with relief as the noise of the banquet hall faded away behind her. She and the Prince walked together through the gardens in silence. Annabelle led the way, following the path to the edge of the great cliff and to the sea.

The prince walked along beside her, hands in his pockets, saying nothing. She hadn't asked for his company as she rose from her seat at the high table, but he had followed anyway. Questions bloomed in her mind, winking into existence like the stars overhead, burning and bright.

Why had he followed her? Why wouldn't he speak to her? Look at her? Was all of this really just duty to him? Did he not long for the power and position that their union would bring to him and to his kingdom?

Annabelle stumbled a bit on the uneven ground, and the prince reached out a hand to steady her, but she waved him away.

"I'm fine," she said, voice slurring a bit. The world was spinning, those stars swimming above her head. She needed to sit. There was a stone fountain gurgling nearby. Annabelle sank gratefully onto the edge of its basin, gulping down the salty air.

The prince sat next to her, watching her, his expression grim. Something in it made her say, "I suppose I'm not making much of a first impression."

He said nothing, those sapphire eyes steady as he watched her.

"I'm not usually like this, you know. I usually have more self-control than this, I mean. Well…I suppose that's not exactly true…My aunt always says that if I don't watch my tongue, one day someone is going to cut it out." Annabelle was babbling, but she couldn't help it.

"Your aunt sounds…intimidating," the prince said quietly. Annabelle could have kissed him for saying something, anything to fill the silence between them.

"She can be," Annabelle said, giggling, "but she just cares about things, about my father, about the kingdom." *About me*, she thought but did not say.

"It must be a lot for you to live up to," he observed mildly.

It was suddenly painful to breathe. What would Aunt Penelope say if she knew Annabelle was carrying on like this in front of her betrothed. This was precisely the sort of behavior her aunt had always condemned. She had taught Annabelle better than this.

"I just—I just can't stand it!" Annabelle said then, more loudly than she had intended. The words bursting from her before she could stop them.

His eyes widened in surprise, but his voice was calm as he asked, "What can't you stand?"

"Everything. My father, this place, these people." Annabelle didn't know why she was telling him all of this but couldn't stop herself as the words came spilling out. "The pressure, the expectations. And I was handling it, too—not *well*, but I was working through it in my way, and then..."

She trailed off, fighting against the sudden burning at the corners of her eyes, the back of her throat.

"Then I saw you, and I don't know..." she continued, voice hoarse. "You were this other person. And I thought—I don't know what I thought. That you might be just as scared as I was. That maybe I wouldn't be so alone anymore. But you were so cold, and you didn't want to talk to me, and my father..." she trailed off again, shaking her head as if she could rid herself of the memory of seeing his empty chair, of knowing that he had abandoned her again, just as he had that afternoon, just as he had when she was a child. "And I suppose I couldn't take being a disappointment to you too."

And there it was; that oozing, festering wound at her core, laid bare. Tears of shame began sliding silently down her cheeks, and she couldn't look at him—this stranger to whom she had so readily bared her heart. But hadn't that been what Aunt Penelope had said? *Show them your heart, Annabelle, and don't let them tell you that it makes you weak.* Well, this was her heart, every broken piece of it. She braced for the blow that would come, that would shatter her to pieces.

"You aren't a disappointment."

The lie was so soft, so gentle. It broke against Annabelle's raw soul like a wave, cleaning and soothing. She met his eyes, pawing at her wet cheeks.

"Thank you for lying," she said. "It may be the nicest thing anyone has ever done for me."

"Annabelle."

She turned to see Sam hurrying up the garden path toward them, relief painted all over his frantic face. He gripped her shoulders, inspecting her face and body as if scanning for injury.

"I'm fine, Sam," she mumbled, shying away from his penetrating gaze.

"Is that so?" he frowned, and her cheeks flushed with embarrassment, realizing he could smell the wine on her breath.

"It's my fault," the prince stood and placed hands on his hips as he met Sam's questioning stare. "I asked her to walk with me. I thought she could use the fresh air."

Sam considered the prince for a long moment before he inclined his head respectfully. "Thank you for taking care of her, your Highness. But I think it's time the Princess goes to bed."

Annabelle went with him without protest, unable to bear even a backward glance. Shame coiled like a snake in her belly—shame for her behavior and her vulnerability. So she let Sam lead her away by the arm, leaving the prince, her betrothed, standing alone in the dark garden.

Chapter Nine

The darkness pressed in on all sides as she ran down the deserted corridor. Her feet slapped, aching, upon the cold stone floor of the corridor, but she pushed her screaming legs to keep going, keep running. Time was running fast, and so she must run faster.

A flash of lightning illuminated the corridor ahead, and she saw the door—closer than she had thought. Skidding to halt with a groan of pain, she pressed her hand against the large iron lock. It sprung open beneath her touch, and she threw herself into the room. Booming thunder covered the sound of the heavy oak door as she slammed it shut behind her. Another touch, a muttered word, and the lock sealed itself again.

Behind her, the child slept in the little bed hung with gossamer curtains. Pain twisted like a knife in her heart as she approached the tiny sleeping figure, but she shoved it aside. He was coming for her, and she must work quickly. There was no time for pain, for heartbreak, for goodbyes. A few more words and a pass of her palm across the child's forehead ensured that she would continue to slumber, to wake in the morning rested and happy, with no recollection of the night's events.

Kneeling before the foot of the bed, she ripped the ornate rug aside, revealing the bare floor beneath. The spell took form on her lips, so effortlessly it was like breathing, and she began to trace symbols across the stones, blue light streaming from her hand as it moved in intricate patterns; bright as the lightning that flashed once more, illuminating the room in a flat silver glow.

With the next roar of thunder came a mighty pounding upon the door. She ignored it, working with such speed that her words and gestures became a blur. The spell rose into the air, and she along with it. Her toes barely grazed the floor, and still, she worked with furious intensity, caught up in a trance. The pounding increased in urgency, accompanied now by shouted words that were rendered unintelligible by the storm banging against the shuttered windows.

As the spell moved to hover above the little bed, guided by her outstretched arms, there came a mighty crack, and the door burst open, swinging creaky and crooked on its hinges. He stood on the threshold, tall and hooded, face hidden from view.

She turned, smiling as tears poured down her cheeks, every last effort pouring into the spell that now glowed so bright that the entire room was bathed in its warm light. She saw him cringe away from the sudden brightness.

"You are too late," she said. "It is done."

"No," he reached out a hand but did not dare come closer. "Please. Stop this madness."

"I'm sorry." Her voice was a cracked whisper. "Please...Please, try to understand. And forgive me."

And she brought her hands together in a swift motion, the final words ripping from her throat. There was a flash of light, the sound of screaming, and then nothing at all.

Annabelle woke suddenly in a pool of sweat.

Trembling, she threw herself from the bed and seized the chamber pot just before her stomach rebelled, hurling the contents of her stomach into the porcelain basin. When the retching subsided, Annabelle sat back on her heels, wiping at her face and streaming eyes. Her limbs shook, and her face was clammy with sweat. Stumbling a bit, she heaved her trembling body onto the balcony and gulped down lungfuls of cold, salt-tanged air.

As her breathing and heart rate returned to normal, Annabelle's head cleared enough that she could think.

The strangest part about the nightmare was how real it had felt. Annabelle had nightmares in her childhood—some sending her screaming and bawling into Lord Roger and Lady Ellen's bedchamber. Those nightmares had been terrifying and had felt real at the moment, but the finer details usually began to melt away even minutes after waking.

This nightmare was something else. If Annabelle closed her eyes, she could still recall its details with perfect clarity. She opened her eyes again when her stomach roiled in protest. No, Annabelle had never had a dream like this before, but what else could it have been? A vision? The thought was so absurd that Annabelle actually chuckled aloud. Such things were the stuff of stories.

Mopping her wet forehead with the sleeve of her nightgown and mentally chastising herself for being a fool, Annabelle returned to her bedchamber.

Emily waited there, holding a glass of water and trying to hide her amused expression.

"Drink it," she said. "All of it."

Annabelle took the glass from Emily, groaning as her head began to pound. "Thank you."

"Don't mention it," Emily said with a smirk.

"I curse wine and all wine-related activities," Annabelle moaned, sinking back onto the mattress.

"I wouldn't worry about it, your Highness," Emily said reassuringly. "You weren't the drunkest of the lot by far. I doubt we'll see Lord Velton before supper."

"Mmph." Annabelle drank deeply from the glass, draining it, and held it out to Emily. The maid took it and filled it again from the pitcher on Annabelle's nightstand.

"I curse wine all the same," Annabelle grumbled as she accepted the glass once more and took a small sip this time, relishing the feeling of the cold water on her dry lips. "It is the beverage of lunatics."

"It can be," Emily agreed, "but it also reveals the truth. Maybe some truths that we would rather avoid."

Her words triggered something, and suddenly the events of the previous night came crashing back to Annabelle, and she covered her face with a hand. *Oh, by the Gods…*

"I'm guessing from your expression," Emily continued, her voice light and airy, "that you did some truth-telling of your own last night."

The garden. The prince. What she had said? The nightmare had driven the memory from her mind, but now Annabelle thought she would die from embarrassment. She had to fix it, to find him. But she couldn't just apologize. She couldn't tell him it was a lie because it hadn't been.

"Annabelle," Emily's eyes were kind when Annabelle lowered her hand from her face. "I'm sure there's nothing you said or did that will make anyone think less of you. The maids hear all the gossip, and this morning there was nothing about you—though there was quite a bit of tongue-wagging on the subject of the prince's cousin, that warrior Raphael Kane." She smirked. "The servants have a bet going to see which of the ladies makes it into his bed first."

But Annabelle wasn't listening. "Do you know where I can find the prince? Where are his rooms?"

"The Eìrlani delegation is occupying a suite of rooms in the east wing," Emily said. "But you won't find him there. He and his commander left a few minutes ago for the harbor."

Annabelle threw her legs over the side of the bed, wincing as a stab of pain shot through her head. "I need to catch them. Can you get Sam? And tell someone to bring my carriage around. Oh, and if you see my ladies," Annabelle called out to her as she buried her head in the armoire, "tell them I'm still asleep—anything to keep them from noticing I've gone."

Emily flashed a wicked grin and nodded before hurrying from the room.

Annabelle set about dressing, thinking hard. She had been expecting a prince—someone spoiled and power-hungry, like Gustav—someone who would woo her, spurred on by the pursuit of her throne, her kingdom. Prince Mica's cold indifference had come as a shock, and it had hurt her to realize that he may be utterly disinterested in marrying her or in the titles that came with such a match. But maybe she could use that disinterest to her advantage.

By the time Sam knocked on her door, she was fully dressed, and her headache had begun to recede, burned away by steely resolve. She had a plan.

$$\text{)}\text{)}\text{)}\bullet\text{(}\text{(}\text{(}$$

The noon sun made the bay sparkle as Mica stood upon the wharf, waiting for the longboat that cut its way through the choppy water, its peaks rising in the stiff breeze off the ocean. *A good day to sail*, he thought darkly. How he longed to give the command, to watch as his crew hoisted the sails and feel the wind in his face as the great vessel turned out to sea, out to freedom.

Beside him, Raphael was recounting the previous night's events in great detail. Mica could not have cared less.

"I saw you slip off with the princess," Raphael said, waggling his brows. "And you were worried that the night would be a complete waste of time."

Mica kept his expression smooth as he remembered his walk in the garden, what she had said to him. Intoxicated and upset as she was, her words had chimed in harmony with something in his heart. To see her so distraught, so sad and lonely—it was how he had felt but hadn't dared say. Her fearless vulnerability terrified him.

"I'm surprised you noticed," he said instead, "surrounded as you were by admirers."

Raphael chuckled. "Yes, I did make rather a spectacle of myself, didn't I?"

"Yes," Mica replied wryly, "you did."

"All for your sake, cousin." Raphael inclined his head, grinning wickedly.

"How on the Goddess's green earth was that…scene for *my* sake?"

Raphael tapped a long finger against his nose, winking. "Throw them off the scent. I'm invisible now. Those puffed-up lords will think I'm nothing more than a womanizing brute and pay me no mind. Clever, eh?"

Mica was about to tell him another word for such a ridiculous scheme when a clear voice rang out behind them.

He turned to see Princess Annabelle striding purposefully down the wharf, the same tall knight he had seen in the garden the night before trailing after her.

She was beautiful, he had to admit, her raven hair shining as it rippled behind her in the breeze, her proud face, the softness of her mouth, those startling green eyes…

"Prince Mica," she said, stopping before them. "Commander Kane."

Raphael moved forward and bowed low, taking her hand. "Raphael, please, your Highness." He dusted the back of her hand with a soft kiss before releasing it. She beamed up at him, and Mica thought the light in that smile could have chased away the sun itself, so great was its brightness. He blinked.

"Are you headed to your ship?" the princess asked, turning her eyes to him.

He nodded. "We are."

"Good," she said, placing her hands on her hips. "Then we will come with you. I've always wanted to stand aboard a ship, and I can think of none better than one that is to purchase my hand in marriage. I'd like to make sure it is worthy of me."

Mica did not know what to say to this, but Raphael was grinning from ear to ear as he said, "You are most welcome to join us, Your Highness. Sir..."

"This is Sam," the princess gestured toward her companion, who looked sternly back at her. "I mean," she corrected, grinning up at her companion. "Sir Sam Fisher."

The knight inclined his head but did not smile as he glared at Raphael. Mica had a feeling that this was the same knight Raphael mentioned meeting during his inspection of the palace. His suspicions were confirmed when Raphael's grin widened, and he said, "I believe I have already had the...pleasure."

Sir Sam said nothing. The princess frowned, looking back and forth between the two men.

"I don't know that it would be appropriate for you to accompany us without a chaperone," Mica said, hoping to leave the princess and her knight safely ashore.

"Nonsense," Annabelle turned to him, bristling. "Sam will be chaperone enough. He is sworn to protect me, and I have given him permission to defend my honor to the death if needs be. Come. I think your longboat has arrived."

And she pushed past them to where the boat had come to rest along the end of the wharf.

Raphael let out a low whistle. "I like her," he said to Mica before following the others into the longboat.

Mica's feet had barely hit the solid boards of the deck before the princess seized his arm and led him toward the bow of the ship, asking questions about the rigging, the sails, the helm, smiling warmly as members of the crew raised their hands in greeting. He allowed himself to be steered away from where his cousin and the knight stood together on the stern.

"I don't know if we should leave those two alone together," he said as they went, but the princess waved away his concern.

"Sam can handle himself," she said. "Trust me. Now, what is this big rope called?"

Mica began explaining the purpose of the mainsheet, doubting the princess had truly understood his concern but knowing better than to elaborate. He continued to answer her seemingly endless flow of questions until they reached the bowsprit. They were alone up there, and the breeze picked up, lifting her hair and wafting her scent toward him—rain... and flowers... and fir trees. She released his arm then and turned to him, face set and resolute.

"I want to make you an offer," she said, clear and serious—her light and airy tone evaporated in the morning breeze.

"An offer?" Mica blinked, caught off guard by this abrupt change in her.

She nodded. "Yes. Will you agree to listen until I have finished and then decide whether or not to accept my offer? Know that I will take your word as truth, and if you reject me, I will not bother you again."

He nodded, suddenly very curious to hear what she had to say.

"You do not wish to marry me," she said boldly. "And I do not wish to marry you, but I have always known that I do not have a choice. From birth, I knew that I would make a match for the kingdom's benefit one day, and I have had nearly twenty years to make peace with that fact. When I met you, I only hoped to make the best of my situation. I still do, but only if you want the same.

"My offer to you is simple. I offer you friendship. I want to get to know you, to be your ally and not your enemy. We can both be miserable about the hand we have been dealt, or we can realize that we are together in our misery and that it does not have to be a lonely life.

I do not expect that you love me, now or ever. I only offer the possibility that we can one day be friends and that we might start building toward that future right now. But I can't do that without your consent, without your desire to see me as something other than an anchor weighing you down."

She sighed then, and he could still see the shadow of the pain he had glimpsed the night before in her eyes.

"Your reasons to despise me are your own. I don't need to know them. I only ask that you realize that I am not the prison. I am a fellow prisoner. We may fare better if we endure our sentence together."

The picture she painted was so brutal, so honest, that all he could do was stand and let her words break upon him like waves against the cliffs in the distance. When she was finished speaking, he considered her.

She was right. He had behaved unfairly toward her, though she was generous enough not to accuse him of such treatment outright.

Raphael liked this young woman and had said that her kindness was genuine. There was never a better judge of a person's true character than his cousin, but still, Mica had withheld from her. But now she stood before him, chin held high, eyes clear and resolute, and he knew he had a decision to make.

Yesterday, trusting this woman had felt like giving up, like surrendering his freedom willingly. Now it felt like a glimmer of hope on a stormy horizon.

"I am the youngest of five sons, prince of a hidden kingdom." He began slowly. "I grew up learning to fight with the Branai warriors, spent my time sailing the world. My father had no dreams of seeking out allies beyond our shores, so I grew up free to pursue my own interests. When my father died and my brother ascended the throne, his ambition to make powerful allies meant that I was expected to be a prince for the first time in my life. You saw me as another person when we met. I admit that I did not see you as the same. I saw you as the agent of my destruction. But I want the future you describe. I want to believe that my life can still have purpose and meaning and joy." He held out a hand. "I accept your offer, Princess."

She took it, her hand warm in his. "Annabelle," she said.

He smiled. "Mica."

"It's nice to meet you, Mica." She returned his smile with her own, dazzling him once more.

Annabelle.

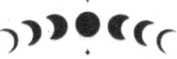

"Where are you going?"

Sam glared after Annabelle as she took a turn down a corridor in the opposite direction of her rooms. He had been surly all the way back to the palace, and now he glowered at her, hands on his hips, as she stopped and turned.

"I'm going to find the library," she said innocently.

"Why?"

She crossed her arms in front of her chest and raised an eyebrow. "Because I'm hungry. We keep the food in the library, right?"

"Annabelle, be serious."

"Oh, come on, Sam!" She sighed, exasperated. His overprotective older brother routine was growing old, fast. "There's no harm in a little exploring. Besides, the Eìrlani will be with the king and his cabinet all day, and there's nothing else for me to do."

He didn't look convinced. "I know you, Annabelle," he growled. "I know what you get up to when you're bored, and I am not going to let you sneak off to the Gods know where."

"I am going," Annabelle said through gritted teeth, "to the library. You can come with me if you like. I'm sure the place is filled to bursting with little corners where you can stand and glower."

They stared each other down for a long moment before Sam held up his hands in surrender. "Fine. Go to the library. I have better things to do than watch you read, but I'm telling Emily where you are, and she'll come to find you in two hours if you haven't returned."

"Fair enough," Annabelle said, turning uncertainly on the spot before asking, "Um…where *is* the library?"

Sam pointed back down the corridor in the direction they had come. "That way. Straight, two left turns, and you're there."

"My hero," Annabelle trilled and skipped off. Men really were such grumpy, unreasonable creatures. She marveled at how they had ever managed to conquer the world in the first place.

Chapter Ten

The palace library was a massive, vaulted space filled with shelves of so many books, scrolls, and tablets that Annabelle stood on the threshold, struck dumb to see so much knowledge spread out before her. Yes. She would surely be able to find the information she sought among these hundreds of tomes.

She strode among the shelves, searching the titles, wondering where to begin, when a voice somewhere above her head said, "Would you mind catching this please?"

Annabelle looked up to see a little man with white hair stuck out from the sides of his head and small, round spectacles set upon the bridge of his nose looking down at her. He was perched atop a ladder that reached all the way to the ceiling, holding a stack of books in one arm. The book that sat atop the pile was sliding precariously, about to tumble to the floor.

"Oh, dear!" The man said as the entire stack began to wobble. "Better run for it, I think."

Annabelle stepped hurriedly out of the way as the entire stack of books slid from the man's arm and crashed to the floor. She stepped forward, gathering the books as the man descended the ladder. He thanked her as she handed over the stack and bustled over to set them upon a long wooden table.

"I should know better than to try to carry so many," he said as he went, "but one does not like to admit that one is losing one's youthful reflexes."

Annabelle did not know what to say to this, so she said nothing. The little man wore the gray robes of the priesthood, which he adjusted briefly before asking. "What can I do for you, Princess?"

"So you already know who I am," Annabelle said with a sigh, feeling disappointed. What she wouldn't give for one soul in the palace, or in the entire world, who did not know her name.

The man chuckled. "The many times I saw your mother in here, curled up with a book, lost to the known world. I'd be a fool not to recognize her daughter—though I'd wager you're sick of hearing how much you look like her?"

Annabelle shrugged, "It's nice, in a way. It makes me feel closer to her."

The man peered at her through those spectacles and nodded his understanding.

The knowing in those beady eyes made Annabelle shift uncomfortably, so she changed the subject. "You know who I am, which means you have me at a disadvantage, priest."

He waved a wrinkled hand dismissively. "Call me Herbert. Everybody does. Well, it's my name, isn't it? We have names for a reason. The others of my order love being called "Priest" or "Father" or "Eminence," but I find it gets a bit confusing, don't you?"

"I suppose..." Annabelle had no idea what to make of this funny little man, but she liked him all the same. "Listen, I was hoping you could help me with something."

"Anything at all," Herbert said, throwing his arms wide. "I am a disciple of the Gods, but I am foremost a librarian, and these books are my flock."

Encouraged by his friendly demeanor, Annabelle said, "I'd like to see any books you have—*all* the books you have on the kingdom of Eìrlan."

Herbert chewed his lip, considering her request. "One moment, Princess." And he bustled away, vanishing among the shelves, though she could hear the sound of him whistling a cheery tune as he went.

She settled herself in one of the chairs by the long table and waited. A few minutes later, Herbert reappeared. He carried one small book in his hand, and this he lay upon the table before her with a flourish.

"There you are," he said with a cheery smile. "Everything I have about the kingdom of Eìrlan."

Annabelle inspected the small volume, certain this had to be a joke. "It's a book of children's stories," she said.

Herbert nodded. "It is, Your Highness. Stories passed down from generation to generation and preserved," he tapped the cover of the book with his index finger. "Right here, for your reading pleasure."

"But..." Annabelle didn't know what to say. She had known there wouldn't be much. After all, knowledge of the mysterious kingdom was hard to come by, and what most people *thought* they knew was only the product of rumor and speculation. But this was a royal library of Dunea. She had imagined that, if there was any information to be found, it would have been here.

Herbert was watching her as she sat there, staring down at that sad little book, her plans shattering before her eyes. "Hoping to learn more about your intended, were you? His home?"

She nodded sadly. "I was. But I doubt I'll find much that will be any use in an old book of children's stories."

"Oh, now!" Herbert exclaimed. "Don't underestimate the power of a good story, Princess."

"I just thought there would be more," Annabelle said, sighing heavily. "This was definitely not a part of the plan."

Herbert clicked his tongue, looking thoughtful. "Well, I can keep looking for you if you like, but I wouldn't get your hopes up. All books about Eìrlan, all save this little book of stories, vanished ages and ages ago—after the war."

"Vanished?" Annabelle asked. "What do you mean, 'vanished'?"

"I mean, one day they were here," Herbert explained patiently, "and the next—*poof!* Gone. No idea where or why. There is a logbook kept by one of my predecessors that cataloged the event. Beside himself with grief over the loss, poor man. Though if you ask me, that one went a bit loony in his head toward the end," he added with a wink and a waggle of his shaggy brows.

"How is that possible?" Annabelle demanded, disbelieving. How is it that so much knowledge, so much history, could vanish, just like that?

Herbert chortled, and his eyes lit up as he said, "Why, the only way anything inexplicable or impossible happens, my dear." When Annabelle continued to look confused, he leaned in close and whispered, "*Magic*, of course."

Annabelle laughed. A joke, she had thought. Well, she had been right. This was preposterous in the extreme. She fully expected that Herbert would join in the laughter. When he only continued to watch her, no humor in those piercing eyes, she stopped laughing.

"Oh, come now. You cannot be serious! *Magic?*" She protested.

"Why not?" He asked.

"Because it's impossible," Annabelle said, feeling slightly foolish to have to explain such a simple concept to a man so much older than she. "There is no such thing. Our ancestors believed in magic only to explain what they could not, but we know now that it was a trick—a lie used to control people."

"That," Herbert stated with the dignity of a king, "is utter poppycock."

"You're saying it's a lie?" Annabelle raised a skeptical eyebrow.

"I am saying…" Herbert paused, his lips pursed, thinking. "I am saying that you want to know about Eìrlan, but the knowledge you seek has vanished without a trace. I am saying that the answers you seek may require you to open your mind and see beyond the world as you believe it to be. I am saying that you may not believe in magic, yet I know you have seen it with your own two eyes."

A flash of lightning. Glowing symbols sketched upon the air.

Annabelle shook her head to clear it of the onslaught of visions as she stood, hands balled into fists at her side. "I have seen no such thing," she said, suddenly angry and afraid.

Herbert tilted his head to the side. "No? Have you never seen the work of a healer, then?"

"I have. But their ability to heal is a gift from the Gods in exchange for devotion," Annabelle protested. "Not…not *magic*."

Herbert only smiled, a bit sadly. "Oh, my dear girl. If healing the sick, if bringing those we love back from the brink of death is not magic, I do not know what is."

Annabelle seized the small book from the table, desperate to bring this conversation to an end. "Thank you for your help," she said. "Do you mind if I take this back to my rooms?"

Herbert gave a slight bow. "As you wish, your Highness."

And Annabelle turned on her heels and fled, his words chasing her from the library.

꜒꜓꜔ ● ꜕꜖ꜗ

The clang of steel on steel rang out in the practice ring as Sam and Damon dueled within, their bodies twisting, entangling, and breaking apart in a lethal dance. Bright as lightning, Sam's blade flashed through the air, and Damon spun, just barely blocking his advance. His eyes popped wide in surprise.

"Easy does it, Sammy" he said before they broke apart once more.

Sam flashed a feral grin. "You could always yield," he said.

Damon barked a laugh before bearing down on him, his blows brutal and swift. Sam danced out of the way, his body twisting and flowing across the pounded earth of the ring. Sweat gleamed on his face, his arms. The movement, the strenuous exercise cleansing him of his cares—his worries about Annabelle, about the king, about…

Sam missed a step as he turned to see Raphael Kane standing at the edge of the ring, leaning against the fence, a sultry smile twisting his lips.

Pain lanced through Sam's side as Damon landed a blow, at last, taking advantage of his distraction. When Sam turned, his friend's face was pale. "Gods, Sam, are you alright? I thought for sure you'd block me..."

But Sam only shook his head, stretching his side and wincing slightly. He would have a bruise, but the blow hadn't been hard. "I'm fine," he said. "Don't worry. You pulled back enough when you realized I wasn't blocking."

But Damon was still frowning, concerned. "Are you sure you're alright?"

"I'm fine." It came out harsher than Sam had meant it, and Damon's eyes narrowed as he shrugged.

"Good, then get ready."

Damon came at him again, taking Sam so by surprise that he acted on instinct before his rational mind could catch up to what was happening. In two swift movements, he sent Damon hurtling to the ground, his sword skittering away across the dirt, Sam's own blade leveled at the knight's throat.

Damon blinked up at Sam, opening and closing his mouth like a beached fish. "How..."

"I..." Sam backed away hurriedly, shocked and ashamed by what he had done. He had lost control. "Damon, I'm..."

"Great show, lads!" Sam looked around to see that Kane had leaped the fence and was now strolling toward. "Either of you fancy a tussle with me next? I haven't had a worthwhile sparring match in weeks."

Sam didn't reply but stared at Damon pleadingly as his friend got to his feet, wanting to explain what had happened, to somehow mend whatever hurt was causing Damon to look so coldly back at him. But that chasm between them widened as Damon backed away.

"I'm out," he said and stripped off his shirt, wiping at his dripping face with the already sweat-soaked material. "Though perhaps Sammy will be more of a match for your talents."

Sam watched as Damon walked away toward the soldier's barracks, pain twisting like a knife in his gut. He wanted to chase after him, to tell him he was sorry, to do something to fix this. But what could he say? That he had been holding back? That the days of Damon beating him in battle were long gone? That he...No.

No, the truth would only make everything worse.

"So. How long have you been in love with him?"

Sam whirled to see Kane standing close, too close. He backed away.

"What are you talking about?" he snarled, gripping the hilt of his sword tight in his fist.

Kane's face was earnest as he said in a low voice, "It's alright, you know. Nobody can hear us. And it's not a crime to love someone."

"I don't know what you're talking about." Rage, icy and swift, swept through his veins.

Kane raised an eyebrow. "No?"

"Did you want to spar or not?" Sam's voice was sharp and decisive, a challenge.

The commander straightened, his expression going hard as he reached up and pulled two axes from their straps across his back. Sam watched the two gleaming blades as they began to swing loose in Kane's hands, the movements fluid and practiced. And then, without warning, with the speed and swiftness of a viper's bite, Kane struck.

Sam barely had time to bring up his sword to block that first blow, the power in it radiating through his blade, down his arm, and into his shoulder. With every ounce of strength he possessed, he threw the warrior off, but those axes came back around again in a swipe to his midriff, forcing him to roll over backward to avoid it.

He and Kane circled each other, and each time the warrior attacked, Sam only just managed to block or avoid being cleaved in two by those axes. His breathing became labored, and his limbs screamed as he blocked, jumped, and weaved, applying every scrap, every drop of his training in the face of Kane's ferocity.

Their battle began to draw a crowd. Guards, knights, and even stable boys gathered around the ring to watch a knight of the realm battle the Branai warrior. Sam hardly noticed as they cheered and jeered in equal measure each time he evaded Kane's advances, each time he narrowly avoided those swinging, crashing axes.

Even as Sam battled to maintain his footing, he saw a fierce gleam in his opponent's eyes. Kane was enjoying this. Sam was scrambling just to meet his blows, and Kane was toying with him, playing with his food before he finally sent Sam tumbling into the dirt. The knowledge made the anger rise anew, like fire in his blood.

"You don't know me!" He shouted, not caring if the onlookers overheard. "How dare you speak to me as if you know the first thing about me."

"Oh I *am* sorry," Kane retorted, his arms wide, the blades of those axes gleaming in the afternoon sun. "My mistake for wanting to help. But you don't need my help, do you, *Sammy*."

Sam loosed a roar and charged, his arm rising and falling, driving Kane back toward the fence for the first time.

"I... don't...need...help...from...someone...like...*you*," he said, blows falling with each word.

Kane's back hit the fence, and Sam pounced, his blade arching down toward the warrior's face. Just in time, he raised his weapons and blocked. They wrestled for dominance, locked together. Sam gasped with the effort. Despite his efforts, Kane was gaining the upper hand.

The warrior could smell victory, and he bared his teeth as he said, "Yield, lad. There's no shame in admitting you're beaten."

"I'll never yield to Eìrlani scum like you," Sam hissed.

Kane's eyes went cold with fury. "That's it," he growled.

In one swift movement, he sent Sam crashing, hard, onto his back. Before Sam could catch his breath, Kane was upon him, Sam's own blade pressed against his throat.

The onlookers cheered and groaned in equal measure, dispersing as Sam glared up at Kane, gasping to catch his breath. The warrior only leaned in, so close that nobody else would hear, and said into Sam's ear.

"I know who you are, little knightling. I've seen your pain, and I know that anguish will tear you to pieces at best or turn you into a hateful little shite at worst. You can hurl insults at me all you like, but it won't do you a bit of good. I offered you friendship, and you spat in my face. I'll give you one last chance to have someone to talk to—someone who won't judge you for who you are. Right here. Right now."

"Go to hell," Sam rasped, angry tears burning in his eyes.

Kane's lips pressed into a thin line, and those eyes, those soft brown eyes, were so sad as he murmured, "Goddess deliver the little boys from this forsaken kingdom."

And then he was gone, striding from the ring and out of sight as Sam lay gasping in the dirt.

Chapter Eleven

Ronan paced the floor of his study, deep in thought. It had been one week since the negotiations with the Eìrlani delegation had begun. One week, and already things were starting to break down as the king descended deeper into the madness that gripped him.

He had worked tirelessly to bring the Eìrlani to the table, and the king had signed off on every communication. The treaty was a simple one—the marriage of Prince Mica to Princess Annabelle in exchange for the forces needed to end the conflict in the north. They were out of resources and out of time, hardly in a position to bargain.

So it was shocking to the delegation and the cabinet alike when talks ground to a halt on the third morning.

The king had not been himself; Ronan had known it the moment he entered the cabinet room. He had listened to the ambassador talk, but Ronan was distracted, waiting for the explosion he feared would come. Finally, the king had stood and declared that there would be no wedding until after Dunea declared victory in the north.

"We do not have reason to trust your word," he snarled at a speechless Cerre. "You make grand claims about the mighty Eìrlani navy, but what evidence have we seen to support your claims?"

Of course, the room had erupted at this insult. Dunea was in no position to make such a demand, but the king would hear no objections, and he stormed from the cabinet room before long. The ambassador and his companions left not long after, informing the cabinet that they expected the king to concede his point, or they would leave, and there would be no treaty and no alliance, no help for Dunea against their enemies.

Ronan frowned, staring out of the window toward the bay where those majestic ships sat anchored. He was losing control of the situation quickly. The king's paranoia where Annabelle was concerned had grown beyond where even Ronan could have predicted, and it worried him more than anything else could have. It was time for him to intervene, to set specific plans in motion.

A knock sounded on the study door, and Sir Sam Fisher entered the room.

"Close the door behind you," he bade the knight, who did as he was asked at once.

Ronan settled in the chair behind his large oak desk, which Sam approached warily.

"You sent for me, my Lord?"

"I did. Please sit," Ronan said, gesturing to one of the chairs before the desk.

Sam sat.

"We must speak plainly with one another," Ronan said. "I am troubled, and I believe you can help…alleviate my troubles."

"I will do what I can, my Lord," Sam said.

Ronan smiled. "I do hope so. I have heard reports of your deeds in the north. You are a good knight—the best, in fact. But we are beyond the days when one good knight can make a difference in this conflict. We *need* this treaty. Badly."

"I understand, my Lord."

Ronan said nothing for a moment, studying the knight. It was impressive how one so young, born into such low circumstances—a fisherman's son, Ronan had discovered—had managed to rise so high to become the best. It was an ambition, a fire, a drive to excel beyond all others that he knew well.

"I have noticed your friendship with the princess," he said, "and I know that the Duchess personally requested that you be reassigned to her protection."

"Yes, my Lord."

"I am curious, how are you enjoying your new position?"

"I am honored to protect my princess and future queen," Sam said without hesitation.

"Naturally," Ronan said dismissively. "But, forgive me, I find it hard to believe that a knight of your…talents would find playing personal guard to one woman, even a woman as…spirited as our princess, to be fulfilling."

Sam hesitated before he said, "Respectfully, my Lord. The princess is my friend and my childhood companion. I would lay down my life for her."

"You misunderstand me," Ronan said. "I only mean to inquire if you would find it objectionable to take on some additional responsibilities."

"I am at my Lord's disposal."

So careful, so polite, with a perfectly impassive expression and sharp eyes that missed nothing. Yes. This man would do nicely.

"No one desires a successful alliance with Eìrlan more than I do," Ronan explained. "Yet I cannot shake the feeling that something is…amiss."

"You think the negotiation is likely to fail, my Lord?" Sam inquired, frowning slightly.

"I…I simply have a feeling," Ronan said. "The last time I had a feeling like this one, the queen was murdered within the walls of the palace. If the same were to happen to her child…I could never forgive myself. Do you understand me?"

"I do."

"Of course, I have no reason to think that this feeling has any basis in fact," he continued. "But it would make me feel better to know that I have eyes and ears that can keep watch when I am otherwise occupied."

"What would you like me to do?" Sam asked, his expression resolute.

Ronan fought the urge to smile. It had been as he thought: any threat to Annabelle's safety, perceived or otherwise, would be the trick to bring the young knight to heel.

"Continue to protect the princess," he said, expression carefully somber. "Report anything suspicious to me. Even I have limits to my power. I cannot be in all places at once."

"Very good, my Lord."

"You will do this for me?"

"Yes, my Lord. Of course, my Lord."

"I should tell you," Ronan said. "That I reward those who serve me loyally. You are a good man, Sir Sam Fisher. Do your job well, and the next talk we have will be about your future."

The knight's expression was unreadable as he inclined his head respectfully. "Yes, my Lord. Thank you, my Lord."

"You may go."

Ronan sat for a long time in the wake of the knight's departure, thinking. It was risky to bring such a man as Sam Fisher into his confidence, but nothing was safe these days. Everything was on the brink of either success or collapse, and the time for cautious action was long gone. He needed Sam Fisher on his side if he was to see his plans through.

He only hoped that Sam Fisher would prove worthy of his trust.

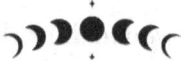

"Are you *sure* this is all you have?"

Herbert looked between Annabelle's irritated expression and the little book she clutched in her fist and sighed.

"As I told you before, Princess, that book is all that's left."

Annabelle slumped into a chair, defeated. She had spent every spare moment she'd had trying to glean what information she could from the book—when she wasn't being primped and powdered and shoved in front of some noble lady, some countess, or some royal committee. There just wasn't much to be found. The book was a collection of stories, tales of strange otherworldly creatures who possessed a wild, raw sort of magic that was tied to the land and the elements. They were morality tales, full of lessons for children on fairness, friendship, loyalty, love, and responsibility. Charming, certainly, but essentially useless.

"Why don't you just ask the prince what you'd like to know?" Herbert suggested, sitting beside her.

Annabelle laughed mirthlessly. "People lie, Herbert. Besides, we are...*trying* to be friends, but it's hard. He doesn't like to answer my questions."

"People write books too," Herbert pointed out. "The printed word is no guarantee of truth. And perhaps the prince would be more forthcoming if he knew that you wanted to learn about his home. Tell him that you care, and maybe you will be surprised."

Annabelle fought the urge to roll her eyes. She liked the old librarian, despite his somewhat ludicrous opinions on magic. He knew about all sorts of fascinating things, and she found her aimless steps brought her toward the library again and again. But now, she felt stuck, at a dead end.

She sighed. "Perhaps you're right, old man. I suppose it's time I sought answers from the horse's mouth."

He flashed a grin, eyes sparkling from behind those spectacles. "No time like the present, wouldn't you say?"

Her brow furrowed, the question forming on her lips just as someone gave an awkward cough behind her. She turned to see Mica standing in the middle of the library, looking uncomfortable.

Annabelle rounded on Herbert.

"What did you *do*?" She hissed.

But Herbert only winked and hurried off into the depths of the library.

"I was wondering," Mica said when the librarian was out of earshot, "if you wanted to spend some time together this afternoon?"

Annabelle cocked her head, "What did you have in mind?"

Mica shrugged as he said, "Anything you like."

Annabelle's interest piqued at once. "Anything?"

"I need an adventure," he explained. "This place is so massive, it seems impossible that I'm always being watched, and yet that's exactly how it feels."

"I know what you mean," Annabelle said, frowning. He was right. The walls in the palace had eyes. There was no way she would be able to go for a walk in the gardens alone with him, much less sneak out of the palace altogether—at least not without Sam or her ladies trailing after them. "As wonderful as an adventure sounds, I don't think we would make it three feet out the front door before someone came to shepherd me back inside."

"Who says you need to go out the front?"

Annabelle turned to see Herbert standing in the far corner of the library. He reached up and pulled a book from the shelf. Annabelle gasped as the entire bookcase swung forward on hinges, revealing a passage beyond.

"Funny thing about this passage," he said as Annabelle and Mica exchanged excited smiles. "It lets out by the temple of the Gods, which happens to be just out of sight of the palace. I believe I am the only one to have discovered it in ages. Funny thing, that." He gave a little wink and then turned his back on them. "I think it's time I took my nap."

And he vanished into the stacks of the library.

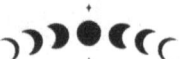

The city was everything Annabelle had dreamed it would be. She had Mica take her to the open-air market, where she purchased a meat pie from a vendor with bright blue hair and one gold tooth that gleamed as he accepted her money.

The pie's crust was crisp and golden, and the filling was so juicy that it dripped down Annabelle's chin. When Mica offered her his handkerchief to wipe up her mess, Annabelle giggled and blushed with embarrassment.

They spent most of the day wandering through the arts district, and Annabelle thought her eyes would pop out of her head at the colors and the people and the music. Oh, the *music*. Street performers at every corner serenaded them, playing lutes and flutes and accordions of all the colors of the rainbow. Annabelle's heartbeat in time with the rhythm of the city, its drumbeat resonating in her bones.

At first, she hovered on the sidelines, tapping her feet to the music and feeling self-conscious, but before long, she became swept away— dancing and laughing as she lost herself among the merrymakers, with Mica at her side.

It was different to dance like this, free and unencumbered by silks. *This is how parties should be*, Annabelle thought dazedly as Mica spun her around and around so many times she thought she would topple over. It was pure bliss, all of it, and Annabelle felt she could have kept spinning forever.

But eventually, her feet began to ache, so Mica suggested they stop in a tavern for a pint of ale. Annabelle gripped her pint anxiously, wondering if this would be a good time to probe Mica with questions about his homeland. But just then, a woman with a towering column of hair, her bosoms laid bare for the world to see, spread herself in Mica's lap and said, "Three coppers for the best night of your life," her voice a sultry whisper.

Annabelle laughed so hard that ale spurted from her nose as Mica politely extricated himself from the woman's clutches.

They left the tavern at sunset and wandered together down to the harbor, striding along in companionable silence. Annabelle gazed up at the forest of masts with a wistful expression.

"Three coppers for the best night of your life?" Mica asked, earning himself a swift elbow to the ribs. He laughed, rubbing his side and grimacing. "Fine. Just for your thoughts, then."

Annabelle sat upon a low wall, the water in the harbor lapping against the stones below. Mica joined her, and she smiled up at him as she said, "today has been the best day of my life. Thank you."

"You're welcome," he said, his eyes glinting in the light from the streetlamps. "Ellasport is a beautiful city. I can see why you love it so much."

Annabelle's smile faded, and she looked out across the harbor. "I love it, and yet I never even knew it before today. I was born here, and I spent my first few years here, but I don't remember it. After my mother…died, I was raised far away from here. But I suppose this place is still home to me, in some corner of my heart."

"You said something at the feast; I didn't know what it meant. Now I understand." His voice was kind. He didn't mock her for claiming a home that she'd never seen. She was grateful for it.

"Tell me about your home?" The question fell from her lips before she could stop it.

He didn't say anything for a long while as they sat upon that wall, looking out at the hundreds of ships in the harbor. Annabelle thought he might not answer her question, but then he said, "I like Danaa the best in the spring."

Annabelle didn't say a word, didn't move, didn't breathe as he continued.

"It would be about this time, I suppose. They'll be setting up for the spring festival, which will happen in a few days, I think. I've lost track of time with...with everything. The whole city will be covered in flowers and color. The festival will go on for a full week of parties, sailing regattas, food, and drink set on tables in the street for anyone who wants it. We celebrate the warm weather and the coming warmth of summer. Though...some people look forward to the festival because they see it as a week-long excuse to engage in debauchery."

"Raphael?" Annabelle asked knowingly.

He chuckled. "Yes. Though he's not nearly the worst of them if you can believe it."

"Don't try to convince me you're too noble to engage in a little debauchery yourself, Prince," Annabelle said, raising an eyebrow.

He gave her a wolfish grin. "Why, Princess? Curious about what a night out with me at the spring festival would be like?"

She scowled, and he laughed out loud, the first time he had done so since they had met. The sound was so pure and deep that Annabelle's heart splintered to hear it.

"I've had my fair share of good times during the festival," he continued, "but those escapades were never my favorite part. I just love how everyone in the city steps out of their houses and roams the street. No crime. No fear. We shed our titles and our walls and become one people. It's like..." he fell silent.

"Magic," Annabelle whispered.

His gaze snapped to her, and his eyes went wide. He was so close just then. So close that she could count his eyelashes. Annabelle's lips parted, her heart hammering against her ribcage.

And then he was gone, and the night air was cold with his absence.

"I should get you back," he said and extended a hand to help her to her feet.

They returned to the palace without speaking. The journey seemed to take hours longer than it had that morning. Annabelle felt wretched, but she had no idea why. What had happened? Had she said something wrong?

Twice she opened her mouth to say something—though she didn't know what. But one look at Mica's stony countenance, illuminated by the silver light of the moon, caused any words of reconciliation to die on Annabelle's lips.

They bid each other a hasty goodnight at the cold and silent threshold of the library, and Annabelle watched him go with a pang of longing for something she had only barely grasped before it had slipped away.

The walk back to her rooms was long after the excitement of the day, and Annabelle's limbs felt heavy as stones. She longed to fall into bed, to lose herself to the world and sleep away the confusion that gnawed at her.

But that glorious oblivion was not meant to be.

As she pushed open the door to her sitting room, she had one glimpse of the Duchess, seated on her sofa, lips pressed into a thin line, and Emily pacing nervously in the background before Sam stepped in front of her—face pale, eyes livid.

"Where have you *been*?" He demanded, nostrils flaring.

Annabelle pushed past him into the room. "What's going on?" She asked her aunt.

"Answer the question," Sam barked, closing the door behind her with a snap.

Annabelle rounded on him. "It's none of your damn business where I was."

"I beg to differ," he growled. "We are all trying to keep you safe because we love you, and you just go galavanting off—"

"I was with the Prince," Annabelle spat. "I was having fun. I was taking a well-deserved break, and I was perfectly safe."

Which had seemed the truth at the time. Though Annabelle would have rather bowed before Baron Gustav Wallace than admit it, she was beginning to think her actions had been a bit rash and foolish.

Sam took in her wind-swept hair, her dusty hem, her flushed cheeks. "You went into the city," he said accusingly.

Annabelle stared him down, defiant. "So what if I did?"

He looked like he was likely to explode, and Annabelle felt a sudden thrill of fear as he pulled himself to his full height.

"Enough."

They both turned to see the Duchess glaring at the pair of them.

"Sam, go to bed. You two can kill each other in the morning, but right now, I need to speak to my niece."

There was a pause in which nobody moved.

"*Alone*," the Duchess snapped, pounding her walking stick on the floor for emphasis.

"I'm not done with you yet, *Princess*," Sam growled before he stalked from the room.

Emily caught Annabelle's eye and mouthed, *I'm sorry*, before she too hurried out of sight.

"Annabelle, sit," the Duchess commanded.

Annabelle sat, fuming. He wasn't done with her? Good. She was ready for a fight, yearning for it. That time in the city, those shining hours with Mica when she had been free and happy seemed only a bright memory now, pale as the moon in the morning sky.

"As much as I would like to scold you for your behavior," the Duchess began, her tone severe, "I understand why you did it. But Annabelle, it must not happen again."

Annabelle opened her mouth to protest, but her aunt held up a hand, and she closed it.

"This evening, your father and the delegation from Eìrlan reached an agreement. They signed the treaty an hour ago."

Annabelle froze. "Th—they...they," she stammered, her thoughts spinning out of control as the weight of her aunt's words slammed into her.

The Duchess nodded. "Tomorrow, there will be a feast to celebrate the signing of the treaty, and the King will announce your engagement to the court. The wedding will take place in three days."

Engagement. Marry the prince. Three days. There was a rushing sound in Annabelle's ears, and she sat still and staring as her aunt rose to her feet.

"I hope you had a nice time today, Annabelle, but you must put it behind you now," she said as she moved to the door. "The time for being young and foolhardy has passed. The moment has come for you to do your duty to your kingdom and your people."

Three days. Annabelle did not move as her aunt left her. Her thoughts were filled with color and music, and meat pies. She watched, enraptured, as those light-filled memories faded, faded, and then snuffed out—leaving her in darkness.

The shroud of night hid her surroundings from view as she slowly regained consciousness. Panic, sharp as talons, scratched down her back as she struggled against the ropes that bound her. She lay on her side upon a hard stone floor, and her shoulder and hip barked in protest as she wriggled in her attempts to get free. If she could only sit up... but it was no use. A cloth was tied tightly across her mouth, and the exertion and lack of oxygen made her lightheaded.

Breathe. She forced herself to become still and take deep, even breaths through her nose. Calm down. Focus.

As she lay there breathing, the details of the room began to take shape out of the blackness. It was large and cavernous, with a great stone altar at one end. The temple of the Gods. But where were the priests? Why had the candles upon the altar been extinguished?

There was a noise behind her that stilled her breath. The door to the temple had opened and closed with an echoing click. Footsteps crossed the floor toward her, and she shut her eyes, feigning unconsciousness, forcing her breath into a slow and easy rhythm.

The newcomer passed her by without pausing. Soon she heard new sounds, a scratching and a shuffling of objects in the direction of the altar. She dared to open one eye. A hooded figure stood in front of the altar with his back to her, arranging candles, bowls, bottles, and stones upon its smooth surface. A spell. Her pulse quickened, and she once again resumed her efforts to free herself, as quietly as she could manage, gathering her strength, pooling it deep within.

A bang reverberated through the chamber as the door was blown wild on its hinges. Footsteps thundered upon the floor, and she fell limp once more as a man's voice demanded, "What are you doing?"

The figure by the altar said nothing, not even acknowledging the voice.

"You cannot do this," the man sounded agitated. "You have to listen to me. You have no idea what this will—"

Using the disturbance of his pleas as cover, she muttered a single word, and the world exploded. Blue light flashed in the temple as both figures were thrown backward from where she lay. She leaped to her feet, bonds disintegrated from the force of her spell and, without so much as a backward glance, tore from the temple. They wouldn't be out for very long, and she needed to hurry.

The temple was set upon a rocky slope, and the stones cut into the pads of her feet as she climbed, but she pushed the pain aside, intent upon her destination as she ran. The first fat drops of rain began to fall, and still, she ran.

When she finally crested the slope, a flash of lightning illuminated the world, and she saw it—a gleaming palace, so close she could have wept with relief. But there was no time. They would be coming, and she did not have a moment to lose. She repeated one word with each footfall as she ran, driving her forward, acting as a balm against pain and terror.

Annabelle, Annabelle, Annabelle...

Annabelle was moving before she realized she was awake. Hurtling for the balcony, she wrenched the doors open and stood there in the fresh air, gasping, fighting against the urge to heave the contents of her stomach across the stone floor.

It was a dream, she told herself firmly, *a dream*. But she could not clear the images from her mind: the altar, the hooded figure, and the name that still echoed in the chambers of her mind.

Annabelle.

She was losing her grip. It was the only explanation for the nightmares. The first one had happened the night she came to the palace; the night her father humiliated her in front of the entire court; the night she made a drunken fool of herself in front of her betrothed.

And now? Well, Annabelle did not need to imagine why she was once again sent running from her bed in the gray hours before dawn. In three days, she would marry the prince, and he wanted—well, after last night, she had no idea what he wanted anymore.

On top of everything else, Sam was mad at her. Annabelle groaned when she remembered the anger and betrayal on his face. It was his job to protect her, and she had deliberately betrayed him by running away. How he must have felt...

Guilt, hot and furious, threatened to overtake her. When Herbert opened that secret passageway, all Annabelle had thought about was her own freedom, her own desires, and her own life. What kind of Princess did that make her? What kind of *friend* did that make her?

There was nothing for it. Annabelle needed to find him. There was too much that she did not understand, and that could not be fixed—but she could fix this. She had to fix this. There was no surviving whatever was to come if she didn't have Sam by her side.

A fissure ran up the stone face of her determination, sending Annabelle to her knees. There had been many times over the years since her mother died when Annabelle felt her absence. It had never been quite as bad as now, though, with the entire world growing and changing by the minute.

For a few minutes, she allowed herself to feel the wave of grief that ravaged her heart. Then Annabelle picked herself off the floor, wiped her tears, and went to take responsibility for her own future.

Chapter Twelve

"I'm sorry."

"I don't want to hear it."

"I'm *sorry*."

"Go away, Annabelle."

Annabelle did not go away. She trailed after Sam as he stalked across the gardens, rage rolling off of him like waves of heat.

"Come on, Sam," She begged. "Please talk to me."

He rounded on her, and she backed up a step, startled.

"Did you even once think about what it would do to me to find you missing?" he demanded. "Did you consider my feelings at all?"

"Well…" She shifted on her feet, uncomfortable. "In my defense, you weren't supposed to find out."

He let out a harsh, cruel laugh, and Annabelle flinched.

"Wonderful!" he shouted, throwing his arms up in the air. "Just perfect. I spent all day worrying about your safety, and this is the thanks I get? I thought you understood, Annabelle. I thought you finally grasped the seriousness of your situation." He lowered his voice until it was barely more than a hissing whisper. "You are betrothed to the prince of a foreign kingdom that has spent the better part of the last century hating our guts. Your mother was murdered in this very palace, right under the nose of about a hundred guards. Your father, our *King*, seems on the verge of a complete mental collapse, and—" he stopped, taking a ragged, steadying breath. "And you waltzed out of the safety of these walls without a thought, without a care, without realizing that if someone in that city had realized who you were and grabbed you, we never would have found you. You would have been lost, Annabelle. Gone. I thought you were smarter than to take such a stupid risk."

Annabelle glared up at him. He was right, of course, and she hated him for it; hated all of them for stealing her one day of joy like ripping the rug out from under her feet. She put her hands on her hips and stared him down. "Maybe I'm not."

He blinked. "Excuse me?"

"Maybe I'm not smarter than that. Or maybe I am? And maybe I weighed that stupid risk against the fact that I'm about to be married, I'll be expected to have children right away, I'll be locked inside that palace, and I'll never be free another minute of my life. Maybe I am smart enough to put one likelihood against the other and realize that I'd rather die than live the rest of my life without knowing what it's like to be free—to be truly free, for once."

Annabelle sighed then, and the fire in her heart guttered as her shoulders sagged.

"I'm sorry I didn't think of you, Sam. I know you're just trying to protect me. But I didn't want to be protected, just for one day. I wanted something to happen to me because something happening to me would be better than nothing ever happening to me."

Sam let out a long, vocal sigh and scrubbed his hands through his mop of hair. "You are going to be the death of me," he groaned.

"Tell me something I don't know," Annabelle smirked.

He pulled her into a hug, and when they broke apart, he gave her a crooked smile. "Incidentally, how was your day galavanting all over town with the handsome prince?"

"Wonderful," Annabelle sighed. "Perfect. And then…not."

And she told him everything as they walked through the gardens—how Mica had opened up to her, the moment they shared, and how he had turned from her in an instant. Sam frowned in the wake of her story.

"I can't pretend to be any kind of authority on people," he said with a shrug. "Maybe you should ask him about it. What's the worst he could do?"

Annabelle shrugged. "Oh, I don't know…hate me for the rest of my life."

"Why would he hate you?"

"It's hard to explain." She wracked her mind for the right words. "It's like…there's the person who I am, who I show to the world, and then there's this other person. She's who I truly am when everything else is stripped away. I'm just afraid that if I let him in, let him see her, he'll hate me…and then there will be nothing I can do because he hates who I am at my core. That's the part of me that I'll never be able to change, and then we'll be trapped forever. Do you know what I mean?"

Sam's jaw clenched, and his eyes were far away as he said, "Yes, I do."

Annabelle peered up at him. There was something in his expression that made her ask, "Sam, is everything okay?"

He looked down at her, brow furrowing. "Yes, of course. Why do you ask?"

"I don't know," she said. "You're just always worrying about me, and I've noticed that Damon hasn't been around, and I haven't seen the two of you together much since we came here…so I just figured someone ought to ask you if you're okay."

He smiled sadly. "I'm fine. Damon's just…" he trailed off. "We'll figure it out."

"I hope you do. I don't like the idea of you two fighting."

Sam made a noncommittal noise, which Annabelle interpreted as his way of asking her to drop it. Annabelle, however, would do no such thing.

"I'll make you a deal," she pushed. "I'll talk to Mica about my thing if you promise to talk to Damon about yours."

He pulled a face. "We don't really do that—*talk* about things."

"Oh, I forgot, you're *men*." Annabelle rolled her eyes. "Fine. Well… you don't have to talk to me about it, as I can tell you don't want to, but talk to someone. Please?"

Sam's expression was unreadable as he stopped and looked at her for a long moment. Finally, he smirked and said, "Come on. We've got to get you dressed for the party."

And though she pestered him all the way back to her rooms, he would not say another word on the subject.

Sam and Annabelle spent the rest of the day together, Annabelle avoiding her responsibilities and Sam making sure Annabelle didn't get into too much trouble. Things between them seemed back to normal, and Annabelle was relieved. It felt terrible to be at odds with Sam after they had already spent so much time apart.

Their day together put Annabelle in such a good mood that, by the time she entered the banquet hall for the feast, her worries seemed far smaller when they had that morning. Despite everything that had transpired the day before, she and Sam were back on good terms, and she felt more beautiful than she had in her entire life.

She wore one of the gowns that Barrick's tailor had made for her—a gown of red and silver brocade, with a latticework of pearls stitched into the bodice. The skirts spilled out from her waist, and she felt like she was floating as she crossed the candlelit hall, drawing awed stares from all around as she passed.

Ladies Malisa and Rose had outdone themselves, curling and braiding her hair into an intricate woven knot at the back of her head. On top, nestled in the soft piles of her curls, sat her mother's tiara, winking prettily in the flickering light.

The king and Mica stood before the dais, waiting for her. Annabelle was startled to see her father looking as good as she had ever seen him—clear-eyed and beaming as she approached and sank into a bow before him. When she straightened, he reached out and pulled her into an embrace. "You look breathtaking," he whispered into her ear. "Your mother would be so proud."

Taken aback but pleased, all the same, Annabelle turned shining eyes to the prince.

He was dressed in black, his jacket decorated with the same embroidered symbols he had worn on the day he arrived at the palace. Against the dark of his hair and his clothes, his sapphire eyes glowed so brightly they caused her breath to catch in her throat. He was so handsome, so perfectly beautiful that her heart ached. But when he looked upon her, those sapphires burned cold.

"Lords and Ladies of the court," the king said in a voice that reverberated through the hall, strong and clear. "Honored guests. It is my great pleasure and honor to announce the engagement of my daughter, Annabelle Ilenna Alexandria Penelope Isren, Princess of Dunea, to his Highness Prince Mica of clan Rian of Eìrlan."

Mica, please, Annabelle begged silently, staring at Mica, willing him to hear her. *Please. I'm your friend. Smile. Do something, anything to show me it's going to be okay. I'm scared. Please, Mica.*

"Let their union stand as a symbol of the budding friendship between two great and ancient kingdoms."

Please, Mica. I can't do this alone. Please. I am begging you. Show me I'm not alone. Show me that you're here, that you're with me, please.

The king lifted his goblet from the table behind him and raised it high into the air. "To Prince Mica and Princess Annabelle."

Mica's eyes slid away from her as every goblet in the hall was raised high into the air, and Annabelle wanted to scream in frustration.

No, Mica. Look at me. Please. Look at me. LOOK AT ME.

"Prince Mica and Princess Annabelle," the court intoned as one and drank.

And he was walking away from her, climbing the dais and taking his place at the high table. Annabelle just stared after him, lost and adrift. The memory of his beautiful laugh haunted her as she took her place beside him. What had she done to deserve this treatment? What could she do to fix it?

As the rest of the court feasted, her father's booming laugh sounding through the hall at regular intervals, Annabelle only sat and combed through the events of the previous night, hunting for some reason why he should treat her so coldly. She could discover nothing. Hopelessness, cold and unyielding, settled upon her shoulders.

"Annabelle?"

Annabelle turned to see her father looking at her, those green eyes, *her* eyes, so clear and bright.

"Father," she murmured, hardly daring to breathe, bracing herself.

"I wanted to say," he began, his voice deep and quiet. "That I know I have not been...myself as of late."

She said nothing, only waited as he continued.

"This treaty, the war in the North," he sighed. "They have weighed upon me, and I have not borne my worries gracefully. I would have liked our reunion to come at a happier time, a time when we could sit together and talk." He hesitated. "When this is over, I'd like us to have some time together before I return to the capital."

"Am I not coming with you?" She asked, confused. The Duchess had always told her that she would join her father in the capital once she was married.

The king took her hand in his and kissed it. "No, my darling child. I need you to remain here, where it is safe. The prince will accompany me, of course. He is to command the fleet that will help us stomp out the rebellion in the north for good. Once that is done, once it is *safe*, you will join us."

Fury, white-hot electrifying rage surged in Annabelle's blood, burning everything away—all the pain and hopelessness and fear—until there was nothing left but crystalline clarity. How dare he? How dare *they*? These men and their changeful hearts, with their whims and pleasures. How dare they lock her up and abandon her to rot in a gilded cage. How *dare* he treat her so unfeelingly, only to apologize for…what? Having a bad week?

He said that her mother would have been proud. Proud, indeed. Her mother would not be proud of the meek, caged little doll she had become. Her mother had been wild. She had walked the streets of the city. She had helped people. Annabelle knew the stories; she'd collected them in her heart like shining treasures. Her mother would not have accepted this, accepted *him*. She wanted to yank her hand away, to tell him to shove his apology and leave her be. But she did not.

Instead, she lifted her hand to her father's cheek and smiled sweetly.

"I would like that very much," she lied. "Time, with you. To talk."

He beamed at her, those green eyes shining with happiness, and returned to his supper.

Annabelle sat seething silently for only a heartbeat before turning to face Mica. She was resolute. They were not married yet, he held no sway over her for the next two precious days, and she would have answers.

But his chair was empty. He was gone.

She found him in the garden. The prince stood by the wall, staring at his ships anchored in the harbor. He turned as she approached, and she watched his features harden as that cool mask slid into place when he saw her. That only stoked the fire of her anger as she stormed up to him.

"What did I do?" She demanded.

He just looked at her, face impassive. "I don't know what you're talking about."

But she was having none of it. "Don't pretend with me. We were having an enjoyable time together. We were having *fun*, and then you shut down. Why? *What did I do?*"

His gaze was so cold it burned. "I don't know what you're talking about."

"Yes, you do."

"No, I don't."

She gaped at him. Could he really be this stubborn?

"Was it the flirting?" She asked. "Could it possibly be the absolutely harmless flirting?"

"I did not flirt with you," he growled.

Her shriek of laughter sent several birds scattering from the nearby bushes. "You flirted with me. Big deal. We're only going to be married, so I don't exactly see the harm in—"

"You offered me friendship," he said, cutting her off. "Friendship, Annabelle. Not questions about my home, not those memories, not…not…."

His mask was cracking. He dragged a hand through his hair, eyes wide.

"What?" Annabelle pressed, baiting him, desperate to break through his defenses, to learn the truth. "What did I do that was so terrible?"

But it was too late. His features hardened, and the prince gave her a withering glare. "I do not owe you an explanation."

It felt as if he had struck her. Annabelle actually stumbled back a step as she gasped, "This…this isn't you."

"You don't *know* me," he said. "We've known each other, what… less than one week? What makes you think you know the first thing about who I am?"

But Annabelle shook her head. "One week was enough. I know you enough to know that you are not cruel. I am not going to let you get away with pretending otherwise."

"What is it that you want me to say, Annabelle?" he said, throwing his arms wide. "What do you want from me?"

"I want you to stop this," Annabelle whispered. "I want you to stop pretending that…that there isn't something between us."

Mica didn't say anything for a long moment, and when he did, the words were like shards of ice in her heart.

"I'm not the one pretending. You are. You want everything to work out perfectly, for me to be the prince of your dreams. But I'm not a dream, Annabelle. I'm just a man. And one night does not erase the fact that I didn't choose this—that *we* didn't choose this. You cannot force love, or else we'll only ever have a ghost of the real thing. I don't want that for me, and I certainly don't want that for you. Can you honestly say that you do?"

His words stung, but only because of the truth in them. Standing there in that beautiful garden, with that cruel truth echoing in the space between them, Annabelle realized that she *had* been pretending. The thought had been there, lurking beneath the surface, driving her on, that maybe everything was working out just the way it was meant to be. Maybe they were meant to be together all along. If he had looked at her, he had decided that she was the one he wanted, even if there was no treaty, no ships, no war—maybe that would make it better, somehow. Maybe she could have found a slice of true happiness.

But he was right. That wasn't love. That wasn't *real*. It was just pretending—just the beautiful, hopeful dream of a desperate girl.

"This is going to be hard," she murmured into the silence. "Isn't it?"

Mica sighed heavily. "It was never going to be anything else."

Wordlessly, Annabelle turned and walked away from him so that he would not see the tears that rolled down her cheeks, scattering to the dirt like rain. Annabelle hoped that the vast well of tears she had cried since coming to the palace might water a garden as grand as this one; something beautiful and good from so much pain.

$$)\mathbf{)}\mathbf{)}\bullet\mathbf{(}\mathbf{(}($$

Sam wandered the paths of the garden, muttering under his breath as he searched for Annabelle. After their fight the night before, after her apology, she had run off again. The Gods save him; he was going to attach a bell to that girl if he ever found her. Turning a corner, he found himself at the wall. There was nobody in sight.

Cursing, he turned and saw a dark figure lurch to its feet and stroll casually into the light from the full moon above.

"You know we have to stop meeting like this," Kane said with a sultry smile.

"Have you seen the princess?" Sam asked, too tired, too worried about Annabelle for games.

"She was here," Kane said. "She left. Gone to bed, I'd wager. I'd be surprised if she returned to the party. My cousin can be a right little prick when he wants to be."

Sam frowned at him. "What are you talking about?"

"Well," Kane sighed, "The princess and my cousin got into quite the melodramatic tiff. They didn't know I was here, but then *I* don't let my charges wander off unsupervised."

"What did he do to her?"

Kane gave him an exasperated look. "Stand down, soldier. She'll be fine. She's a big girl—more than equal to the task of handling a little shite like Mica, anyway."

He was right, of course. Annabelle could handle herself. That was the problem. Exhaustion hit Sam like a tidal wave. He was so tired of this, of waiting for something to happen, worrying about Annabelle, dealing with everything else. He just wanted one good night's sleep, free from the worries that drove him from his bed in the grey hours before dawn and kept him lying awake well into the night.

Kane was watching him closely. "Are you alright, knightling?"

"Why does everybody keep asking me that today?" Sam grumbled, rubbing his middle finger against a sudden pain in his forehead.

"Maybe because you look like shite and have the manners to match?"

Sam actually laughed tiredly. "If I do, I don't see why you should care."

"Maybe I do," Kane shrugged. "Maybe I don't. Maybe I just fancy the opportunity to dump your sorry arse in the dirt one more time."

Sam's smile faded. "Look, Kane…"

"Raphael," he interjected.

"I—sorry?" Sam blinked his confusion at this request.

"Call me Raphael," Raphael repeated. "Kane is the name of my clan, not my surname."

"Oh," Sam hadn't considered this. "Well…alright. Raphael."

He felt awkward calling the man by his first name. It felt too...personal.

"Look," he said, trying to regain his bearings. "About the other day...I am sorry. For what I said to you, I mean."

"I've been called worse." Raphael sat on the wall, his long legs stretching out in front of him.

"I'm sure," Sam smirked. "But not by me. I don't like it when... when I get angry like that. I become someone else, someone I really don't like."

"I told you," Raphael said quietly. "That self-hatred will rip you to pieces or turn you into someone hateful. Most likely both," he added with a grimace.

Sam didn't say anything. He couldn't admit it, not out loud, and not yet. But he didn't deny it, either. He just stood there, letting the silence be his confession. Raphael did not say a word; he did not move. For the first time since they had met, mere footsteps away from this very spot, he let Sam be alone with his thoughts and his demons.

"I don't know what to do," Sam said at last. Terror ripped through his chest, but he beat it back, thinking of Annabelle. *Talk to someone.* His friend was brave. He would be brave too.

Raphael considered him before saying, "Well, for starters, I'd stop falling in love with unavailable men."

Sam's cheeks flushed with embarrassment, but the grip of that terror eased somewhat. It felt good to speak this way, plainly. No lies. No carefully constructed mask. No excuses. Just the truth—or as much of it as Sam felt capable of laying bare.

"There's no such thing as an available man in Dunea," he said with a grimace.

"Maybe yes," Raphael said, cocking his head to the side, "maybe no."

Sam couldn't say anything, couldn't give voice to the one small hope that he had guarded, that lay coiled in a secret corner of his heart. But he didn't have to because Raphael knew what he was thinking.

"He isn't one of them."

"And how would you know that?" Sam grumbled, rebelling against that sad truth.

Raphael barked a laugh. "Please, lad. Never have I seen a man so enamored with the fairer sex. I believe he'd live with his head buried under a woman's skirts if he could."

A pause as the warrior's grin faded, and he said in a voice so soft, so gentle, that Sam could have fallen to his knees and wept, "I don't say these things to hurt you, Sam. I say them because you have to move on because there's a whole life—a whole *world* waiting on the other side of that pain. Trust me."

Sam didn't believe him. He couldn't believe him, not when his entire life had taught him that he must shut out a piece of himself or else live in the darkness—like those poor wretches on the streets of Rengon City, running from guards and dying slowly in the dark.

"Nothing is waiting for me," he said and turned to leave.

A warm, calloused hand gripped his arm, and Sam barked in protest as Raphael pulled him into a crushing embrace, their bodies pressed together and covered Sam's mouth with his own.

It was like waking up after a dreamless slumber. Sunlight burst behind Sam's eyes, and hot sweet fire ignited in his blood, in his bones, as Raphael kissed him. No fear gripped him, no terror that they might be seen, no panic over the fate of his friends. It was all gone, and all that was left in its wake was pure ecstatic oblivion.

Raphael pulled away, and Sam wanted to scream, to pull him back, to punch him across his horrible, beautiful face, to run away and hide. But he did none of those things, only stood transfixed to the spot as the warrior took two steps back and said, his voice ragged, "Something to think on."

Then he was gone, and the cold came to find Sam once more.

Annabelle couldn't sleep. How could she have? Her whole world was coming to an end, and she felt that it was the least she could do to bear witness to its slow death.

How foolish she had been to think that her life could have been different—could have been something worth living. She had become like a child reading a book of faerie stories. Naive, gullible, actually convinced that there was magic in the world. But Herbert was wrong. There was no such thing as magic, and she would do better to lock that naive little girl in a dark room and throw away the key.

Annabelle hugged the blanket closer around her shoulders and tucked her knees into her chest—a shudder running down her spine that had nothing to do with the sudden chill in the air that blew in from the bay.

She sat upon her small stone balcony, lounging in one of the wrought-iron chairs, listening to the sounds of the banquet, still in full swing, floating up from below. Here and there, she spied darkened figures moving about the gardens. A stab of envy made her squirm in her seat. How unfair that they should enjoy themselves when she was so miserable and alone.

Salt found her on the air, and Annabelle breathed deep, welcoming its caress inside, begging it to soothe her, to heal her. But that pure, clean salt air had lost its magic too. It belonged to another time, another world, wherein anything had still seemed possible.

How she missed Lord Roger, missed his warm smile and his big muscled arms that had closed around her and kept the cruel truths of the world at bay. Fat tears slid down her cheeks as she remembered those sunlit days of her childhood.

"Mind if I join you?"

Annabelle wiped her face and smiled up at Emily as she settled into the other chair, a wool shawl wrapped tight around her thin shoulders.

"What are we drinking?" Emily asked, helping herself to some of the wine from a pitcher that sat upon the little table between them.

"Oh, you'll love this vintage," Annabelle replied, swirling the dark red liquid around the edges of her goblet. "A classic. Full-bodied self-pity, with notes of regret on the nose, and black cherry heartbreak on the tongue."

"Ah," Emily replied with a knowing nod of the head. "One of your favorites, if I am not mistaken."

"You are not," Annabelle grimaced and took a sip. "It's a good thing my ladies haven't realized I've left the party yet. Could you imagine their reactions if they saw us drinking out here together?"

Emily giggled. "I do enjoy shocking them."

"It is good fun."

"Shame I locked the bedroom door," she sighed.

"Quick," Annabelle urged, "unlock it. Let's be discovered. I long to hear the dulcet melody of my favorite tune...."

"Behavior unbecoming of a princess," Emily crooned, holding her glass high in the air.

Annabelle joined in, "Scandalous that a maid should take such liberties. I should have you flogged, you know."

"For intruding so rudely?"

"No," Annabelle raised both eyebrows. "For neglecting to bring more wine."

Emily pulled a face of mock solemnity. "A hanging offense, if you ask me."

"Truly."

They fell into pleasant silence for a while, sipping their wine and enjoying the company of their friendship, and Annabelle wondered how long it would last once she was married.

"Do you remember Billy Edwards?" she asked.

Emily gasped. "Oh, my word. I haven't thought about Billy in ages!"

"He was so in love with you," Annabelle recalled with a smile.

"And I thought I loved him for a time."

Annabelle snorted at this. "You did no such thing. If I remember correctly, you told me that...what was it? He was pretty to look at...."

Emily shook her head. "I said he was like a beautiful box with nothing inside. By the Gods," she said, crinkling her nose, "was I really *that* cruel?"

Annabelle shrugged. "It was true enough. Besides, you were too intelligent for him. He and Eddie Wallworth, the butcher's son."

"And Ryan Hill, the baker's boy," Emily chimed in.

Annabelle laughed out loud. "I forgot about him! Poor boy. He was the one who wrote you the poetry, wasn't he?"

Emily nodded, scowling. "I told him to stop seven times. Seven! I never understood what got all of them, so…riled up over me."

"What are you talking about?"

"I never knew why any of them liked me, really." She said, picking absently at some pilling that collected on her shawl. "Not when Susie Merchant—"

"Susie Merchant could never hold a candle to you," Annabelle cut in, leaning forward in her chair and staring pointedly at her friend. "And I never want to hear you say otherwise. Am I clear?"

Emily's face flushed, but she sighed. "Fine. The words will never cross my lips again."

"See that they don't." Annabelle refilled her goblet and sat back in her chair. "Besides, I was glad for your endless string of village admirers. I lived life through you, imagining it was I who had a dalliance with the farmer's son."

Emily pulled a face. "Gods preserve me; I would never have a dalliance with Raymond Billings!"

"It's just a figure of speech, darling," Annabelle said, smirking.

"Even so…" her friend gave a slight shudder.

"Do you think…" Annabelle began but stopped.

"What is it?"

"No…" Annabelle wished she hadn't said anything at all. "It's nothing. Nevermind."

"Please tell me," Emily urged, her eyes wide. "If something is bothering you, I'd like to help if I can."

"Well…" Annabelle was so embarrassed, and she couldn't look her friend in the eye as she said. "I was just wondering if maybe…I don't know…the fact that I never had a love—even something silly with someone pretty like Billy Edwards—if maybe it has made me a bit…naive."

Emily frowned. "I don't think so, but I'm guessing that you do."

"I've made a mess of things with the Prince," Annabelle admitted, sighing heavily. "Because I let myself believe that he and I could have something that was…well, if not *love*, then maybe something like it. But he'll never see me as anything other than the woman he was forced to marry. And now I'm terrified that I've missed my chance to experience anything remotely resembling love. And I'm afraid that it's my fault, that I pushed too hard."

Emily considered what she'd said for a long moment, and Annabelle's heart swelled with gratitude. That was one of the things she loved about Emily—she took her time with her thoughts, especially when advising her friends.

"Look," she said finally, "if he's decided that his situation is somehow your fault, that is his problem, not yours. Annabelle, you are beautiful, intelligent, a wonderful friend, and a good person. If he doesn't want to get to know you, if he doesn't even want to *try* to love you, then to hell with him, I say."

"I suppose you're right," Annabelle grumbled, not yet ready to stop moping.

Emily sniffed at her wine. "You know…I think I do smell that self-pity you mentioned earlier."

Annabelle pulled a face. "Be serious, Emily."

"Fine." Emily set her wine glass down on the table, and Annabelle actually shrank away from the stern look her friend gave her. "Annabelle, you are the Gods-damned Princess of Dunea," she said. "You are going to be Queen someday. Don't you think you have better things to do with your time than worry about whether or not some stupid man thinks you're worthy of his attention?"

"I...I guess I do," Annabelle said into her wine glass.

"Yes, you do," Emily said, standing imperiously. "Now, you get the rest of tonight—one more night to mope about your lot. The Gods know that your life is not easy, and it won't get any easier. But you, my dear friend, are more than up to the challenge. So tomorrow morning, I want to see you up and ready to fight. Do I make myself clear?"

Annabelle grinned sheepishly up at her. "Yes, madam."

"Good," she huffed, walking off toward her room. "I'll see you in the morning, then."

"Hang on a moment."

Annabelle reached down and lifted the book from where it had lain on the floor of the balcony beside her chair and held it out to her friend. "Would you return this to the library for me, whenever you get the chance? I was trying to learn about Eìrlan, to..." She couldn't meet her friend's eyes as she said, "to try to please him. I can't face returning it myself. It's too shameful."

Emily took the book, and her voice was kind as she said. "I'll do it. Don't worry."

"Thank you."

Emily nodded and then left Annabelle alone once more. Gods above, she was so grateful for her friends. They made everything in life so much more bearable. Not for the first time, Annabelle wondered if she would have made such good friends had she grown up in the palace or the castle at Rengon. Somehow she couldn't see Lady Rose or Lady Malisa speaking to her with such candor as Emily had just done. Pleasing her was not the same as being her friend. She supposed if there was one thing in her whole childhood that she could be grateful for, it was her friends.

For it had been a real childhood, she knew now. It would not have been the same growing up in this place, not without her mother. Her heart swelled with gratitude, even as it split in two; gratitude for the people who had granted her that time to be free, to be a child. Lord Roger, Lady Ellen, the Duchess, Damon, Emily, and Sam; their faces swam before her eyes as something shifted within her—a bright beam of light sparking to life, in the middle of the darkness.

Perhaps she would not know her father's love, maybe Mica would always see her as the agent of his imprisonment, but that did not matter. She had known the love of a father and the love of a family. Love was all around her, shining in the eyes of her friends.

Her friends had sacrificed so much to keep her safe, to keep her protected, because they loved her as she loved them. She had disrespected that sacrifice to chase…what? To chase a love that would never exist? No more. She knew better now. Annabelle finally understood that the love she already possessed was worth a thousand promises of future happiness that may never come to pass.

The love of her friends, her *family*—that was the real magic.

There was a noise behind her, and Annabelle said with a grin, getting to her feet, "You'd better have brought more wine this t—"

White-hot pain blazed as something hard struck her across the back of the head. She fell, her goblet shattering upon the hard stones of the balcony as darkness swallowed her whole.

Chapter Thirteen

As the faint hum of music died away, the banquet guests dwindled, and the numerous candles were extinguished, Sam sat at the edge of the garden, thinking.

Raphael left him there alone, and Sam was unable to move for what felt like hours, his thoughts filled with the past; the first time he had realized his feelings for Damon and the first time he realized that he must never share the secrets of his heart with another living soul.

Hot anger and irritation swelled in his blood as he thought about that kiss. Of all the presumptive, arrogant, not to mention *dangerous* things to do. If Raphael so much as looked at him sidelong again, he would pummel the man into the dirt as retribution for taking such liberties. And yet...

And yet, that kiss had changed something. Sam had never let himself give in to what he wanted, not once. By the Gods, he hadn't even confided in Annabelle his true feelings, even though he knew she would never scorn him—hoped she would not, at least.

But now? Now, something was tugging, deep within his gut, pulling him forward toward something. He had spent his entire life running away, trying to smother the voice that begged to be free. Now Raphael's words floated to the front of his mind, *It's alright. It isn't a crime.* Well, maybe not where Raphael was from. Could such a place indeed exist? He had never considered it before, never dared hope. *There's a whole world waiting for you on the other side of that pain.*

Damon. His friend. The man whom he loved above all others, the man he had left behind because that love had nearly shredded him to bits. The thought of coming clean, of truly baring his heart to Damon sent a cold shiver down Sam's spine. He knew that such a thing was impossible.

Damon would never understand, had openly sneered at men like Sam. Sam himself had joined in the taunting, not wanting to draw attention to himself, but then cried himself to sleep at night. Breaking. Broken. He had only been a boy then. Afterward, he had resolved to make himself strong—so strong that not even Damon could hurt him.

And he had failed. He had not understood the kind of strength that was required to remain resilient against attacks of the heart, the blows to his soul that rendered it ragged and bloody. Annabelle knew that kind of strength, but Sam could not imagine it. He had shown Raphael a crack, the barest sliver of himself, and that alone had taken so much effort that it left him trembling and weak as a kitten in the snow.

Sam longed to let his walls come tumbling down, so desperately longed to feel more of that freedom and rightness that he had tasted as Raphael held him. But how?

Suddenly, every muscle in Sam's body tensed as the hairs stood up at the back of his neck. The world had gone still and quiet, so deathly quiet. Something was wrong.

The crunch of footsteps on the gravel path had him whirling around to see Damon running toward him, eyes bright with alarm, face set and grim.

"Thank the Gods I found you," he said, breathless as he skidded to a halt before Sam.

"What's wrong," Sam demanded, every muscle in his body tensing as if preparing for an attack. "What's happened?"

"It's Annabelle," Damon gasped, trying to catch his breath. "She's been taken."

"What?"

The words didn't make sense. It couldn't be true. Sam's heart pounded and raged even as his mind went deathly calm, sharp as a blade.

"Emily raised the alarm," Damon went on. "She heard a noise in the princess's bedchamber and went to investigate to find the room deserted."

"Maybe she only went for a walk," Sam suggested, even as the words screamed in his head, *Wrong, wrong, wrong!*

Damon shook his head. "The guards outside her door were knocked out, and her wine glass was broken, and..." Damon's throat bobbed. "Sam, there was blood on the floor."

It didn't make sense. Sam's mind was working furiously, running through potential scenarios, each one more unlikely than the last. "I still don't understand," he growled. "Who would have taken her?"

"The king has ordered that the delegation be placed under arrest, and the prince too," Damon said. "All available men, knights, guards are to head into the city to round up any Eìrlani who try to flee."

No. *No*. Sam wished he could seize time and keep it from moving until he could piece this chaos together into an explanation of events that made any kind of sense. "He wouldn't be so stupid," Sam said, more to himself than to Damon. "There has to be a better explanation for what's happened."

But Damon was shaking his head again. "It's done, Sam."

As if beckoned by his words, as if that final statement had been the call to arms, light flared at the corner of Sam's vision, and he turned to see an avalanche of flaming arrows soar free from the harbor, from the roofs of buildings, from the city wall. He watched, mouth falling open in horror, as those arrows found their mark, and the Eìrlani ships began to burn.

"Gods preserve us," Damon gasped as the great sails caught fire, but Sam didn't hear him.

A roaring sound had filled his ears, his mind, his very soul as he stared down upon the bay. Raphael was down there, somewhere. Sam was standing there, safe on dry land, with Damon, and Raphael was down there, perhaps burning along with his ship, with his countrymen. Sam had let the warrior walk away. He wanted to leap from the cliff into that black abyss, to swim for the ships, to find him.

But then words that had been spoken to him in the privacy of a fire-lit study echoed through him, bringing him back to the present, to sanity.

The last time I felt this way, the Queen was murdered within the walls of the palace.

Annabelle.

He had to find her. *But she's gone*, a voice in his mind argued. No. Whatever reason the king had to accuse the Eìrlani, Sam knew better. The attack against those ships had come as a surprise to everyone on board. Even now, tiny dark figures were running across the decks, trying to put out the fires even as the second volley of flaming death fell from above. No, whoever had taken Annabelle, he would bet his life that they lived much closer to home.

Something clicked into place, and cold spread down Sam's spine, extinguishing the fire of panic and anger that raged in his heart. This was why he had been chosen—why the Duchess and Lord Barrick had entrusted Annabelle's safekeeping to him, above all others. He had been trained for this. There was a fox in the palace, but he was the wolf, and he had scented his prey.

He turned to go, but Damon reached out and grabbed his arm.

"Let me come with you," he begged. "Let me help."

And he knew what Damon saw in his eyes as he dropped Sam's arm, as if it burned him—knew what had caused the shock and anger, and fear. The awkward boy Damon had known, his brother, and his childhood companion was gone. In one instant, Sam had shed the last lingering vestiges of youth, revealing the knight, the warrior, the *man* underneath.

"I will find her," he said as he turned his back on Damon and strode from the garden.

At first, Annabelle did not realize that she was awake. It was dark, and she lay, hands and feet bound, upon a hard stone floor. A dream; this was the same dream that had sent her rocketing from sleep only a few nights ago. She was once again captive, unable to move. There was that same panic gripping her, forcing reason and breath from her body, the same pain lancing through her head as she moved, trying to see her surroundings. But she'd had this dream before. She knew what to do.

Forcing herself to breathe, slow and steady, she waited as the details of her surroundings came into sharper focus.

A cavernous room with pillars set at regular intervals, holding up a roof that was not visible in the darkness. The faint smell of incense. A large stone altar, and a figure, shrouded in darkness, standing before it.

Just breathe, Annabelle thought as fear welled once again within her. *Just breathe.*

A flame burst to life as a candle was lit, and in the flickering light from that single candle, Annabelle saw his face. At the moment that he turned to face her, eyes burning red, a manic smile twisting that handsome face into a gruesome mask, she knew that this was no dream.

"Hello daughter," said the king, his voice a rasping husk of what it had been only hours ago.

"*No*," Annabelle groaned, trying to wriggle her body away from him, and the king laughed. It was a cold, brutal sound.

This didn't make any sense. What was going on? "What…" Annabelle fought against the pain that threatened to drag her back into unconsciousness as her head throbbed. "What is going on? What… what has happened?"

"You were in danger," the king said as if stating something obvious. "I had to keep you safe."

"But...then why am I tied up?" She struggled against her bonds. "Cut me loose. Father...please."

He shook his head, almost managing to look sad, "I cannot do that, daughter. If I untie you, you may try to run to him, to help him. I see the way he looks at you, the way you look at each other. I will not allow it. You are blind to his treachery, and I will—*I will keep you safe*."

She stopped struggling then as his words sunk in and stared in horror as the flames danced upon the altar. "What have you done?"

The king said nothing, turning his back to her, lighting more candles. "What have you DONE?" Annabelle howled, struggling with renewed vigor. "What did you do to Mica?" She had to get free. She had to help them.

"Only what needed to be done," he said, whirling to face her once more, and those eyes flashed crimson. "Only what others have failed to do for centuries. It is already underway. The order has been given. I only need to be patient, and soon the supposed great, untouchable kingdom of Eìrlan will be brought to its knees."

"*Why?*" She whimpered. Gods, her head hurt so badly that tears welled in her eyes.

The look he gave her was pure madness, those green eyes so wild and fearsome that Annabelle began to shake as he took one step toward her, then another.

"Because I will not let them have you. The savages seek to destabilize me, to take what is mine. But I say they have taken enough. This time I will take what is theirs. One ship is all I need to build my own fleet, and then the north will fall, and *you*..." He was so close, leaning over Annabelle, that dagger flashing dangerously close to her face, "You will be safe, locked away where I should have left you these long years, where I should have left your mother."

Tears welled in those horrible, red-rimmed eyes, and they spilled down his cheeks and onto Annabelle's face. As they fell, he continued to smile maniacally, his breath hot and sour with wine.

"Please," she begged him, her voice barely more than a whisper. "Please let me go."

The king snarled and stood, striding away from her, his footsteps echoing in the empty chamber.

"You should be thanking me," he hissed. "I alone have sought to protect you. I alone will keep you safe, keep you pure." He began muttering as if to himself. "I see the way he looks at you, the way his eyes fall upon your body. But you are mine. He will not have you, Ilenna!"

"I'm not Ilenna," Annabelle sobbed. "I'm Annabelle. I'm your daughter, *please!*"

But it was no use. The king was gone, lost to whatever madness gripped him as he said, "I will lock you away where only I can reach you, where nobody can take you from me. You will be mine, forever."

A cage. Another cage. Annabelle howled and writhed on the floor, pitching and bucking, the stone singing painfully against her shoulder and hips and back, but she did not care. Agony tore through her body, her head, but she kept struggling as the high stone walls of the temple began to close in around her. She had to get free. She couldn't let him lock her away. Rooms flashed before her eyes—the manor, the palace, cages, cages, *cages*.

"*NO!*" The scream tore from her throat, from the deepest darkest part of her soul, as light flashed through the temple, illuminating it in brilliant white light up to the highest corner of the vaulted ceiling.

The king yelled as he was thrown backward off his feet by an invisible force and slammed against the altar behind him. As the light faded, the king slumped to the floor and lay motionless.

Annabelle stared at him, horrified, unable to move, to think. Was he dead? What had happened? Where had that light come from? *No more cages, no more cages, no more cages.* Panic, terror, and revulsion gripped her and squeezed. Pain, hot and blinding, once again speared through her skull, and Annabelle shoved to all fours, vomiting upon the stone floor of the temple.

It was only when she raised a shaking hand to wipe her mouth that she realized her bonds had been reduced to dust. She was free.

Run. The voice clanged through her bones, through the panic, through the pain. *Run, Annabelle. Run!*

And she ran, flinging the door wide and hurtling into the night.

She stood, panting, on the front steps of the temple of the Gods. Annabelle knew this place, had seen the tall marble building as she and Mica exited the passageway that let out just up the hill from where she now stood.

Annabelle made for the hillside without pausing to consider what she ought to do next. The king—her own *father*—had kidnapped her, bound her, and threatened her. There was nobody she could trust. She needed a friend.

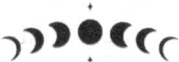

The library was deserted and dark when Annabelle pushed open the bookcase and stepped cautiously into the room. She knew a moment of panic as she scanned the shadowed stacks and alcoves, trying to think of what to do.

She needed to find Sam. But how? She couldn't simply go traipsing through the palace, could she? Surely if she let someone know she was safe…but what would she say? Instinct told her that whatever was going on in the palace and the city outside, it was better to stay hidden.

A flicker of light sent Annabelle cowering into the shadows as a figure appeared holding a candle aloft. A sigh of relief escaped her as Herbert's bespectacled face came into view around the edge of a bookcase.

"Who is there?" He asked the darkness, eyes widening in shock as Annabelle stepped into the light cast by his candle. "Gods above," he breathed, taking in her bedraggled hair, bruised wrists, and dirty nightgown. "Princess. What—"

"There's no time," she said, rushing forward. "Please, Herbert. I need your help."

Herbert asked no further questions nor raised any objections as she communicated what she needed.

"I will return as soon as I find your friend," he said when she had finished. "I urge you to hide. Dangerous things are happening in the palace tonight."

"I know," she replied. "Don't worry. I'll stay hidden."

And so she watched, feeling helpless and small, as Herbert took the comforting light of his candle from the library, leaving her in darkness. Shaking, Annabelle retreated into the stacks, sitting in a shadowed corner, knees tucked up under her chin. The books seemed to loom above her from their shelves, whispering of horrors to be found within the pages. Annabelle cowered, trying to block out the fear of what might happen next as the minutes ticked slowly by.

꒛꒜●꒚꒚

It was the quiet that disturbed Sam the most as he moved like a shadow through the cavernous halls. The frenzy following the attack had been smothered like a blanket upon a fire. Now the only sign that anything was amiss were the guards who patrolled the corridors at intervals, sending Sam backtracking and ducking into empty rooms, slowing his progress.

Every available man had been ordered to descend into the city, to hunt down Eìrlani fugitives, but Sam could not afford to waste a single minute. He would not hunt men but clues. Annabelle had been taken, and Sam would discover where and by whom.

His first stop was Annabelle's bedchamber. As its only occupant had vanished, he found her rooms unlocked and unguarded. On the floor lay scattered the remnants of the shattered goblet, and beside it, Sam spied two dark stains—one was wine, the other was unmistakably blood.

Chilling evidence, perhaps, but useless. Sam returned to the door and inspected the frame. There was no sign of forced entry, no splintered wood, no sign of a struggle in the corridor beyond. Strange. This room was always locked, always well guarded. There should have been a struggle. It was all wrong. *Wrong.*

Barrick. Sam needed to find Barrick. He had known this would happen, had felt the same wrongness that Sam had felt since arriving at the palace. Sam would tell him what he observed, what he guessed. It was his only option. For all the power that Sam had acquired for himself, every scrap he had fought and clawed for, he did not have enough to find the princess on his own—not if someone within the palace was responsible for her disappearance. Sam made for the hidden panel in the wall of the bedchamber. The maid's passageways would be empty—the fastest way toward the cabinet room and Lord Barrick.

There were two guards posted on either side of the cabinet room door, each holding a long spear in his fist.

As Sam approached, one of the guards stepped forward with his palm raised. "I am sorry, Sir," he said. "His lordship is not to be disturbed."

"This is an urgent matter," Sam said, making to step around the guard, but the man lay a hand upon Sam's arm, restraining him.

"You really want to remove your hand," Sam said, his eyes flashing dangerously. "Now."

The guard swallowed hard but did not release Sam. "I am s—sorry, Sir," he stammered, "But we have strict instructions not to disturb his lordship, for any reason. He said to use all necessary force, Sir."

"Oh really?" Sam's lip curled back from his teeth as he sneered at the guard. "Care to give it your best shot?"

The guard who held Sam winced at these words as if Sam had struck him, and his companion shrunk back into the corner. *Pride of the king's guard, these two*, Sam thought to himself with disgust.

Just then, the door creaked open, and Barrick's voice said from the darkened chamber beyond, "There will be no need for that, Sam. Come in."

Sam jerked his arm from the guard's grip, who looked more than a little relieved to let him go and stepped past his cowering companion into the cabinet room, shutting the door behind him.

No sooner had the catch clicked into place than Sam was thrown back against the wall, a long forearm pressing against his throat, closing off his windpipe.

Barrick was upon him, his face a mask of fury as he hissed, "How could you. *How* could you let this happen? I trusted you. I trusted you to protect her, and you *failed.*"

"W—what—" Sam gasped, trying to draw breath, but Lord Barrick only bore down upon him.

"You failed me," Barrick growled as he choked Sam. "You failed *her.*"

"I di...didn't...get...can't..." Sam sputtered. He needed to breathe. He couldn't think. He struck Lord Barrick in the abdomen with one swift move, and the arm fell away from his throat as the lord let out a grunt and stumbled away.

"I'm sorry, my lord," Sam rasped, rubbing his sore throat. "I'm sorry I did that, but I had—"

And then Sam took in the rest of the room, and the words he was about to say died on his lips.

The cabinet room was simple. A large fireplace stood to the right, and there were maps and charts hung upon the walls. In the center of the room stood a long table surrounded by many straight-backed chairs, and laid out upon that table...

But...it couldn't be. Sam blinked as his legs bore him forward, unbidden until he was looking down upon the corpse stretched out upon the wood. She looked so peaceful, hands set upon her stomach as if she merely slept. But she was not sleeping. She could not be sleeping, not with that ugly twisting gash splitting her neck from ear to ear.

"It can't be," Sam breathed as he just stared down upon Annabelle's lifeless form.

"She was found in the temple of the Gods," Barrick said, his voice thick and halting with emotion. "The...king found her, b— brought her back."

It was over—life itself. Sam stood frozen as every inch of his body, every spot of light in the world, screamed in agony, in fury, in rebellion against the chilling truth that lay before his eyes. It was as if the world had shrunk down until it was only himself, staring down at his cold dead friend.

This was beyond tears, beyond wailing, beyond mere grief. This was brutality that Sam had faced countless times on the battlefield. Yet, this was something he had never encountered before—not when he lost his parents as a baby, not when he saw those mutilated bodies in the north, and not when he had looked down upon the lifeless face of Lord Roger.

Sam knelt beside the table so that his eyes were level with her head.

"I...I am so sorry," he whispered. "You deserved more than this. You deserved the whole world."

With a trembling hand, Sam reached out to tuck a stray lock of hair behind her ear. It was such a futile gesture, the last sad attempt to care for her, even in death.

As he swept the hair back, revealing the bit of pale skin behind her ear, Sam froze. He stared at that spot, hardly daring to believe what he saw: smooth skin, unmarred by a single mark or scar. But...how was that possible?

It's not her.

Barrick let out a miserable howl and yanked Sam's hand away. "You do not get to touch her," he moaned. "You do not get to grieve her. You failed her."

Sam let Barrick drag him away from the body without protest, his mind working furiously. Annabelle had a scar behind her ear. He had been there when she received it, had endured Lord Roger's lectures for letting her climb trees, had felt the dizzying relief when the healer said she would be alright. The wound would only leave a scar, a mark that Annabelle would bear for the rest of her life.

As Barrick fell to his knees before the table, Sam stood behind him, dazed by the realization that swept through him like an icy wind. This person—whoever it was—was not the princess. Annabelle, the *real* Annabelle, might still be alive. It was impossible, and yet it was the only explanation.

But should he tell Barrick what he knew? This...copy was yet another piece of evidence in an evolving situation that did not make Sam trust the floor beneath his feet, let alone this man he barely knew.

And there was something about what Barrick had said that struck Sam as odd. The king brought her body up from the temple, he had said. But what had the king been doing there in the dead of night? How had he known where to look? The questions multiplied in Sam's head, each one birthing two more.

No. Better to keep his theories to himself until they could be proven. Better to retain what little control he had over the situation until he could find the princess...*if* he could find the princess.

This was another problem. Even if Annabelle was alive, he hadn't the first clue where to look for her. With the news of the princess's death, so too would cease all efforts to find her. Surely it would be better to have more eyes on the lookout, more feet on the ground.

One hour, Sam resolved at last. He would give himself one hour to look. If he found nothing, he would return and reveal to Barrick what he suspected.

"I will leave you to your grief," he said quietly as he backed toward the door. Though something gave him pause as his hand rested on the knob. He turned. "My lord?"

Barrick's eyes were full of pain when they met his own.

"I will avenge her," Sam said steadily. "This will not go unpunished."

He would find his friend, and this time she would be safe—because *he* would be the one caring for her. And once she was safe, he would find out who had tried to hurt her, and they would pay.

Barrick's eyes flashed as he nodded once. "See that it doesn't, Sir Knight."

The grisly scene in the cabinet room shut safely behind him, Sam began to walk. He had no ideas and no clues to guide him, and so he would start with the temple. Perhaps if this fake Annabelle had been discovered there, he might find some sign that would lead him to her captors.

Lost in his thoughts, Sam turned a corner and nearly bowled over a small man clutching a candle in his upraised hand, hurrying in the opposite direction.

"I am sorry…" Sam mumbled absently, barely noticing the man's robes. "Priest. I was not watching where I was going, forgive me."

"That is quite alright," the priest said, retrieving his spectacles from the ground and replacing them atop the bridge of his nose. He squinted up at Sam. "Tell me, are you the knight Sam Fisher?"

Sam blinked down at the man. "I am."

The priest let out a relieved sigh. "I am glad to hear it. I have been searching high and low for you, and here I run full-tilt into you on my way back to the library. The Gods do love their little jokes, do they not?"

"I suppose…" Sam was hardly listening to the priest, his impatience begging him to stop wasting time. "Forgive me, Priest, but I do have to be on my way…."

"No," the priest shook his head vigorously. "No, you must come with me at once."

"I…"

"We have a mutual friend," the priest interrupted before Sam could protest. "She needs your help."

"She?" Sam's heart nearly dropped out of his chest. She. *She*? But it couldn't be…

As if sensing his need for proof, the priest stepped close to Sam so that no one would hear the words he whispered in his ear. "She is a daughter of Ella and may one day be Mother to us all."

Ella. The wife of the first king of Dunea and mother to Annabelle's royal lineage. *Mother to us all. Queen. Annabelle.*

"Take me to her," Sam said without further hesitation, his heart hammering in his chest. "Now."

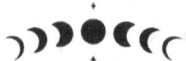

Alone, crouched in a hidden corner of the library, questions began to circle Annabelle in the dark.

Would Herbert be able to find Sam? What would happen if he could not? Would she be locked away, as her father had threatened? Would Sam be able to stop him? Would the Duchess? Would she become just another story in a book? Or would she be forgotten, a missing page not worth worrying over. The lost princess. Caged and dying like a bird with clipped wings.

Footsteps had her heart leaping into her throat, and she pushed to her feet as the door to the library creaked open and closed—ready to do…what? She did not know. But then a voice called out into the darkness.

"Annabelle?"

Sam.

She hurtled for him, throwing herself into his arms. He caught her and held her tight as she began to cry into his shirt. "Thank the Gods, you're alright," he whispered against her hair, gripping her so tightly she thought she might burst.

The mention of the Gods brought back pain-edged memories of the temple, and she stepped back, wiping at her face. She had to collect herself. It wasn't over.

Sam's eyes roved her appearance, the dirt on her nightgown and face, the blood on her feet, his face ashen. "What happened?"

What happened? Such a simple question. And yet, Annabelle didn't have the first idea of what had happened. So she settled for the truths she could currently wrap her head around: her fight with Mica; her conversation with Emily; how someone had kidnapped her from her rooms; how she had woken in the temple, bound and terrified; how her father had threatened her.

When it came time to tell Sam how she had escaped, Annabelle faltered. What would she tell him? The truth? She didn't know if she even believed it or if she even knew what *it* was. So she told him as much of the truth as she could manage.

It was not altogether convincing, but Sam did not press her for more detail. He simply listened, staring at her with a kind of hunger as she spoke, as if he had thought never to look upon her face again.

"We need to get you out of here," Sam said when Annabelle had finished her story. "It isn't safe for you to remain in the palace—not if the king himself is willing to hold you hostage for his own ends."

"But surely, if I let my presence be known, we can stop whatever it is that he's planning," Annabelle protested, her voice high and strained with desperation and fear. "If I'm alive, and I tell everyone that nobody from Eìrlan was involved...."

She fell silent as she beheld Sam's expression—so dark, so *angry*.

"It's too late for that now," he said gravely. "Shortly after you disappeared, the king ordered the delegation be placed under arrest, and..." He paused, searching her face as if hesitant to deliver any further bad news while she was in such a state already.

"Tell me," Annabelle whispered.

"He had his guards burn the ships," Sam said. "It's over. Nothing we do now can change what has already been set in motion."

The three of them stood together in stunned silence, the truth and horror of Sam's words breaking against Annabelle's heart—relentless and painful. Her friends. Those beautiful ships. Tears began to leak from her eyes as she thought of those glorious white sails reduced to ash on the water. How many innocent lives had already been lost, and for what? She began to shake.

"No," she whispered, tears welling over and tumbling down her cheeks as she buried her fingers in her hair. "Gods, no."

"That is grave news indeed," Herbert said. "Grave news."

"Annabelle, listen to me," Sam lay a warm hand upon her shoulder and squeezed gently. "I plan to do everything in my power to get to the bottom of what has happened and to help our friends, but I cannot do that if I continue to worry about your safety. It is my job to protect you. Please let me do my job."

He was right, but doubt still clawed at her belly. "I know you want to protect me," she said, "but if all the guards in the palace are hunting for me, I don't see how you can."

Suddenly Sam wouldn't meet her eyes, and Annabelle frowned up at him. "Sam. What aren't you telling me?"

He loosed a long breath before he said, hesitantly, "The guards aren't looking for you, Annabelle. Not anymore."

"What are you talking about?" She demanded. "Why?"

He looked as if he would rather be anywhere else in the world. "A… body was found in the temple. A body that looks exactly like you."

"What? But…" Annabelle shook her head, confused. "You're saying there was a dead woman who looks like me?"

"The body didn't just bear some resemblance to you, Annabelle," Sam said patiently. "This body…it *was* you. I saw it with my own eyes. I thought it was you, that you were…" He didn't finish the thought.

Dead. Sam had thought that she was dead. Annabelle's mouth worked for a moment as she tried to think of something to say. It was utterly ridiculous—impossible! And yet Sam was looking at her as if…as if…

As if she had risen from the grave.

"Let's say that what you are suggesting is even possible," Annabelle said, her mind still rebelling against the sheer incomprehensibility of what he had just told her, "How did you know that the…that it wasn't me?"

"Your scar," he said simply. "The one behind your ear. I don't know why or how such a convincing copy was made, but whoever made it had no idea about the scar. When I saw the bare skin behind your ear, I hoped it meant that you were still alive, somewhere. When the priest found me, I knew."

Annabelle reached up to touch the patch of skin behind her ear where that scar still cut through her hairline. How could it be possible? How could something so horrible as a dead woman wearing her face be possible?

She met Herbert's eyes then, and the memory of their first meeting clanged through her.

Magic.

The very thought sent a thrill of foreboding through Annabelle, and she shuddered. This was starting to be too much. She needed to get the discussion back to solid ground, or she would fall to pieces.

"Do you know anything about what is happening?" She asked Sam and Herbert desperately. "We know *what* has happened, but do you have any idea *why?*"

They exchanged a look.

"No," Sam said. "I have theories, but nothing more substantial than that."

"Fantastic," Annabelle said, starting to feel a bit overcome with fear and pain, and exhaustion. "One minute I'm up in my rooms, determined to drain every pitcher of wine in the palace, and the next minute I wake up in the temple of the Gods with my head splitting in two, bound and bleeding, with my father standing over me. By sheer luck, I manage to escape and make it back here, only to find out that my dear father-turned-kidnapper has arrested or murdered the Eìrlani and that *someone* has decided to try to fake my death—though to be perfectly honest, I'm still not sure I believe that what you saw was even possible. So now I'm battered, bruised, exhausted, and *dead*, apparently—and you're telling me that you have no idea *why?*"

"There will be time for why," Sam said soothingly. "But for now, I'm going to get you out of the palace and, eventually, out of the city. You are my priority. Once you are safe, I promise you, I will find out all I can."

"And how is that possible?" Annabelle demanded. "I am the princess, Sam. Where could I possibly go?"

"I have friends who will help us," Sam explained calmly, "there is a house in the city. You will be safe with them until the gates reopen. From there, I know a place where you can go to hide for a while, at least until we learn more about the situation."

"I only wish there was someone who could explain to me exactly what the situation *is*," Annabelle said, more a prayer than an actual question.

Nobody spoke for a long moment, each of them mute in the enormity of what they faced. Finally, Herbert cleared his throat.

"The situation," he said, "is very, very bad."

Chapter Fourteen

The city was so transformed by the events of the night that Annabelle did not recognize it as the colorful, sunlit paradise it had been before. Houses and businesses were shut up tight as she and Sam crept down the narrow streets, flitting from shadow to shadow. There was no laughter, no merriment, only distant shouts and the horrible tapping of guard's footfalls echoing off the stone walls.

Annabelle shivered, clutching the cloak more tightly around her shoulders as she tried to keep up with Sam. Herbert had lent her clothes for the journey, a cloak and a pair of soft shoes, but underneath she still wore only her nightgown. There had not been time for a disguise. There had not been time for goodbyes either.

She had only planted a kiss on Herbert's cheek, saying into his ear, "I know what you risk by helping me. I will never forget it." And then Sam was pulling her away, into the dark passageway, and away from the palace.

One day Annabelle might know whom to trust, and one day it might feel different—this fear of everything, of the world around her, of the people she thought she knew, and of the unknowable world beneath her own skin. But for now, Annabelle felt she was drowning in a sea of uncertainty and peril, each step she took in Sam's wake a desperate clawing stroke toward fresh air.

It was not easy to make their way undetected. There were a few heart-stopping moments when Sam had to pull her into a shadowy alley, pinning her to the wall as a contingent of guards marched past, and Annabelle was sure they would be discovered.

But it turned out that Sam rather knew what he was doing, and just when Annabelle felt she might expire from terror before they reached their destination, Sam paused.

"Listen closely," he said, turning to face her. "The woman you are about to meet is a friend of mine. She trusts me, and if you do exactly as I say, she will help you. But you must let me do the talking, do you understand?"

Annabelle nodded mutely, afraid that if she opened her mouth, she would vomit across the cobblestoned street.

Not seeming entirely convinced, Sam added, "These are not the sort of people with whom you are used to interacting, but take care not to offend them. We need their help, Annabelle, or I will not be able to protect you."

"I know," Annabelle managed to say. "I promise to keep my mouth shut, Sam."

"Good," was all Sam said before he strode away down the street, Annabelle hurrying to catch up.

It was a narrow street, but very long, stretching down the hill toward the bay that Annabelle could only recognize as a flat expanse of black in the distance. There was no sign of fire anymore, but Annabelle could smell the tang of smoke upon the air. The houses that lined the street were old but clean, and red lanterns hung by the doors of many.

The pleasure district.

Annabelle expected to be horrified that Sam would bring her to such a place, but instead, she felt a thrill of excitement as Sam approached one of the doors, his face illuminated hauntingly by the soft reddish glow from the lanterns, and knocked.

The door swung wide a moment later, revealing a petite woman standing on the threshold. She was so small that her towering, curled pile of hair barely reached Sam's chest. Her pretty face was perfectly colored and powered, even though she looked as if she had just come from her bed, a pink silk dressing gown tied about her waist and fur-lined slippers on her dainty feet.

The woman lifted one pencil-thin brow as she glared up at Sam.

"Well, if it isn't my liege," she said, cocking her head to the side. "My Lord. My puffed-up princeling."

"There's no time for that right now, Ilya," Sam said urgently. "May we please come inside?"

Ilya frowned, taking in Sam's pale face, and then her heavily lined eyes slid to Annabelle. They widen a fraction as they alighted upon the princess's face. *Damn.* She didn't know how, but this woman knew exactly who Annabelle was. Even so, Ilya stepped aside, allowing them to enter her house.

They stepped into the foyer, Annabelle's eyes roving curiously over the bits of the house that she could see. It was immaculate and prettily decorated. A salon stood to the right of a long staircase with a carved wooden banister leading to the upper floors. Everything was velvet and lace, and it felt…comfortable, luxurious, and even a bit dangerous. Annabelle felt the tension in her body begin to ease.

The door slammed shut behind them with enough force to shake the house, and Annabelle whirled to see Ilya standing before Sam, the silver blade of a knife leveled at his privates. He held up his hands and went very still.

"What game are you playing, Sam Fisher?" Ilya snarled as she let the knife's tip rest gently against the fabric of his trousers, "What are you thinking, bringing her here?"

"I'm sorry, Ilya," Sam replied, his tone measured. "But I was desper—"

"Your *desperation*," Ilya interrupted with a twist of the blade, "is going to put my entire operation in jeopardy."

"Listen to me, Ilya, please," Sam said, and Annabelle could hear the pleading in his words. "I didn't have another choice. She isn't safe in the palace."

And he began to tell Ilya everything that had happened, starting with the attack and ending with their flight from the library. Annabelle stood in horrified silence as he spoke. He was telling this woman everything—*everything*. But she trusted Sam, and so she kept her mouth shut, just as she had promised, and let him spill their secrets to this stranger.

Ilya listened to his story without interrupting. When he finished, she considered him for a long moment before lowering the knife. She let out a low whistle, shaking her pretty head. "Gods, Sam. You've really gotten yourself into it this time."

He shrugged. "That's my job, Ilya."

"That it may be," Ilya said, scrubbing a hand across the back of her neck and grimacing. "But it isn't *my* job to clean up your messes."

"Usually, I'd agree with you," Sam said with a hesitant smile. "But even you have to agree that this time I am not the one responsible for creating a mess."

"You, the king, the rutting *princess*." Ilya waved a hand in Annabelle's direction. "It's all the same to us common folk."

Sam grinned down at her. "Since when have you ever considered yourself 'common'?"

The corner of her mouth twitched. "It is good to see you, Sam Fisher," she said with a sigh. "You are, as ever, a pain in my ass."

"It's good to see you too, Ilya." Sam's grin faded. "I am sorry to bring this to your doorstep."

Ilya waved him away as that knife vanished into some hidden place.

"It was already at my doorstep," she said. "The guards have come knocking twice already tonight. Terrible for business, as you can see." The sweep of her hand took in the entirety of the empty salon. "But, good for you, as there is nobody here to witness you commit treason, save for my own Gods-forsaken self."

She smiled sweetly at Annabelle. "Hello, treason."

"A pleasure," Annabelle said without returning the smile.

Ilya cocked her head to the side, expression amused. "A bit rude, I think. But you'll do. Come on, child. I'll show you where you can stay. You'll need a bath, of course, and a meal." Her little nose crinkled as if she could smell something abhorrent. "Bath first."

Annabelle made to follow Ilya, but Sam held her back. He turned her to face him, his hands gripping her shoulders, gaze intent.

"I have to leave you now," he said. "But I will come back."

"But...why?" Annabelle didn't want to stay here by herself, with this stranger in this strange place.

"There are others who are in danger tonight," he reminded her. "And I need to go to see if there is anything at all that I can do to help them."

Mica. Raphael. So many others who had been lost to the night in flame and smoke. They were still out there somewhere, and Sam was right. He was the only person who could help them.

She nodded, gathering what little courage she still possessed. "Go," she said quietly. "I'll...I'll be fine."

"You will," he said earnestly. "Trust Ilya. I do; with my life, and with yours."

Annabelle nodded again, feeling as if her bones were suddenly filled with lead.

He squeezed her shoulders once and then looked over her head to where Ilya stood on the stairs, glaring at him.

"My time to be angry with you this night is not over yet, is it Fisher?" She demanded.

"I'm sorry, Ilya," Sam said. "But you knew as well as I did that something like this was coming. Tonight, these events—*this* is what we do it for. If we sit on the sidelines now, we were only ever looking to protect our own precious skins."

Ilya sighed heavily, and there was the weight of worry in her voice as she said. "You're right, of course. Though I hate you for it. Go, then. Do what you need to do. I'll take care of the princess and wake the girls. It would seem we still have work to do tonight."

Sam nodded his approval, and then he was gone.

Annabelle opened her mouth to ask what on earth *that* had all been about, but Ilya was already climbing the staircase to the upper floors. So Annabelle swallowed her questions and hastened after the madam.

Sam followed Ilya's street down to the waterfront, swift as a shadow. Dawn was approaching, and there was no time to waste on stealth. For the first time that night, Sam had a perfectly reasonable explanation for being exactly where he was and a perfectly truthful explanation of what he was doing.

Hunting for Eìrlani survivors.

The waterfront and the harbor were still crawling with guards, and Sam cursed under his breath as he saw the light of their torches bobbing in the distance. He would need to be smart about this.

Pausing before the wharf, Sam took stock of the scene before him.

It was a grisly sight, made clearer by the ever-lightening sky above. Where those magnificent ships had once sat anchored in the bay, there was only a still-smoldering pile of wreckage floating on the water. On the beach below where Sam stood: bodies washed up by the tide, cast upon the shore like flotsam, scattered and broken across the sand.

Here and there, guards picked their way among the debris, checking for survivors. They moved in groups of two, stopping every now and again to kick a body or a piece of driftwood before moving on.

Sam watched them for a moment, learning their pattern. He held no torch of his own. It might be possible for him to move across the beach undetected if he was very, very careful.

A disturbance farther down the beach drew Sam's attention. He moved toward it, straining his eyes to make out its source. The two guards farthest down the coast away from the harbor appeared to be struggling with something. One of their torches had gone out, fallen to the ground, perhaps.

Sam was closer now, nearly running toward the spot where he could now see a hulking figure standing between two smaller men, a jagged piece of wood gripped in both hands, swinging it wide. Sam leaped over the wharf, landing lightly upon the beach below, and broke into a run.

The first guard didn't even have time to turn around before Sam's blow sent him tumbling to the sand. His companion out of commission and seeing himself suddenly outnumbered, the second guard made to flee, but the big man hurled the plank of wood at the guard's head. It made contact with a sickening thud, and the guard fell, his torch extinguishing in the wet sand beside him.

Panting, Sam stared up into a familiar bearded face.

"Hullo knightling," Raphael said, his voice a shallow rasp, a shadow of that playful smile tugging his lips. "Nice of you to turn up."

"Good of you not to finish them off before I arrived," Sam quipped, relief at the sight of the warrior making his legs a bit wobbly.

"Would have waited," Raphael said in that same haggard tone. "But these two wanted to dance. Happy to oblige them. You know I'm an excellent dancer."

"We need to get out of here," Sam said with an anxious glance over his shoulder to where the other torchlights bobbed up and down, drawing ever nearer.

"Aye," Raphael said and took a step but staggered on the sand.

Sam rushed to help him, lifting Raphael's arm over his shoulders. "Take a moment," he urged the warrior. "It won't do me any good if you pass out. I won't be able to carry you."

"I'm fine," Raphael said. "Just..."

He trailed off as they began to move together up the beach. Sam didn't need an explanation to know that Raphael was in bad shape. Even in the dim light, he could see the cuts to his face and the tattered remnants of his clothes. The sickening smell of burned flesh hung about the warrior, and Sam knew that if he didn't get Raphael to Ilya's, and soon, he was likely to die.

Somehow they managed to make it back over the wall and up into the relative safety of the city streets. Sam gave Raphael his cloak, and the two made their way back up the hill.

It was slow going. Raphael's breathing became more labored as they walked, and Sam got a better look at the extent of his injuries in the light of the lamps they passed. It was a miracle that the warrior was standing.

"I've been in worse shape than this, knightling," Raphael muttered when Sam glanced up at his face in concern for the tenth time. "I'll be right as rain in no time. Just...need some rest."

"Don't...talk now," Sam urged, panting with the effort of supporting Raphael's considerable weight. "We're nearly...nearly there."

Sam didn't bother knocking this time, heaving Raphael through the door to the brothel and closing it quickly behind them. The warrior stood, swaying on the spot, before slumping heavily to the floor.

"Raphael!" Sam fell to his knees beside the unconscious man, rolling him onto his back.

"Who are you?" Demanded an unfamiliar voice. Sam looked up to see a pretty brown-haired woman wrapped in a dressing gown similar to the one Ilya had worn, staring down from the stairs at the two of them on the floor.

"I need your mistress," he said without answering her question, unfastening the cloak from around Raphael's neck. "Quickly."

"Excuse m—" But the woman fell silent, gasping in horror as Sam removed the cloak and ripped through the tattered remnants of Raphael's shirt.

Sam froze horror and nausea, causing his stomach to flip over.

A burn, red and black and oozing, covered Raphael's left shoulder from his neck down his chest. It was so gruesome that Sam felt himself recoil inwardly from the injury.

"Your mistress," he said gravely to the woman who still stood, frozen on the stairs. "Now."

Without another word, the woman scurried up and out of sight. Sam returned his attention to Raphael, gently removing any bit of cloth that he could reach, careful not to let anything touch that horrible burn.

He could feel tears threatening at the backs of his eyes, but he forced himself to keep it together. It made no sense that he should feel this panic, this desperation. But all Sam knew as he worked, as he waited for Ilya and tried not to think about the terrible wounds he exposed with every bit of shirt he pulled away, was that Raphael must live. He *must* live.

Thundering footsteps heralded the arrival of Ilya and three of her girls, including the one he had sent to fetch her.

"He needs a healer," Sam said to Ilya as she knelt beside him, her face going pale at the sight of Raphael's wounds.

She looked at him then, and he saw the doubt in her eyes, saw the words he silently begged her not to say: that Raphael was beyond help. But she did not question him.

"Vera," she said. "Fetch Lyddia. She should be finished patching up our other guest by now. Carmen and Louisa help us get him into the kitchen. Gods, he's a big man. We won't be able to get him upstairs until he's well enough to get there on his own two legs."

Vera retreated back up the stairs as Ilya and the others helped Sam drag Raphael back to the kitchen and up onto a long wooden table.

Vera returned with a petite blonde woman who must have been Lyddia. She couldn't have been older than sixteen. To Sam's dismay, Annabelle stepped through the door behind them.

Lyddia approached the table without hesitation, rolling up her sleeves, already giving orders to the other women. Sam stepped back, marveling at the command and bravery of this young woman as she set about tending to Raphael's many wounds.

"You shouldn't be here," he said as Annabelle came to stand beside him.

"I heard Vera tell Lyddia about Raphael's wounds," she said in a small voice. "And I had to come. I had to…to be here, to help if I can."

Sam wrapped an arm around her shoulders, watching as Lyddia applied salves to Raphael's burn. "I don't think there's anything we can do for him now but pray to the Gods he pulls through this."

"He needs a healer," Annabelle said. "That burn…"

"Lyddia is a healer," Ilya said sternly before Sam could reply. "But you'll be keeping that fact to yourself."

Looking confused, Annabelle reached up and touched the back of her head. Then her eyes popped wide. "But…how?"

Nobody answered her. All attention was on Raphael and Lyddia as she worked her gifts upon him.

Sam knew he ought to leave at once, ought to return to the palace before his absence was noticed, but he couldn't move. Annabelle did not ask him about his strange need to stay. She only stood beside him. Though he knew she had to be dead on her feet, they waited together.

The morning sun filled the kitchen with soft golden light by the time Lyddia stepped back from the table, mopping her brow with the sleeve of her nightgown.

"I've done all I can," she said weakly. "All we can do now is wait, but…I think he will pull through."

Sam loosed a sigh of relief, and Annabelle smiled tiredly up at him, squeezing his hand.

"Thank you," he said to the healer. "He's…a friend."

"It's not over for him yet," Lyddia warned. "He'll need rest. A week at least."

A week. Sam's eyes sought Ilya. She was looking at him with a curious expression, and he thought she might refuse, but she said, "He stays here until he is well enough to travel."

"Thank you," Sam said again. "All of you."

The women dispersed then, clearing away the dirty linens, bowls of water, and jars of salve, vanishing into the depths of the house. Vera approached to take Annabelle in hand as the princess was already dozing against his shoulder. Sam watched Annabelle stumble sleepily toward bed, overwhelmed with gratitude that, despite the horrible events of the night, his friends had made it to the other side.

The kitchen was empty now, and Sam gazed at the table where Raphael lay, bandaged and unconscious, but alive. He was not healed yet, not out of the woods yet. That would take time, time they didn't have. But that was a problem for another day.

Ilya met him in the foyer.

"I will send word when he wakes," she said as he retrieved his cloak from the floor and fastened it about his neck. "The girls will make him a bed in the storeroom. It won't be much, but it's warm in there, and hidden."

"I'll return as soon as I can," Sam said. "I owe you, Ilya."

"You know," she said, expression thoughtful. "I was just thinking the other day how things were getting a bit too boring and predictable around here."

"Happy to oblige," Sam muttered, thinking that he would give a vast sum of money for normal and predictable.

"It's bad, isn't it?" Ilya said then, and Sam saw fear in her eyes for the first time in the years he had known her. "Everything that happened tonight…and you, bringing the princess here of all places."

He met her gaze as he said, "Yes. And I fear it will only get much, much worse."

Chapter Fifteen

Annabelle was so drained by the night's events that she slept through the next day and most of the following night as well—waking only long enough to gulp a cup of water before sagging back against the pillows and losing herself to dreamless sleep once more.

When she finally did wake, she simply stared up at the canopy above the bed for a long while, thinking, reminding herself of what was real.

My name is Annabelle Isren, Annabelle thought to herself over and over and over, *I am the daughter of King Alexander and Queen Ilenna. One month ago, I was betrothed to Mica, a prince of Eìrlan. Last night my father, the king, kidnapped me and held me against my will. I escaped him…and I don't know how I did it. Sam got me out of the palace to this place. Now I am hiding in a brothel, surrounded by strangers, and Raphael is wounded and unconscious in the kitchen. This is all fine. This is all going to be fine.*

It was not fine, of course. Annabelle had no idea how things would ever be fine again, but it felt better to tell herself that one day this would all make sense, and she would somehow—*somehow*—make it through to the other side and into something that resembled a life.

Not feeling any better, Annabelle sat up and examined her surroundings.

She had been too exhausted the previous morning to take in the details of the room. It was lovely—large and richly furnished, with velvet drapes and upholstered armchairs by the fireplace.

Rising from the plush, canopied bed, Annabelle went to the large picture window and pulled one of the heavy velvet drapes aside, peering out into the street below.

The city was pale and ghostly in the gray light of dawn, the golden stone of the buildings and walls glowing white like the face of the moon. Annabelle's gaze traveled up, seeking the sight of water. The faraway horizon where the sky met the sea emerged from the shadows as the seconds ticked past. The waters of the bay were flat and calm. The world was still minutes from beginning to shake off the last vestiges of its slumber.

It seemed incredible that there could be so much peace when everything in Annabelle's life had shattered to pieces, but the sight of the sleeping city, of the massive expanse of sea, calmed her nonetheless.

The door behind her opened, and Annabelle turned to see Ilya backing into the room, bearing a tray in her arms. The smell from the dishes set upon the tray made Annabelle's stomach rumble and her mouth water. She was starving.

"Good morning," Ilya said pleasantly, placing the tray upon a small table by the fire. "You'll be happy to know that your big friend made it through the night. He's had some water and some broth and is now sleeping peacefully."

"That is good to hear," Annabelle said, settling in one of the armchairs. "Thank you for helping him." She eyed the food hungrily. Sausages, toast, and tomatoes; It smelled divine.

"Dig in, child," Ilya urged her. "No need to stand on ceremony here. You must be famished."

Annabelle was famished, and the food tasted better than it smelled, but she forced herself to go slowly. She hadn't eaten in a while, and it would be very bad manners to be sick all over her hostess's gorgeous ornamental rug.

Ilya sat in the other armchair and helped herself to a cup of tea while Annabelle ate, watching the princess with curiosity in those large blue eyes.

"You seem to be taking all of this rather well," She observed when Annabelle finally sat back in her chair with a contented sigh, her own cup of steaming tea clutched in both hands.

Annabelle blinked at her. "I do?"

"You do," Ilya said with a kind smile. "If it were me, I'd be having some kind of fit, I promise you."

Annabelle considered this for a moment. She certainly felt confused and terrified enough to throw a fit, but it wouldn't do her any good.

"I don't feel…I don't know that I am handling everything well," Annabelle admitted. "But I trust Sam, so…" She trailed off with a shrug. "I'll have to wait for answers, I suppose."

Ilya scowled. "Damn it, Fisher," She cursed. "Princess, after what has happened to you, you deserve answers. Don't let that idiot knight of yours get away with keeping you in the dark. It's a bad habit of his—one I spent years trying to stomp out of him."

"I don't think he knows more about what's happening than I do," Annabelle protested, feeling a bit defensive of her friend. After all, he had saved her life. Didn't that act alone deserve her trust?

"Oh?" Ilya raised a slim eyebrow. "So he did explain to you exactly where he was taking you? I suppose you already know who I am and why you can trust me."

"Well, no," Annabelle admitted. "He didn't exactly have time to—"

"And do you know his plans for you?" Ilya interrupted her. "Where he intends you to go next? You obviously can't stay here forever. Does he have a plan? Does he have no plan? When is he coming back to fetch you?"

"I don't...I don't know," Annabelle flushed, suddenly feeling a bit ashamed. These questions not only seemed obvious to her now, but she felt foolish for not having asked them, demanded answers.

"Princess, forgive me for being blunt," Ilya said, "but you cannot afford to be an idiot. Fisher may have saved your life, but it is *your* life. Your questions deserve answers. So" She said, splaying her arms wide. "I will answer them—the ones that I can."

Annabelle didn't say anything for a moment. She felt a bit wounded by Ilya's words, but there was truth in them. And, if Annabelle was honest, she liked this woman's direct way of speaking. It made Annabelle trust her.

"Well...where *am* I going when I leave this place?" She asked at last.

Ilya nodded her approval of this first question. "Fisher and I have a mutual friend who will hide you for the time being. I've written him to let him know I'll be sending you with his man tomorrow. We don't have time to wait for his response. The longer you stay here, the more danger we're all in."

Tomorrow. So soon. Annabelle took a sip of tea to ward off the new surge of panic that twisted her gut.

"You've already risked so much to help me." She said. " I don't know if I'll ever be able to repay you, but I will try."

"As Queen, I believe you will be in an excellent position indeed to repay your debt to me," Ilya observed.

"There's not much of a chance of that happening now, what with me being dead and all." Annabelle pointed out wryly.

"Dead, and yet sitting before me drinking tea and carrying on a conversation." Ilya considered her for a moment. "Would you like that, Princess—to use this as an excuse to escape this broken kingdom and live a normal life somewhere far away?"

Annabelle opened her mouth, then closed it again. She hadn't considered it before, but now that the question was asked, she had to admit it sounded like a very good idea.

"I don't know," she said instead. "I don't know what I'd be running away from, exactly."

Ilya frowned. "What do you mean by that?"

"I mean…" Annabelle searched for the right words. "You called this a 'broken kingdom'…and I am a bit embarrassed to admit that I do not know why."

She had expected Ilya to be angry, but the woman did not seem the slightest bit surprised by this statement.

"Of course, you don't know why," she said impatiently, waving a dismissive hand. "Nobody in that palace was ever going to teach you why—to explain the truth of things. It is *your* job to learn to *see* and to ask the right questions. So…" Ilya gestured for her to continue.

"Alright…" Annabelle thought for a moment. "The healer, Lyddia…she's not a priestess."

It wasn't a question exactly, but Ilya seemed to know what Annabelle was getting at.

The madam's expression darkened. "No." She said flatly. "She is not a priestess. Nor will she ever be if I have anything to say about it."

"But," Annabelle was confused by this statement. "I don't understand how that is possible. How can she be gifted with healing and *not* be a priestess?"

Ilya shrugged. "You know, I don't know the full story, only that she has managed to keep her secret since childhood and begged me to do the same when she came to me. Of course, I did as she asked; anything to keep one young woman safe from the reach of the temple. She helps this house in exchange for room and board. Her history is her own."

Annabelle drank her tea to cover her shock. What Ilya had said implied that Lyddia had the power to heal *without* the blessing of the temple priests and, through them, the Gods. Had Herbert been right all along? Was healing simply a form of magic? After everything Annabelle had seen, it seemed more possible than ever.

But she did not wish to reveal her ignorance to this woman. Annabelle feared that her questions about magic would lead to more questions that she was not prepared to answer.

"What did Sam mean," she said instead, steering the conversation toward safer territory, "when he said 'this is what we do it for?' What is it that you…do?"

"I'm impressed," Ilya said with a wide smile. "You remember that detail when you were already dead on your feet. I may have misjudged your powers of perception, Highness."

She paused, chewing her lower lip as if considering whether or not to answer the question.

"I'll say this," she said finally. "There are those of us who…disagree with certain aspects of the law, the way it hurts the people it is supposedly designed to protect. So we work outside of the law to help those who need it most."

"That is…impressive!" Annabelle was suddenly far more intimidated by the woman in the chair opposite her. It was as if she sat in the presence of a different kind of monarch—the Queen of the city.

Ilya chuckled at Annabelle's evident shock and awe. "It's not glamorous work, but it helps me sleep at night."

Annabelle nodded her understanding. She had often felt the weight of responsibility, knowing that one day she would hold the lives of so many people in her hands. It made her feel better to know that there were people like Ilya who would risk everything to even the odds. It made her feel worse to know she had yet to do anything in her power to help them.

Ilya sat in expectant silence, waiting for Annabelle's next question. She still had hundreds of them vying for priority in her dizzied mind, but only one that she dared to ask.

"Why are you helping me?"

Ilya's gaze was intent as she said, "Because Sam Fisher asked me to help. Because I trust him. And…because I have a sense about you. It is…let's call it a *talent* of mine, to feel the truth of people. It is what makes me so good at my job; both of them," She added with a wink. "I know what people are like. You…" Her eyes narrowed a bit as if she was peering into Annabelle's soul. "You feel like a promise, like potential. I think we have yet to see what you will become. But I think you need my help if we are ever to see the truth of who you really are."

Annabelle sat in numb silence. She felt stripped bare by Ilya's words, and it was not a comfortable feeling. It was a painful thing to be seen as someone with a destiny yet to be fulfilled when Annabelle's own legacy was already drenched in blood, her birthright tarnished by unspeakable crimes.

"I'd like to see Raphael," she said, pushing to her feet.

Ilya seemed a bit taken aback by this request. "I assure you he's perfectly…."

"I know, but I'd like to see him all the same," Annabelle cut across her. Then, not wanting to be rude, she added. "You've done so much for him, for both of us. But I'd like to look after him if that's alright. I'd like to help."

Ilya said nothing to this, only stood and walked to the door. Annabelle was afraid Ilya would refuse her request, but then the madam opened the door and held it ajar.

"Come on then," she said impatiently. "Before we both die of old age, or the crown comes for our heads."

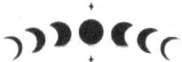

Raphael was stretched out along the far wall of the storeroom. He lay upon a pile of blankets and pillows that had probably been taken from the parlor above. A fur throw covered his legs and stomach, leaving the rest of his torso and arms exposed to the air.

Annabelle knelt beside him, feeling a terrible pang of shame and guilt as her eyes roved over his bandaged shoulder and the cuts to his face and arms. Her father, her *people*, had done this to him. And the physical marks were only the surface of the terrible harm they had caused. It was irreparable, the damage.

"Are you sure you want to stay down here with him?" Ilya asked from the doorway. "My girls are perfectly capable of tending to him if you want to rest."

"I've had enough rest," Annabelle replied. "I will take care of him. It is…it is the least I can do, and I have to do something."

Ilya left her there without further protest, though Annabelle thought she saw a curious look pass over the madam's features that Annabelle neither recognized nor cared to understand.

"S…S…am…"

The sound had Annabelle turning to Raphael's side as the man began to stir, his breathing distressed and ragged, eyes snapping wide with apparent distress.

"Shhh," she hushed him, laying a hand upon his uninjured shoulder. "It's alright. You're safe."

Raphael tried to speak, but his voice came out as a ragged croak, and Annabelle retrieved a cup and filled it from a pitcher that sat nearby.

"Drink this," she commanded, lifting the cup to Raphael's lips.

"Princess…" he breathed when she set the cup aside. "What—what are you doing here?"

"Same as you." Annabelle settled beside him. "Hiding."

"But…I don't understand…."

And so Annabelle told him what she could about her capture and escape, how Sam had brought her to Ilya before running off to look for him. Raphael listened, wide-eyed, mouth slightly agape.

When she finished, Raphael loosed a long breath. "That is…" he cleared his throat and tried again. "That is quite a tale, lass. Goddess… but I am glad you're alright."

Tears welled in Annabelle's eyes at his words. How he could care for her safety, after everything that had happened, everything that had been done to him.

"I'm so sorry, Raphael," she choked, swatting at the tears now pouring down her cheeks. "It's all my fault."

He frowned up at her. "And how is that?"

"He did it because of me," Annabelle explained, her heart breaking. "Because he wanted to protect me."

Wincing, Raphael reached over to take one of her hands in his. "Did you give the order? Did you wield bow and flaming arrow? Did you even wish me or my people harm?"

Annabelle shook her head, unable to speak now.

"No, of course, you did no such thing," Raphael said earnestly. "Because you are a good person with a kind soul. This was an act of evil, Annabelle. It was not done to protect but to harm. I'll not have you blaming yourself. It doesn't do my men or me a bit of good, do you understand me?"

Annabelle nodded. "Yes," she managed to whisper. "I understand."

"That's a good lass. Now, what was done to you and to me is horrible. But we're in this together now, alright?"

"But…Mica…" His name fell unbidden from her lips, and she saw Raphael's eyes alight with fire, his jaw set. He looked so forbidding then, even maimed and weak as he was.

"We'll find him," he said, and the words were a promise. "We'll get him back, and then we'll leave this Goddess-forsaken land together."

Annabelle's tears dried, and she felt Raphael's resolve kindle a fire in her belly as their eyes met.

Together.

)〉⟩●《《(

The air was stifling in the cabinet room. All the shutters had been closed, long heavy drapes pulled closed against the fading light of the day. Braziers of candles had been set burning day and night, and their smoky smell mixed with the sweet aroma of flowers to barely mask the stinking stench of death that seeped into the corners.

Ronan fought the urge to stop up his nose as he approached the figure kneeling by the foot of the long table, averting his eyes from the sight of the body still stretched upon it, now surrounded by heaps of flowers from the gardens; rose, lily, primrose, and lavender. To Ronan, they were all weeds compared to the angelic creature withering between them.

"What is it, Ronan?"

The voice was sharp and ragged, and the kneeling man did not turn.

"Your Majesty," Ronan said, careful to keep his tone soft and kind. "I have come to fetch you for supper."

"You needn't have troubled yourself," the king growled. "I will eat nothing."

"You must eat something, Sire. If you do not wish to go to supper, I can have the servants bring some broth, or…"

The king lurched to his feet, whirling around. His red-rimmed eyes glowed wild in the flickering candlelight. "Leave me in peace," he spat into Ronan's face, "Lord Barrick."

"No, your Majesty" Ronan replied calmly. "I will not."

The king snarled and reached out a hand to seize Ronan by the lapel of his coat. "Your King has given you an order."

Ronan met the king's eyes without flinching, even as his wine-soaked breath brushed hot and rotten against his cheeks.

"As a lord of your realm and a servant of the king, I am duty-bound to obey your command. As your friend, I am worried about you. You have not slept nor eaten a single bite of food in nearly two days, Alex. Respectfully, I do not care what orders you give me. I will not leave your side until you have taken at least one step to take better care of yourself; if not for your own sake, then for mine."

The king's eyes widened, and his face drained of what little color still remained. Risky. Risky to be so bold when the king was so distraught, raging with grief and drink. But this man had been his friend long before he had been king, and though Ronan would have joined him in his misery, though he felt the keen sting of grief splitting his own heart in two, he had a duty to ensure the king did not waste away.

"She is *d-ead*," The king said finally, voice cracking, shoulders slumping as he released Ronan's lapel. "*Dead*. First my…my Queen and now my daughter…slaughtered by my enemies. Why? Why can they not leave me in peace?"

"I do not know, Sire."

The king wandered back toward the table, gazing upon the face that had become so white in death that it looked like it had been carved from marble.

"She was so beautiful," he murmured. "Just like my Ilenna." He whispered the last word as if it were a prayer.

A muscle in Ronan's jaw twitched at the sound of the name. It had been years since he had heard the king speak it, nor had anyone dared to say it in the king's presence, for it usually set him into a fit of rage or a miserable stupor that would cling to him for days at a time. Ronan braced himself for the inevitable meltdown, the collapse as his friend realized the mistake of giving voice to the one thing in this world that had ever held sway over him.

But it did not come. The king only stared down upon his daughter's face, frozen in time by death. "We will lay her to rest tomorrow," he said. "At sunset. I...I think she would have liked that. To be here. With her mother."

"I think that is an excellent idea, Sire."

Ronan watched as the king leaned over the body and pressed a kiss to the white forehead.

"Rest, my darling child" the king whispered so quietly that Ronan could barely make out the words. He straightened then and looked at Ronan. Those eyes that only moments before had been burning with grief and pain were suddenly clear, and what glowed within them was not the unbridled fury of a broken man but a steely resolve and clarity that sent a shiver down Ronan's spine.

"Those who have taken my future from me will pay," he said, voice deep and resonant. "They have come into my home and taken what is mine, and I will not forget."

Fear, bright and burning, rose like bile at the back of Ronan's throat at these words. He found that he could not speak as he and the king looked at one another across the long oak table, across the princess's body. A child. *Her* child. That light of consciousness flared bright in the king's eyes—suddenly the eyes of a much younger, much stronger man.

And then, as quickly as it had come, the light was gone. A shadow passed across the king's features, and he crossed the room, stumbling a bit as he caught the toe of his boot upon the corner of the decorative rug that covered the cold stone floor.

"Tomorrow," was all he said before leaving Ronan alone, his eyes watering from the stench of flowers and death.

Chapter Sixteen

Annabelle was dressed and waiting in the foyer when Sam returned to the brothel the following morning. He inspected her appearance as she stood before him, fidgeting nervously.

The illusion wasn't perfect, but it would do well enough. At the very least, nobody would suspect Annabelle of being a princess—dressed as she was in a plain cotton dress and soft leather shoes, her hair covered by a lilac scarf and no paint or colors upon her face or lips.

"Very good," he said, turning to Ilya. "You have her identification?"

"Right here," Ilya said, handing him a rolled-up sheaf of paper. "It won't hold up to much scrutiny, but there shouldn't be any need. Wilkin knows what he's doing."

Sam nodded his agreement and slid the paper into his jacket pocket. "How are you?" He asked Annabelle quietly.

"I'm alright," she said with a shrug. "Ilya's taken good care of me."

"And…" he hesitated. "How is Raphael?"

"Alive," Annabelle said with a smile. "And healing, but Lyddia says he isn't well enough to travel yet."

"We finally got him up to one of the bedrooms, though," Ilya added with a grin. "Took the whole house, but we managed it in the end."

"I'd like to look in on him before we leave," Sam said, moving toward the staircase.

Ilya nodded her agreement. "Third floor, last door at the end of the corridor," she said before taking charge of Annabelle. "I'll get the girl some provisions for her journey."

Sam climbed the stairs alone, feeling inexplicably anxious. He had been able to think of little else for two days than seeing Raphael again, to know he was alive and healing. Now that the moment was at hand, he felt the sudden urge to run.

Raphael looked up from the book he was reading when Sam entered the bedchamber, his battered face splitting into a broad smile.

"Hello, knightling," he said pleasantly, setting the book aside. "Come to weep by my sickbed?"

"I don't think weeping will be necessary," Sam observed wryly. "Seeing as you're hardly at death's door."

"Still, a lad can dream," Raphael sighed, winking.

Sam pulled a chair up beside the bed. Relief made his limbs a bit wobbly, and he didn't want to endure Raphael's teasing if he noticed.

"You look like hell," Raphael observed as Sam sat.

Sam raised an eyebrow, "Look who's talking."

"I've endured worse," Raphael grunted, expression darkening. "Though never at so steep a cost, I'll admit."

The ships. His countrymen. His friends. All gone. His prince captured.

"I'm sorry for what you lost," Sam murmured.

"What was taken from me, you mean" Raphael growled.

Sam nodded. "For all of it. If I had known..." He didn't finish the sentence because there was no way to know what he would have done or *could* have done. Even if he had been able to help the Eìrlani, would it have made any difference at all? Anything he could say now was pointless, so he said nothing. Instead, he asked, "How did you survive?"

Raphael huffed a laugh. "Sheer luck, plain and simple. I was restless when I returned to the ship, after...well, you know."

He trailed off, and Sam's face heated as he realized what Raphael meant: he was restless after he left Sam in the garden. After they...

"The arrows hit our ship first," Raphael continued. "I was just climbing aboard when it happened. There wasn't time to do anything except react. I tried to save my men, but I've never seen fire act like that before. By the time I raised the alarm, the entire damned vessel was burning."

"Did any of your men escape in the longboats?" Sam asked, but Raphael shook his head.

"If they did, I have no knowledge of it. When the rigging snapped, something knocked me into the water. After that, it was all I could do to just stay alive. I couldn't tell you how I made it to the shore. Like I said before, it was dumb luck." The corner of his soft mouth jerked in a smile, but there was no joy in it. "For all my luck, though, it wouldn't've made a lick of difference if you hadn't turned up when you did."

Sam loosed a long breath, dragging a hand through his hair. "I still can't believe I found you. It was such a long shot, but I had to try."

"How did you even know to look for me? Goddess, *why* did you try to save me at all? Not that I'm not grateful...."

Memories of fire filled Sam's head—the cruel glow of the flames, the plumes of smoke, the sound of screaming. Even if he closed his eyes, he could see it burned into the backs of his eyelids, as if that fire could melt time and space as well as wood and flesh.

His voice was hoarse as he said, "I saw it, Raphael. I saw the whole thing."

Raphael frowned. "You saw it?"

"I was still in the garden when the first ship went up in flames. It... it was like watching the whole world come to an end."

"Did you know?"

Sam's eyes snapped to Raphael's, horrified. But there was no accusation there, just exhaustion and pain. Not for the first time, Sam marveled at this warrior with the open heart.

"No. I had nothing to do with the attack against your people." Sam bit back against the cold fury that threatened to overtake him at the very idea. "And if I had known, I would have done everything in my power to stop it."

"But I still don't understand why. Why go against your king and country? You're a knight, Sam!" Raphael sighed. "If anyone finds out what you have done...."

"It's too late now," Sam shrugged. "Whether or not I'm found out makes no difference. It's done, and I would do it again. As for why..." he considered his answer carefully. "Wrong is wrong," he said at last. "What was done to you was done out of spite, or madness, or malice, or the Gods know what. That was not honor, and it was not right. As a knight, I am sworn to protect those who cannot protect themselves and to uphold everything good and right and honorable. I knew at once what my duty was, and it was not to my king. Not this time."

"Annabelle told me what he did to her," Raphael said darkly. "Her own father, Sam."

The king. Something dark and sinister slithered, wrapping oozing tendrils around Sam's mind, something he had been avoiding thinking about. Sam could not escape the tendrils of dread any longer, so he gave voice to his fears.

"There is something that doesn't add up," he said. "I understand his reasons for doing what he did—twisted though those reasons might have been. But then, why fake her death? Why use…I can't even believe I'm saying this—why use *magic* to do it?"

"Annabelle said the king was rambling about keeping her safe, and after what happened to the queen…maybe he believed she would be safer if everyone believed she was dead," Raphael offered.

"I thought of that," Sam said, nodding. "It would be the perfect way to make her disappear. He had an enemy ready-made, delivered right to his doorstep. Framing you for her murder while spiriting her away somewhere—elegant and simple, if you possess that kind of power, I suppose."

"But that isn't what happened," Raphael's eyes lit with comprehension as he followed Sam's train of thought. "He doesn't have her…and still the guards have called off the search?"

Sam nodded. "The patrols stopped hours ago."

"And now that they have stopped looking for her…." Raphael supplied.

"It's easy to get her out of the city," Sam concluded the thought. "Too easy."

That night there had been no time to think about it. Sam hadn't had the luxury of worrying over his good fortune. Now, though…he wasn't entirely sure the fortune was good. But he had no choice. Annabelle had to get out of the city, and he would take every advantage the Gods granted him. Only time would tell if he was the greater fool for it.

"Do you think someone is trying to help you?"

Sam looked up, the question dragging him back to the present. "Help? I'm not sure. It's like the world has turned on its head. Either Annabelle has an identical twin sister who is now dead, or we have a witch somewhere in the city. If the latter, I am only glad that their plans seem to align with mine for now. I only pray that situation does not change before we can discover who it is…or before she's safe."

"I don't envy you," Raphael said with a low whistle. "This is quite the mess."

"Yes, it is." He pushed to his feet. "Speaking of which, I have to go. If Annabelle spends one more minute in this city, I'll go mad with worry."

"Tell her goodbye from me," Raphael said. "I'll miss having her as my nursemaid. Though I suppose you'd do just fine, if you wanted to come back and see me."

"I'll tell her," Sam assured him, "And…and I'll be back as soon as I can."

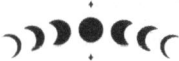

Ilya met him in the corridor. Around them, the house was still quiet, its nocturnal inhabitants sleeping in the rooms below.

"Thank you for looking after him," Sam said as she approached. "I hate to think of how large a favor I now owe, but I'll gladly pay it."

"That you will, laddie," she quipped. "And if you ever want me to do a thing for you again, I'd start buttering me up now. I like things that sparkle," she added, indicating the glittering baubles hanging from her throat and wrists.

Sam grinned at her. "I'll keep it in mind."

"Oh, Sam Fisher." Ilya grimaced. "The Gods help me, but I do have a soft spot for you. Try not to get yourself killed before you have a chance to pay me back."

Sam grinned. "I promise not to get myself killed."

"And Sam?"

He waited as she chewed on her bottom lip.

"That warrior of yours…be careful there."

Sam's heart gave an extra loud thump as he tried to school his expressions into neutrality. "I don't know what you—"

"Don't bother," she cut across him. "I don't care about your pride. This isn't Eìrlan or Petra. I've seen what happens to the men who get caught. If you two are discovered, even I won't be able to save you."

Sam didn't know what to say to this, so he nodded. Ilya's talent had always been reading people; it was what made her such a skilled madam. For the first time, Sam began to wonder if this talent might be something more than pure intuition and practice.

In this new world where dead women could wear the princess's face, anything now seemed possible.

꜀꜀꜀●))) ⸮⸮

Annabelle walked beside Sam in silence as they made their way toward the market, suspended in an in-between place, relieved to be leaving the city at last but knowing that her journey was far from over. The thought sent Annabelle's heart leaping up into her throat.

There was so much life in the city that it took her breath away. Memories of that day spent in glorious freedom with Mica, tracing these very streets, came back with every step she took. There was the vendor where he had bought her a pastry, and over there was the square where she had danced herself into exhaustion.

How different the city had seemed to her then, how different the whole world had appeared. But that day had only been one day—and though she had walked through the city, she had not been a part of the life here. It had only been a window. She did not know this life or these people. And she likely never would.

They did not pause until they reached the market. Everywhere Annabelle could see, there were stalls and people and commotion. Sam lingered for a moment, scanning the square. Not possessing Sam's considerable height, Annabelle could not see far. So she contented herself to wait until Sam had spied their quarry. A moment later, he beckoned, and she followed through the crowd, snaking between stalls and patrons, toward the far side of the square.

A solitary wagon stood there, already loaded full of boxes, barrels, and crates. The driver leaned back in his high seat, feet braced against the edge of the wagon in front of him, wide-brimmed hat pulled low over his eyes.

"Wilkin!" Sam called as they approached the wagon.

The man sat up and lifted the hat to reveal a lined, kind face. His white beard matched his hair, which was tied back in a horsetail at the nape of his neck. The man leaped down from the wagon with the agility of a much younger man, grinning.

"Master Fisher," he said, extending a hand. "It is good to see you, young man."

Sam gripped the man's forearm, face splitting in a wide smile. "Good to see you too, Wilkin. Thank you for doing this."

Wilkin waved away his thanks. "Say nothing of it. Always a pleasure to help a friend in need. Well, it is my job isn't it?"

"Here is her identification," Sam said, producing a small scroll from his jacket pocket and handing it to Wilkin.

Wilkin unfurled the scroll and scanned its contents, loosing a low whistle. "My that Ilya does some fine work. This is the precious cargo then?" He nodded in Annabelle's direction.

Annabelle, who had been lingering awkwardly behind Sam, took a step forward and bobbed a hesitant curtsy. "Anna Baker, at your service," she said, giving the name Ilya had assigned her.

The corner of Wilkin's mouth twisted as if he found something amusing. Annabelle worried that she had already done something wrong, but Wilkin only inclined his head respectfully. "A pleasure to meet you, Miss Anna. Well, we ought to be on our way. Quite a journey ahead, and daylight is wasting."

Annabelle turned to Sam, suddenly drowning in panic. "Can't you come with me?" She pleaded.

He smiled sadly down at her. "I can't. You know I can't. If I'm away from the palace any longer, my absence will be noted."

Annabelle had to blink rapidly against the emotion swelling within her. Every instinct in her body begged her not to let him leave her. Instead, she said. "Be safe, Sam."

"Of course I will be." There were tears in his eyes as he pulled Annabelle into a tight embrace. "You'll be alright," he whispered against her hair. "I promise you, I will come to you when I can."

She nodded into his chest, unable to speak. And then he was pulling away, helping her up onto the seat beside Wilkin. A heartbeat later, before she could say goodbye, he was gone—vanished into the bustle of the crowded square.

"Right then, young Miss," Wilkin said. "Shall we be on our way?"

"Where are we going?" Annabelle asked. Maybe this man would be more forthcoming about their intended destination than Sam had been.

"North," was all Wilkin said before he clicked his tongue and the wagon jerked as the draft horse began to walk. They were on their way at last.

Chapter Seventeen

Princess Annabelle's funeral had been tragic, but at least it was over. *Finally*, Sam thought as he walked alone through the temple district, up to the palace. The guests were still filing out of the temple of Kings, lingering, crying, whispering amongst themselves, but Sam was not in the mood to feign grief, not now when he was next to giddy with relief.

He had waited near the city gate that morning, unable to return to the palace before he knew that they had made it out. Lingering near a butcher's shop, Sam watched as Wilkin's cart approached, as Wilkin exchanged words with the guards stationed there.

Annabelle had looked appropriately meek, but she had not looked scared. When the guards questioned her, she even managed to look appropriately harassed. Sam had never been prouder of his friend and of her incredible bravery in the face of incomprehensible danger.

When at last the guards stepped aside to allow Wilkin passage through the gate, Sam had sagged against a wall, relief temporarily robbing him of the ability to stand upright.

Sam inhaled deeply, relishing the cool air in his lungs after holding his breath for days. His work was far from over, but at least Annabelle was out of the city and out of immediate danger. There was some time now, time for him to find out the truth of things, to figure out what to do next.

"Sam."

Sam turned to see Damon striding up the path toward him. He waited for his friend to catch up, and then the two of them set off side by side.

"I didn't think I could feel worse than when my father died," Damon said after a while. "But this is...this is too terrible."

"I know," Sam said, careful to keep his tone appropriately somber, even though he was irritated at the unwanted intrusion on his solitude. He didn't want to see Damon. He wanted to go back to the palace, to his rooms, and wait for nightfall before returning to the brothel. He wanted to be among people who knew his secrets. He wanted...

"At least the scum who did it have paid the price," Damon said grimly. "I only wish I could have found a few of the Eìrlani bastards myself, made them suffer as she suffered."

Sam balled his hands into fists by his sides to keep from losing his control. *Damon doesn't know what he's talking about,* he reminded himself. *As far as he knows, he's in the right to speak this way about them, about...him.*

"We shouldn't have let her leave the manor," Damon continued. He stumbled on his words a bit as he spoke, and Sam realized with a stab of annoyance that he was drunk. "Shouldn't have agreed to let her marry that…that…" He trailed off, apparently unable to think of an appropriately offensive slur.

"It wasn't up to us, Damon," Sam said, trying to calm his friend. "There was nothing either of us could have done."

"We could have kept a closer eye on her," Damon retorted, growing more agitated still. "We should have never let her out of our sight, not with scum circling her like buzzards."

"We did our best," Sam said. "We did everything we could have done, Damon."

"Buzzards," Damon carried on as if Sam hadn't spoken. "That prince drooling over her. And that man, that commander, pawing at our women. Scum. As if he had a chance with a true Duncan lady. As if they would touch such a ruthless, Godless, brute."

Fury surged through Sam's veins, dissolving his self-control and good sense. He seized Damon by the collar and slammed his back up against a nearby tree.

"Sam—what the…." Damon sputtered as he fought to free himself from Sam's iron grip.

"Do you think she would thank you for it?" Sam growled in his face. "Do you think she would admire you for carrying on like this? She was good and kind, and she would be ashamed of you, Damon."

"Don't you speak for her!" Damon shouted back, his eyes wild. "She's dead. *Dead*, Sam. And it's your fault."

"*My* fault?" Sam roared, shoving Damon back against the trunk.

"Yes," Damon spat, finally throwing Sam off. "You were supposed to protect her. *You* were supposed to be her new knight, her new hero.

Even after I served as her protector for years, she still wanted you. But she never turned up dead on my watch, did she, Sam."

Sam punched him, straight and hard, across the jaw. Damon stumbled back, hand clutching his face. Sam just watched as he straightened, spitting blood onto the ground, cold and unfeeling.

"What is wrong with you, Sam," Damon said, hurt in his eyes. "I feel like I don't know you anymore."

"No," Sam said, turning on his heel and walking away, still seething. "You don't."

)))●(((

The atmosphere at the brothel was loud and bawdy when Sam finally returned. Richly-clad men lounged in the parlor with women draped around them like silk scarves, bosoms exposed, laughter like the tinkling of bells filling the air to mingle with the haze of pipe smoke. Unmistakeable sounds of satisfied customers drifted down from the floors above like a rhythmic beat that underscored the symphony of flesh that was Ilya's house of pleasures.

A slight, blonde woman whom Sam didn't recognize answered the door, the sheer fabric that covered her body leaving nothing at all to the imagination. She smiled, slow and sultry when Sam lowered his hood.

"Why aren't you delicious," the woman said, eyeing Sam from top to bottom. "My lucky day."

"I'm looking for your mistress," Sam said without amusement.

"My mistress is indisposed," said the blonde woman. "But I'd be happy to see to your pleasures, sir." She batted her eyelashes in what

Sam assumed must be an alluring way, though it held little of interest for him.

He was about to say so when another woman sauntered up to the door. Sam recognized this one; Vera, the dark-haired beauty from the night Sam had brought Annabelle and Raphael to the house. She wore a green jacket with gold buttons—the uniform of the city watch—and nothing else besides a gold sash tied about her narrow waist. She leaned against the doorframe and looked Sam up and down, face inscrutable.

"Let him in, Ellie," she said in a deep, husky voice. "I'll take him to the mistress."

Ellie pouted, her red mouth plumping like a ripe strawberry, but stepped aside. Sam crossed the threshold, sparing her a respectful nod before trailing after Vera, who was already making for the staircase. She led him up the stairs and down the hall to the room Raphael occupied. There she stopped and rapped twice on the door.

"Sam Fisher here to see you, Mistress," Vera said in response to a muffled sound from within. Another muffled acknowledgment followed, and she opened the door and stepped aside to permit Sam entry.

Raphael and Ilya sat in armchairs by the fire, facing each other across a magnificent chessboard with tall carved pieces. Both were leaned forward in their chairs, staring at the board with rapt attention.

"That will be all, Vera," Ilya said without turning.

Sam thanked Vera, who gave him a little bow before sauntering back down the corridor. When she had gone, he closed the door and turned to frown at Raphael.

"Should you be out of bed?"

Raphael waved a dismissive hand, not taking his eyes from the board. "I'm fine, lad—aha!" He reached out and moved one of his pieces into place, putting Ilya in check.

Ilya lifted an eyebrow. "Awfully confident in your strategy, aren't you?"

"I am," Raphael said, shrugging. "With good reason."

"Hmmm." Ilya took the piece he had moved, setting it aside and replacing it with one of her own. She leaned back in her chair, her smile feline in its satisfaction as she announced, "Checkmate."

Raphael's face fell, and his eyes darted around the board for a long moment as he searched for evidence that she was wrong. A moment later, he threw his head back and roared with laughter.

"Goddess, be good!" He exclaimed. "You do know your way around a board, mistress."

"I told you I never lose."

"And you never lie either, it would seem." Raphael leaned back and snatched up his goblet of wine from a side table, drinking deeply. His eyes fell upon Sam, and he lowered the goblet. "What?"

For Sam had been watching the entire exchange from his position by the door, seething with disapproval.

"You should be in bed," Sam said.

"Come now, Sam," Raphael replied. "I really am doing much better, and it's just a game of chess. It isn't as if I've been running mad through the streets or trying to swim to Petra."

"Even so." The fight with Damon still hummed in Sam's veins, making him irritable.

"Calm down, Fisher," Ilya sighed, rising from her chair. "Lyddia has done a fine job with him. As long as he doesn't exert himself, he'll be alright.

"I really ought to be paying for the kind of attentive treatment I've received at the hand of your ladies," Raphael added with a wink.

"Don't encourage her," Sam said with a scowl.

Ilya and Raphael exchanged a look, and the madam got to her feet. "Best of luck with this one, Raph. I have customers to attend to. Try not to cluck over much, Fisher. Mother hen is not an attractive look on anyone, least of all you."

"Oh, I don't know about that, Illy," Raphael chimed in with a smirk. "I quite like it when he makes a fuss."

"Perhaps he can teach you how to play chess," Ilya suggested, winking.

Raphael's face fell, and he adopted a look of mock solemnity. "You know I think I ought to lie down after all. Suddenly I feel quite weak."

Sam glowered as Ilya closed the door behind her with a snap. They could hear the tinkling sound of her laughter all the way down the corridor beyond.

"What a delightful lass," Raphael said, lounging back in his chair with a lazy smile. "She's become quite fond of me, you know."

"Is that so?" Sam crossed the room and stood before Raphael, hands on his hips. "I need to inspect your injuries."

Raphael's eyebrows rose slightly. "You don't trust me? I'm offended, knightling."

"How about this," Sam offered. "Let me inspect you, and if you are faring as well as you say, you will not hear another word from me about rest. If not…" he jerked his chin toward the sizeable four-posted bed. "You go to bed."

The look Raphael gave him at these last words made the heat rise in Sam's face, but he only nodded and stood, stripping off his shirt. White bandages stretched across his broad muscled chest and encased his left shoulder and upper arm. Sam moved forward and set about peeling back the edge of the bandage to check the burns underneath. Raphael watched him as he worked, but Sam kept his eyes on what he was doing.

To Sam's shock, he discovered that Raphael's skin was healing fast. It should have taken two more days at least for such progress, even with the help of a skilled healer.

"How is this possible?" He murmured as he pulled back more bandage to reveal more of the same.

Raphael shrugged. "I'm a fast healer."

His words reverberated in his big chest, into Sam's fingertips. Flushing crimson, Sam replaced the bandages and quickly stepped away from the heat of Raphael's body, retreating to the relative safety of the chair that Ilya had recently vacated.

"No one is that fast a healer," he pointed out.

Raphael slipped back into his shirt and resumed his seat. "Lyddia knows what she's doing. Impressive for one so young."

Sam was still skeptical but didn't press the matter.

"I'm glad Ilya is taking such good care of you."

"I am grateful to her," Raphael said. "Incidentally...how does a knight of the realm happen to have such a close personal relationship with a madam?"

Sam smiled grudgingly. "I know it's unusual, but then again, I suppose I'm an unusual sort of knight."

"What do you mean by that?"

Sam shrugged. "I had an uncommon beginning. For a knight, I mean. My father was a fisherman. I was born in this very city, in fact."

"Is it so uncommon for the son of a fisherman to become a knight?" Raphael asked. There was no judgment in his face or his words.

"Very," Sam nodded. "My parents died when I was a baby. Lord Roger Wallace took me in as his ward—another unusual occurrence. I never heard the whole story, but I managed to piece together enough over the years. From what I could discover, my mother was the daughter of a farmer who worked the old Lord's estate. She and Lord Roger knew each other as children. Lord Roger fell in love with her, I think, though I cannot know for certain. Whatever happened between them is still a mystery to me. All I know is that she left to seek work in the city, and Lord Roger married Lady Ellen."

"It can't have been as simple as all that," Raphael said. "Not if you wound up as his ward."

"It's a regret of mine that I never asked him what happened," Sam admitted. "I managed to find an old letter of my mother's, telling him she was dying and begging him to find me a good home. Well, he did her one better, I suppose."

"And did he—did Lord Roger want you to become a knight?" Raphael asked.

Sam shook his head sadly. "I don't know. I never asked. Damon and I were…close growing up. Like brothers, more so than Damon and his elder brother Gustav ever were. And, well…" he trailed off, afraid that Raphael would make mention of his exceptionally non-brotherly feelings for Damon. But he did not say a word, and so Sam continued. "Anyway, Damon wanted to become a knight. Gustav was going to inherit the estate and the title, and Damon saw the knighthood as his way to bring honor to his family name. I saw it as a way to carve out a place for myself in the world and as a way to stay by his side."

Sam fell silent, staring at the chessboard between them without seeing it.

"I suppose my wishes came true and did not, in equal measure."

"You did manage to carve out a place for yourself in this world," Raphael observed.

Sam nodded. "In a way. It took a long time and many rather unorthodox methods for me to win my knighthood. That is how Ilya and I met. Damon and I had arrived in Rengon City, and he had a position as a squire for Lord Velton, ready and waiting for him. Velton was able to arrange a position for me in the household of a knight, Sir Falcoun, but I was no squire. Such patronage must be earned or bought. As I had no money to my name, it was upon my shoulders to win my own place."

Raphael stood and moved stiffly to the sideboard, pouring two glasses of wine. "And how did you manage that?" He asked as he handed Sam a glass.

Sam accepted it with a grateful smile. "That is very much due to Ilya. Sir Falcoun was an older knight from a wealthy family in the west. He liked wine and gambling and…well…the pleasures of the flesh. I attended him every time he went out into the city at night. I performed many duties that a squire might. The arrangement was perfect for Sir Falcoun, who wanted to have a squire to serve him, but did not desire the responsibility of training such a man to win his knighthood. If not for Ilya, I might have been trapped in such an arrangement forever."

Sam sipped his wine, settling back in his chair. It was quite comfortable and warm by the fire. He had already spoken more words than he had in a long time, but it felt good to tell his story. So much of his time was spent in secrecy, protecting his history in order to protect his friends. But Raphael had joined him behind the curtain, had become a companion, and now that Sam was no longer alone in the darkness, he found that he wanted— he *needed* to share who he was. In case the worst happened, it felt good that another soul would know who he had been.

"And how did Ilya help you out of your undesirable predicament?" Raphael prompted when Sam didn't say anything for a long while. "Was she the madam of the brothel your master visited?"

Sam shook his head, a bit embarrassed to be caught daydreaming. "No. Ilya is young for a madam even now. Back then, she served Madam Raiya, who ran one of the oldest and most renowned pleasure houses in the city. Her specialty was catering to unusual tastes." Sam grimaced. "Ilya was one of Sir Falcoun's favorites. I knew who she was, but we didn't have the opportunity to become acquainted until one night when my master had taken longer than he was accustomed. I went upstairs to check on him and found that he had passed out drunk in Ilya's bed."

"Charming," Raphael drawled, taking a sip of wine.

"Indeed. She begged me not to wake my master. You see, she would get paid more the longer he stayed put. I agreed, of course. I was in no hurry. We sat there together in the room while he slept it off, talking about our lives, our dreams. Her mistress could be cruel. My master would never make me a true squire. We both wanted out, but we knew we could never manage it alone. So we agreed to help each other. The men who frequent those sorts of places are important and wealthy, and they talk when they've had too much to drink. Ilya agreed to pass me information from her clients and from the rest of the girls."

"And in exchange?"

"I use the information and my freedom to roam, to release her from her bondage to Madam Raiya."

"A tall order," Raphael observed, raising an eyebrow.

Sam's mouth twitched in the shadow of a smile in spite of himself. He knew he had a captive audience.

"I used the information that Ilya passed me to win a position as a squire to a young Lord Allbrook. He agreed to have me trained and be my patron when I petitioned the king for a knighthood. Damon and I were finally reunited as Squires together, but my life had already changed—*I* had already changed. During the day, I attended his lordship and trained in the yards with Damon and the other squires, but at night I roamed the city's streets, acquainting myself with the seedier aspects of Rengon.

"I managed to learn that Madam Raiya was stepping outside the king's law in her role as a purveyor of pleasures to the nobility. Her list of wrongdoings was long indeed, including kidnapping, torture, rape—all in the service of the great lords of the land. Of course, I could never have ruined such powerful men, but I was not trying to do so. All I needed to do was expose the madam, and her customers would turn on her. I did, and they did. Raiya was ruined and imprisoned. Ilya was free. She left the city a month later with enough gold from the patrons who favored her to open a house in the south and never looked back."

Raphael gaped in the wake of his story. "Gods above," he breathed. "No wonder you trust her."

"I trust her with my life," Sam said plainly. "She earned it. She passed me information when all she had in return was my word that I would not forget her."

"And you two never...." Raphael waggled his eyebrows suggestively.

It was a casual question, but suddenly the air felt hot and tense, and Sam shifted in his seat. "It was only ever friendship between us. She knew from the beginning what I was."

Raphael's shoulders tensed visibly at Sam's words. "And what is that, exactly?" He asked, tone clipped.

Sam shrugged, unable to meet Raphael's eyes. He said nothing. What was he? A monster, he had thought many times. Broken. Wrong.

Raphael flinched as if he had shouted the words aloud. With a grumble that sounded a lot like a growl, he stood and walked to the bed, leaning against one of the posts. Sam watched him without speaking, inexplicably afraid.

"It disgusts me," Raphael spat. "I mean, I've heard stories about this pestilential place, but to see it...to hear about it. Gorgeous, fearsome creatures like Ilya forced to serve lecherous old beasts. Noblemen left unblemished while women are kidnapped and tortured for their pleasure. And you!" He whirled on Sam, fury all over his rugged, beautiful face, fire in his eyes. "You are the worst of it!"

"What have *I* done?" Sam objected, shoving to his feet, ready for the fight.

"You have not done a bloody thing," Raphael growled. "That's the point, Sam. You think there's something wrong with you, that you're broken in some way."

"I—what? I don't—" Sam was flustered. His cheeks were burning, and his fists were clenched tight at his sides. Raphael was pacing now, and he continued his tirade as if Sam hadn't spoken.

"You do, and all because this Goddess-forsaken country is so Goddess-damned, bloody—"

"You do realize you are speaking about my *home*," Sam shouted. "It may not be perfect, but there are plenty of us fighting to make it better."

Raphael made a strangled noise of disbelief that set Sam's blood boiling.

"And I suppose you are going to tell me that life in Eìrlan is *so* much better." Sam snapped.

"Eìrlan may not be perfect," Raphael shot back, expression ferocious in its intensity. "But at least we do not enslave our women and terrorize our boys with fear of persecution and the noose."

"I have not been terrorized," Sam said through clenched teeth.

Raphael barked a mirthless laugh. "Haven't you? Goddess save me, Sam. They prepared me for this place, prepared me for the things I might witness and how it may not make any sense to me. I thought I would handle it well enough. And then I met you."

"And what exactly is wrong with me?" Sam demanded. He had close to had enough. Who was this man to criticize and badger him? Who was this man to know anything about who he was or what he felt? He didn't want Raphael's anger or pity or self-righteousness.

"*Wrong* with you?" Raphael's face was stricken, and his voice was cracked and raw with emotion as he took one step toward Sam, then another. "You poor, sweet, beautiful man. There is *nothing* wrong with you. Nothing."

And then Raphael was kissing him, and Sam's entire world melted away into fire and sweetness and light. This was not the same kiss from the gardens, secret and swift. Raphael gripped him hungrily, his mouth firm and soft at the same time, his tongue claiming. Sam could not think, didn't want to think, didn't want to do anything except cling to the warm muscled body and slowly fade away. Nothing had ever felt like this. Nothing, he was sure, would again.

Even I won't be able to save you.

The words swam in Sam's mind, unbidden, accompanied by memories: a man stripped naked and strung up in the village square, the makes of his stoning blooming red and angry across his broken body; the taunting jibes made by the boys, by Damon; the things they threw; the approving nods of the fathers who looked upon their sons' hatred.

Sam tensed. "Stop," he said, his voice muffled against Raphael's entreating kisses.

Raphael stopped, moving away from Sam so quickly that the sudden absence of his body and warmth left him breathless, dizzy.

"I'm sorry," Raphael rasped. "I shouldn't have... I'm.."

But Sam was already moving to the door. "It's not your fault, I..." His mind was a disaster of pain and confusion. "We can't," he breathed. "Not here. Ilya—she has already risked her life and livelihood for us, and I can't put her in more danger, no matter...no matter..." No matter how much he wanted to reach out and pull Raphael back to him. The thought made his bones turn to ice. He reached for the doorknob.

"I understand." Raphael dragged a hand through his hair, sighing. "I'm sorry, Sam."

Sam's heart constricted at the words, at the sorrow in them. "It's alright. I'll come back to check on you in a couple of days. We can figure out how to get you out of here once everything has calmed down."

Raphael nodded. "Very well."

They just stood there—Raphael sitting on the end of the bed, Sam standing with his hand resting on the doorknob—neither sure what to say or do. Finally, it was Raphael who broke the silence.

"Do you have to leave right now, or do you have some time?"

Sam blinked at him. "I have some time."

"Stay," Raphael offered. "Let's have a game of chess and some wine."

Sam hesitated. "I don't know...."

"Please." There was real pleading in Raphael's tone now. "I promise to keep my hands to myself."

"It's not that." Sam lifted a brow. "Only...after Ilya handily bested you I'm just not sure if your ego could handle another thrashing."

Raphael tipped his head back and laughed, full and deep. The corner of Sam's mouth tugged into a smile.

"Come," Raphael said, pushing off the bed. "You set up the board, I'll pour the wine."

Chapter Eighteen

Annabelle and Wilkin traveled together across the southern country-side for three days. After the first day, it became apparent to Annabelle that they were heading northeast in the general direction of Rosewood Manor. Though she knew that the manor was changed, no doubt for the worse under the rule of Baron Gustav, Annabelle couldn't help feel a lightness in her heart the closer she came to home.

Wilkin was friendly company, entertaining Annabelle with stories from his youth. If one of the tall tales was true, Annabelle would eat her hat, but it was still a welcome distraction to listen to the pleasant rise and fall of Wilkin's soft voice as they trundled along the country roads.

Despite the dangers of traveling in the open, Wilkin never stopped at an inn or village, instead giving these populated places a wide berth. When Annabelle asked his reason, Wilkin only smiled and said, "What, are you tired of my company already miss? And here I was thinking we were having a grand time."

They never met with trouble. Wilkin knew this land well and found secluded places for them to make camp and to water his horse, Sally. Annabelle had difficulty sleeping—being out in the open brought back fears of kidnap and danger—so she spent hours each night staring up at the stars twinkling above until she eventually fell into fitful dreams full of fire and death.

By the third day, Annabelle felt terrible. She sat up in the front of the wagon beside Wilkin in bleary-eyed silence. After only a few hours' travel through green rolling hills and lush forest, Wilkin pulled the wagon to the side of the road.

"Why don't you lay down in the back," he suggested. "I can create some space for you easy enough, and you look at the edge of death if your Highness will pardon my saying so."

Annabelle sighed. "I'd like that. Thank you, Wil—"Then her sluggish brain finally registered what he had said.

"You…I…you know who I am," she stammered, suddenly fearful. "Who…who told you?"

Wilkin chuckled. "I didn't need telling. The second I laid eyes on you, I knew who you were. The way you walk, the way you hold yourself, the way you speak—I knew you were no farmer's daughter."

Annabelle didn't know what to say.

"As if that wasn't enough on its own," Wilkin went on, smiling sadly. "I was lucky enough to see the Queen once with my own eyes, one day when I was selling in the city markets. She strolled right into the square, bold as you please, no guards or anything following her. I didn't know who she was then, but when folks in the market began bowing and scraping and falling all over themselves, I caught on quick enough. Couldn't believe it. It was like seeing something out of a faerie tale appearing in the flesh."

His eyes were far away as he told his story, his face transported. Annabelle couldn't breathe, drinking in every word like they were the nectar of life itself.

"And then, if you'll believe it," he continued, "her Majesty the Queen of the whole damned kingdom walked right up to my stall and bought a bushel of apples off me for five times what I was asking for them. Said they were the most gorgeous Goldens she'd ever seen in her life. Took a big bite out of one right then and there. Well… you could have knocked me down with a feather. Proudest day of my whole life, that."

Annabelle could see it, could picture it all in her mind's eye. It was the most precious gift, this story. She could hardly breathe.

"And then you strode right up to my carriage, and it was like I was staring at her ghost. At that moment, I knew exactly who you were."

He met her eyes then, and she saw that his eyes were wet. "I don't know what's happened to you that you've found your way into my wagon when you're supposed to be dead and buried, but I am grateful for it. I don't need to know more. I will do what I can to do right by you and by a queen who would buy a bushel of apples off of a poor farmer for a whole gold coin just because it was the right thing to do."

Gratitude for the kind old man swelled in Annabelle's chest, and she reached out to take Wilkin's hand.

"Thank you," she said. "Thank you for doing this for me and for sharing that story."

He squeezed her hand. "I can't speak for any other soul, but it broke my heart clean in two to hear that she died. And I can't say I know what it is like to stand in your shoes, but I just thought it might help ease your mind to know that you're among folk who are loyal to her and to you."

"It does help," Annabelle said. And it was the truth. She climbed into the back of the wagon, with Wilkin's help, and stretched out beneath the canopy of canvas. She hardly noticed as the wagon began to move once more, her mind far away in a marketplace, surrounded by golden apples.

Annabelle did not remember falling asleep.

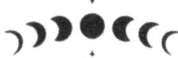

It must have been the absence of movement that roused Annabelle, for when she opened her eyes, everything was quiet, still, and dark. The canvas covering had been pulled back from the wagon's bed, and the stars winked down from the inky sky above. Off in the corner of the sky, a full moon gleamed white. Annabelle sat up, yawning into the back of her hand as she took note of her surroundings.

The wagon was parked in front of a small farmhouse with a wood-shingled roof covered in moss, ivy creeping up the stones of the front wall, and a garden peeking out from behind. Beyond the quaint house, she could see a large barn and a field surrounded by a split-rail fence that contained—as far as she could see in the dim light—a smaller structure that looked to be a chicken coop and several deep feed troughs.

It was peaceful in this place. The only sounds she could hear were the jingling of the harness as Wilkin unhooked Sally and the serenade of crickets on the wind.

"Well, look who has decided to join the land of the living!"

Annabelle cricked her neck as she whipped around to see a man leaning against the other side of the wagon, grinning from ear to ear.

He had a youthful face, no beard, and a waterfall of golden hair that he brushed out of his soft brown eyes as he stood and addressed Wilkin.

"Everything go smoothly?"

"Smooth as Petran silk, Charlie," Wilkin replied. "The young lady is a fine traveling companion." He winked at Annabelle, who gave him a small smile in return.

Charlie nodded, "Good." Then he looked back at Annabelle. "Come on, then." And without another word—without any further explanation as to who he was, where this place was, or what on the Gods' earth she was doing here—he turned and strode away up to the house.

Annabelle tumbled out of the wagon, brushing off her skirts, and bade Wilkin a quick farewell before hurrying after him.

The inside of the farmhouse was just as quaint and cozy as the outside. A rickety staircase stood on the right, leading into the darkness of the second floor, and an arch to her right revealed a small parlor beyond.

Charlie walked straight ahead down the hall and into a spacious kitchen where the last embers of a fire smoldered on a sizable hearth. A long wooden table stood in the middle of the room, and as Annabelle couldn't see any separate dining space, she presumed that the family must take their meals in here.

Charlie retrieved a clay bowl from a high shelf, ladled something into it that looked like stew and smelled tantalizingly rich and sweet, and plopped it down on the table.

"Sit," he commanded, setting a spoon down beside the bowl with a clack. "Eat. You must be starving."

Annabelle's stomach gave an audible gurgle in response, so she slid onto one of the long benches beside the table without protest and seized the spoon.

The stew was one of the best things Annabelle had ever tasted. It was an effort not to forego the spoon altogether and simply pour the contents of the bowl down her throat.

Charlie slid onto the bench opposite her and gave a deep chuckle. "Easy does it. You don't want to be ill and let that liquid gold go to waste. Bess's stew is the best in the region."

"Best in the world, you mean," Annabelle said as she slid another spoonful into her mouth.

He laughed again. "That I don't doubt."

Annabelle swallowed her mouthful and then paused, her spoon hovering over the bowl. "I don't mean to sound…rude," she said, hesitating. "But who are you, exactly?"

"Charlie Rabbold," he said, extending a calloused hand, which Annabelle shook. "Rabble Farm, which is where you are now, is mine."

Annabelle raised an eyebrow. "'Rabble Farm?'"

"It didn't use to have a name," Charlie said with a shrug, "But my father and his brothers were such troublemakers when they were growing up that the village started saying 'Rabble' instead of 'Rabbold' and the name just kind of…stuck. Didn't bother my father in the slightest, but then again, the man always did have a soft spot for a nice turn of phrase."

"And where exactly are we?" Annabelle asked, helping herself to another spoonful of stew.

"North of Ellasport—well, northeast, I should say. In the Falls Hills."

Lord Velton's lands, Annabelle realized. The knowledge made her feel better, closer to home in this strange place.

"And Wilkin?"

"He works for me, as does his wife Bess—whom you have to thank for the stew. They both worked for my father before he died, helped him run the family business."

"The farm, you mean?" Annabelle asked. Her spoon clanged in the bottom of the bowl, and she frowned down into its empty depths.

Charlie snatched it from her and went to refill it with stew.

"That, and other things." He set the newly filled bowl in front of her. "We run an underground network, of sorts."

"Ah. You mean smuggling runaways across the country," Annabelle said, smirking.

"You would be our first live cargo, actually," Charlie replied with a wink. "Usually, we trade in things that the people couldn't get otherwise, not with all the useful goods being sent north. Healing remedies, leather for new shoes, seeds, books, tools—anything to make life a bit easier."

"So you steal these things." Annabelle winced inwardly as the accusation slipped out. She didn't want him to think she was ungrateful; she just wanted to know the kind of person she was dealing with.

Charlie's smile faded as he said, "The real stealing is what's being done to people who were barely scraping by before the king's tax collectors come knocking to take what little they had. All to sustain a conflict that has been going on since before many of us were even born. If there's even the smallest bit I can do to ease their suffering, I'll do it, just as my father did before me."

"I'm sorry," Annabelle said. "I didn't mean anything by it. I'm only..." She trailed off. She didn't know what to say.

Charlie sighed, scrubbing a hand across his face. "You're only tired and scared, and you wanted to figure out if you ought to sleep with a knife under your pillow tonight. Is that right?"

Annabelle nodded, face flushed with embarrassment.

"Well, I don't blame you," he said. "I'd feel the same if I were in your shoes. And here I am, prattling on about things I probably shouldn't. It's just been so wretched dull around here for days, and it's nice to have someone to talk to for a change. I'm sorry for my bad manners."

"No, don't apologize," Annabelle insisted. "I'm grateful to you for answering my questions."

"If you have any more of them, I'd be happy to give you answers—*nicely* this time, I promise," he said, holding up his hands in mock surrender.

Annabelle only had two.

"How do you know Sam?"

Charlie's face lit up as he said, "Sam's a good friend. One of the best men I've had the pleasure to know. We met when I was serving as a part of the king's infantry in the north. Of course, that was before my father died, and I had to come back here to make sure things kept running and the farm and with...everything else. Sam offered to help in any way he could when I told him I had to come back here. Introduced me to Ilya—best thing to ever happen to our little operation, let me tell you."

It was nice to hear about Sam from someone who knew him at a time when Annabelle did not. She yearned even more to hear the whole story of Sam's life but would content herself with this small piece for now.

She hesitated before asking Charlie her final question.

"Do you know who I am?"

Charlie did not blink, did not show any sign of discomfort. He only met her eyes and said, without any explanation or preamble, "Yes, I do."

"Did Wilkin tell you?"

Charlie shook his head. "Ilya warned me. Don't worry," he added when Annabelle looked alarmed. "We use a strong code, and it's Gods damned near indecipherable without the key."

Annabelle chewed her lip, thinking. The number of people who knew that Annabelle lived was growing every day, and it made her uneasy. Still, there was nothing to be done about it now.

"You should know," Charlie continued, "that Wilkin and Bess won't ask you why you're here. I've said that we are to give you a safe haven, and they trust me enough not to question my reasoning. But I will want to know why I am putting my people's lives in danger. Not tonight; tonight, I will leave you in peace and let you rest. But I will need an explanation at some point, from either you or Sam. I think it only fair compensation for what I'm risking to help you."

Annabelle thought that if he wanted explanations, he could damn well get in line, but she didn't say that. Instead, she said, "Whatever explanation I can give, you will have it."

"Thank you."

They sat in silence as Annabelle finished eating. When her bowl was once again emptied, and she was so full she could not have swallowed another bite, Charlie stood.

"Follow me," he said. "I'll show you where you can sleep."

The room was small and simple but comfortable. A woven rug lay upon the floor, and the little bed was made up with a patchwork quilt of blue, pink, and green squares. A water jug sat in a basin on the nightstand, and a chest of drawers stood in the opposite corner, a vase of wildflowers sitting on top. The sight of the room made Annabelle feel warm and comforted. She turned to Charlie with a smile.

"It's lovely," she said.

He shrugged, scanning the little room. "It's not much—nothing near what I'm sure you're used to, but it's warm and clean."

Annabelle shook her head vehemently. "It's perfect. Thank you."

"It's not a problem," he said with a half-smile. "I put some of my mother's old clothes in the dresser for you. She was near your size, I think, so the fit shouldn't be too bad. Breakfast is at sunrise down in the kitchen, but take your time if you need to rest. Bess'll be cooking all day."

Charlie lingered for a moment on the threshold, looking at a loss for what else to say. For the first time, he looked like a young man playing host in his father's house.

"Good night," he said finally and strode off down the hall.

Annabelle closed the door to the little room and set about rummaging in the chest of drawers for something clean to wear to sleep. There were two cotton nightgowns, and she slid gratefully into one of them and curled under the quilt.

Laying there in the dark, staring up at the ceiling, everything she had forced herself not to think about for the past week came bubbling into the forefront of her mind. Images of horror flashed before her eyes as panic clawed at her chest—her father's face looming over her, his hot tears falling upon her cheeks, a blue light that exploding from nowhere, the sickening sound of the king's body slamming hard against stone, corpses of the drowned piled high, each one wearing her face, Sam's face, Emily's face, Raphael's Face…Mica's face.

Herbert had been right: whatever was happening was nothing good. It was one thing to be grateful for this warm bed, for the safety of this farm and the goodness of the people to whom she now entrusted her safety, but Annabelle couldn't stop herself from wondering—what now? Surely she couldn't stay hidden here forever. Or could she? Could she simply vanish in plain sight, a mere three days ride from the palace, and live out the rest of her days in the country? The promise of such a life was tempting.

But what about Mica? What about Raphael? Could she sit contentedly and leave them to whatever fate? What about Emily, Damon, the Duchess? Could she simply allow them to believe her dead, brutally murdered in a senseless, ruthless attack? As terrifying as it had been to flee, Annabelle doubted very much that she had the constitution to simply fade into the background, abandoning her friends and her kingdom.

But wasn't that precisely what she had done? While her new friends burned, Annabelle ran, helpless as a sick pup. Greater than her fear and more sinister than horror, Annabelle's shame crept in to lay over her like the soft quilt, slimy and sickening.

Feeling lower than the muck that coated the bottom of the sea, Annabelle turned her back on the pretty little window set high on the wall of the cozy little room in the peaceful little farmhouse and cried silently in the dark.

Chapter Nineteen

It took Annabelle a few moments to remember where she was when the morning sun fell across her pillow, dragging her reluctantly from sleep. Stiff and bleary-eyed, she sat up and, stretching, looked around the room. Then it came back to her—she was at Rabble Farm. She had met Charlie Rabbold, the farmer. This was his house, and she wore his mother's nightgown.

There were clothes for her in the armoire, she remembered. There was also a hairbrush and small looking glass set on top. Quickly, she dragged the brush through her mussed hair and selected a simple brown cotton dress, savoring the softness of the fabric and the forgiving fit. At least there were no restricting ballgowns to be found in the room.

Spirits a great deal lighter thanks to a fair night's sleep and clean clothes, Annabelle splashed some water on her face from the basin on the nightstand and followed her gurgling stomach in search of breakfast.

Heavenly smells drifted up the stairs from the kitchen. Annabelle discovered that their source was a skillet of sausages frying on the hearth, tended by a plump woman in an ash-colored frock. When Annabelle approached, the woman straightened and turned. She smiled warmly when her eyes alighted upon Annabelle.

"You must be our new guest," she said, bouncing a little on the balls of her feet.

"Yes. I'm Ann—Anna." Annabelle faltered, nearly forgetting her newly acquired identity. That would not do. She had to be more careful.

Thankfully, the woman chuckled and said. "Oh my dear, no need to look so terrified. I know well who you are. Wilkin is my husband, you see." She said by way of an explanation.

"Oh." Annabelle returned her smile, relieved. "So you must be Bess."

"That I am," said Bess. "Cook, laundress, housekeeper, and anything else you please. Between you and me," she leaned in conspiratorially, "I'm the reason this place survives one day to the next."

Annabelle giggled. "I believe you."

"Charlie told me not to expect you for some time yet. Said you'd want to have a bit of a lie-in after your journey."

"I slept a bit yesterday," Annabelle said with a shrug. "And I smelled breakfast."

The woman's grin widened. "Well then, you must sit and have some, miss Annabelle—do you mind if I call you Annabelle? Saves a terrible amount of time to do away with the titles and nonsense. After all," Bess took Annabelle's hands in her own, "we are all family here."

"Annabelle is perfect," she said, squeezing Bess's hands. "I prefer to be called by my own name."

"And a lovely name it is," Bess agreed. "Now, sit."

Annabelle slid onto the bench by the long table, mouth-watering. Bess set a plate in front of her and heaped it with sausages, wilted spinach, eggs, and mushrooms. Everything smelled divine and tasted even better. Annabelle inhaled her food, thinking all the while that the finest palace chefs would have a thing or two to learn from this country cook.

"Finished already?" Bess asked, raising an eyebrow at Annabelle's clean plate.

Annabelle's cheeks flushed. "I'm sorry…it was just so delicious."

"Oh my dear," Bess laughed aloud. "Never apologize to a cook for enjoying her food. I'd take it as a compliment if you weren't so regrettably *thin*. But never you mind." She leaned over and squeezed Annabelle's shoulder as she retrieved the plate. "We will put some meat on those bones in no time."

Annabelle did not object to this. She had always had a healthy appetite, but the weeks at the palace had taken their toll. Somehow, even surrounded by the most sumptuous meals she could ever imagine, the constant feeling of being watched had made it hard to eat.

Once the meal was cleared away, Bess offered to show Annabelle around the farmhouse. Annabelle did not imagine there was much to see but accepted, not wanting to appear rude. Upstairs were the three bedrooms, Bess explained at the foot of the stairs before showing her the small sitting room and the study beyond.

"Where did all of these books come from?" Annabelle asked, marveling at the large shelf that occupied one wall, laden to bursting with books of all shapes and sizes, in varying states of wear and tear.

"Master Jonathan loved to read," Bess explained with a sad look at the shelf. "Brought one back with him from the city every time he returned from the market. Poor man," she added with a sigh. "Terrible what happened to him."

"What happened?" Annabelle didn't mean to pry, but she rather suspected Bess had been hoping she might.

"Carried off by plague, two years ago. Terrible tragedy, a man of his age and health. But he wouldn't leave the people of the village to face the sickness alone. Delivered healing remedies to them until he could no longer walk or drive a wagon. If he had only left well enough alone. Everyone knows that no healer's potion can cure a plague that is Gods-sent. But that was Jonathan. Always cared more for others than his own well-being. Still…" Bess's eyes drifted toward the window and far away. "I don't think Master Charlie was ready for the responsibility of running the farm. A soldier was all the lad ever wanted to be, and I still think it hurts something inside of him to be here while his friends are fighting and dying in the north."

Annabelle could not think of a single thing to say. She suddenly felt so small and selfish, knowing that her most significant concerns had been an arranged marriage to a good man and a father who did not love her properly. Charlie had a father and a life, and it had still been ripped from him. Annabelle's thoughts turned to Lord Roger. He had been a good man, just as this Jonathan Rabbold had been. It was so unfair that the Gods should take the good men before the bad.

"I'm sorry," Annabelle said quietly. "I lost someone close to me recently. He was a good man too."

Bess smiled kindly. "Thank you, dear. And I, too, am sorry for your loss. It is easy to forget that even a princess can know suffering and heartbreak, no?"

Annabelle's eyes were burning now, and she turned from the woman to hide her distress. Something caught her attention, and she approached the window.

Charlie was out in the field beyond the garden. He wielded a broadsword in one hand and was moving through a sequence of complex movements with the weapon—his muscles straining, shirt stuck to his body with sweat, face set and focused.

"He does that every day," Bess said, coming to stand beside Annabelle at the window. "I think it soothes him to remain sharp and ready. For what, I cannot imagine."

Annabelle could imagine. She had believed herself safe from harm, and yet harm had come knocking at her door more than once. Even sequestered in this secluded place, she could not blame Charlie for maintaining his combat skills.

She watched him for a while, mesmerized by the flash of his blade in the morning sun, the way his muscled body expanded and contracted with every movement. It was the most beautiful dance Annabelle had ever seen, almost too intimate and private to witness, and yet she could not look away.

"Would you excuse me, Bess?" She asked. Turning, she saw that the woman had gone and could hear her whistling a merry tune from the direction of the kitchen.

Annabelle turned back to the window, finishing her thought aloud. "There's something I have to do."

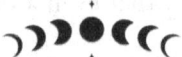

"Very impressive."

Charlie was rubbing his blade down with a cloth when Annabelle reached the fence at the end of the field.

At her words, he looked up and shrugged. "The exercises keep me limber. Still, there's no substitute for a good sparring match."

"I know what you mean," Annabelle said, leaning against a split wood post. "I've had the notion to banish Sam to the sparring ring when he gets in a mood, once or twice."

Charlie grinned wolfishly. "Now there's a partner I would give much to have a go with again. He knows his way around a sword, our Sam."

"That he does," Annabelle said. Memories of those pleasant days on the road, watching Sam and Damon spar together, glittered in the morning sunshine.

"Did you find Bess?" Charlie asked, sliding his sword into its leather sheath.

Annabelle nodded. "Her breakfast is just as good as her stew."

"I think you'll find," Charlie said, "That there is little our Bess makes that doesn't make one want to lie down and pass from this world from sheer confidence that nothing more wonderful could exist in this life."

"I believe that." Annabelle hesitated. There was something she wanted to say but was unsure about how to begin.

Charlie, somehow sensing her intention, said, "Out with it, Princess. I have a farm to care for, and my animals start biting if they don't get fed in a timely manner."

Annabelle frowned. "Don't call me that."

"What?" Charlie's brows raised. "'Princess'?"

"Yes."

"It's what you are." Charlie cocked his head. "But fair enough. What would her Highness prefer to be called?"

"My name will do just fine," Annabelle said, rolling her eyes.

Charlie smirked. "Very well. What it is you would like to say to me, *Annabelle*?"

"I…" Annabelle took a deep breath. "I wanted to offer you an explanation for why I'm here. I know you said sometime, but I don't want to spend even one minute here if you aren't comfortable taking the risk."

Charlie considered this for a moment. "Fair enough. I'm listening."

Annabelle told her story as best she could. Though she had promised to tell Charlie everything, Annabelle didn't think she could explain exactly how she had managed to escape the temple. She knew she would have to confide the truth in someone, sometime. But for now, she resolved to keep the details vague until she had a better explanation to give.

When she reached the part about Sam, the mysterious corpse, and how he had discovered that Annabelle must still be alive, Charlie frowned.

"But…how is that possible?" He asked.

"I don't know," Annabelle admitted. "I never saw the body, so I still find it hard to believe…but I don't think Sam would lie."

"No," Charlie agreed. "Still…it is alarming."

"I don't know why this is happening," Annabelle said, feeling a bit tired after reliving the details of that horrible night. "But I do know that I can't go back. Sam thinks that this is the place for me, and I trust him. If you disagree…well, I'd rather know now."

Charlie did not say anything for minutes. His silence was terrifying, but Annabelle made herself wait.

"Thank you for telling me," he said at last. "I can't pretend I understand all that has happened to you...but I do agree with you. Sam Fisher is nearly always right about these things, and you cannot go back. So, you will remain here for as long as it is the safest place for you to be."

Annabelle was glad to hear it, but she did not relax yet. "There's... something more I have to ask of you."

The corner of Charlie's mouth twitched in amusement. "You mean more than harboring a missing princess who is supposed to be dead, putting my life and the lives of my friends and family at risk in the process?"

"Er...yes." Annabelle was suddenly anxious he would refuse her, but Charlie only looked curious.

"Well," he sighed and folded his arms across his chest. "Let's hear it then."

"I want to learn to fight," Annabelle said. "I'm sick of being helpless, relying on my friends and the kindness of strangers for my protection. I put everyone around me in danger. The least I can do is know how to pull my own weight."

The silence that followed this request was deafening. Even the insects in the field seemed to quiet as Charlie considered his answer. Annabelle waited, chin held high, meeting his gaze unflinchingly.

Finally, Charlie sighed, his shoulders sagging a bit. "Fine. Sam will beat me bloody when he finds out, mind...but you're right. You should at least know how to defend yourself."

Annabelle could have kissed him. "Thank you," she breathed. "I owe you a great debt, Charlie Rabbold."

"And you'll begin paying it back," he said, striding away toward the barn. "This morning."

"I'm sorry, how exactly?" Annabelle hurried after him.

Charlie led her toward the chicken coop that stood at the back of the barn. Grinning widely, he retrieved a basket from the ground beside the coop and gestured toward the little wooden structure that seemed to hum with clucking and rustling.

"Chores," he said. "Everyone at Rabble Farm has them, and now you do too. Each morning, before breakfast, you will collect the eggs."

Annabelle grimaced, eyeing the basket with trepidation. "Chickens?"

Charlie held the basket out for her to take. "Yep," he said. "Chickens."

$$\text{)}\text{))}\bullet\text{((}\text{(}$$

The crackling and popping of the guttering fire filled the silence of the bedchamber as Sam watched Raphael consider the chessboard between them, eyebrows jammed together.

"Just pick a piece and move it," he suggested after a few more minutes had passed. "It's only a game, Raph."

Raphael grunted in response, but he did not make a move.

Sam sighed. Raphael had been like this since he had arrived. Usually, the man was cheerful, glad to see Sam and to partake in their daily game. Today, however, he had been quiet and prickly. With every piece that Sam captured, his expression grew stormy. This was unusual, as Raphael was always such a gracious loser. Now that Sam had him in check, Raphael was refusing to make a single move.

"What is wrong with you today?" Sam demanded, finally losing his temper. He didn't like to admit how much he looked forward to the time they spent together, cloistered in this room; sometimes talking, sometimes not talking. But he couldn't help but feel angry at Raphael's behavior, feeling as if something precious was being stolen from him.

"When were you going to tell me?" Raphael demanded, finally looking up at Sam, his eyes molten with anger.

Sam watched him, suddenly wary. "Tell you what?"

"When were you going to tell me that you're leaving?"

Of course. Sam had spoken with Ilya the day before. He had explained the situation—that he was to leave the city with the court to return to the capital. And she had told Raphael. He should have realized she would.

"I was going to tell you," he lied.

"Were you?" Raphael barked a mirthless laugh. "Because I don't think so. I think you weren't ever going to tell me and that you were planning on leaving me trapped here."

"I was planning no such thing," Sam argued, heat blooming in his belly and across his face. "I have to leave in two days, but Ilya will still be here. When you've healed, she'll be able to smuggle you out of the country, and then—"

Raphael slammed his hands down onto the table, causing several chess pieces to topple over and roll to the floor. "I have told you, Sam Fisher," he growled. "I will not leave this kingdom without Mica."

"And I have told you, you stubborn oxhead, that to rescue the prince would be a suicide mission," Sam snapped. They'd had this argument already, but Raphael had yet to admit defeat. "The king has already had him transported to the capital," he continued. "The castle is swarming with guards, soldiers, noblemen, knights—but you know all of this, Raphael."

"I've beaten you in the ring," Raphael continued on doggedly. "And aren't you supposed to be one of the best?"

"Your humility astounds, as always," Sam drawled, rolling his eyes, "But if there were one hundred of me and only one of you, I'd like those odds."

They glared at each other across the table, neither willing to give ground. Sam was angry, but he wasn't worried. Raphael needed his help, and Ilya's, if he had any prayer of escaping—not to mention if he planned to carry out his harebrained scheme to rescue the prince.

"Look, Raphael," Sam said after a moment, trying to defuse the situation. "I understand your frustration. But there is nothing you can do for him here. The best chance you have to see your prince returned safely home is to go back to Eìrlan and convince King Leo to negotiate for his release."

"Don't you think I've already considered that?" Raphael snorted. "I may be a brute, Sam, but I am capable of some strategic thinking. I *am* the leader of the finest warriors in the world, am I not?"

"Are you? I hadn't realized," Sam said sarcastically.

Raphael ignored this. "Leo is a good man and a good king. He loves his brothers, all of them. But he is not the only ruling voice in the kingdom—something your king seems not to understand. Our council of elders won't allow him to negotiate with a monarch who has so loudly declared himself our enemy. Mica would not want him to either. There will be no negotiation. If Mica is getting out of here alive, I am his only hope."

"I understand," Sam said. And he did, honestly. "But that doesn't make the doing of the thing any less impossible."

Raphael let out a roar of frustration. "It wouldn't be so impossible if you would help me like you helped Annabelle. But no. You'd rather ship me away. Do you really want to be rid of me so badly, Sam?"

"No!" Sam objected before he could stop himself.

Raphael's eyebrows lifted in surprise. "No?"

"I…" Sam cast about desperately, searching for what to say. He settled on the truth. "I don't want to be *rid* of you. I want you to be safe."

And there it was, the reason for everything he had done to help Raphael, to save him. The night of the attack, they had barely known each other, but when the ships went up in flames, Sam had understood, like it was instinct, that he would not be alright until he knew that Raphael was safe. That feeling had only grown in the days they had spent together, and the thought of Raphael running off to the capital to stage a rescue was enough to make Sam want to chain him to the floor.

At his words, the molten anger in Raphael's eyes changed. Sam had seen this heat before. He froze, breathless, terrified that Raphael was going to kiss him again, and also wanting him to so badly he could feel it in his toes. But the moment passed, and Raphael took a deep, steadying breath.

"Sam," he said, and his voice was no longer gruff but soft and kind. "You can't run around keeping everyone you love safe. You're doing it with Annabelle, and now you're doing it with me, and it can't work."

"It has worked," Sam argued, upset at how petulant he sounded. "Annabelle is safe."

"Annabelle is a princess who is supposed to be dead, hiding in the Goddess knows what place, from her own father: a man who will, at best, lock her away for the rest of her life or, at worst, think her a skinwalker wearing his daughter's face and have her executed on sight if she is found. She is not *safe*." He said the words kindly, but still, Sam felt each of them as a challenge.

When Sam continued to look mutinous, Raphael sagged back in his chair, expression solemn. "I *will* try to rescue my cousin, Sam," he said. "There is nothing you can do to stop me. So, you can help me and give me a fighting chance, or you can refuse. Those are your choices. There is no third option."

It was no choice, and Raphael knew it. Sam was in misery. Yet, even as his heart rebelled against this insanity, his mind whirred to life. He began to plan. Raphael waited patiently as Sam worked it through, putting together the pieces of the puzzle. He had been so quick to dismiss the chance of rescuing the prince that he had not considered how it might be done.

And it might. If Sam used every tool in his arsenal and called in every precious favor he had cultivated over the years.

"Very well," he said, at last, meeting Raphael's eyes. "I will help you."

Raphael did not laugh or gloat. He only nodded. "Thank you."

Sam grimaced. "Don't thank me yet. I'm still not convinced that this will work."

"Well, we have two days to plan," Raphael said, retrieving the chess pieces that had fallen to the floor. "Now. Where were we...."

He replaced the pieces on the board and considered for a moment before moving his queen clear across the board.

Raphael grinned at Sam, his eyes dancing. "Checkmate."

Chapter Twenty

The howling rain and wind slapped her face and pulled at her cloak as she made her careful way down the rocky coastline toward the beach. At regular intervals, the flash of lightning illuminated the world—the hulking outline of the wreck, driven onto the rocks by the storm; the foaming curse of the waves as they battered the island; trees bent double against the onslaught.

Despite the ferocity of the storm, she pressed on, searching. She could hear them as if their voices were carried to her on the wind. The vitality that still flickered in their veins tickled her face with every drop of rain. Life. Despite the horror of the wreck and the unforgiving sea, there was life on this beach—two guttering flames, weak but undeniably real.

Movement caught her attention, and she moved more quickly toward the dark outline of a figure upon the beach. The man pushed to his elbows as she approached, vomiting seawater onto the already sodden beach. She knelt in the sand beside him and helped him to a sitting position. His life force grew brighter with each passing moment.

"Are you alright?" She had to shout to make her voice heard.

The man nodded and attempted to stand, but she held him in place. "Wait here," she said. "I will search the beach for more survivors."

She made to stand, but firm hands gripped her cloak, and wide eyes found hers. She could see the whites all the way around. "Find him," the man begged her. "Find—he...he can't be...."

"I will do what I can," she replied. "But you must let me go."

The desperate man obeyed, and she was free, setting off again down the beach in search of the second flame that even now was growing dimmer and dimmer. There was another dark figure, illuminated in another flash of light. This one was not moving. Rushing now, she fell to her knees beside the man and, with great effort, turned him onto his back. There was a gash in his forehead, though the wound looked shallow, and he was breathing.

After several unsuccessful attempts to rouse the man, she stood and returned to the first survivor. If she wanted to get the unconscious sailor to her cottage, she would need help.

"There is a man further down the beach," she told him. "He's alive but unconscious. Do you think you can stand? I'll need help to get him inside."

The man pushed unsteadily to his feet, wavered, and then stood tall. "Lead me to him," he croaked.

They returned together to the unconscious man. At times, her companion stumbled. She moved to help him, but he waved her off, eyes bright with intent. When they, at last, reached the unconscious man, her companion fell to his knees, his strangled cry swallowed by the roar of thunder and the crashing of the waves. Together, they carried the man up the beach toward the cottage.

Safe within the walls, they lay the man upon her small bed. He was so tall his feet hung over the edge, but it was the best that could be done. The other man sank into a chair beside the table, looking gaunt and haunted.

"You have to save him," the man rasped. "Please."

"I will do my best." She took stock of the man's injuries. He was young and strong, like his friend. There was no reason he could not recover if only she could find...there. A dark shadow moved through his body, leaving destruction in its wake. It must be expelled and quickly.

Moving to the cabinet where she kept her remedies, she selected a small glass bottle with a cork stopper. Sending a prayer to the Goddess, she unstoppered the bottle and poured the contents down the man's throat. The shadow paused but was not expelled. One minute. Two minutes.

Frustrated, she lay her hands on either side of the face. Words formed and tumbled from her lips in an uninterrupted stream, and light began to glow at the places where her skin touched his. The other man gave a chirp of alarm, but she ignored him, completely and utterly focused on her task.

The body lurched, and she moved aside as the man leaned over the side of the bed and vomited seawater, sand, and something black and oozing onto the wood floor.

"That's it," she soothed, rubbing the man's back as he expelled the death from his body. "That's it. Get it all out."

When the retching ceased, the man fell back against the pillow, scrubbing his mouth on the back of his hand. "W—what happened?" He stammered, shaking. "The ship...we—"

"Shh," she said, laying a hand upon his. "It's alright. You're safe now."

He looked up at her, and their eyes met—his own shone with fear and confusion in the light from her fire, two orbs of the clearest emerald green she had ever seen.

)))●(((

Annabelle jerked into consciousness, gasping and trembling. Her head was pounding, and she pressed the heels of her hands into her eyes. Images swam in her mind, looming out of the darkness.

The storm, so much like the other storm she had dreamed—that shipwreck. The man...those eyes; they were just like her eyes.

Her father's eyes.

Suddenly restless and very much awake, even though the sky outside her window had only just begun to pale with the coming dawn, Annabelle fetched her dressing gown and wandered down to the farmhouse kitchen.

Annabelle plopped onto one of the benches with a sigh, cradling her head in her hands. How she wished she knew what these dreams meant and why they were so much more than dreams—terrifying in their clarity and detail. She had been so hopeful that they would stop now that she was safe from the danger of the city and the palace.

But you aren't out of danger, a little voice reminded her. *You are in a new place, surrounded by strangers.*

Annabelle sat alone in the kitchen until the gray of pre-dawn filled the room and spilled across the field and trees beyond. It was so peaceful that for a moment, Annabelle forgot all about the dream and just stared out the window, watching the world outside come into focus.

A noise disturbed her reverie, and she turned to see Charlie stepping off the stairs.

He was once again dressed in simple clothes, the neck of his shirt open to reveal his muscled chest, thick hair tousled from sleep. If he was surprised to see her there, he didn't show it as he sauntered down the hall to the kitchen. He was carrying a bulky pile of...something.

"You're awake," he said. "Good." He placed a set of clothes—soft brown breeches and a cotton shirt—upon the table, setting a pair of boots beside them. "Get dressed. Training starts now."

)))●(((

By the time the sun had fully risen, Annabelle felt like she had been chewed up, spit out, chased by wolves, and then pounded by hammers on every inch of her body.

Charlie began her training with a run around the outer edge of the field. The first circuit went well, and Annabelle felt flushed and warm when they reached the barn again. But then Charlie kept running, and Annabelle's heart sank. Of course, it wasn't over so quickly.

They ran and ran, around and around, until Annabelle vomited. Only then did Charlie agree that it was time to stop—time to stop running, anyway. Next, he set her performing a seemingly endless set of drills to condition her arms, legs, and core.

"I thought you were going to teach me to defend myself," she complained when he told her to carry two buckets filled with water down one length of the animal paddock and back, twenty times.

"I am," was his terse reply. "I am making you strong. I am giving you endurance."

"But what use are those things?" Annabelle protested. "I need to learn to fight and to wield a blade."

"A blade won't do you any good if you aren't strong enough to hold your own in a fight," he replied calmly. "Only when I believe you aren't more of a danger to yourself than others can we talk about weapons. Now, get on with it. Those buckets aren't going to carry themselves."

While she performed her seemingly endless list of tasks, Charlie moved through his usual morning routine with the broadsword. *I may not be allowed to hold a blade yet*, Annabelle thought mutinously as she hefted the buckets once more, *but I can still watch and learn*. So she did watch him closely as she carried her buckets.

His movements were so fluid that one might have thought his weapon weighed no more than a feather in his hand, though Annabelle was confident nothing could be further from the truth. The sight of him was distracting—the way his body tensed and lengthened with each step and thrust of the blade, the lines of his strong jaw, the way the dawn sun made the gold streaks in his hair glow.

There was a crash, and Annabelle yelped in shock as water sloshed over her legs and down into her boots. She had been so distracted watching Charlie that she had walked right into a fencepost and dropped both her buckets of water. Charlie turned to see her standing there, red-faced and dripping, and roared with laughter.

Face burning with humiliation, Annabelle seized the empty buckets and stomped off to fill them again, resolving not to speak to Charlie again for the rest of the day.

Eventually, Charlie dismissed Annabelle, allowing her to limp back up to the house to clean up before chores and breakfast. As she scrubbed the dirt and sweat from her aching body as best she could in her tiny washbasin, shivering at the frigid water, Annabelle wondered what she had gotten herself into.

It will be worth it, she admitted to herself, *if I stop putting all the people I care about in danger. It will be worth it. I hope it will be worth it.* Still, she was in such a foul mood that she knew if one of the chickens tried to peck her, she could not be held accountable for her actions.

When Annabelle stomped down the stairs for breakfast, Bess took one look at her stormy expression and enlisted her help in the garden, pulling weeds. Annabelle thought this might be as much to keep her away from Charlie as anything else, but she was glad to be spared the more exciting barnyard chores all the same.

Annabelle knelt gratefully on the soft earth, happy to have the repetitive work and the company of the jovial housekeeper who kept up a ceaseless stream of stories and gardening tips that well and truly distracted Annabelle from the weight of her cares and questions.

When half the garden was free of weeds and pests, and Bess's wicker basket was brimming with vegetables for the midday meal, Bess suggested they pause to prepare lunch.

Annabelle, whose stomach grumbled in agreement, rose from where she knelt among the beanstalks, brushing the dirt from her hands and smiling. It surprised her how much she enjoyed such work, but there was something entirely satisfying about doing something worthwhile—something that could be begun and completed.

Before she can follow Bess into the kitchen, Annabelle was distracted by the sound of hoofbeats. She lifted a hand to shield her eyes from the sun in time to see a lone horse and rider galloping up the dirt road toward the farm.

Fear gripped her as she watched the rider approach, and she quickly ran through her story in her head: who she had been and why she was here. Charlie had said that nobody they trusted would ever betray them, but his assurances did nothing to quell her alarm.

The approaching hoofbeats summoned Charlie from within the barn. He was clutching a shovel and looked solemn as he approached the road. Annabelle watched the entire scene, wanting to run, to hide, but knowing that she could do nothing of the sort. If she ran, if the rider saw her run, that would only arouse suspicion. And so she waited as the horse stopped before the farmhouse, and a small woman dismounted, throwing back the hood of her cloak.

A moment later, Annabelle was running for the front of the house, fear and worry replaced by joy that pricked at the corners of her eyes.

"Steady on!" Bess squawked as she tore through the kitchen on her way to the front door, but Annabelle ignored her, wrenching the door open and stepping out onto the path beyond. She stopped, breathless, and smiled at the young woman who stood before her, clenching a saddlebag and looking at her with wide eyes.

"Emily," Annabelle breathed, staring in disbelief, tears welling in her eyes.

Emily dropped the saddlebag, hands going to her mouth. "No," she gasped, shaking her head as if attempting to disagree with her own eyes. "It can't be…."

"I'm sorry I couldn't tell you." Annabelle's smile faded as she realized that her friend might not be entirely pleased to see her. "I'm…Sam said I couldn't, but Emily, I *wanted* to so badly." She was desperate for Emily to believe her, to forgive her.

Emily did not seem capable of speech. "Y…". She tried once, then swallowed, tears rolling down her cheeks. "Y—you're alive. Oh…oh *Annabelle*."

And then the girls were running into each other's arms, crying and laughing and clutching each other so tight they could have cracked a rib. But Annabelle didn't care. Having Emily there, being able to hug her and look into her face was like not being so alone anymore.

"But what are you doing here?" Annabelle said when she had calmed down enough to let go, pawing at the wetness on her cheeks. "Did Sam tell you to come?"

Emily frowned quizzically. "Sam? No, of course not. This is my home."

Annabelle blinked at her. "Your...what?"

"Hullo, Em." A deep voice sounded behind Emily, and she turned to see Charlie standing a few paces away, grinning from ear to ear.

"Charlie!" Emily squealed, leaping into his arms. He lifted her off her feet and spun her around in the air once before setting her back down.

"Little sister," he said, clutching her hands to his chest. "It is so good to see you."

"*Sister?*" Annabelle gaped at the pair of them. Emily giggled.

"I told you I used to live on a farm," she explained. "And that my father died two years ago, yes?"

"You did, but I didn't realize...." But the truth Annabelle had missed finally clicked into place.

This was the farm. The farmer who had died was her father who had died. And Charlie was Emily's brother. Now that she saw them together, Annabelle didn't know how she hadn't seen it—the two siblings had the same shape to their faces and the same amused tilt of their smiles as they watched Annabelle reel in the wake of this revelation.

"How did this happen?" Emily asked, looking between Charlie and Annabelle with a bewildered expression. "I mean, not that I'm displeased...."

"Come inside," Charlie said, scooping her bags from where they had fallen. "We'll tell you everything over lunch. Bess is just making it now."

Emily let out a groan of longing. "You know I still dream about Bess's cooking sometimes."

"I know what you mean," Annabelle said, wrapping her arm around her friend's shoulders as they walked up the path toward the house together. "And I also finally understand your grudge against chickens."

The peal of Emily's bright laughter rang in Annabelle's soul, breathing life into a piece of her heart that she had not realized had died.

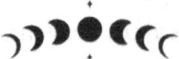

"You have to be joking."

Emily sat across from Annabelle and Charlie at the kitchen table, fork suspended over her plate of food, a piece of boiled potato skewered on its end. She put the fork down without eating and let out a long breath, eyes wide. "To think you were alive the whole time." She shook her head. "I cannot believe you managed to escape."

Annabelle couldn't believe it either, really. "I wouldn't have managed it without Sam, and if Charlie hadn't been willing to take me in, I don't know where I would have gone."

"I'm only happy to have had a safe place to offer you," Charlie said.

He had remained quiet while Annabelle told Emily her story.

Emily nodded her agreement. "The maids talk," she said. "As you know. From the gossip, I'm certain that things were bad before we ever arrived at the palace. The horrible part is that, when the king attacked the Eìrlani delegation, nobody was surprised." She gave an involuntary shudder. "Horrified, obviously, but not shocked. I heard Lisa telling

Rosemary that the cabinet ministers were already unhappy with the king, but they hoped that your marriage to Mica was a sign that he had come to his senses at last. But now…" she shook her head, falling silent.

"Without the alliance with Eìrlan, we will begin to lose ground in the north," Charlie said, expression grim. "And now we've made a powerful enemy in King Leo."

"We *think* we've made a powerful enemy," Emily reminded him. "But we don't really know anything about the scope of Eìrlan's forces, do we?"

"We don't," Charlie admitted. "Still, it won't help us to be fighting a war on more than one side."

"Would he attack, even if the king holds his brother hostage?" Annabelle asked, alarmed.

Charlie sighed, thinking. "Perhaps not. But nothing is stopping him from providing aid to the rebellion in secret. I don't know how… but that doesn't mean it's impossible. With his own children and many brothers in line for the throne, he may take the risk."

Annabelle groaned. "This is a mess," she said. "And now I'm in no position to do anything about it. Perhaps I ought to have stayed. Maybe I could have…I don't know…persuaded the king to see reason?"

Emily gaped at her. "How can you say that? It sounds like he was willing to lock you away in…a tower or a dungeon or something. You did the right thing running from him."

"It was lucky that you managed to escape," Charlie agreed with a solemn nod.

Annabelle felt a slight twinge of shame. She had once again omitted the more…fantastic details of that night. Annabelle began to lose her grip on the truth with every retelling, and it felt terrible to lie to her friends.

"I suppose you're right," she said with a heavy sigh. "Anyway, Sam wouldn't hear of me staying, not after he saw my…the body. Though I admit, I still have a hard time believing what he *thinks* he saw is even possible."

Emily and Charlie exchanged a long, silent look.

"What?" Annabelle asked, feeling suddenly left out and cranky.

"It's nothing," Emily said soothingly, extending a hand and laying it atop Annabelle's. "We're just worried about you. You've been through such an ordeal already, and…and you're right. It is strange. And there's so much we still don't know…."

"I know," Annabelle said. "And it's alright. I mean," she winced, "it isn't. But I'll be alright. I promise."

"Good," Emily smiled sadly at her. Then, abruptly, she got to her feet. "Well," she said, "I'm off to father's study."

"Whatever for?" Charlie demanded, frowning.

"Answers," she replied simply and headed off in the direction of the study.

Charlie watched her go, frowning slightly, before muttering something about checking on the animals and sauntering out the back of the kitchen toward the barn. Needing some occupation to calm her busy mind, Annabelle decided to help Bess clear the table.

She had lied to Emily when she said she would be alright. She didn't know if she would be alright, not after everything that had happened and everything that might still happen. Yet, as she scrubbed the plates clean, it occurred to Annabelle that perhaps she had been more truthful than she knew.

Now that Emily had returned to the farm, and Annabelle once again felt that strength that came from being surrounded by her friends, she could not deny that she felt better.

Chapter Twenty-One

"Focus, Annabelle."

"I'm *trying!*"

"Try harder."

Annabelle was exhausted, and every inch of her body screamed in pain. She had been at the farm for two weeks, and Charlie had only begun to show her some self-defense drills that morning. So far, the experience was proving more disheartening than Annabelle could have imagined. She was weak, her responses were slow and clumsy, so she was sent careening to the ground, often.

Charlie was not deterred by her inability to perform even the simplest defensive maneuver. He simply waited for her to pick herself up before moving forward to put her body into another inescapable bind or lock. Annabelle very much regretting bullying him into showing her more practical techniques, thinking longingly of her strengthening exercises and those infernal buckets of water.

"You're so much larger than me," Annabelle complained as she pushed herself to her feet for what felt like the millionth time that morning. "I'm sure if I could practice with someone my own size—"

"If you could practice with someone your own size who had my skill and training, you'd still wind up brushing dirt off the backside of your breeches," he cut in. "Size is just an excuse, Annabelle. There is no reason you shouldn't be able to throw me off with enough time and practice. Now, we go again."

"I need a break," Annabelle groaned, stretching out her aching back. "And water."

"What you need," he argued, crossing his arms in front of his chest and looking stern, "is to run the drill again."

They stared each other down. Annabelle felt like screaming at him. It was hot out, and she was dirty, tired, and thirsty. This was nothing like she had imagined. *This* was not glamorous. *This* was not fun. *This* felt less like being taught to do something and more like having something beaten into her.

"Come on, Charlie," Annabelle said, turning toward the well and walking away. "Just let me get some water, at l—"

Muscled arms seized her from behind, wrapping around her waist, pinning her arms to her sides. Annabelle shrieked, writhing in Charlie's iron grasp, unable to do a thing as he lifted her off her feet.

"Fight back," he growled in her ear. "I've taught you what to do. Now fight back."

But Annabelle could not think. She was only terror and rage and pain. Trapped. He had her *trapped*. Something searingly hot and cold stabbed down the back of her throat like a knife as she fought for freedom. *No more cages, no more cages, NO MORE CAGES!*

Bright light flashed, and Annabelle was suddenly falling painfully to her knees as Charlie's grip loosened, and he was blasted off of her, slamming hard to his back several paces away.

Annabelle lurched to her feet and whirled around, suddenly gripped by an entirely different kind of panic. Charlie still lay on his back, limbs splayed wide across the grass, gasping as if trying to find his breath. Annabelle ran to him and dropped to her knees, frantic.

"Charlie!" She gasped. "Charlie, I—I'm so sorry. I—" But precisely what she would say to explain what had just happened, she did not know.

But Charlie was already recovering his breath and his senses. Sitting up, he gave her a look that turned her blood to ice. He didn't look afraid or confused. Charlie looked enraged. Annabelle fell silent, scrambling backward away from him as he stood, cursing.

"Gods above, Annabelle," he snapped. "You should have told me!"

Annabelle blinked up at him, very much wrong-footed. "I… what are you—"

"What's going on?" Emily had joined them. She was breathing hard as if she had run from the farmhouse. "Charlie, I saw—"

Charlie rounded on his sister, cutting her off mid-sentence. "Did you know?"

Emily looked just as taken aback as Annabelle felt. "Charlie, what are you talking about?"

"I am talking about," Charlie said through gritted teeth, clearly trying to rein in his temper, "the fact that in all the time that I have given this woman shelter—risking the lives of everyone I care about, and everything that father built—nobody thought to mention that *she*," he brandished an accusatory finger in Annabelle's direction, "is a *witch*."

Annabelle knelt in the grass, staring down at her hands, sitting palm-up in her lap, Charlie's words echoing in her mind. Witch. She's a witch. These were stranger's hands. This body was unfamiliar to her. How could it be hers when it could do things without her consent? When it could lash out? When it could hurt not only her enemies but also her friends.

And yet, what he had said could not be possible. Could it?

"How?" The word escaped her like a sigh, quiet as a prayer.

Emily knelt beside her. "How?"

Annabelle looked up, meeting her friend's eyes. They were so wide and concerned that her heart ached.

"How can I be a...a *witch*?" Annabelle asked, voice breaking. How is it possible? Magic...magic is not..." She fell silent again. *Magic is not real*, she had wanted to say, but she remembered what Herbert had said, and Ilya, and all that she had seen since she had left the sheltered halls of Rosewood Manor.

"You truly did not know?" Emily's voice was soft and kind.

Annabelle shook her head, tears springing to her eyes. "I...I didn't mean to do it. Charlie, I'm so sorry. I don't know what's happening to me."

Charlie's face had gone very still as he looked at her. "You didn't do it on purpose?"

"No."

"But..." his wild eyes sought his sister's. "Emily, that's not possible."

Emily wrapped her arm around Annabelle's shoulders. "Come inside, Annabelle," she urged. "We'll get you some tea, and we'll... we'll talk. Alright?"

Without protest, Annabelle allowed Emily to lead her back into the house. The boundaries of her world feeling more fragile than they ever had before.

)））●(((

"It all happened so fast. One minute I was tied up, and the next...I just ran for it. I didn't have time to think about what had happened. After a while, I think I convinced myself it hadn't happened...or that I'd imagined it? I'm not sure."

The three of them sat together in the study. Annabelle clutched a mug of tea and spoke into its depths as she told them the truth, beginning with her dreams and ending with her flight from the temple of the Gods.

Emily and Charlie listened without interruption, but Annabelle had not been able to bring herself to look at them. It was easier to just look at the mug in her hands without really seeing it.

"I hoped the dreams would stop now that I'm away from the palace," she continued. "But I had another one, just before we started training. I should have said something then."

"Was it a new dream?" Emily asked.

"Yes," Annabelle replied, looking up at last. "I was...on a beach, and there had been a shipwreck. I found two men still alive on the shore. One of them was my father. I...healed him, I think. Though it was unlike any healing I've ever seen."

Annabelle hesitated before letting the final truth spill from her like blood from an open wound.

"I think…the woman, the person that I become in these dreams…I think it's my mother. I think I'm reliving her memories."

Charlie and Emily exchanged dark looks.

"If the queen was a witch," Charlie said, "that would explain your abilities well enough."

"It would," Emily agreed. "But that is about all it explains. Why didn't anybody know that the queen was a witch? And why would she not tell her own daughter if there was a chance that Annabelle would inherit her abilities?"

"I don't know," Charlie admitted, scrubbing a hand across his face. "Gods, this is a disaster, isn't it?"

"It also doesn't explain the nature of the magic," Emily continued. "Annabelle worked a spell, without meaning to, and without any object to focus her power. I've never heard of any witch being able to do such a thing."

"We don't know that," Charlie argued, eyeing Annabelle closely. "She could have used…something. And as for her dreams—"

"Don't be an idiot, Charlie," Emily cut across him. "You two were sparring, for the Gods sake. She's wearing a shirt and trousers. She's not wearing an amulet, and she can't have had time to cast a proper spell."

"How do you two know all of this?" Annabelle cut in, suddenly irritated at being talked about like she was no there. "Only weeks ago, I thought magic was a thing of stories, and now I feel like the rug has been ripped out beneath my entire world. But you two are going on about…about witches and magic like…like you see such things every day. What aren't you telling me?"

They exchanged a guilty look.

"We don't see magic every day," Emily hastened to explain. "There aren't many witches left in the realm. But…" she hesitated, looking desperately at her brother for assistance.

"You're right," Charlie said simply. "We do know some things about witches. Our father taught us about them, and we have some books on magic hidden away. But we have to be careful, Annabelle. Witchcraft is forbidden in Dunea. Even speaking about such things is considered treason against the crown."

This revelation sent Annabelle's mind spinning. "But…why?"

"Ask Em," Charlie shrugged. "She's the history enthusiast, not me."

Emily gave her brother a disapproving look but asked Annabelle gently, "What do you know about the Great War?"

"I…" Annabelle tried to remember what Lord Roger had told her. "I know that it began two hundred…no, two hundred and fifty years ago, when Prince Elthre led a revolt against his brother, King Isre."

"Your ancestor," Emily nodded. "Do you know why Elthre rebelled against his king?"

"The priests say he was an evil man who served a false God, but Lord Roger believed he just wanted power for himself, and he nearly got it." Annabelle shrugged. "It's why Eìrlan has always hated us. The clans fought on Elthre's side."

"That is what is told," Charlie chimed in. "But it is only one piece of the full story."

"What we know—and it isn't much," Emily said apologetically. "Is that there is magic in the rest of the world, and there used to be magic here—*more* magic—before the war. There was even a place within the realm that was sacred to the witches, though we don't know where—though we think it was somewhere in the north."

Magic. In Dunea. And only a hundred years ago. Annabelle tried to imagine it but was unable to fathom such a thing.

"There was also a council of kings," Emily went on. "Rulers from the kingdoms of Dunea, Petra, Aelnìr, Pharos, and Demos. Ennen, the first king of Dunea, founded the council as a way to maintain balance and peace between the kingdoms."

"Fat lot of good it did, in the end," Charlie grumbled.

"Well…it did work for about five hundred years," Emily pointed out, then she sighed sadly. "But then there was a plague; the worst plague our kingdom has ever seen. It took Isre and Elthre's father, King Owen, as well as his queen, and countless others."

"Isre had not been king for long when things went bad," Charlie said. "His wife fell gravely ill with the sickness."

"This is where the history gets a bit tricky," Emily added, frowning. "It's hard to tell if Elthre was himself a witch or if he was simply a man of learning who associated with the witches of Dunea. Either way, Isre ordered the witches who had gifts of healing to cure his wife… but they failed."

Annabelle's insides felt cold as she listened to this story. She was beginning to see where it was leading, and she dreaded its conclusion.

"There was a priest by the name of Crispin, who was the spiritual advisor to Isre," Emily continued. "He took advantage of the king's grief—convinced him that the plague was punishment for allowing magic to run unchecked in our world, which was why it was so resistant to magical healing."

"But the plague has always been resistant to healing," Annabelle said, unable to keep quiet a moment longer. She felt, irrationally, that if she could convince Emily that this way of thinking was madness, she could change the course of history itself.

"I know, Annabelle," Emily said sadly. "But King Isre had lost his father, his mother, and now his wife. He needed someone to blame, and so he blamed the witches. Elthre tried to convince his brother to see sense, of course, but Isre banished him from the kingdom. He fled north and joined with Pharos and the clans of Eìrlan to try to reclaim the kingdom and protect the witches. Ultimately they failed, obviously, and the kingdom of Pharos was reduced to ashes."

"The northern province," Annabelle murmured. "That's why they keep rebelling against the crown."

Emily nodded, but it was Charlie who said, "It wasn't enough for Isre to decimate their land, but he lay claim to it as well. Though it's hard to control, isolated as it is on the other side of the mountains."

"But…" Annabelle frowned. "You fought them, Charlie."

"I did," he said. "And I'd do it again. It was terrible what happened to them, but they don't have a real chance of winning this rebellion. Their ceaseless attacks are causing suffering for people here who never did a thing against them."

"I'm sorry," Annabelle said quickly. "I didn't mean to accuse you of anything. I'm just trying to wrap my head around all of this."

"That's alright," Charlie said, and the corner of his mouth tugged into the shadow of a smile. The sight of it filled Annabelle with the hope that she was indeed forgiven.

"What happened to the witches?" She asked, fearing the answer.

"Isre had them rounded up and slaughtered," Emily said grimly. "Every man, woman, and child he could get his hands on."

"That's horrible!" Annabelle breathed. "Even the children?"

"Magical abilities run in families," Emily explained. "Many powerful bloodlines were extinguished in a matter of days. After that, Isre established the priests as the moral guides of the kingdom, and they began erasing magic from our history."

"And the healers?" Annabelle asked.

"That bit is unclear," Emily admitted. "I think that Crispin convinced Isre to spare the women with healing magic and send them to serve as priestesses. Managing to seize power in the kingdom, only to drop dead from a cold or infection...I don't think that was a very attractive prospect."

"Ilya has a girl, a healer," Annabelle remembered. "She said she was keeping her safe from the temple."

"And it's a good thing, too," Charlie said. "the life of a healer is a horrible one. They are...bred, to create new generations of healers," he added, face twisted in disgust, "by members of the priesthood."

Annabelle's stomach heaved at his words, rebelling against this new horrible revelation. "Surely not...all members of the priesthood," she asked, her thoughts filled with Herbert. He had been her friend, and he had spoken of magic.

"No, not all," Emily said kindly. "Remember that joining the priesthood is the only option for some men in the kingdom. Some men join for the ability to learn and to travel. But...some seek power."

Annabelle nodded her understanding, relieved. "So...just like that, magic vanished, and the entire kingdom forgot it ever existed?"

"Well, not the entire kingdom," Emily said. "Discussing such things is forbidden, and so it's no surprise that you would have grown up without ever hearing of it. No lord or lady would raise a child to believe in magic or witches. But there is still a fair amount of general knowledge and superstition among the common people."

"Your father knew," Annabelle pointed out. "And he taught you both."

"He never told us how he knew so much," Charlie said, chewing on his lower lip pensively. "No matter how much Emily pestered him about it."

"I never pestered him!" She protested. "It was a fair question to ask."

"Our father cared about people," Charlie said with a shrug. "I always figured it was just another way he was teaching us to help."

They sat in silence for a while, each of them lost in their own thoughts about all that had been shared. Annabelle's head hurt, and her heart was so tired from absorbing the atrocities perpetrated by her own people, by her own family. Once upon a time, she had felt the weight of responsibility to uphold her family's legacy. Now it felt like a legacy of ashes and blood.

But there were still loose threads tugging at Annabelle's mind— nagging questions, holes that the story had yet to fill.

"Witches. Can…can they…could they transform a body—a dead body?" Annabelle asked haltingly.

"I'd never heard of such a thing before," Emily admitted, looking a bit sick. "But…it is possible."

"And…" Annabelle paused, considering the best way to ask the next question. "Before…you said that I did magic without," She frowned, trying to remember, "Without something to focus my power. What does that mean?"

Emily shifted uncomfortably in her chair. "Witches require objects to perform spells: plants, stones, water—something to channel the power into the desired result. There are incantations and rituals required, even from the most powerful witch. Without the objects or rituals, the spell cannot work. When you...when that light came out of you, there was no object and no incantation. You just..." She trailed off, waving a hand vaguely through the air.

"From the sound of it, your mother didn't require a ritual or object to perform magic either," Charlie added. "Unless there's something you can remember—something that didn't seem significant to you before."

"There's nothing," Annabelle said. "It just came from within her, just like it did with me."

"What interests me most," Emily said thoughtfully, drumming the tips of her fingers against the side of her mug, "is the first dream you described to us. You said your mother used symbols to do...well... whatever it was she was trying to do."

Annabelle nodded. "Yes. She...drew them, I suppose, in light that came from her hands."

"Do you remember the symbols well enough to draw them? In ink, I mean," Emily added when Annabelle looked alarmed.

Annabelle closed her eyes, trying to remember. The image of the circle of light, the symbols drawn within it, formed clearly in her mind's eye. She opened her eyes again and took the quill Emily held out to her. With as much detail as she could manage, Annabelle recreated the symbols on a piece of parchment.

Emily took the picture when Annabelle was finished and inspected it, frowning. "I feel like I've seen symbols like this before," she said, almost to herself. "I'll have a look through father's books. I haven't discovered anything yet about the kind of magic required to transform a dead body, but perhaps this will yield greater results."

So that was what Emily had been doing, shut up in this room all day. Annabelle felt a surge of gratitude and affection for her friend. The panic that had gripped her began to dissipate.

Charlie was staring out the study window and bouncing his leg as if itching to escape through it. Annabelle did not know what to say. She wanted to fix whatever rift had split open between them. All at once, she felt how precious their budding friendship had become to her and the pang of fear that she would lose it in one ill-fated split-second flash.

"Thank you," she said quietly, "Thank you for teaching me. But you don't have to train with me anymore. I mean…I understand if you don't want to anymore."

Charlie's attention snapped back from the window, and he frowned at her as he rose from his chair. "You'll not be rid of me so easily, princess," he said, moving toward the door. "I'll fetch you from your room tomorrow at dawn. No tricks this time, mind. I expect a fair fight from you from now on."

Annabelle smiled at his back as the door swung wide. "You've got a deal, soldier."

Emily watched this exchange—the way Charlie paused on the threshold, the sudden flush rising in Annabelle's cheeks—without comment.

Annabelle and Emily sat together for a while, staring down at the drawing on the table between them.

"Why would he have married her?" Annabelle asked, the question bubbling up from some secret, fearful corner of her heart. "If he knew she was…whatever she was—a witch, or something else…why did my father marry her?"

"Maybe he didn't know," Emily suggested. "Maybe he didn't care. Either way," she sighed. "Your guess is as good as mine."

There had been countless moments over the years when Annabelle missed her mother so much it stole the breath from her body. Now, staring down at her awkward drawing, cold and lifeless upon the page, for the first time, Annabelle felt angry that the one person who could answer all of her questions had left her alone in one great burst of light.

Chapter Twenty-Two

The camp was tranquil as Ronan made his way to the king's tent. When they had made their way south to Ellasport, the night was always filled with the sounds of celebration. The nobles of the court loved a good expedition, especially with teams of servants seeing to their every whim and a legion of guards to keep their precious possessions and bodies safe.

In the wake of the princess's funeral, however, the court had been subdued. A more forgiving person might have called this change of behavior a sign of respect, but Ronan knew better. It was a sign of fear.

Even as he moved among the tents, he could feel eyes following him, could hear mutterings. It was an unwelcome feeling, but not entirely unexpected. He was the king's most trusted advisor and friend, his right hand. In the court's eyes, he was as much to blame for recent events as the king. He could not blame them for their suspicions—all the more reason to make preparations for their arrival in Rengon, now.

The king was sitting at his table when Ronan arrived—his plate of food untouched, wine goblet hanging loosely in his hand, staring into nothingness.

"Sire," Ronan said, bowing low.

The king jolted a bit and looked around. "Oh, it's you. Ronan. Sit down, would you?"

Ronan sat, feeling a bit apprehensive. He had known Alex for many years and seen him in many states of passion, heartbreak, sorrow, and even madness. This vacancy of spirit alarmed him in ways that the other versions of himself had not.

"Is there anything I can do for you, your Grace?" He asked soothingly.

The king only looked down into his wine goblet, sighed, and set it on the table. "I miss her," he said. "Is that the oddest thing? The child spent her whole life away from me, but I miss her now all the same."

"I am not a father," Ronan said carefully. "But I do not think there is anything at all strange in how you feel."

The king smiled then, his eyes wet. "You are a good friend, Ronan. You have always been a good friend, to me, and to…Ilenna."

A friend. Yes, he had been a friend. And look what good his friendship had done. Ilenna was dead. Annabelle was dead. And the king? That remained to be seen.

"It is because I am your friend that I come to you now," he said, eager to have the matter settled and to escape this macabre tent.

"There is something wrong," the king said, regarding Ronan as if he were seeing him sitting there for the first time. "Tell me what it is."

"It is the court, Sire," Ronan said. "They are afraid."

"But the danger has passed, has it not?" The king remarked. "Why should they be afraid now?"

"Forgive me, your grace…but there have been questions about the succession."

"Ah." The king took up his goblet again, swirling the wine within. But he did not drink from it. He simply stared into it once more, expression anguished. "I do not wish to speak of this now," he said.

"We must speak of it now," Ronan pressed. "I am sorry, Sire. I know this is a…a horrible time to think of such things, but we have no choice. You are not young as you once were, and if you were to be taken from this world without an heir, the kingdom would plunge into chaos. The rebels in the north would have us between their teeth. It is imperative that you marry again, and soon, if for no other reason than to quell the tide of unrest sweeping through your court."

It was a bold and risky move to pressure the king in this way, but Ronan was out of time and options. The king needed to hear these hard truths, and it was Ronan's lot to be the one to speak them.

The king took a long sip of wine, and for a moment, Ronan feared he would lose the man to another fit of madness. But when the king once again set the goblet upon the table and looked up, his eyes were clear.

"You are right, as always" he said. "I consent to marry, even though I do so reluctantly. I assume you have a candidate in mind?"

Ronan nodded. "I do, Sire. Lady Emilia Adalara."

"The Countess of Lamara?" The king frowned slightly. "But she is Aelnìra."

"Exactly so, your grace. The lady is wealthy and a favorite of King Francis. An alliance with Aelnìr would go far toward putting the minds of the court and the cabinet at ease. Lady Emilia's wealth would help fund our war with the northern rebels and cement our unsteady alliance with her homeland. Perhaps in time, she may even convince Francis to intervene in the north on our behalf."

"Yes, I see." The king sighed. "It is a good plan, Ronan. You have done well."

"Thank you, your grace." He hesitated. "May I arrange the marriage for when we arrive in Rengon?"

"You may—but Ronan," the king placed a hand on Ronan's before he could rise from his chair. "Let's not make a fuss. This is a marriage of strategy and convenience. I will not treat it as anything more. Do you understand?"

"Yes, Sire. I understand."

"Very good. You may go."

Ronan rose from his chair, bowed, and moved toward the exit.

"You have always been a good friend to me, Ronan" the king said again from behind him. Ronan turned and met those piercing emerald eyes. "I can trust you, can't I?"

"Of course you can, Sire."

The king said nothing more, and so Ronan stepped out of his tent and into the cool night air, feeling more unsettled than he had before entering.

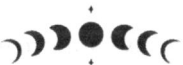

Despite the excitement provoked by Annabelle's recent outburst of power, life at the farm began to fall into something like a routine.

Each morning Annabelle awoke and dressed in the soft breeches and shirts that Charlie and Emily provided for her and waited patiently on her bed for Charlie to unlock her door. She then followed him, usually in stony silence, down to the field to undergo that morning's beating.

She was getting stronger and better. Though Charlie was so much stronger and better than she was that she hardly seemed to be making any progress at all.

He sent Annabelle tumbling to the ground so many times that her backside was bruised and aching by sun-up. Still, Annabelle always stood and brushed herself off, ready for another go. She didn't want to give Charlie any more reason to disapprove of her.

As it was, he could barely look her in the eye these days. His cold silence, and the curt, businesslike manner in which he conducted their training sessions, made Annabelle's heart ache. She hadn't realized how fond she had become of the farmer. Now that his laughter and flashing smiles had faded away, she felt their absence like a knife to the gut.

Annabelle sought guidance from Bess whenever they worked together in the garden, but the old woman would only chuckle and say, "Men need their own time to wrap their minds around things. Just give him space, and he'll be back to his old self in no time. Just you wait and see."

This, though unhelpful, was far more helpful than Emily's advice, which was to "Forget about my stupid brother and his moods and help me with my research."

"Um…" Annabelle eyed the ominous stack of books set upon the desk that nearly obscured Emily from view. "Actually, I'm meant to help Bess in the kitchen."

It wasn't that she didn't want to help Emily. She yearned for answers as much as anyone. It was just that every time she cracked open one of the books, she would be dead asleep in her armchair before she reached the second page—so tired from her training and the rigor of life on the farm.

It was as if Charlie was venting all the frustration he felt with her person upon her physical body. When Annabelle dressed each morning, she read the bruises and scrapes like the marks of his anger, sense of betrayal, and abiding fear. Yet she continued to rise early and dress, all the same, patiently awaiting that morning's torment.

From his look of disappointment when he knocked on her door to find her ready and waiting each morning, Charlie expected her to give up. But she would not give him the satisfaction. It was a challenge, and their friendship was the prize at stake. Annabelle would not allow him to forsake her so easily.

She cared for Charlie, for his kindness and his loyalty to his home and its people. The soldier in him felt so trapped in this small, quiet place. And yet, he never complained about his lot but worked hard day and night to care for his father's legacy. Annabelle envied him that love and sense of duty. Charlie was one of the most admirable men she had ever known.

And so she dressed, trained, helped Bess in the kitchen and the garden, and spent time in the study with Emily, poring over endless books. Another two weeks passed, and Annabelle did not dream again.

"*DAMN* it all to the Gods' hell!" Emily shouted, slamming a heavy tome down upon the desk with a bang.

Annabelle was so startled that she nearly dropped her own book.

"Emily!" She gasped, recovering her composure. "Gods have mercy. You gave me a fright!"

In fact, Annabelle had been nearly dozing, unable to keep focused on *Lost Languages and Symbols*. Her friend's sudden outburst had brought her sharply back to consciousness.

"I'm sorry," Emily said, glowering. "But it's just no use. I cannot find anything remotely helpful. And I've combed through every book in this library. What I wouldn't give to be back at the palace. I'm sure your librarian friend could have helped us find *something*."

"Any books on magic in the royal library would have been locked away or burned long ago," Annabelle pointed out. "I doubt he would have been much help."

"Perhaps." Emily scrubbed her hands over her face, looking weary. "I'm sorry, Annabelle. But I've looked through everything twice. Even silly novels and romances."

"What about this one?" Annabelle spied a small leather-bound book that sat upon the shelf beside her chair. It looked strangely familiar. She slid it from the shelf and plopped it down on top of the open book in her lap. One look at the cover, and she knew where she had seen it before. It was the book of stories that she had borrowed from the palace library.

"You kept it?" Annabelle breathed, running a hand over its embossed title.

Emily nodded, blushing. "I couldn't face returning it. It—it felt like a piece of you that I still had. I'm sorry. I should have done as you asked."

But Annabelle was already flipping through the pages. "No, I'm glad you..."

She froze, completely forgetting what she had been about to say. A thrill of excitement ran all the way through her body and into her toes.

"Emily," Annabelle breathed. "Emily...I found it!"

Emily sat forward in her chair, looking alert. "You what?"

Annabelle held the book out to her, grinning widely. "I found it! Look."

They looked together, the book spread open upon the desk between them. On the title page was a drawing of a circle filled with strange symbols.

"I can't believe I never noticed it before," Annabelle said excitedly. "Only...I suppose I hadn't been looking for it at the time."

"This isn't the same image" Emily pointed out, indicating several places on the illustration. "Look. Some of the symbols are the same, some are set at different positions, and others are symbols we haven't seen before."

"Do any of the new markings look familiar?" Annabelle asked.

"Well..." Emily tilted her head to the side, considering the image. "This one looks a bit like a fish hook." She crinkled her nose. "But no."

The two women leaned over the desk until their foreheads were almost touching, lost in the wild excitement of discovery. Annabelle could not believe their good fortune. This was something! This was a start! This...this was a book of stories. Tales. Falsehoods.

And just like that, the burning flame of her excitement was extinguished in a puff of smoke.

Emily did not seem to share her trepidation. "Annabelle, this is wonderful!" She exclaimed, bending low over the paper.

"How is it?" Annabelle asked, failing to see the fortune in this discovery. This was a book of old Eìrlani folktales. Even if it meant something, the only people who could have provided any answers were both far away and out of their reach.

"I don't know yet," Emily said, infuriatingly. "But we are going to find out."

And with that, Emily snatched the book up off the table and buried her nose between its covers.

Annabelle stretched and yawned. "Well, you have fun. It's late, and I have my morning punishment with your brother. I should get some rest."

Emily said nothing, already lost to the known world within the pages of the book. Smiling to herself, Annabelle left her friend to read in peace.

She made for the stairs, thinking longingly of bed, when a knock sounded at the front door. Annabelle frowned. She hadn't heard any horses approach the house. Had Charlie been locked out again? It happened from time to time when he was out late visiting the village.

Too tired, her mind too filled with thoughts of the little book to remember who she was or where she was, Annabelle unlocked the door and opened it.

"*Annabelle, no!*"

Annabelle turned to see Charlie standing on the stairs behind her, expression white and horrified. Suddenly she realized her mistake. She ought not to have answered the door, no matter the reason. She ought to have fetched Emily at once. But it was too late. The door was already swinging wide, revealing two tall hooded figures standing on the stoop.

Without asking for an invitation, they pushed past Annabelle and into the foyer.

"What the—"Annabelle exclaimed at the same time as Charlie bounded down the rest of the stairs, stepping into the men's path.

"Please leave my house," he growled. "Now."

Annabelle knew a moment of sheer terror. Both men were larger than Charlie, and the one he faced down was wearing a sword. She could see its outline pressed against the fabric of his cloak.

But then the man pulled back his hood, and Annabelle gasped.

It was Sam.

"Close the door, Annabelle" Sam said. "I'm certain that we weren't followed, but I'd prefer not to risk it."

Annabelle did as he commanded, legs and arms shaking. She turned to see that Charlie's look of anger and challenge had been replaced with one of surprise and delight. That smile she hadn't seen in weeks stretched wide across his face, making her heart do a little flip in her chest, and he clasped Sam's arm.

"Gods above, Fisher," he exclaimed with a laugh. "You do know how to make an entrance."

Sam grinned a bit sheepishly. "Sorry for the theatrics, friend. We had to approach the farm in the dark."

"He *insisted* we approach the farm in the dark," the other man corrected. "In case hostiles lingered about the place. A bit paranoid, if you ask me."

The man pulled his hood back as well, revealing Raphael's grinning bearded face. He turned twinkling eyes upon Annabelle. "It is good to see you again, Princess."

Annabelle looked from Raphael, standing tall and whole, to Sam, grinning down at her, and burst into tears.

"Oh! Now…" Raphael explained, drawing Annabelle to him in a warm embrace. "There's no need for that. We're here now, and everything is going to be just right and dandy. You hear me?"

Annabelle nodded and pulled away, wiping her face and feeling embarrassed. "I d—don't know what's wrong with me," she said, hiccuping a bit. "It was just…seeing you both *here*. And…and, oh Raphael." She looked up into his eyes, feeling fresh tears welling up. "I'm so glad you're alright."

"Bit charred, but I pulled through" He said with a wink. "It would take more than that to keep me down for long. Now I won't have you crying over me, lass."

Annabelle took a deep breath, wiped her tears, and smiled.

Raphael beamed at her. "That's my girl."

"Come into the kitchen," Charlie urged. "I sense we have much to discuss."

"Indeed we do," Sam said, following Charlie down the narrow corridor.

Annabelle went to fetch Emily, and they joined the men in the kitchen that had at one time seemed spacious but now was full to bursting. Charlie set about gathering cups and a pitcher of ale. Emily rushed forward to embrace Sam and introduce herself and her brother to Raphael—a courtesy that Annabelle and Sam had entirely forgotten in the shock of their arrival.

Annabelle hovered in the doorway, watching her friends—smiling and safe, and together.

Sorrow lanced through her heart at the sight as Mica's absence struck her, leaving her breathless. Where was he now? Was he trapped in some dungeon, or worse? Did he have enough food to eat? Of course, he did not. He was captured, grieving, and alone. It seemed so terribly cruel that they were all together, warm and well-fed, while he was not.

"Annabelle?" Sam was watching her, concerned. "What is it?"

She shrugged. "I was just thinking about Mica. Sam, we have to do something to help him."

Sam nodded knowingly. "I know. Please, sit down. We have a plan."

Chapter Twenty-Three

Annabelle lay in bed for a long time the next morning, staring at the ceiling. Her mind danced with everything she had learned the night before. Sam and Raphael had told them the plan to rescue Mica. Annabelle was still didn't know how she felt about it. The plan was good, all things considered, but there was still so much that could go wrong.

As it was, the two men were fortunate that Raphael hadn't been caught and killed when they smuggled him out of the city. Ilya had played an instrumental role, of course. Apparently, she smuggled more than just crates of food and medicine for the needy. Certain nobles paid a premium to enjoy luxuries that had been hard to come by during the escalating conflict with the north, and the madam used those connections to keep scrutiny off her back.

"I spent a full day hiding in a giant crate of furs," Raphael had explained with a grimace. "Ilya's people let me out on the shore a few miles east of Ellasport. That's where I met Sam."

"Did you have any trouble getting here?" Charlie had asked.

Sam had shaken his head. "No," he'd said. "But that's not surprising. The king and court left the palace the day before we did, taking the extra guards and high alert with them. All eyes will be turned to the north now."

"The north and the capital, where we're going to attempt to free the most important political prisoner," Annabelle had pointed out. "Please tell us your plan is good; otherwise, we're all going to wind up dead."

Sam and Raphael had exchanged a look, then Sam said, "If all goes *exactly* to plan, we should be able to free Mica and get you both out of the country."

Annabelle had started to object, but Sam cut her off with a look.

"You cannot stay in Dunea," He explained patiently. "It is too dangerous to remain when there is still so much we do not know or understand."

And so Sam would leave to rejoin the king and court on the road north. Once he arrived in Rengon City, Sam would find out where the prince was being held and lay the groundwork for his rescue.

Ilya had arranged for a ship to pick up Annabelle and Raphael on the coast to the east, then they would sail north, to the east of Rengon City. If Sam managed to free Mica and escape, that's where they would all meet and sail to Eìrlan.

"Which is as likely to go off without a hitch as the apple tree in the garden sprouting gold coins this year instead of fruit," Charlie had grumbled.

He and Sam had begun arguing about strategy and planning, back and forth until Annabelle was yawning and Emily had fallen asleep with her head on the table, her hand still clutching her cup of ale. Raphael had suggested it might be time to get some sleep and that they could resume their bickering in the morning.

And so they had all gone to bed, though Annabelle did so reluctantly. After the excitement of the evening, she dreaded the added distress of another dream. But after a while of tossing and turning, Annabelle was finally able to drift off into a restless sleep. She knew she had dreamed, but as she watched the morning light grow steadily through her window, Annabelle realized that she didn't remember the dream at all.

)))●(((

Charlie hadn't come knocking at her door at dawn, so Annabelle went looking for him, desperate to do anything else but lay in bed drowning in worry. She found him in the kitchen.

"I thought you could use the rest," he said with a shy smile when she asked why he hadn't woken her. "After last night, we all could."

This small act of kindness made Annabelle's cheeks go pink. "Thank you," She said. "I did need a good night's sleep."

"You're welcome."

He met her eyes then, and the warmth in their golden depths made Annabelle's breath catch. There was an awkward silence, followed by a moment when Annabelle was sure Charlie was about to say something. But the moment was interrupted by the appearance of a tousle-haired Sam.

"Morning," he yawned. Then Annabelle saw him freeze, his eyes going from her cheeks, which were beet red by now, to Charlie, who was suddenly very busy with the frying pan.

Annabelle set about fetching plates and cutlery, painfully aware of Sam's gaze following her, but she ignored him. Once Raphael and Emily joined them, they all sat down to breakfast together, but Annabelle had trouble joining in the pleasant conversation and banter.

She still felt off—had felt off all morning—but now she knew why. There was still something she needed to do, a secret she had yet to confide in her closest friend. If this plan was going to succeed, and if Sam would risk his life for her, he needed to know everything. But how and when should she tell him? Now?

Annabelle watched Raphael as he laughed at something Emily said, chewing on her lip. He, too, deserved the truth. After everything that had been done to him, he deserved whatever truth she could give him. The prospect of honesty was terrifying, but Annabelle had no choice. It had to be now, or she would definitely lose her nerve.

"I have to tell you something," she said.

The conversation died at once as all eyes turned upon Annabelle. She shifted uncomfortably in her seat.

"I'm sorry I didn't say anything last night, but in all honesty...I forgot."

"Are you sure?" Emily asked quietly. "You don't have to do this now."

Charlie didn't say anything, but he was watching her. Annabelle could not read his expression. Sam and Raphael simply looked confused.

"I do have to do this now," Annabelle said, gripping her mug of tea to keep her hands from shaking. "They have to know everything."

And so Annabelle told Sam and Raphael about the dreams, about the magic, about all of it.

"Goddess be good," Raphael breathed when Annabelle was finished speaking. "*That* is quite the twist in the story, lass."

"I know," Annabelle said. "I'm sorry I didn't say anything before now. I was afraid, and I didn't know *what* was happening to me. At least now I know that I'm not losing my mind."

"Charlie and I know about magic, but we've never seen anything like what Annabelle did," Emily said. "She doesn't seem to be doing it on purpose, and she doesn't need any charms or spells, which is odd."

"Have you tried using your magic intentionally?" Raphael asked.

"Of course not," Annabelle gaped at him, shocked by such a suggestion. "I'm terrified I'll… I'll blow up the farm, or something."

"Well…that is interesting," Raphael muttered. He looked thoughtful then but said nothing more.

Annabelle felt a bit better now that this final truth was out in the world, but she couldn't stop looking at Sam. He hadn't said anything, hadn't so much as moved a single muscle since she began speaking. There was something in his eyes—not anger, nor fear—but something that made her nervous. What was he thinking? Why wouldn't he look at her?

"Sam?"

He looked at her then, and he must have seen the pleading in her eyes because he gave her a small smile. But he didn't say anything. Instead, he got to his feet.

"Let's take a walk," he suggested, extending a hand toward Annabelle. She took it without hesitation. If there were things they needed to talk about, she knew Sam would feel better having space and time to think and to have his feelings.

They left the kitchen through the back door into the garden, and Annabelle followed Sam down the slope toward the barn. Together they circled the field, following the fence line. Sam was quiet for a while, and Annabelle did not rush him into speech. It wasn't until they turned the corner, the forest on one side and the fence on the other, that Sam stopped walking and turned to face her.

"I need you to know," Sam said, at last, turning to her, "I don't understand what you're going through—I couldn't possibly understand—but it's alright."

"Is it?" Annabelle asked doubtfully. "You aren't...scared of me now?"

He frowned at her. "Why would I be scared of you?"

Annabelle shrugged, picking at a splinter sticking out of the split-rail fence, not looking at him.

"It's Charlie, isn't it?"

She looked up at him then. "I *attacked* him, Sam."

"You didn't know what you were doing."

"Still," she grumbled. "He's never going to forgive me."

"Oh I don't know." Sam cocked his head. "He seemed pretty friendly this morning."

"You don't know what you're talking about," Annabelle said dismissively. But he had a point. Charlie *had* been kind to her this morning, and it had felt like a small, special gift.

"Thank you for telling me."

She looked up at him. His expression was unguarded, his eyes wide and trusting. It was for a moment like they were children again.

Annabelle smiled. "You deserved the truth, especially if you're going to risk your life for me *again*. You deserved to make up your own mind if it was still worth it."

"Why on earth wouldn't it be worth it, Annabelle?" He looked so taken aback, so horrified by what she'd said that Annabelle actually laughed.

"Oh, come on, Sam. If we'd heard a story like the one, I just told you, even a year ago, we both would have thought the person insane, at best."

"Maybe you would," he retorted. "Give me a bit of credit. I have seen more of the world than Rosewood Manor in the past few years, you know."

"Fair enough," Annabelle threw her hands up in mock surrender. "I yield, Sir Knight."

Annabelle picked at the fence again, a large piece coming off in her hands. She then began ripping the piece of soft wood into shreds and discarding them, one by one.

"There's still something on your mind," Sam probed, watching her restless fingers.

"Well, yes. There is," Annabelle admitted. "There's one thing I don't understand about your plan."

Sam snorted. "Only one? The entire thing is utter lunacy. We'll all be killed or imprisoned for sure. But," he sighed. "We will probably be killed or imprisoned anyway for having kidnapped the princess so, might as well risk it."

"I've never known you to be so cavalier about safety," Annabelle remarked, raising an eyebrow.

Sam shrugged. "I'm not, but...well, it has been pointed out to me that I can be a bit...over-cautious. I don't want to put off doing the right thing just because I'm afraid for the people I love. And rescuing Mica, or attempting to, is the right thing to do."

"But, that's the thing. You'll be rescuing him—*you*. After that, it's unlikely that you will be able to return to the capital or to Dunea, possibly forever. Are you certain you're okay with that?"

Sam didn't say anything for a long moment. He seemed to be deciding whether or not to tell her something. Annabelle waited patiently. Whatever he decided, she would accept it, as he had accepted her, without question.

"I think I want to leave Dunea," he said at last. "My place is at your side now. I have no loyalty to the king, not anymore. And...and there are other reasons."

"You don't have to tell me," Annabelle assured him. "It is good enough for me to know that you have reasons and that they are enough to convince you to go."

But he shook his head. "No, I—I want to tell you. You have more than earned it." He took a deep breath. "I want to leave because I have not been...myself here."

"What do you mean?" Annabelle asked. She had no earthly idea where this was going but could sense that Sam was building up to something important.

"I never felt comfortable at the manor—not like you did," Sam explained. "Growing up there was...was like something out of a dream. Every day I was grateful to Lord Roger for bringing me to live there, but I was always afraid that one day I would wake, and it would all be gone. The possibility was terrifying."

This was one of the reasons Annabelle and Sam had been so close. They often felt exactly the same way for entirely different reasons. Sam was afraid that his life at the manor would be taken from him because he was only a visitor. Annabelle had feared that her life at the manor would be taken from her because she was only a visitor. The princess and the fisherman's son—so different, and yet so alike.

"So I followed Damon to the city, hoping to become a knight," Sam continued. "I told myself that I wanted to prove I belonged with him, prove that I was his equal in every way that mattered. I told myself I went because I wanted to earn my place in this world. But...in truth, I think I would have done anything to be near him."

"That's not really a surprise," Annabelle said with a small smile. "You always wanted to be just like Damon."

"I did," Sam agreed, returning her smile. "When I was a child, I followed him wherever he went. He was like the brother I never had, and I idolized him. When we were older...that feeling changed, became something...more."

"More?" Annabelle wondered where this story was going but didn't want to rush him. It was clearly important that Sam say everything he wanted to say, the way he needed to say it.

Sam's cheeks flushed, and he wouldn't meet her eyes. "I loved him, Annabelle."

"Well, of course you..." But the words died on Annabelle's lips as she realized exactly what Sam meant. His feelings had changed. *Love.*

Everything in the forest became suddenly very quiet as Annabelle considered what Sam had just confessed. She knew without having to be told that this moment was important—how she reacted to this declaration had the power to change their friendship forever. The moment felt like a robin's egg that she held in her palm. So precious and so fragile.

It was a shock to learn that Sam had been in love with Damon; Annabelle couldn't lie about that. Such things were forbidden in Dunea, but Annabelle had never considered how she felt about it one way or another. Nobody had ever confessed such feelings to her before.

But now that Sam had trusted her with this secret, she needed to consider how she felt, and she needed to do it fast.

In truth, there was nothing to consider. She loved Sam. Sam loved her, and he had loved Damon. Annabelle could not fathom how love in any form could be wrong. And so she had her answer.

"Thank you for telling me," she said. "And… I'm so sorry you've had to carry this secret. But, Sam, you have to know that I don't care. I don't think it matters who you love, as long as you *can* love."

He met her eyes then. "Really?"

"Of course." She smiled in earnest, opening her heart so that he could see how much she meant what she said. "Although, I suppose you haven't been allowed to love—not really. Not in the way you want to."

"No," he sighed, running a hand through his hair. "And that's why I'm not sorry to go—to have the chance to be who I am without being afraid. I know this is an…odd way to explain it. But you deserve my secrets if you're going to trust me with yours."

"I appreciate your trust." Annabelle chewed her lip for a moment, thinking. "And…and did Damon ever…do you know if he ever felt the same way about you?"

Sam laughed. "Damon? Gods, no. He would live under a lady's skirt if he could."

"Sam!" Annabelle giggled. "I don't think I've ever heard you talk like that."

"Technically, that was Raphael's way of putting it," Sam said, his cheeks going red again. "But I think it illustrates the point effectively."

"He knows, doesn't he. About you, I mean," Annabelle said, a thought occurring to her—an answer to something she had seen or thought she had seen. She remembered how Sam had stared down at Raphael's unconscious body while Lyddia worked on his burns. She had been too tired then, too overwhelmed to ask questions. But now...

"He does," Sam said, his blush deepening. He did not elaborate.

"Good," Annabelle said. "I'm glad you've had someone to talk to."

"Raphael is..." Sam paused, chewing his lip. "He isn't what I thought he was. I think he's a good man."

"Well, I like him," Annabelle announced as if that settled the matter. "And he is rather gorgeous, isn't he?"

"Let's make a deal," Sam suggested, raising an eyebrow. "If you don't tease me about Raphael, I won't tease you about Charlie."

Now it was Annabelle's turn to blush. "Fine," she said with a sigh. "You have your deal."

Because Annabelle could not help it any longer, she hugged him. "Thank you for telling me," she said into his shirt.

Sam's arms tightened around her. "Thank you for being such a good friend," he said. "I should have told you sooner."

"Well, I don't know about that," Annabelle said with a wink as they started back toward the farmhouse. "It could have saved you years of needless brooding, and we both know what a tragedy that would have been."

Sam's laugh drifted light and free upon the morning breeze as they walked together, arm in arm, back to the farmhouse.

Chapter Twenty-Four

Sam left the farm the following morning. It broke Annabelle's heart to say goodbye to him when it had only just started to feel like their friendship was returning to its former ease. But she knew it was a necessary heartbreak all the same.

At least her training sessions would serve as an adequate distraction. No sooner had Sam vanished into the forest beyond the farm than Charlie ordered her to meet him in the field. "One day's rest is enough, I think," he said, striding off around the farmhouse.

"Do you mind if I join you?" Raphael asked. He had been quiet that morning, which was unusual for Raphael. Annabelle had her suspicions about why but kept them to herself.

"Of course," She said with a warm smile, confident that Raphael needed a distraction as much as she was. "I'm sure Charlie won't mind."

"Thank the Goddess," Raphael said as they walked to the field together. "I need a bit of training after my extended convalescence."

Charlie, it transpired, *did* mind that Raphael joined their training session, but there was hardly anything he could do about it. Raphael was an accomplished warrior in his own right and was perfectly able to conduct his own training regimen with or without company.

"Why are you so bothered by this?" Annabelle asked him under her breath as they ran drills, and Raphael stretched out his body nearby. "I thought you'd be pleased to have someone who you can't beat so easily."

Charlie said nothing to this and proceeded to send Annabelle crashing to the ground with perhaps a bit more force than was entirely necessary.

"Ow—*Charlie*," Annabelle protested, wincing as she sat up. "I don't know what's wrong with you, but would you try to use only *necessary* force? My entire body will be black and blue at this rate."

Charlie helped her up, looking a bit ashamed of himself. "I'm sorry, Annabelle," he said. "I just don't trust him."

"You don't know him yet," Annabelle pointed out. "Sam would not have brought him here if he wasn't a good man. And furthermore, based on recent events, he has more reason to mistrust us than we do him."

Charlie assured her that he would try to be more pleasant, and he even concluded their training early so that he and Raphael could spar together. Annabelle watched them, thinking that she had never seen such an incredible spectacle.

Charlie was smaller than Raphael, but Raphael was stiff and only barely healed. They wrestled bare-chested, and it made Annabelle's heart constrict painfully to see the rippling scars that now covered Raphael's left shoulder and stretched down his chest. It was a miracle that he had healed so well and in so little time too. Annabelle was glad to look upon the damage her father's insanity had wrought. It kept the anger and determination alive and burning within her heart.

Raphael turned out to be an excellent addition to their little group of outlaws. Bess adored him, Emily laughed so hard at his jokes that she cried, and Annabelle found him good company in those sad moments when she missed Sam so much she could feel it like a physical injury. At these times, she would seek Raphael out, and they would sit together, swapping stories. Annabelle told Raphael about what it was like to grow up at the manor, and he told her about his life in Eìrlan.

It fascinated Annabelle to hear about his birthplace, and she never tired of hearing about their great cities with colorful houses and festivals that lasted weeks and weeks. When Raphael told her about how sometimes the islands in the archipelago looked like they floated in the clouds on a misty day, Annabelle could only stare. She longed to see this wondrous place for herself one day.

Despite the many reasons why Annabelle was glad Raphael had joined them at the farm, his most helpful contribution came on their third day together.

It was just after a particularly brutal training session, and Annabelle was drawing water from the well to pour over her sweat-drenched body. The summer heat was upon them now, and it was nearly unbearable to be so active, even so early in the morning.

"I was watching you today," Raphael said as he approached. "You are making incredible progress, little princess."

Annabelle scowled at him. Raphael was full of nicknames for everyone, but she couldn't say she cared much for hers. "I don't feel like I'm making progress," she said.

"Don't you enjoy being tossed around by such a fine soldier as young Charlie?" he asked, waggling his eyebrows at her mockingly.

Annabelle threw the bucket at him, and he dodged the spray of water easily, laughing.

"Was there something you *wanted*, Raph?" She demanded.

"Actually, there was." He leaned casually against the side of the well. "Have you ever heard of meditation?"

Annabelle shook her head.

"Meditation is a process of calming and clearing the mind," Raphael explained. "I can tell from watching you that you'll never get the upper hand on Charlie because you're still thinking too much."

"There is quite a lot to think about," Annabelle said. "Foot placement and…and…what?" She demanded because Raphael was shaking his head.

"There is a lot to *learn*," he said patiently. "You have to memorize those things because you don't want to be thinking of them when you finally face an opponent. A busy mind misses things. A clear mind, on the other hand" he tapped his temple with a finger and winked, "sees all."

Annabelle lifted a skeptical eyebrow. "I don't think there's a way I could best Charlie, clear mind or no."

"And that right there is why you have yet to do so. But that isn't the only reason I mentioned it." He hesitated. "I thought it might help with the…little *outbursts* you've been having."

He had Annabelle's attention now. "It can?" She asked.

Raphael shrugged. "Can't hurt to try, can it? My father had a bit of magic. Always said meditation is what kept things…organized."

Annabelle's jaw dropped. "*What?*"

"It's true," Raphael said, nodding sagely. "He had a particular affinity for healing and for navigation spells. I never showed a talent for magic myself, but I suspect that I inherited some of his gift because I heal from injury so quickly."

Annabelle's eyes roved over the place where his burns had healed so inexplicably well, without infection, and in a fraction of the time they ought to. "That explains a lot," she said.

"Indeed," Raphael agreed. "It was my father who taught me to meditate. I thought, well, I *hoped* that if you wanted to give it a try, it might help you keep things…calm. Maybe give you enough control to stop another outburst, in case it happens at the wrong time, in front of the wrong sort of people."

Annabelle considered this suggestion. Though there hadn't been another incident like the one when she had accidentally blasted Charlie off his feet, it would be comforting to know she was doing something to ensure such a thing never happened again.

"Alright," she said. "If you are willing to teach me, I will try."

"Excellent," Raphael exclaimed. "We'll begin tomorrow after training, shall we? Meditation is a wonderful way to rest and restore the body after exercise."

"Is there anything meditation can't help?" Annabelle was amused by Raphael's excitement, even though she still felt a bit skeptical.

Raphael thought for a moment. "You know, try as I might, I still can't seem to strip a person naked only using my mind. The old-fashioned way works best," he waggled his fingers in front of him, and Annabelle let out a snort of laughter.

Not for the first time, Annabelle marveled at Raphael's power to cast things in a better light, to put even the most troubled corners of her soul at ease. Though they had not known each other long, Annabelle trusted the warrior with her life.

"Would you come with me?" She asked him, deciding something. "I have something you need to see."

It was time to show Raphael the book.

Emily was helping Bess with breakfast, and so they had the study to themselves. Raphael settled himself in an armchair, and Annabelle retrieved the little book and her drawing from the desk. She offered the picture to him first, explaining that she had tried to recreate the symbols from her dream. When she showed Raphael the little book, he frowned.

"This is a book of Eìrlani faerie stories," he said. "Where did you find this?" It almost sounded like an accusation.

"In the library at the palace," Annabelle said. "But we don't know the significance of this symbol or why it so resembles the one I saw in my dream. I was hoping you might be able to shed some light on its significance."

Raphael let out a long breath and sat back in his chair. "I don't know if I can explain how this drawing wound up in your dream, but I do know a bit about the legends of the faeries and these symbols."

"Anything you can tell me will be helpful," Annabelle said encouragingly.

"There are symbols and drawings like these all over Eìrlan, in places that are sacred to us," Raphael said. "We don't know for certain who made them or why, but legend says that they were made by faeries—beings of extraordinary power, spirits of the earth itself."

"The book talks about faeries," Annabelle interjected. "But I never considered that they could be real, of course."

Raphael shrugged. "Maybe they were, at one time. If so, they're gone now. People with magic say that the places where these symbols are found have power, but I don't know if there is truth in those claims. The sites are sacred to us, but stories of the faeries have never been more than legends."

"My mother used these symbols in my dream," Annabelle pressed, unwilling to admit defeat. "It has to be connected, somehow. Don't you think?"

"It's possible," Raphael said slowly. "But hard to know for certain."

Annabelle sighed. "True. Well, thanks anyway, Raph."

"I am sorry I couldn't be more of a help, Annabelle," he said, laying a comforting hand upon her shoulder. "Maybe you'll be able to find someone in Eìrlan who can better answer your questions."

"Maybe. If we ever get there." Annabelle was grumpy now. She had been so sure that Raphael would be able to give her some sort of clarity.

"Annabelle, listen to me." He turned her to face him, expression earnest. "We will find answers to this. You just have to keep looking, lass. Don't give up."

Someone standing behind them cleared his throat. Annabelle looked over her shoulder to see Charlie glowering in the doorway.

"Don't you have chores?" He demanded. "Eggs don't collect themselves, you know."

"Well…I think I'd best get cleaned up," Raphael said, getting to his feet. "Charlie. A pleasure as always." He slid carefully past Charlie and, whistling a merry tune, left them alone.

Annabelle stood to face Charlie, feeling exceptionally irritated. He had been stomping about the place in a temper for days, and she'd had enough of it.

"What is your problem?" She demanded.

"*My* problem?" Charlie's face was red with fury. "I'm not the one shirking my responsibilities to lounge about with…with…."

"Don't you dare insult him," Annabelle growled, cutting him off. "Don't you do it."

"I wasn't going to insult him," Charlie said defensively. "I was going to call him a…a pretty distraction."

Annabelle was seething. She had been aching to confront Charlie, and now here he was, willing to bait her. Fine. If he wanted to fight, it was about time they had it out.

"Are you serious, Charlie?" She demanded, placing her hands on her hips and glaring at him. "Every morning, I drag myself out into the field before the sun is even up so you can pummel me into the dirt, and do I complain about it? No, of course not. So don't *you* suggest that I'm distracted."

"I would never suggest that," he retorted, "Not when it comes to your training. But what about your other responsibilities, Annabelle? I thought I made it clear that this was an exchange. I protect you, I teach you to fight, and you help out around the farm. But these days, it seems like every time I want to find you, to ask you to help with something, you're off somewhere with *him*."

This was so ridiculous and unfair. What was he talking about? Before Raphael came to the farm, Annabelle had rarely ever seen Charlie outside of their morning sparring matches. Just because he had suddenly decided to hang around more, that didn't mean that...

But now that she thought about it, Charlie *had* been around more often—not that he'd done more than sulk about the farmhouse.

"Charlie...are you *jealous*?"

"M-me?" He sputtered. "Jealous? Of *him*?"

"You are jealous!" All anger left Annabelle, and she actually laughed aloud. Of course. She hadn't even considered it before. After all, he barely spent any time with her, barely looked in her direction. But now it made perfect sense. The realization delighted Annabelle. She had been so terrified of losing his friendship after everything that had happened. Clearly, she ought not to have worried at all.

He wasn't looking at her. He had his arms folded across his chest and was staring at the floor before his feet. "If you're quite finished," he said through gritted teeth.

"Charlie, listen to me," Annabelle urged, moving a few steps closer to him. "Raph and I are friends—that is all. It's just...it's just nice having someone to talk to who was there, who knows what I went through at the palace. I like spending time with him because it makes me feel better. But, Charlie, if you want to spend time with me too, all you need to do is ask me."

Charlie looked up at her then, looking suddenly awkward. "You would like to? Spend time with me, I mean?"

Annabelle beamed at him and nodded. "Of course I would. But only if you stop stomping around the place like you're about to explode. Poor Bess is having kittens over you."

He scrubbed a hand across the back of his neck, looking embarrassed. "I have been acting like a bit of an idiot," he muttered. "I should apologize to her."

"And maybe you should stop treating Raphael like he's some kind of criminal," Annabelle suggested. "Truth be told, I think it amuses him for some reason. But even so."

"I will," he said. "I promise. I'm so sorry, Annabelle. I've behaved badly."

She sighed. "You aren't the only one who needs to apologize. I've felt terrible about…about what happened. And we never had the opportunity to really talk about it."

"I know we haven't. But…" he hesitated. "I know you can't help it, and I know you didn't do it on purpose. I was just scared. Can you understand that?"

Annabelle could, but she still needed to know one thing.

"Are you scared of me now?"

"No," Charlie said without hesitating. "I promise you I am not."

"That's very good to hear, Charlie."

Charlie smiled in earnest then, and he was so beautiful Annabelle found it suddenly hard to breathe. "Come on," he said, extending a hand to her. "Let's go have some breakfast."

Chapter Twenty-Five

Sam reached the royal camp in the middle of the night. All was silent and sleeping save for the guards stationed at regular intervals through the moonlit avenues of temporary animal paddocks, crackling fire pits, and a city of tents.

He was exhausted and hungry after days of hard riding, barely stopping for food or rest on his way. The success or failure of the rescue plan rested solidly upon his shoulders, and it was his determination that fueled him. This was not just about Annabelle anymore. This was about rescuing an innocent man and seeking freedom for the people he cared about most in the world.

And maybe finding a little corner of freedom for himself as well.

The memory of his talk with Annabelle burned like a warm talisman in his heart. She had been so wonderful, so lovely—but of course she had been. It was who she was, and Sam felt more a fool than ever for not realizing that she would have accepted him no matter what. But it was useless to regret his hesitation. She knew now, and it felt wonderful to have one other person in this hostile world with whom he could be wholly himself.

When he was finished erecting his tent at the edge of camp, Sam wandered off in search of food. He would eat before he slept or risk waking up groggy and miserable. That would not do. From tomorrow morning onward, he needed to remain sharp.

The mess tent was silent and dark, but there was a pot of cold stew still sitting atop one of the serving tables. Sam retrieved a bowl and spoon and helped himself. The fire beside the tent still had some life left in it, and so Sam settled himself on a log beside it and began to eat.

No sooner had he swallowed his first spoonful than he heard a woman's voice say, "Why, young Sam. This is a surprise."

Sam looked up from his bowl to see the dignified figure of the Duchess walking toward him from out of the shadows. He leaped to his feet at once, but she held up a hand. "Please sit, eat. I didn't mean to disturb you."

"Not at all, Duchess," he said, resuming his seat.

"Have you only just arrived?" She asked, settling near him with all the grace as if she lowered onto a throne and not a fallen log.

"Yes, Duchess."

"It is good to see you again."

Sam returned her smile. "It is good to see you again as well, Duchess." He hesitated, then asked, "If I may, your Grace…I am surprised to see you awake at this hour. Is everything alright? Is there any way I can assist you?"

"No. No, I'm fine. Thank you. I only find it hard to sleep these days." Her expression saddened, and she stared into the fire, eyes far away. "It's her birthday next week," she said after a time. "Did you know?"

"I…" Sam paused, trying to remember how many days he had been riding. "Yes, I suppose it is, your grace."

"I always used to visit her on her birthday, if I could," the Duchess said, still looking into the fire. "She was always so difficult, but still…I like to think that I had some impact upon her."

"She loved you dearly, your Grace," Sam said.

She looked at him then, expression thoughtful, the shadow of a smile playing about her lips. "Did she. Well, isn't that a thing all on its own."

"It makes me happy to know that you visited her," Sam said. "I missed too many of her birthdays."

The Duchess only nodded, and so Sam continued to eat his stew. They sat together in silence, watching the fire slowly go out. When the bowl was empty, Sam set it aside and got stiffly to his feet.

"With your Grace's permission, I should get some sleep. I have been riding very hard the past few days," he said.

The Duchess sighed. "Well then, I suppose you ought to help me to my feet before you go, else I'll be trapped on this infernal log until dawn. My joints aren't what they used to be, young man."

Sam didn't know what to make of this request. He had never witnessed the Duchess display a single ounce of frailty, but he moved to stand in front of her and offered his hand all the same. She took it, grasping her cane in the other, and stood smoothly.

Then, with a speed and strength that took Sam utterly by surprise, her fingers released his hand and gripped the front of his coat, pulling him down until his ear was level with her mouth.

"Tell me she's alive," the Duchess whispered. "Tell me you got her out and that she is alive."

"W—what," Sam was taken aback. "I'm sorry, Duchess, I don't know—"

"I like to think," the Duchess interrupted, still hissing into his ear, "that I know my grand-niece better than to fall for that horrible, gruesome trick. My idiot of a nephew may have fallen for it, but I know that, whoever we put in the ground, it was *not* my Annabelle. I don't know how you did it or where she is, and I don't want to know. But you will tell me that she is *alive*."

Sam's mind was reeling. What did he say? Should he tell her the truth and risk everything? There was nothing that could have prepared him for this. But she had known that body wasn't Annabelle, just as he had. Only someone who truly loved the princess, who *knew* her, would have been able to see past the illusion. If the Duchess could be trusted, she could make a powerful ally if the time came. He would have to risk it.

"She is safe," he said quietly. "She is alive."

The Duchess's shoulders sagged with relief, but she did not release him. "Listen carefully, Sam," she said, so quietly now that Sam had to concentrate to make out her words. "My nephew has not abandoned his ambitions in the north. He will marry Emilia Adalara, a Countess from Aelnìr before the month is out. He is determined to win this war, no matter the cost. Do you understand what that means?"

Sam knew exactly what it meant. It meant that Annabelle was now in more danger than she had ever been before. He nodded.

"Get her out. Get Annabelle out of Dunea for good. There is no place for her here, not anymore." The Duchess released her viselike grip on his jacket, and she pulled away from him. "Thank you, Sam," she said, resuming her usual crisp, clipped tone. "You have helped an old woman this night, and I will not forget it."

And she left him standing by the fire. As he walked slowly back to his tent, Sam prayed that, whatever he had done to win the grace of the Gods, he never ever lost it.

)))●(((

Another week passed at the farm without incident, not that Annabelle paid much attention to the passing of the days. She was too preoccupied with her training, with Raphael's meditation lessons to add to her daily frustration and the new, delightful, and altogether entirely welcome distraction of Charlie.

They were now spending quite a bit of time together, and Annabelle could not remember a time when she had been happier in her entire life.

He was so sweet. And funny. And so beautiful it nearly hurt Annabelle to look him full in the face—though she did catch her eyes roving over other aspects of his sculpted physique, feeling perhaps less embarrassment or guilt than she ought. She could not help it. It felt heavenly to be able to lose herself in something so new and exciting.

There were moments when Annabelle became lost in fantasies about staying to live at the farm forever. And why not? Raphael and

Sam were more than capable of rescuing Mica on their own, no matter what Sam said. In fact, she suspected that staying behind would significantly improve their chances of making it out of Dunea alive. She would miss Sam terribly, and Raphael, but they would be safe and happy, which would help to ease her pain.

Besides, she would have Charlie and Emily, Bess, Wilkin. Time would pass. They could create a new identity for her, a new life. And if Charlie eventually married her, she would be safe. Nobody would think a princess of Dunea had married a poor farmer. Would they?

Such pathways of thought always led Annabelle to feel grumpy and restless. Why did every single plan for her future happiness have to include marriage? It was never something she had wanted for herself, but then again, she had never really had the chance to discover if she wanted it or not. Marriage was expected; it was required. There was no choice, no wanting, only a planned out future that she could have read from cover to cover like one of the books in the study.

Still, it was the only way Annabelle imagined she might stay at the farm forever, and she desperately wanted to stay.

"Where is your head, Annabelle?"

Grimacing, Annabelle pushed herself to her feet for what felt like the hundredth time that morning. "Sorry, Charlie," she muttered. "I'm just a bit…distracted."

Annabelle was distracted. She had counted the days since she had arrived at the farm that morning while she waited for Charlie to knock on her door and realized that it was her birthday. Twenty years old. So much was to have happened by now that would never happen now. For some inexplicable reason, that realization had filled Annabelle with an oddly empty feeling. She hadn't anticipated feeling such a sense of loss.

True, she was now free from an arranged marriage and had escaped the grasp of a father who might steal the last freedoms she enjoyed. But being the Princess of Dunea had given her life purpose. What was her purpose now? Running away, staying safe, mistrusting everyone outside of her own inner circle.

"Well, un-distract yourself," Charlie encouraged her as they resumed their positions. "You're capable of more than this."

She rolled her eyes but stood in ready stance anyway. This was hopeless. Charlie came at her, and she dodged his first attempt to seize her around the waist, but then his arm lanced out with unbelievable speed to grasp her wrist, which he twisted around until he had her right arm bound behind her back.

The feeling of his body pressed against the length of her back suddenly drove all moody fogginess from Annabelle's mind.

"Come on," he whispered in her ear. "You know how to get free of me."

Oh, but she didn't want to be free of him at all. And so she would not be. Charlie forced Annabelle to her knees, and she yielded the round.

"You're not breathing!" Raphael called from where he watched, leaning against a fencepost. "Remember to *breathe*, Annabelle."

Annabelle shot him an exasperated look. When Raphael had explained meditation to her before their first lesson, Annabelle had laughed at him. All that was required was to sit cross-legged, close her eyes, breathe, and practice releasing her thoughts as they came without attachment.

"So...sit still and don't think, basically?" She had asked, smirking.

The look he had given her was dripping with knowing, but all he had said was, "That's it. Easy, right?"

It had not been at all as easy as Annabelle had anticipated. Her body ached after training, and it was challenging to sit still long enough to allow any thoughts to come, let alone release them.

When she did manage to achieve stillness in her body, her mind was suddenly filled with distracting thoughts—thoughts of Charlie, thoughts about how Sam was faring, and thoughts about whatever it was that she could smell wafting to her on the breeze from the farmhouse.

Far from helping with her sparring sessions with Charlie, meditation became another item on a long list of distractions and frustrations that plagued Annabelle's days.

But she gave Raphael her word that she would try. So Annabelle forced herself to take several deep breaths and attempted to clear her mind of anything other than Charlie—his muscular body, his feet shifting on the ground, preparing.

Ready as she would ever be, Annabelle gave the signal to begin.

Charlie attacked, and Annabelle dodged his first attempt to grab her as she had done before, but he again managed to seize her wrist. This time Annabelle noticed that, while he reached out to grab her, he was momentarily off-balance.

Moving with an agility of which she had never imagined herself capable, Annabelle grabbed his arm with her other hand and shoved her hip into his body. Charlie over-balanced and tumbled over her hip and onto his back.

He stared up at Annabelle in delighted surprise as she pinned him to the ground with her knees. "Do you yield?" She asked, unable to keep a pleased smile from stretching across her face.

"I yield," Charlie said, breathing hard. He looked into her eyes, and there was a heat burning there that set her entire body aflame. She pushed off him hurriedly, glad that the flush of exercise camouflaged the entirely different flush that rose in her cheeks.

"That's my girl!" Raphael roared, applauding raucously.

"Well done, Annabelle," Charlie said, getting to his feet. "You've come far in a short time. You should be proud of yourself."

Annabelle waved him off. "I got lucky. You know I did. The chances of my catching you off-balance like that again are close to zero."

Charlie shrugged. "But it only takes the one time. Attackers will make mistakes. You just need to have the presence of mind to look out for them. Besides," he added, leaning in close so that Raphael could not hear, "you always throw me off balance."

Annabelle took a deep breath and smiled up at the cloudless blue sky. It really was the most spectacularly beautiful morning.

ꜱ꜠ꜟ•ꜞꜟꜱ

"We're having a...*party?*"

Emily smiled pleasantly across the kitchen table. Its surface was entirely obscured by heaps of fruits and vegetables in various stages of preparation for cooking, sacks of flour, baskets of eggs, and a rather enormous slab of what looked like half a cow wrapped in what must be an entire tablecloth.

"We are having a party," Emily repeated calmly, the peel of the potato she held coming away in one long continuous strip under the flashing blade of her paring knife. "For your birthday, of course!"

"But..." Annabelle hadn't said anything about her birthday, and when Charlie and Raphael failed to mention it, she had thought that Emily had forgotten about it too. She whirled to find both men standing in the doorway to the kitchen, both red-faced from trying not to laugh.

"You knew?!" She demanded.

"Surprise!" Raphael trilled, moving forward to steal a handful of figs from the pile on the table. "Did you really think you'd be able to sneak this one by us, lass?"

"Over my dead body," Emily said pleasantly.

"And mine," chimed in Bess.

Annabelle was overwhelmed by the sight of so much food. They would be cooking all day. "How many people are we expecting?" She asked.

"The five of us," Emily said, "And Wilkin makes six."

"This is an awful lot of food for only six people," Annabelle observed. "You shouldn't have gone to such trouble."

"Oh, this is nothing," Bess sang out happily, lifting a golden brown loaf of bread from the oven and giving it a long sniff. "You should see what this place looks like when we hold a feast for the village."

"Besides," Emily dropped her potato, now skinless, into a large iron pot that sat at her elbow, "We all need a celebration. So, take some bread and fruit for breakfast if you want, but you steer clear of this kitchen for the rest of the day. Got it?"

Annabelle held up her hands in surrender. "Fine. Whatever you say, mistress. And…thank you. Really. This is so kind of you."

"Of course, dear," said Bess, crossing the kitchen to take Annabelle's hands in her soft ones. "It has been a gift from the Gods to have you with us. And if that is not a cause for celebration, well, I cannot imagine what is."

Overcome, Annabelle hugged the cook and left them to prepare her birthday feast in peace.

There was plenty to do to occupy her time. Annabelle elected to help with Charlie's duties around the farm while he and Wilkin made some badly needed repairs to the paddock fence. Charlie's tight hug of gratitude made Annabelle so wobbly in the knees that she had to lean against the wall of the barn for several minutes before she felt sturdy again.

While she set about cleaning the stalls in the barn, spreading fresh straw upon the ground, feeding the pigs, and dodging the chickens to collect their eggs, Annabelle couldn't help but marvel at how strong she was becoming.

Mere weeks ago, she had struggled to carry buckets of water one length of the paddock. Now, she slugged bucketfuls from the well to the water trough and back with ease. Though she had quite a way to go until she was as strong as Charlie, who could toss about bales of hay as if they weighed nothing at all, the progress was encouraging.

Annabelle had always been sturdier than most fine ladies. A childhood spent climbing trees she was not supposed to climb, galavanting through the forests of Rosewood province, and traversing a seaside scattered with massive boulders had kept her strong enough.

But combat required a different kind of strength, fitness, and flexibility. Annabelle hadn't wanted to admit what a blow it had been to her self-esteem to find herself so weak. Admittedly, it had been some time since she had climbed a tree, but she had still expected to feel some level of competence when she began training with Charlie.

Now that Annabelle noted the increase in her strength, as well as the very noticeable changes to her body—places that had once been soft and rounded now hardened by muscle—she wondered if she might have been mistaken. Perhaps her active childhood had given her a foundation from which she was building. She was making progress somewhat faster than she felt she ought to be.

Just that morning, as they made their way back up the farmhouse, Charlie had suggested that they might begin to train with knives.

"Small ones," he had rushed to clarify when Annabelle crowed her excitement. "Made of wood."

Annabelle smiled to herself as she worked. The vague absence of purpose she had felt that morning evaporated. She could have laughed at her foolishness. How could she regret the life she had left behind when this new one she had found was so full of light and joy? The person she had been was strong, but the one she was becoming would be stronger—strong enough to withstand anything the Gods could imagine for the future, she hoped.

Chapter Twenty-Six

Emily came to fetch Annabelle at sunset. She found the princess sitting with Charlie and Raphael, lounging on the grass by the garden, talking and laughing.

The day had been one of the best Annabelle had spent at the farm, despite the relatively back-breaking work. With the extra assistance from Annabelle and Raphael, Charlie and Wilkin managed to repair the entire fence, tend the animals, and have enough time to relax while they waited to be summoned for supper.

Emily was already dressed for the party. She wore a very pretty pink dress with little white flowers embroidered into the hem and had woven matching ribbons into her braids, her lips and cheeks dusted with pink stain. Annabelle gaped at her. "Emily, you look beautiful!"

"And is that really such a surprise?" Emily demanded, but she looked pleased all the same. "Come on," she said, extending a hand toward Annabelle. "I have another surprise for you. And you two useless layabouts," she cast a commanding stare upon Charlie and Raphael, whose easy smiles vanished. "Wash and dress, *quickly*. Bess needs your help setting up the table."

Annabelle followed Emily into the house, all the while assuring her that the party was enough and that she didn't need any more surprises, but Emily ignored her. They went to Annabelle's bedroom, where she was stunned into silence by the sight of the dress laid out upon the bed.

It was sky blue, with a wide neckline and long, full sleeves that closed at the wrists. Embroidered stars in white silk thread clustered along the neckline and bodice and spilled out like a cascading waterfall across the skirt to the hem. It was the most beautiful dress Annabelle had ever seen, and her eyes burned with emotion as she looked at it.

"Bess and I have been working on this for a while," Emily explained. "We used one of my mother's old ones and tailored it to fit you. The stars were my idea." She shifted awkwardly on her feet when Annabelle still hadn't said anything. "I…I hope you like it. I remember how much you liked that blue dress when we were at the manor and, well…."

Annabelle pulled Emily into a tight embrace, squeezing her until she squeaked in protest. "Thank you," she said, refusing to release her friend. "It is *exquisite*, Emily."

"It's just a dress," Emily muttered.

"No," Annabelle pulled away, looking Emily in the eyes. "It is not just a dress. Everything that you have done for me, that your family has done for me…" Annabelle shook her head, unable to think of the words. "I don't think I will ever be able to thank you enough."

Emily took Annabelle's hands and squeezed them. "You're my friend," she said simply. "You would do the same for me. I know it."

"Without hesitation."

"Do you want me to help you get ready?" Emily asked.

Annabelle laughed. "Emily, nothing has made me happier these weeks than having you as my friend and *not* my maid. I do not wish you to be so ever again."

"I can live with that," Emily said, beaming. "I'll wait for you downstairs."

Annabelle found another welcome surprise waiting for her on the other side of the bed: a large tub filled with water that was still warm when she slid into it, moaning with pleasure. It had been ages since she'd had a proper bath. Soap lay on a towel next to the tub, and Annabelle scrubbed away happily until her skin was glowing.

The dress was simple enough to get on without assistance, and Annabelle was once again overcome with gratitude. This was how dressing should be—easy and done by one's self. She dragged a comb through her knotted hair until it was smooth and decided to leave it at that. Barefoot, her hair streaming free down her back, and feeling lighter than she had in a long while, Annabelle joined the others outside.

The garden was transformed into something out of a dream. Colorful ribbons streamed from trestles, tied up among the vines. There seemed to be a great deal more flowers than there had been before— bouquets of them stuck in among the vegetables, petals strewn across the grass, and arranged around the bottoms of barrels that stood at regular intervals with cascading towers of candles set on top, illuminating the evening.

The long table from the kitchen stood in the middle of all the splendor, laden with dishes of every variety—steaming platters of boiled potatoes, tureens of vegetable casseroles, pots of sauces and jams. In the center sat a massive filet of beef, sliced crosswise to reveal a perfectly pink middle, brown juices collecting on the plate beneath.

Annabelle's eyes danced with the light of the candles, and her mouth watered at the sight of the food. Her friends had truly outdone themselves.

Charlie looked up as she approached from where he had been lighting the last of the candles. "Annabelle…" he murmured, dazed, looking like someone had hit him over the head with a shovel. "You look…I mean…" he seemed to collect himself then and smiled. "Happy birthday."

Annabelle beamed at him. He looked very handsome in soft brown pants and a forest green jacket over a crisp white shirt. His hair was pushed back from his face as if he had run his wet fingers through it in an attempt to be tidy. "You don't look so bad yourself," she observed.

Charlie opened his mouth to say something, but then they were joined by Emily, Bess, Wilkin, and Raphael.

"Pop your eyes back in your head Charlie, there's a good lad," Raphael said, brandishing two jugs of ale and wearing a mischievous grin. "It's time to eat!"

The food was simply divine, and the company even better. Annabelle nearly did not notice that Charlie chose to sit next to her. She nearly did not notice that every so often, his knee moved to rest against hers. Nearly.

The friends ate and drank their fill, chatting animatedly, Annabelle's laughter rising above the lot of them. Each time she laughed, Charlie looked at her with that same dazed expression. It made her feel beautiful and deliriously happy. Annabelle had never before felt less like a princess and more like something…else…something better.

When the food had been eaten, and the conversation lulled, Wilkin rose to his feet. "Now, is this a party or no?" He demanded. When they all simply looked at him, he ran off into the house and emerged a moment later clutching a fiddle in one hand and a long bow in the other. Wilkin spread his arms wide, sketching a low bow before Annabelle, and then began to play.

The music was bright and lively, rising and falling in loops and trills that made Annabelle's heart race and her body yearn to move. New life was breathed into the little group as they all got to their feet, moving out onto the open grass beyond the garden.

Annabelle hoped Charlie might ask her to dance, but Raphael snatched up her hand first. "Oh no, you don't, little princess," he said with a wink. "I'll have my turn with you before I let the mooning farmer whisk you away. I don't reckon the lad will be able to let you go once he's got you in his big, strong arms."

Annabelle tried to step on his feet, but he evaded her with a laugh, sweeping her away across the lawn. Charlie and Emily joined them moments later, and they all spun and spun until Annabelle felt dizzy and breathless. One song flowed into the next, and Annabelle began to feel a bit dizzy as she and Raphael danced and danced.

Finally, the movement of Wilkin's bow slowed, giving them all a bit of a reprieve. Annabelle looked up into Raphael's face as they stood together, swaying, but his eyes were far away.

"You're worried about him, aren't you?"

He started and looked down at her with surprise. "Now, why would you say such a thing?"

She shrugged one shoulder. "I'm worried about him."

Raphael's smile was sad. "Sam is a capable knight. I'm sure he's fine."

"But you're worried about him all the same."

"I am."

"And you miss him, don't you?"

"My, aren't we full of questions tonight," he said, lifting an eyebrow.

Annabelle hesitated before saying, "Sam told me everything. I know about him…about you. It's alright, of course."

Raphael chuckled. "You know, I told him he was foolish to think you'd ever reject him for being who he is. You've a good heart, little princess. Too big and warm for small-mindedness."

"So, you miss him."

Raphael sighed, and his shoulders sagged a bit. "Like my own left leg. But don't you go running off to tell him such a thing. A man hasn't got a thing if he hasn't got his pride."

"I won't say a word," Annabelle promised. "Though I don't know why it should bother you."

"Well…" Raphael hesitated. "Sam has been a bit…hesitant."

"I can see that. I mean," Annabelle hastened to explain when he looked taken aback, "This is all rather frightening for him, isn't it? Things may be different where you come from, but here…they'd hang you both, just for loving one another. Sam already has enough trouble risking the lives of those he loves. Have you ever considered that the way he is acting with you isn't just about his own reluctance to be with you, but actually his own way of trying to keep you safe?"

Raphael opened his mouth, then closed it again, frowning. "I had not," he said. "But…Goddess, lass. That is quite observant."

"I just know Sam," Annabelle said. "He lost his parents when he was a baby, and he lost the only father he's ever really known. I suspect he feels he's losing Damon as well. It's why he's so paranoid about my safety, I think."

"You may be right," he said. "And it does help. Thank you."

"I miss him too. I feel like I've missed Sam for years, and I have. He will come back."

"From your lips to the Goddess's ears," Raphael replied. He glanced over her head, his attention caught by something, and he smirked. "I sense my time with you has come to an end," he said, pressing a kiss to the back of her hand. "It has been an honor, little princess."

"Call her that name again, and I think you'll be missing some limbs."

Annabelle gave a little jump and turned to see Charlie standing behind her. "Come with me," he said, taking her hand. "I want to show you something."

He held a torch, and Annabelle eyed it suspiciously. "Where are we going?" She asked.

"Not far," he grinned. "I promise."

"Be careful, children," Raphael called after their retreating backs. "Don't do anything I would do."

Annabelle shot him a stern look over her shoulder before she let Charlie lead her away into the dark.

꙲꙲●☾☾☾

Annabelle followed Charlie around the outside of the paddock and into the forest. When they had gone not twenty paces, Annabelle heard the sound of water splashing over stones. A stream. Charlie led her to the stream, and they followed its winding progress through the trees.

She wished Charlie would say something. The silence and the darkness pressing in on all sides were making Annabelle a bit nervous, but she was also excited. This was the farthest she had ventured from the farm since she had arrived, they were alone, and she felt lightheaded and silly from drink and dancing. She might have followed him anywhere.

The stream they followed ended in a small pool at the base of a hill that loomed above their heads in a hulking shadow. Charlie dropped her hand and approached the rocky side of the hill, where a waterfall trickled down into the pool below. Annabelle spied a gap beside the waterfall, its opening illuminated by the flickering light from Charlie's torch.

"In here," Charlie said, indicating that she should follow him. "It's perfectly safe," he assured her when she hesitated.

The rocks at the edge of the pool were slippery, but Charlie held her upright as they made their treacherous way. Bowing low to keep from hitting their heads on the rocks, they entered the cave, Annabelle gripping his arm tight.

They emerged into a cavernous hollow that seemed to take up the entire interior of the hill. Annabelle dropped Charlie's arm, and her eyes popped wide. Every inch of wall and ceiling inside the cavern was coated with crystals—even the bottom of the shallow pool of water in the center of the cavern. The light from Charlie's torch was reflected in each crystal, bouncing from one facet to the next until it was nearly bright as day.

"I found this place when I was a child," Charlie explained as Annabelle gaped at the miraculous sight. "I started coming here again after my father died to get some space."

"This is where you go when you're not at the farm," Annabelle said, tracing the edge of the pool.

"Yes," Charlie admitted. "Though I do go to the village often, too. I just…sometimes I just come here."

"I don't blame you," Annabelle turned back to face him, face transported. "This place is *magic*, Charlie."

"Just as you are," he said, the words stealing her breath away. "I have something for you," he said, reaching into his pocket.

"You didn't have to get me anything," Annabelle protested, walking back to him.

He held out his fist and opened his hand. A pendant tumbled through the air, suspended by a long chain, from his middle finger. The silver of the chain gleamed in the light of the cavern, and a single clear crystal encased in a cage of twisting wire swung back and forth, shining like a star in the torchlight.

"It's beautiful!" Annabelle gasped, lifting the pendant in her hand, admiring it from all angles.

"I bought the chain from a silversmith in the village," Charlie said, his voice oddly hoarse. "I made the pendant myself from a crystal I found in this cave." He slipped the chain over her neck. "I thought it would be a good reminder of this place and of me when you leave."

Annabelle's heart cracked, and she stiffened. "Charlie," she whispered, tears in her eyes, "I don't want to leave. I know that Sam says I must, but…I feel safe here. I'm happy here with Bess and Wilkin and Emily and…, and I don't want to leave you. Please, don't tell me I have to leave you."

Something within Charlie seemed to crumple at her words as if he had been holding his breath for years, and air was finally filling his body. "Never," he breathed, eyes wide and desperate.

And then he pulled her to him—the torch clattering to the floor of the cave as his arms wrapped around her, pulling her tightly to his body, his lips fitting over her own. Annabelle met his embrace with equal passion as they clung to each other in the dark.

She could feel every inch of her skin as if it burned. This was everything, too much and not nearly enough. As Charlie held her, as his hands roamed her body, as his lips caressed hers, Annabelle thought she might shatter into a thousand pieces. She never wanted this to end. She would die of starvation if it meant that she never had to stop kissing him.

But eventually, they did stop, Charlie letting her slide to the ground again. The torch had long since gone out, but he retrieved it from the ground anyway and took her hand.

"We should go back," he said, looking very much like he hated himself for even suggesting such a thing.

They did go back, their way lit only by the full moon that shone above the canopy. It was with regret that she followed Charlie through the garden and into the kitchen. The night was so beautiful, and Annabelle didn't want to sleep. She wanted to run and dance—to lose herself among the stars.

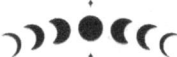

Emily and Raphael were waiting for them, seated at the table, a candle flickering between them.

"Are we keeping the party going?" Charlie asked with a wide grin. "Excellent. I'll go fetch more ale and—"

"Charlie," Emily interrupted him. "Annabelle. Sit down."

It was then that Annabelle realized something was wrong. Without preamble, Emily produced a small scroll and held it open against the table next to the candle so Annabelle and Charlie could read the words scrawled across it.

My friends,

I have happy news. His Majesty the King has announced his intentions to wed the Countess Emilia Adalara of Aelnìr before the month is out. This union will undoubtedly prove fruitful for the kingdom and our righteous campaign to end the insurrection in the north. May the Gods ensure the safety of our future queen.

Sam Fisher, knight of the realm

Charlie swore. "That swine-headed, Gods-forsaken—"

"*Charlie,*" Emily hissed.

"I don't understand." Annabelle felt dazed, shaken by this abrupt tumble back to earth from her flight on high among the stars. "What does this mean?"

"This is Sam's way of telling us it's time," Raphael said, gesturing to the letter. "'May the Gods ensure the safety of our future queen'—he means *you*, Annabelle. He is setting the plan in motion."

"No," Annabelle breathed. "He...he can't be. There hasn't been enough time."

She was dizzy with panic. This could not be happening, not *now*. It was too soon.

"Annabelle, listen to me." Raphael was serious—more serious than she had ever seen him. It terrified her. "If your father plans to remarry, that puts you in terrible danger."

"But they don't know that I'm alive." Annabelle protested. "They don't know—"

"It doesn't matter," Charlie said quietly, and there was such sadness in his eyes that it made her want to fall to the floor and weep. "If the king is betrothed to an Aelnìra countess, then Aelnìr has decided to pick a side in this conflict at last. They can only have agreed if they thought that the line of succession is secure. If they find out you're still alive..." he shook his head.

Annabelle's eyes were wide, pleading with him to stop. She could not bear to hear him say the words that would bring to an end the happiest days of her life.

"Sam's right, Annabelle. We have to get you out of Dunea," he said, his voice hollow, his expression anguished. "And we have to do it now."

Chapter Twenty-Seven

"I don't want to talk about it, Charlie."

Annabelle was exhausted and sad. She had woken to curtains of rain battering the roof of the farmhouse, and a heat that was stifling and suffocating, like a rag dipped in scalding water had been shoved down her throat.

Due to the weather, she and Charlie were forced to train in the barn. He had suggested that they skip the day, but Annabelle did not want to sleep. She wanted to punch something. Charlie, who refused to stand still long enough for any of her blows to make contact, was not helping her mood.

"I know you don't want to talk about it," he said, ducking out of the way of her next swinging attack with casual ease. "But I think we ought to all the same."

"Why?" Kick, sidestep, stumble. Annabelle gritted her teeth.

"You told me you wanted to stay here," Charlie said. "I told you that I wouldn't make you leave, but that was foolish. Of course you can't stay."

Annabelle set her feet and came at him again.

"And now you're angry with me for lying to you," Charlie continued as he blocked her.

"I am *not* angry," Annabelle protested, then she saw an opening at last. He had left his left side unguarded. A swift kick to the ribs ought to bring him to his knees.

However, Charlie shifted just in time and grabbed her foot in midair, three inches from his body. He held it hostage while Annabelle struggled, hopping a bit on the foot that still remained on the ground.

"You are angry with me," Charlie said. "And I won't let you go until you admit it."

"Charlie, let me go!"

"Admit that you're angry with me!"

"No!"

"Well then," he shrugged. "I suppose you'll have to learn to get along with one leg."

Annabelle didn't know if she wanted to pin him to the ground and beat him to a bloody pulp or pin him down for entirely another purpose. "Fine," she said, red-faced. "I am a bit angry with you."

Charlie released her foot. "Only a bit?"

Annabelle half shrugged. "I know why you told me I could stay. I also know why I have to leave—why I could never have stayed here in the first place. The news…the wedding," she sighed. "It all just reminded me why that was always impossible. So yes, I am angry with you, but I'm also just angry."

"Do you know how much I wish you could stay here forever?" His eyes were intent now, and his voice was rough with emotion. Annabelle felt his gaze all the way down in her toes. Her anger left her in a rush, replaced by another altogether more pleasurable emotion.

"Come with me," she murmured, seizing a fistful of his shirt and pulling him close.

"I can't," he said, cupping her face in his big hands. He leaned down and kissed her gently. "You know that I can't."

"I know no such thing," Annabelle protested. "I think it's an excellent idea. You're the one who hates being a farmer." She kept her tone light, playful, not wanting him to realize how serious she actually was, that she had been thinking this over all morning. It was about the only thing that was keeping her from dissolving into tears every other minute.

"I can't abandon this place or these people, Annabelle," He said gently.

She was ready for this argument. "Well…" she paused, expression thoughtful. "You could always leave Emily in charge."

"Oh, could I?" He raised an eyebrow, expression amused.

Annabelle shrugged. "She basically runs the farm for you now that she's here, and she'll take care of Bess and Wilkin."

"She would," Charlie said with a sigh. "But there would be nobody to take care of *her*."

Annabelle opened her mouth to argue, but he swallowed her words with another kiss. This one was deep and so slow that Annabelle was trembling by the time he broke it.

"It makes me very happy to know how badly you want my company," he said against her hair as they held each other. "But I cannot abandon my family. Emily would be a fine mistress of this place, but she is a woman and, as such, cannot legally own property. She needs my protection. I want her to be able to count on this place."

Annabelle suddenly had to blink back tears. "So, what?" She demanded. "We just never see each other again?"

"We don't know that."

"But we do." He wouldn't meet her eyes. "Charlie, what is it you aren't saying to me?"

Charlie sighed heavily, scrubbing one hand across the back of his neck. "Annabelle...there was never a future for us."

"And why not?"

"Are you serious?" He gaped at her.

"Deadly serious." She faced him, hands on hips, daring him to do it—to list the obstacles facing them.

"You are a princess, for one thing, and I am a farmer and a soldier—"

"I don't know if you've noticed," Annabelle cut in, "but I am about to be smuggled out of my own kingdom by my friends because it's too dangerous for me to stay. I may be a princess by name and by birth, but each day it looks more and more like I will never be anything more than that—and honestly, I don't know that I want to be."

"You don't mean that."

Now it was Annabelle's turn to avoid his eyes. She sat on a bale of hay and braced her elbows on her knees. "I've been thinking about it a lot recently. Even if I could—if there was even the slightest chance that I could become queen one day...I wouldn't want it. Being a princess has taken so much from me already. Being queen took my mother's life from her." She shrugged. "I never thought about it before because it never occurred to me that I might actually have a choice in what I wanted my life to be. It's why I refuse to let you tell me why we can't be together if that's what we want."

Annabelle met his eyes then. She wanted him to understand her completely. "Someone out there has killed me. The princess is dead. Whether their intention was to help or to harm me, I no longer care. Sam has been right all along—it is a gift and an opportunity."

"How can you say that?" Charlie's expression was stricken. "An innocent woman had to die to give you that gift."

"And if I could change that, I would," Annabelle retorted. "But there is nothing more I can do to honor her sacrifice than refuse to be manipulated—to take up the reins of my own life and refuse to relinquish them."

"You would abandon Dunea, its people, to whatever fate?" There was such coldness in his voice that Annabelle was momentarily shocked, speechless.

"I—what are you talking about?" She finally choked out. "I'm not abandoning anyone."

"Aren't you?" Charlie snorted derisively. "You have no idea how it has been for us, Annabelle. You have been through so much recently that I've held off saying anything—for that reason, and also because I never imagined you could be so...so...."

"So, what?"

"Selfish," he snapped. "And spoiled."

Annabelle's face, eyes, and throat all felt like they were on fire. Rage was choking her, ignited by the shame that coiled in her belly. He did not understand. She *was* thinking of her people. What good to them was a queen who must always fear for her life or become a pawn to be used by others?

"So this is what you truly think of me," Annabelle said to her knees.

"It isn't what I think of you," Charlie said, settling onto the bale of hay beside her, voice a bit kinder now. "Not really. I always knew you had to leave. It won't do anyone any good at all if you're killed. But…I always assumed you'd return to help us fight."

"Fight what?" Annabelle sighed. "For all the dangers I've faced in the past few months, I cannot honestly say I even know what the real danger is, what I'm actually running away from or fighting against."

"We fight what has already happened," Charlie replied with a shrug. "The laws and religious doctrines that keep the people poor, shackled, and too scared to fight for the change they deserve. And we prepare to fight what is coming."

"What *is* coming?"

"We don't know, but everything that is happening—the rebellion in the north, the growing unrest at court, the king's betrayal of Eìrlani trust, your apparent murder, and the king's marriage to a lady of Aelnìr—these things are not random, they can't be, and they are tied to something far larger than you or I can imagine right now."

"You don't even have a theory?" Annabelle pressed him.

Charlie chuckled. "Sam is the one with the strategic mind. I am simply his sword arm—the brute muscle. When the time comes, he will point me in the right direction. I must sharpen my edges so that I am ready to be used."

They were quiet for a while, listening to the rain hammering the sides of the barn.

"I cannot make you any promises," Annabelle relented at last. "There is so much we don't yet know and so much still to come. What I do know is that I will be useless to my people without help, without strength, and without knowledge. I cannot obtain these things here, and you cannot come with me. But…will…" She took a steadying breath. "Will you wait for me?"

Charlie lifted an eyebrow. "Are you asking me to play the pining maiden, princess?"

Her cheeks flushed. "No, I just…I want the chance to figure out what this is between us, and we will never have that chance now. I can never leave if I'm afraid it means the end of this, and I don't know if I'll have the strength to return if you aren't here waiting for me."

Annabelle waited for him to make fun of her, but he did not. Instead, he took her hands in his own and kissed the back of each one solemnly.

"I think you will find," he said with a sad smile, "that there was never any doubt of *my* waiting for *you*."

Annabelle's eyes narrowed, and she frowned. "What are you implying?"

"It doesn't matter," he said, kissing her softly. "All I mean is that I will do whatever you ask of me."

Annabelle did not believe him but did not argue the point as she lost herself within the warmth of the barn, the heat, and Charlie's arms—at least for a little while.

Annabelle, Charlie, Emily, and Raphael set off at dawn on foot, leaving Rabble farm in the care of Wilkin and Bess until Charlie could return. He would accompany them as far as the coast to meet with the ship that Ilya had arranged to carry them north to the capital. They would leave him there to meet Sam in the north.

Despite Annabelle's protests, Emily had resolved to accompany her on the journey to Eìrlan.

"This is my chance to see more of the world, not just read about it in books," Emily had said firmly on the morning of their departure after Annabelle took that one last opportunity to try to convince her to stay. "And there is nothing you can say to me to change my mind, Annabelle."

And so Annabelle let the matter go. Her objections had been half-hearted, in any case. Despite knowing that the path ahead would be dangerous, Annabelle was glad to know she would have one more friend by her side. Saying goodbye to Charlie would be horrible enough without having to leave Emily behind as well.

I hope I do not come to regret this act of selfishness, Annabelle thought, fingering the hilt of the knife she now wore strapped to her waist. Charlie had given her the weapon the day before, though he begged her only to use it when she must.

"Run," he had urged her. "Run from any danger and only fight when you have no other choice."

Emily wore a similar weapon as well as a bow and quiver of arrows on her back. Both women were dressed in the same brown trousers and simple cotton shirt. They required more ease of movement than skirts could provide, as they were forced to make the journey to the coast on foot, traveling under cover of the trees and across the countryside to avoid notice.

Charlie wore his broadsword and a leather jerkin, and Raphael was covered with blades from head to toe—small knives concealed at his wrists and ankles and two short blades strapped across his broad back.

It made Annabelle feel proud to stand beside her friends—these strong, brilliant warriors—and not feel quite so helpless. Charlie's words from the day before came back to her: *We fight what has already happened—the laws and religious doctrines that keep the people poor, shackled, and too scared to fight for the change they deserve. And we prepare to fight what is coming.*

Her friends, like the weapons they carried, had been forged in the fires of an unjust world. Others had shielded her from the world for so long. Now that she ventured forth into that world, Annabelle realized it was forming her too. Would she become a weapon someday? If she did, Annabelle couldn't help but feel a sting of fear to think of the purpose to which she might be turned.

)))●(((

They made good progress the first night, only stopping briefly to refill water skins in a nearby stream or stretch aching limbs. The journey was not easy, but Annabelle refused to give in to her exhaustion or the way her legs began to scream in protest by the time the sun was high in the sky. She would not be weak. Now more than ever, she needed to put her discomfort from her mind and press on.

After all, this was not just about her safety anymore. They were going to free Mica, and in doing so, they would right a terrible wrong. Annabelle could not bring back the dead or make those glorious ships whole again, but she could do this. And so she would keep quiet and press on, no matter the discomfort.

When they eventually stopped to sleep, Annabelle found it a challenge to get any rest at all. Nerves kept her awake and alert—jumpy when they stopped to rest and anxious to press on as soon as the sky turned orange and gold in the light of the setting sun.

As they pressed on, the terrain became more forested and mountainous, and Annabelle realized with a jolt that this landscape was painfully familiar to her.

"We are close to Rosewood Manor," Emily said to her on the fourth night of their journey as they picked their way across a rocky ridge, deep in the forest.

"Is it wise to pass so close?" Annabelle asked. Her heart yearned to see the place again, but she knew that danger waited within its walls in the form of Gustav Wallace.

Emily shrugged. "It's a risk we have to take. The safest place for a ship to anchor unseen is south of the manor. But we shouldn't have cause to worry. We will only be within Gustav's territory on our final day of the journey."

Tomorrow. They would be passing into Rosewood province tomorrow. The thought should have terrified Annabelle, but she instead felt a strange thrill of excitement and a fresh surge of energy. It was like her home sensed her closeness and was offering her the strength to continue.

They were so close, so very close. Despite all the odds, the first stage of the plan had nearly been completed without incident. It made Annabelle feel the first stirrings of hope that they would actually be able to pull this off.

Annabelle's only regret was that her time with Charlie was rapidly drawing to a close—not that they had any time together on the journey. There was no time to talk or to be alone as they silently raced across the country. It didn't matter. The time they'd had together would never be enough, not for forever, but she prayed it would be enough for now.

The one thing that continued to bother her was what he had said, about how it had never been in doubt that *he* would wait for *her*. It seemed to imply that there was a doubt that *she* would wait for *him*—a ludicrous idea, to be sure. Annabelle could not imagine ever wanting someone else.

It was a girlish notion, and Annabelle was painfully aware of how it would sound if she expressed such thoughts aloud. But she didn't care. She may be inexperienced when it came to love, but she was no idiot. Charlie was handsome and kind. He cared for his family and felt his responsibilities acutely. He could be hot-headed, but he had a big heart. How could she ever want more, ever find better qualities in a man?

If she had been a country girl living in the village, or he had been a nobleman's son, such a match would have been beyond her wildest dreams—in fact, other ladies would call her the silliest idiot who ever drew breath to walk away from such a union.

Time would reveal the truth, but for now, she would let Charlie keep his foolish illusions. Maybe it helped him to let her go, to think that they were never meant to be in the first place. She would not take that comfort from him, but she would be happy to prove him wrong someday.

So lost was she in her daydreaming that Annabelle nearly collided with Charlie's back, as she had not noticed him stop. They had come to a clearing nestled against a rocky slope, surrounded by tall pine trees on all sides.

"We will rest here for the day," he announced to their group. "You three set up camp. I'll go fetch some water. There is a stream not far off."

"Oh, please let me go, Charlie," Annabelle begged, stretching her legs and wincing. "I'm dying for a wash."

Charlie frowned, and she knew he was about to tell her that it was too risky, but Emily said quickly, "I'll go with her. I won't let anything happen to her, Charlie."

Charlie still looked uneasy, but he relented, and Annabelle and Emily set off in the direction he indicated.

The stream was farther than Annabelle had realized, and she felt uneasy as she stripped off her boots and waded into the freezing water. Emily didn't seem concerned, though she kept her bow in her hand at all times and scanned the surrounding forest with sharp eyes at regular intervals.

"Are you excited to see Eìrlan?" Emily asked as Annabelle splashed water on her arms, face, and neck, sighing in relief as the icy liquid soothed her heated skin.

Annabelle shrugged. "I'd not given it much thought. Maybe I was excited about the possibility back when I was meant to marry Mica. It feels different now."

"That makes sense," Emily said, nodding. "Even so, little is known about the kingdom. It will be very intriguing to see such a place."

"Ever the researcher," Annabelle said with a smirk. "You know, you really missed a true companion in Herbert."

Emily's expression brightened. "You know, I wanted to be a scholar when I was young. For years I talked of little else. My poor father never had the heart to tell me it was impossible, but I figured it out eventually." She giggled. "I was so furious, I threatened to burn down the farm."

Annabelle gaped. "You did no such thing!"

Emily nodded. "Of course I did! But then I realized that burning my family home to the ground would do nothing to change the law, so I decided to memorize every book in my father's collection instead."

"A much more productive activity."

"I thought so."

"And who knows," Annabelle added. "You may become a scholar yet."

"Maybe." Emily sighed wistfully but said nothing else about it, so Annabelle returned to rinsing the dirt from her hair.

Her washing complete, Annabelle turned back to Emily. "Toss me the water skins?" She asked, extending a hand.

But Emily did not toss her the skins, which lay on the ground at her feet. She was staring over Annabelle's head, face pale, and she had drawn her bow.

Annabelle turned to see what had caused this alarm, and her heart stopped. Men were walking out of the trees—five of them, all bearing an assortment of weapons. One man carried a bow, which he had pointed, not at Emily but at Annabelle.

"Don't think about it, girlie," the bowman called out. "One move, and I drop your pretty friend."

Emily did not lower her bow, but nor did she shoot.

Annabelle tried to breathe calm and slow, just as Raphael had taught her, to keep from panicking. What were her options? She stood knee-deep in the stream, her feet bare against the slippery stone bottom. Slowly, she adjusted her position, trying to find a better purchase with her feet that would allow her to move without tumbling onto her rear in the shallow water.

The men continued their approach, each wearing an expression of lazy amusement. Annabelle could now see that their clothes were ratted and mismatched, and their hair and beards were gnarled and unkempt. *Bandits*, she realized with horror.

"We don't have any money," Annabelle called to them, holding her hands high in the air. "We only wish to pass through this place in peace."

A few of the men laughed.

"Nobody has any money," said one who carried a long curved knife. "But you have weapons."

"And the clothes on your backs," said another.

"And a pretty trinket around your neck," continued the first man, pointing toward Annabelle's chest with the point of his blade.

Annabelle looked down. Charlie's gift, the crystal necklace, hung low and heavy between her breasts. "You will not touch this," she snarled.

The men laughed again. "And you're gonna stop us, dearie?" Said a large bearded brute brandishing an ax.

"That's right," Annabelle snarled, her hand flexing as she longed to reach for the knife belted to her waist.

"Annabelle, don't!" Emily hissed from behind her.

But Annabelle was angry now. They were so close to getting away from this place, and these idiot thugs were going to ruin it for her—for all of them. Like hell would she go down without a fight. Her breath was now coming easy and clean, her mind clearing. If she could scream for help, and if they could hold these men off long enough, Charlie and Raphael would make quick work of them.

Annabelle did not think; she just breathed, waiting for an opening. All the while, the enemy closed in, and she stood, her feet going numb in the rushing water.

Then it happened—the man carrying the bow stumbled on the uneven ground. It was barely more than a moment of distraction, but Annabelle was ready.

"Now!" Annabelle screamed as loud as she could, falling to her hands and knees in the stream. The bowman's arrow sailed harmlessly over her head, and a moment later, he crumpled to the ground. Emily's arrow had flown true, striking the man clean through the throat.

Annabelle had just enough time to get to her feet before the first of the men was upon her. The knife now in hand, she dodged under his first attack and slammed her body into his. He went down hard, and she was on top of him before he could catch his breath.

The blood was hot as it spurted up around the hand that clutched the blade now buried in the man's heart. She released the hilt of the knife and scrambled away from him, splashing in the shallows of the stream that was turning red with blood. The only sound she could hear was the pounding of her heart in her ears.

Thought was impossible. Everything was impossible. She had killed a man, and yet she still needed to stand up to get to her friend. Why weren't the other men attacking? Annabelle looked up in time to see that they hid behind trees, the occasional arrow keeping them trapped on the far side of the stream.

Maybe it would be alright. Maybe Charlie and Raphael had heard her shout. Maybe they would make it in time. She needed to get back to Emily. They needed to retreat.

But when Annabelle turned toward her friend, what she saw sent her heart rocketing up into her throat, choking her. Three more men emerged from the forest behind the girl, whose attention was still fixed upon the far bank. The men grabbed her, one forcing the bow from her hands and another wrapping his thick fingers around her throat, cutting her scream short.

Panic and fury rose within Annabelle as a familiar force surged in her veins. A scream ripped from her throat, from deep inside of her soul, and white-hot light flashed as bodies scattered, blown off of Emily. The men landed hard, scattered through the wood, and did not rise again.

There were shouts of alarm from behind Annabelle, but she did not pay them any attention.

"Run!" She shouted at Emily, who still stood too far away from her, gasping and shaking. "Run and get the others. I'm right behind you."

"I'm not leaving you," Emily sobbed, reaching out a hand. Annabelle was moving as fast as she could, bare feet sliding in the muck, the sounds of pursuers at her back.

"She's a witch!" A man's voice shouted, too close. "Grab her! Now!"

"Emily, *RUN!*" Annabelle screamed before she felt a sharp pain at the back of her head and the world around her vanished into nothingness.

Chapter Twenty-Eight

Sam was not happy to be back in Rengon City. This place would never be home to him, no matter how familiar the streets and alleys.

Night had long since fallen, but Sam still wandered the city, unable to sleep. How could he rest when his dear friends had left the safety of the farm and were traveling across the country? There were so many reasons they might not make it. But he could not think about that now, lest he drive himself forever mad.

He had never been very good at waiting, not like this. Sam was a creature of action. A knight, perhaps, but little better than an assassin. Track the target, eliminate the target, move on. But this enemy was invisible. Like shooting an arrow at a target that he could not see, all he could do was hold his breath and pray.

And so he walked until he found himself standing before the door of a tavern. Light, warm and friendly, glowed within, and he could hear the sounds of laughter and someone playing the lute. The smell of good food and ale and the joy of good company wafted through an open window. A distraction and a meal might be welcome.

The tavern was warm and lively, and Sam picked his way through the assorted tables where patrons sat, drinking ale and laughing as a long-limbed man sat in the corner and played his lute as an accompaniment to their merry-making.

One particular group of patrons drew Sam's attention. Five men and one woman sat crowded around their small table, laughing and drinking as a fourth man entertained them with a story about a boar.

Sam smiled to himself. He knew that voice and that story.

"Sammy! Is that you?" Damon spied him as he approached the table and threw his arms wide. "Gods save me. Sam Fisher, in a tavern of all places. I never thought I'd see the day."

Sam grinned and crossed the room to greet Damon, who extricated himself from his companions and clapped Sam on the back, eyes alight with drink and laughter.

"It is good to see you," Damon said.

"You as well," Sam replied. "Though I am a bit surprised. I hadn't realized you were in the city."

Damon shrugged. "Nowhere else to go, really. I heard you'd left Ellasport with his majesty's entourage and figured I'd tag along. Rented myself a room in this fine establishment and soon after met these scoundrels." He lifted the mug in his hand to toast his companions, who all jeered, laughed, and drank to his insult in equal measure.

"New friends," Damon announced, wiping his mouth on the sleeve of his jacket. "I would like you to meet my oldest friend— Sir Sam Fisher."

Sam returned their smiles, feeling suddenly uncomfortable. These sorts of things, these impromptu social occasions, were so much more Damon's forte than his own.

"Nice to meet you, Sir Sam," said a large bearded man with quiet gray eyes. "Sam Fisher...where have I heard that name before?"

"Come on, Fletcher, you know who he is. He's that knight everyone can't stop talking about," Piped up a small cherry-headed man with a smooth face and wide green eyes who looked like he could not be older than seventeen or eighteen. He eyed Sam with great interest. "The one who was responsible for killing all those rebels in the north last year."

"Oh, leave off him, Erik," chided the woman. Of all those seated about the table, this woman was the most interesting to Sam. The finery of her attire—the jewels at her neck and the pearls threaded through her dark hair—did not match her surroundings. This woman was a lady, and a great one.

"My Lady," Sam said, bowing deeply before her.

She chuckled. "Oh, I like this one, Damon. Wherever did you find him?"

"We grew up together, Lady Asby," Damon said jovially, resuming his seat. "He was my father's ward."

Asby. Sam's interest in the lady intensified. Everyone at court knew that Lord Asby's wife had been taken in childbirth. This, he realized, must be his eldest daughter, the Lady Cressida Asby. Her younger sister, Malisa, had attended Annabelle during her stay at the palace, but Cressida had remained in the north. She was an infamous fixture in the city, though Sam had never before had the pleasure of enjoying her company. Now seemed his chance to discover the truth behind the rumors.

"Your father's ward?" Lady Asby raised a thin eyebrow, looking Sam over from head to toe. "How fascinating. You must tell me your story one of these days, Sir Sam."

"It would be my pleasure, Lady Asby," Sam replied, pulling up a free chair. "Name the day."

Damon snorted. "Don't let him fool you, my Lady. I've never seen Sam willingly offer up more than a string of five words at a time."

"Luckily, I have you to speak for me," Sam said with a shrug. "And that was eight words, in case anyone is counting."

Everyone, Damon and Lady Asby included, laughed at this.

"You're alright, Fisher," said Fletcher, handing him an overflowing mug of ale. "Have a drink."

It was a pleasant way to spend an evening, sitting among this unusual group of companions. Angus Fletcher, Sam learned, was a court artist, and the young Erik Lessam was apprenticed to a silversmith in the jeweler's quarter. The two other men were called George and Rupert Graham—brothers who owned a small shipping company that transported goods between Aelnìr, Rengon City, Ellasport, and the isles of Petra.

"How did such an odd assortment of people come to be drinking companions?" Sam asked sometime later when everyone else at the table was well and truly lubricated. For his part, he was careful only to give the illusion of imbibing to excess. He did not mean to trick his new friends, only to enjoy the pleasure of their company while keeping his wits about him. Though they did not appear to notice what he drank, nor care.

"Much the same way you and the amiable Sir Damon came to be a part of our little group," Fletcher said. "By chance, and over time."

"But…surely it takes more than chance and time for two merchants, an apprentice, and an artist to come across a high lady of his majesty's court," Sam pressed. "No disrespect meant, of course."

George shrugged. "No offense taken."

"He meant to the lady, dimwit," Rupert said with a smirk.

George opened his mouth to say something, but Lady Asby cut across him. "In answer to your question, I've known Angus here for years. He is one of my father's favorite artists. One day he was painting my portrait, and I asked if he would take me out for a drink in the city, a place I would never find on my own. He brought me here."

"You did?" Sam gaped at the man, who smiled.

"Such a beauty," Angus said with a chuckle. "Of course I did! Haven't regretted it a minute since. She is delightful company. Drinks most of us under the table on a good night."

Lady Asby scowled at him, but the others exchanged knowing looks.

"Well, I am impressed," said Damon. "It is an uncommon woman who would venture out of the castle on her own, unchaperoned and without protection. I raise my glass to you." He lifted his mug into the air and downed it in one.

"What makes you think I am without protection?" Lady Asby inquired with a sultry smile.

Damon eyed her bodice with interest, perhaps imagining that a knife lay concealed somewhere within, but Sam stiffened at once. He had been distracted by his unexpected reunion with Damon and meeting so many new people at once. Now he cast his awareness toward the rest of the tavern.

A man sat alone at the end of the bar wearing a long cloak that, upon closer inspection, was lumpy in places to suggest that more than one blade lay concealed beneath. Two others sat a few tables away, playing a game of cards, but they had not touched their drinks in a long while. As the others at his table continued to drink and talk, Sam noticed three more armed men glance furtively toward their group.

Lady Asby had not come alone but was escorted and protected by no fewer than *six* heavily armed guards. This did not surprise him. She was, after all, the eldest daughter of the third most powerful man in the kingdom. What did bother him was that he had failed to notice the men before now. Sam set his mug down on the table and did not touch it again.

George and Rupert were the first to take their leave, citing an early shipment as their excuse for departing, followed closely by Erik, whose master had instated a curfew. This admission earned him a thorough round of friendly abuse from the others. He bore the quips about his age and foolishness well.

Angus and Lady Asby lingered for a while longer but soon took their leave together. As her ladyship's concealed guard slowly trailed after her, one by one, Sam began to feel more relaxed.

"Is she not the most splendid creature you've ever laid eyes on?" Damon sighed after her retreating back.

The corner of Sam's mouth twitched as he watched his friend's awed and dazed expression. "She is lovely," he said. "Though…I think you have some competition there."

Damon scoffed. "Hardly. Did you notice how she laughed and laughed at my story about Gustav and the pigpen?"

"I did," Sam said, "but did you notice how she left the tavern with *Angus* and not with you?"

Damon's mouth fell open. "Gods take me," he breathed and then laughed aloud, clapping a hand against his knee. "Well, it seems I've been played for a fool. I can't say I don't admire her a bit for it."

"I wouldn't take it personally," Sam offered. "Watching them this evening, I'd wager they've been covering up their affair for some time. They both appear quite practiced at it." It was the truth. The lady and the artist had nearly fooled him; they had seemed so indifferent to one another. That is until they left together. There was a light in Angus's eyes that was unmistakable. Sam had seen that light before, and he was not likely to forget it.

Sam took another sip of his drink, willing the bitter liquid to chase off thoughts of Raphael.

"I don't take it personally," Damon was saying with a shrug. "It isn't as if I meant to court her, anyway."

"No?" Sam was still not really interested but decided he needed the distraction of conversation more than he disliked hearing about Damon's newest object of desire.

Damon snorted. "A low country knight and a high lady of the court? Such a match would be impossible."

"I didn't think you intended to marry her, Damon," Sam said reasonably.

"And why not?" Damon demanded, sounding suddenly irritated. "I could have the ambition to marry."

"I...well, you just said that it would be impossible." Sam could smell another fight on the horizon and was desperate to avoid it if he could. "But if you do intend to marry someone, I think that's...I think that's wonderful, Damon."

"I'll need to marry someday, you know," Damon grumbled into his tankard. "If I'm to have heirs of my own, and a legacy. Not that you care much for those things, do you? I've never seen you so much as sniff at a woman. You're too honorable for your own good, Sammy," he added. Though his smile suggested he was teasing, the hardness in his eyes made it look more like a sneer.

"Look, I know the past few months have been hard," Sam said, attempting to steer the conversation back to safer ground. "But maybe there's a way we can make things better for you. Speak to the Duchess, Damon. She's always been fond of you, and I'm sure she'd do anything to help after everything your family did for Annabelle."

"You would have me ask for charity?" Damon snapped. "I have my pride, Sam. And my honor. I'll not go scrounging at the feet of nobles for scraps."

Sam was confused and exhausted in equal measure. It seemed that he could not have a single interaction with Damon without saying something that set him off. It made Sam horribly sad and frustrated. He wanted this to end. He wanted his friend back.

But maybe Damon was not the one who had changed. Perhaps this was the man he had been all along, and Sam was only capable of seeing the truth now that he had released his desperation for Damon's approval and affection. Regardless of why their friendship was now in free-fall, Sam was out of time.

"I'm sorry," he said. "It was an insensitive thing to say."

Damon wasn't looking at him. "I don't want to argue, Sam." He said, staring into his empty tankard.

"Nor do I."

Neither one of them spoke. The barmaid came by to refill their tankards, and they drank together in tense silence. Then Damon clapped a few coppers on the table and stood.

"Goodnight, Sam," He said.

"Goodnight, Damon," Sam replied.

Damon hesitated, looking as if he might say something. The torn fragments of their friendship floated in the air between them. Sam hoped that Damon would try to grab hold of them, to make some gesture to repair the bond that had snapped and was fading with each passing moment.

But he did not. He turned away and left Sam there alone to mourn something he now knew had long since been lost.

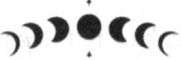

Annabelle regained consciousness slowly. At first, she only noticed bits and pieces about her surroundings before losing herself once again to the dark—The sound of hoofbeats and the sight of the ground speeding past before her eyes as she lay slung over the back of a horse; the gruff rise and fall of male voices as she was lifted and dragged roughly up stone steps; a sudden burst of agony as she was flung to the floor; the feeling of smooth wood beneath her cheek.

It was not until Annabelle's captors hauled her into a sitting position and slapped her hard across the face that she came fully back to herself. Her head ached so badly that stars danced in her vision, and the spot where the man had struck her cheek stung and made her eyes water, but she did not fade away again. She looked around.

How many times had she stood in this very room? She could have described it in perfect detail with her eyes closed—the stone hearth, the wooden bookshelves, the portraits hanging on the walls. Had it not been for the painful grip of the person holding her upright, or the horrible man staring down at her from behind that big mahogany desk, Annabelle might have thought that the past two months had been little more than a terrible dream.

But Baron Gustav Wallace was too real to be denied.

"What is this?" He snapped, eyes staring over Annabelle's head to the man who held her captive.

"A witch, my Lord," the man said, and Annabelle recognized his voice. This was the man who had caught her, one of those who had accosted them in the wood. Annabelle knew a moment of terror, wondering what had become of her friends.

"A witch," Gustav repeated. "Do you have proof of this accusation?"

"She used her power on my men, my Lord," the man replied. "And I found this around her neck."

Annabelle could not see what the man held, but she looked down and realized with a jolt of panic that her pendant was not there. In an instant, she realized what the man was implying: he believed that the crystal was the object she had used to work magic in the forest.

"I see," Gustav said with a nod. "You did well to remove this trinket. Who knows what other evils she may have perpetrated if it had not been discovered. We might all be dead right now." And, for the first time, he looked down at Annabelle.

Gustav's eyes widened in surprise and recognition, and Annabelle could not breathe. He had recognized her. It was over. Annabelle knew it was all over the moment his eyes went cold and his mouth twisted in an ugly sneer.

"Did she have any companions," he asked her captor.

"Er…yes, m'lord," the man said. "A woman."

"And?"

"Er…well…" the man hesitated, and Annabelle wanted to scream with impatience. "We captured this witch for your lordship, but in the commotion…."

"You let the other one escape you," Gustav hissed. "How disappointing."

"Surely—surely one witch is better than none, my lord?" The man's voice was panicked now. He must fear that his payment was in jeopardy. Disgusting. Annabelle silently cursed the man for his despicable cowardice.

Gustav was beginning to look bored. He returned his attention to Annabelle's face. She knew that look—a spider with a fly caught in its web, debating how best to devour its meal.

"Very well. You may go. My men will take it from here." He lifted the lid on a small box that sat upon the desk and tossed a round silver coin at the man, who released Annabelle to catch it.

"Thank you, my lord," he breathed. "I will speak of your generosity."

"See that you do," Gustav purred. "Now, *go*."

The man departed, and without warning, there were more footsteps as two guards moved forward and two new sets of hands seized Annabelle and dragged her into a standing position.

Gustav rose slowly and circled the desk until he was standing in front of her. He leaned down until they were nose to nose, and Annabelle fought the urge to spit in his horrible, wicked face.

"Little witch," he whispered, breath stinking of stale wine. "I suppose it shouldn't surprise me. My father did love you so, and I always wondered why this little girl should mean more to him than his own son. Now I have my answer. Tell me, were they all under your spell?"

"Please, Gustav," Annabelle moaned, hating herself for begging, for pleading with this man. "Please. You have to help me."

Gustav slapped her hard. Annabelle felt her cheekbone crack with the force of it. One of his rings had cut her, and she tasted blood.

"I am not so easily enchanted, girl," he spat. "I have known what you were from the beginning, and now you will get what you deserve. You will hang like the bitch you are, and finally, the Gods' justice will be served. Take her away."

The guards hauled her away from him, out of the study, and Annabelle lost control of herself at last. She screamed and kicked, fear and rage rising up and taking over, along with another feeling, a feeling that was growing ever more familiar to her.

Power—that was the crackle of magic building in her veins. Annabelle welcomed it, bid it to gather its strength, waiting for the moment to release it, to level this place and not caring if she burst apart with the effort as long as she took Gustav with her.

Then, loud as if someone were speaking directly into her ear, she heard someone with her own voice say, *Calm down. Think.*

Annabelle stopped thrashing and fighting, just for a moment, but it was long enough. This could not happen, she realized. The man who captured her had taken her necklace. As long as these men believed that the magical object had been taken from her, they believed she could no longer harm them. If they learned the truth, that would be the end.

And though she wanted to risk it all to enact her vengeance, and damn the consequences, Annabelle forced herself to remember her friends—to remember that Mica was still captive and that the others were still out there somewhere—and she took one long, deep breath.

The fire building within her flickered as if a cool wind had begun to blow. She took another breath, and then another. Painfully slowly, the flow of power slowed and then stopped. Annabelle closed her eyes and took breath after breath as Gustav's men fastened shackles to her wrists and ankles as they lifted her up and threw her onto rough wooden planks strewn with moldy straw.

Annabelle breathed against the power, against the panic and the fear, until she was certain she was no longer out of control—until she had long since felt the rumble of movement against her body and heard the sound of hooves and the creaking of wagon wheels against the dirt road.

She opened her eyes.

People were watching her—four of them, eyes wide and bloodshot, faces pale and streaked with dirt. These people wore shackles at their wrists and ankles too, and they all bore the signs of rough treatment. One woman had a blackened eye, another was bleeding from a cut in her leg. Near the front of the wagon, a small boy of about eight or nine clung to a woman Annabelle assumed must be his mother. Both bore marks of having been beaten.

Around them, iron bars stretched up on all sides and overhead. Annabelle reached out her shackled hands, feeling dizzy, and closed shaking fingers around the bars. Tears leaked from her eyes, rolling down her cheeks in an unending stream as the world closed in around her.

No more cages. No more cages.

No more cages.

Chapter Twenty-Nine

It was over. Gustav knew that Annabelle was alive, and it would not be a matter of if he used that information to his own benefit, but when.

Overcome by pain and terror, Annabelle curled into a ball in the corner of the wagon, huddled against the incessant pawing of her own misery. There was no more fight left in her. She had tried to run, to hide, to escape whatever fate awaited her in Rengon City. But she had lost. It was time to give up.

The only thought that kept Annabelle's heart from shattering into a thousand pieces was that her friends were alright. Emily had escaped the men who had attacked them. They would be fine. Maybe they would continue north. Maybe they would find Sam. Maybe they could still save Mica.

But only the Gods could save Annabelle now. Gustav would tell the king, and the king would lock Annabelle away forever—or worse.

If anyone else discovered that she was alive, if anyone from Aelnìr so much as suspected, then Annabelle was as good as dead.

She was so exhausted and longed for sleep. Sleep would allow her to forget the pain and to forget the fear. Annabelle closed her eyes, welcoming the freedom that would come with the darkness of sleep. A warm hand rested on her shoulder, and Annabelle reluctantly opened her eyes to see that the woman with the black eye had come to sit beside her.

"You mustn't sleep, dear," the woman said. "I know you want to, but you must try to stay awake as long as you can."

"Why?" Annabelle asked, too tired for more words.

"The wound to your head, dear. I have some knowledge of healing," the woman explained. "If you go to sleep now, there's a chance you'll never wake. So keep your eyes open, whatever you do."

Annabelle tried, but it was hard. Her body wanted to rest, and her head ached. But the woman kept her awake and distracted with conversation in the small stretches of time when Annabelle wasn't retching over the side of the wagon.

The woman's name was Phyllis. She came from a small village in the south of Rosewood province—too small and poor to afford its own healer. As an elder and a midwife, Phyllis had been one of the most well-respected members of their community until she wasn't.

"People were getting sick," she told Annabelle on the second morning. "Some died. I didn't know how or what was causing it. By the time we discovered the well in town had gone putrid, it was too late. People were angry and scared, and my family all remained healthy—well, of course we did. We get our water from the spring on my grandson's farm." She sighed heavily. "But nobody wanted explanations; they just wanted someone to blame for their misfortune."

"That's terrible," Annabelle murmured, horrified that anyone could be so unfeeling.

Phyllis shrugged. "I can't blame them. The crown rewards anyone who turns in a suspected witch. It's an old-fashioned law, mind, but with the war and taxes being what they are…One silver coin goes a long way these days."

"Even so," Annabelle said. "I am so sorry that happened to you."

Phyllis eyed her steadily. "It was the same as happened to you, is it not?"

"That is true." Annabelle bit her lip, wondering if she should ask the question that squirmed in her belly, aching to get free. "But you're not…" She hesitated. "You're not a witch, are you?"

"Would you be frightened of me if I were?" Phyllis asked, her gaze intent.

"No," Annabelle replied truthfully.

"Well," Phyllis said with a sad smile, "Whether I am a witch or not, I don't think it matters much now."

"No," Annabelle agreed, feeling a bit disappointed. "No, I suppose it doesn't."

Phyllis made the journey north bearable for Annabelle. The other prisoners kept to themselves, sleeping or staring mutely into the distance. The old woman's company was soothing amidst such gloom and misery.

On the fourth day of the journey, the guards parked the wagon on the outskirts of a small village. Three of them disappeared for a long while, returning with another prisoner. This young woman appeared to be about Annabelle's age, who fought so hard when they tried to put her in the wagon that the other prisoners had to scurry out of her way so as not to be struck by her manacled limbs or flying chains. She spent the journey screaming and keeping up a never-ending stream of insults that she spat at the guards day and night.

"Dear, carrying on like that will do nothing but keep the rest of us from sleep," Phyllis said to the girl after the soldiers had beaten her for the fifth time for wailing through the night.

The girl spat blood at the old woman's feet and gave her a wicked red grin. "I'll not be silenced by anyone, not even you, crone."

This fiery defiance was not to last, however. The guards, evidently seeing an opportunity to make an example for other would-be dissenting voices, began to punish the young woman with chilling consistency. Often, she came back to the wagon, oozing blood from a cracked lip or sporting new purple bruises across her body. Sometimes she bore no sign of injury at all but curled up into a ball in the corner of the wagon and simply lay there, shaking and crying.

It was a horrible thing to witness, and Annabelle was ashamed to feel herself shrink away from the woman as if her pitiable state were catching. Phyllis tried to help the poor thing on several occasions but was swiftly and roughly rejected. All they could do was watch as the cruelty of men slowly broke the woman's wild and vibrant spirit.

What disturbed Annabelle most was that this abuse was happening in *her* kingdom. How could her father allow this? Did he even know? These guards answered to Gustav, and therefore their behavior was more expected than unsurprising. But what did that mean? How much control did the king have over his lords when it came to the actions of their men?

Annabelle knew it was useless to ask such questions. They did not matter—not to her, not anymore. But there was a new feeling stirring deep in her gut. This new feeling reminded her of fear, and yet there was a sharpness to it that chased away the sluggishness of exhaustion and hunger.

Rage. This was rage. Annabelle was no stranger to anger. She often had trouble keeping her temper in check. Anger was a constant companion with whom she wrestled constantly as if she rode the back of a giant serpent. It always made her do and say things she might not have done or said otherwise. Anger made her foolish, irrational, ineffective.

This new feeling was so strong, so all-encompassing, that Annabelle was very nearly distracted from the hopelessness of her predicament. It was like the rage was a white-hot fire that swept through her body and mind, burning away everything cloudy and weak, leaving only bright clarity in its wake.

The injustice that this woman was treated with such contempt, that these people should be taken from their homes, that a wise woman like Phyllis could be so betrayed by her friends—people whom she had cared for when they were sick and dying—had ignited a force within Annabelle that overcame her aching stomach or heavy eyelids.

The next time the guards came to the wagon, looking for their prey, Annabelle was waiting for them. She sat near the wagon door, head bowed like the others, feigning the same fearful indifference, waiting. The second the guard's head came into view, she pounced, clubbing him with her heavy iron manacles and wrapping the chain tight around his neck.

Shouts erupted as the other guards rushed to help their companion. Annabelle had the man pinned to the floor of the wagon, intentionally pressing his face into the stinking hay. "Do you think it's fun to abuse a helpless woman?" She hissed into the man's ear. "Do you think it makes you strong, powerful?"

"Get off me, bitch!" The man choked out. Annabelle applied more pressure to his throat.

"You think you scare me?" She growled. "I've been called worse by better men than you, and I swear to the Gods above that I will live to see the day when each and every one of you kneels before me, you *scum*!"

Hands were grappling at her back now. Annabelle hung on as long as she could manage, but there were too many of them. She allowed herself to be pulled off the man who had fallen into unconsciousness from lack of air. As the other guards carried her off the wagon, Annabelle met the eyes of the red-haired woman—who was staring in open-mouthed shock.

Annabelle wanted to tell her that she was sorry—sorry for sitting silently while she was so mistreated, sorry for allowing herself to be locked away for so long, for letting others take her voice and her power away, sorry for not realizing sooner what was at stake.

It was too late to change much now, but Annabelle could do this. She could share the burden and the pain. She could scream and kick and bite and refuse to be muzzled or locked away again.

Even as the guards beat her, Annabelle felt that familiar nudge of power. It did not rise this time but simmered just below the surface. Annabelle did not know what it was or where it had come from, but she was grateful for its warm presence. It kept her sane, it kept her alive, and it kept her from losing herself in anguish.

When the guards finally took her back to the wagon, both Annabelle's eyes were swollen shut. It did not matter, as Annabelle was still wrapped up within that warm light like a blanket. She did not feel the pain as she curled up in the corner of the wagon and faded away into the warm dark oblivion of sleep.

Emily paced the ground before the campfire, unable to sit still, feeling each moment pass as if it stretched the length of a day. *He's been gone too long*, she thought again. It had been hours, and he would not return. She should have gone with him.

A rustling among the trees to her right startled her, and she turned to see a hooded man approaching the camp. She knew him at once, of course, but relief did not prevent her hand from tightening on the shaft of her bow.

"Relax, Emily," Charlie said, yanking back his hood. "It's me."

"I know," she replied. "But you can't be too careful."

He shrugged, crouching to warm his hands by the fire.

"It's getting colder," she said. "Too cold for the height of summer."

"You've been in the south for too long," he replied with a weak smile.

They were quiet for a moment before she worked up the courage to ask, "Did you find them?"

Charlie's face tightened, and he nodded. "They are still traveling the main road. There's no doubt now that they are headed to the capital."

Emily nodded, feeling slightly nauseated. "So…what do you want to do?"

Charlie let out a low growl and sprang to his feet suddenly, pacing. "What I want to do is go back to their camp and kill every one of those guards and get her out of there," he said agitatedly. "I can't do this, Emily. I can't just sit here while they…they…."

He trailed off, and terror gripped Emily's heart as she asked, "What are they doing to her, Charlie?"

Charlie turned to her, and there were tears in his eyes. "They're beating her, Em," he whispered. "Gods forgive me, they were beating her, and I couldn't—I couldn't do anything to stop them."

She gasped in horror and went to her brother, taking his hands in hers. "Oh, Charlie."

"Remind me why we couldn't have saved her," he groaned. "Please."

Emily took a deep breath. "I know you still want to," she said. "But remember, you agreed with Raphael in the end. Now that we know where they are taking her, we need to ride ahead and warn Sam. He doesn't know what has happened, and he needs to. If it were just about getting Annabelle out of the kingdom, things might have been different, but it's too late now. Raphael is gone and cannot help us. If we were to rescue her, we would need him, at least. All we can do now is trust that we made the right decision and find Sam."

"Find Sam," Charlie repeated. "And Sam will know what to do."

"He will, Charlie. And he needs to know. Annabelle…" She trailed off, swallowing back sudden tears as she thought of her friend. "Annabelle is so much stronger than you or anyone else gives her credit for. She will be alright. But you will be useless to her if you don't start sleeping and eating. You need to take better care of yourself."

He tried to smile but only managed to pull off a kind of wince. "Do I look that terrible?"

He did look terrible. There were dark circles under his eyes, and his short temper was evidence that he wasn't eating as much as he ought to. But she didn't say this. Instead, she said, "You don't—not yet. But I'm your sister, and I know when you are punishing yourself. This isn't your fault."

"It is my fault," he said. "I should never have let you two go off alone."

"Don't be an idiot," she snapped. "Those men were headed in the direction of our camp. They would have found us either way. You don't know that it would have turned out better—it could have turned out worse!"

He shrugged but didn't say anything. She could feel her irritation with him hit a peak.

"I'm the one who was supposed to protect her, Charlie," she said. "Me. And I failed. But you don't see me moping about, do you?"

"It isn't your fault, Emily," he said with a frown.

"Right. And it isn't yours either. So get a grip, Charlie Rabbold, before I box your ears for being an unreasonable mess."

Charlie had the sense to look ashamed of himself. "I'm sorry, Em. You're right. I just…"

"You just love her," Emily said. "I know. I'm not suggesting that this isn't horrible. But we have to hold it together, or we won't be of any use to her."

His face flushed a bit, but he didn't contradict her. "Then I will eat," he said, "And sleep. We leave at dawn. If we ride hard, we can beat them to Rengon by a day, at least. That will give us some time to prepare, but not much."

"It will be enough," she said. *It will have to be enough*, she thought. It wouldn't help to feed Charlie's already heightened sense of alarm, but she was already discouraged about their chances of success.

Raphael had gone on to meet up with the ship meant to carry them all north. If she and Charlie could get to Sam Fisher in time, he might know how to free both prince and princess. Emily, for her part, could only see one way this would all work out:

They would need to get very, very lucky.

Chapter Thirty

It was the dull thrum of pain that eventually roused Annabelle from sleep. It took a while to muster the courage to open her eyes and inspect the damage to her body. When she did, she was surprised to discover that the swelling keeping her lids closed had receded so that she could force her lids wide enough to see the rough wood of the wagon floor. They were moving, and Annabelle gingerly pushed herself to a seated position, looking around.

"Welcome back," said a high, musical voice.

Annabelle saw that the red-haired young woman sat beside her. The bruising on her face was beginning to yellow and fade, making Annabelle wonder how her own face must look. It throbbed, and it hurt to breathe, but at least she was still alive.

"How long have I been out?" She asked the woman.

"Two days," the woman replied. The way she looked at Annabelle, her head cocked to the side, eyes intent, was unnerving.

Annabelle nodded, unsurprised by the answer. "I feel better than I expected. I thought I must have slept for a while."

The woman's eyes narrowed. "Why did you do it?" She asked.

Annabelle shrugged and winced as her side exploded in pain. "I knew it wouldn't accomplish much more than give you one day's reprieve, but I had to do something."

"It was stupid."

"Of course it was stupid," Annabelle smiled ruefully. "But I did it anyway."

The woman scoffed, and Annabelle got the impression that she wasn't impressed. "What's your name?" Annabelle asked.

"Fabia," the woman replied. "And you are?"

"Anna," Annabelle said.

Fabia lifted a skeptical eyebrow when Annabelle gave her name but said nothing. Annabelle suspected that Fabia may have given a fake name as well. The two women sat together, sizing each other up.

"I thought they'd killed you," Fabia said after some time. "When they brought you back, you were banged up so bad I thought you were lost for sure."

"Yes, well. I'm relatively alive," Annabelle said, wincing as her ribs throbbed again.

Fabia shook her head. "You don't understand," she said, dropping her voice to a whisper. "You were…I don't think I've ever seen someone look so bad before. The men were betting each other when you'd die, just to pass the time."

Annabelle didn't know if she should be offended or impressed with her own ability to withstand pain. "I can't say I blame them," she said. "Not much to do."

"This isn't a joke," Fabia said, lowering her voice further still so that Annabelle had to shift closer to be able to hear her. "Are you a healer?"

"No," Annabelle said, wearying of this line of questioning rapidly. "Why do you ask?"

"You shouldn't be alive." Fabia insisted. "It's the only explanation."

"Look," Annabelle said before Fabia could work herself up any further. "Though I may not look it, I'm still in bad shape."

But Fabia was shaking her head again. "You're lying. I know you're lying. Tell me what you are."

This was getting out of hand, and Annabelle was irritated. "I don't know what you think you know," she snapped, "but the men already believe I'm a witch, so if you're thinking of blackmailing me or…."

"Oh, you're no witch," Fabia hissed in Annabelle's ear, "I don't know what you are, but you are *no witch*."

And then her bony hand was wrapped around Annabelle's neck, squeezing as she pushed Annabelle to the floor of the wagon. Annabelle couldn't breathe. Dark spots swam in her vision as she fought for air.

"What are you?" She shrieked as Annabelle tried to dislodge her. "*What are you?*"

She would die soon, and nobody would help her. After all, who was she in this place? The other prisoners would not help her, just as they had abandoned Fabia to her fate. Annabelle had abandoned her long enough, so was it just for Fabia to take her vengeance?

But then Fabia's grip loosened, and Annabelle gasped as life-giving air filled her lungs. She looked up to see that Phyllis had Fabia by the hair and was pulling so hard that Fabia cried out.

"You do not touch her again," Phyllis said, her voice like ice. "Do you understand me?"

Fabia gave a whimper of pain, but Phyllis did not release her until she said, "I won't touch her! I'm sorry, please let go of me."

Phyllis released Fabia, and the young woman scurried away from them to huddle in the far end of the wagon, cradling her head in her hands.

"Thank you," Annabelle rasped, massaging her sore throat.

Phyllis still looked angry. "What happened?" She demanded of Annabelle.

"I—I don't know." Annabelle attempted to shrug off the incident like it was nothing. "We were just talking about my injuries…" Annabelle's mind worked furiously, trying to conjure a believable story. "She mentioned I was healing quickly, and then she just…attacked me."

"Hmm," Phyllis pursed her lips and looked doubtful. "If you say so."

"Maybe she thinks the guards ought to have been harder on me," Annabelle said, desperate for Phyllis to let the matter go. "Really, Phyllis. I think she's just unhinged. Wouldn't you be, after such abuse?"

Phyllis sighed heavily. "I suppose you're right. Even so, we have enough problems as it is without turning on each other."

Relieved that the old woman seemed unlikely to press her for more information, Annabelle lay back against the floor of the wagon, rattled from the altercation with Fabia.

You're no witch.

The words were chilling. Annabelle burned to question Fabia about what she had meant but didn't dare try. From now on, she would need to be more careful. There could be no more outbursts, no more beatings. If she was going to survive, she needed to be inconspicuous.

When her head finally stopped spinning, Annabelle pushed up to a seated position with her back braced against the side of the wagon. She folded her legs the way Raphael taught her to support her spine. Taking a few deep breaths, Annabelle let her body settle into the movement of the cart, allowing her thoughts to flow like water—in and out without stopping. Her eyelids became heavy and eventually closed of their own accord.

Raphael had been a patient teacher, despite Annabelle's reluctance to learn meditation or really anything that she deemed useless against a potential enemy. Well, Annabelle had fought. While she had been far from useless, it would only get her killed to keep rebelling against her captors. With this understanding, the last of her resistance fell away. If she could not fight with her body, she would do so with her mind.

And so Annabelle spent her time making her mind strong. It was more challenging than she expected, and it took discipline not to become frustrated at the endless cascade of thoughts that plagued her.

"I know it feels like it will never end," Raphael had said to her on one of those sun-filled days back at the farm. "But there is no way around this process. You have to let the thoughts come and release them without following. If you do this long enough, eventually they will stop flowing, but not before you have released them all."

Annabelle had rolled her eyes at him and made some smart comment about meditation being easier for people who never had any thoughts in their heads to begin with.

"You're right, it is," he had said, not taking the bait. "Now, try again."

It was painful to think of those happy days now, and yet they were the most challenging thoughts to release. Annabelle missed the farm and her friends. Her pain and longing caused memories to stick to her like sap. Often, Annabelle's attempts to meditate ended in wistful daydreams of Charlie's eyes, his hair, the strength of his arms as they held her.

"*What!*" Annabelle snapped, opening her eyes and scowling at Phyllis. She had been struggling to meditate, distracted by memories of that last day she and Charlie had spent together in the barn—happy and contented to be surrounded by the smell of the hay and the comfort of Charlie's embrace.

Just when Annabelle had decided to drift away upon that memory and never return, Phyllis had lain a warm hand on her shoulder and shaken her gently, jerking her painfully back to the reality of her present torment.

Phyllis frowned. "I beg your pardon," she said reproachfully. "Is that any way to speak to your elders?"

Annabelle instantly felt ashamed. "I'm sorry, Phyllis. I was just… it's not important. What did you want to tell me?"

"Not tell you," said Phyllis, pointing over Annabelle's shoulder. "Show you."

Annabelle turned.

Mountains, so high that their peaks vanished into the clouds overhead, rose like a wall on the horizon. At the base of the mountains, on the banks of a wide river, a vast city stretched out in all directions. It clung to the edge of the river and stretched in cascading clusters of structures into a peak. At the top of the city stood an enormous stone castle—its many towers and spires decorated with flags that snapped in the breeze.

The sight was impressive and imposing in a different way than Ellasport had been. The southern city was stunning in its beauty and color—a visual circus that dazzled the senses and entranced the imagination. This place was a symbol of power and defiance as if it was simply a part of the vast permanence that was the mountain range above.

"I never thought I'd live to see this place," Phyllis murmured beside Annabelle. "I know I should be frightened, but…I cannot help feeling awed by the sight of it."

Annabelle knew what she meant. Despite the fear of whatever horrors might wait within its walls, Annabelle could only watch in wonder as they drew ever closer to the might and mystery of Rengon City.

$$\hspace{1em} \text{)} \text{)} \text{)} \bullet \text{(} \text{(} \text{(} \hspace{1em}$$

The inn stood between two butcher's shops at the end of the long market street bisecting Rengon City from the river bank to the mountain ridge that loomed above. There were so many people rushing about this close to the river and the docks that Sam passed unnoticed through the small door and into the dim light of the common room beyond.

There was little difference between the packed street and the cramped space within the inn. Seafarers coated in varying shades of grime crowded around tables, swapping stories and drinking ale while ogling the few women who picked their way among the men, peddling the wares of the flesh.

Sam turned his eyes from the grim scene. These women were not clean and well cared for like those found at Ilya's house, far away to the south. This was a future that she had feared and had escaped. This was necessity and desperation, neglect and cruelty, and it gave Sam no pleasure to look upon it.

None of the inn's patrons paid him any attention as he climbed the rickety staircase that led to the upper floors. The summons had been specific: the Old Goat Inn, room four. Sam scanned the wooden doors that lined the corridor. Finding the room he sought, Sam knocked.

The door opened a crack, and one eye peered out into the corridor before Sam heard a sigh of relief as the door swung wide to reveal Charlie Rabbold.

"Gods above, Sam. You got here fa—"

"Is she safe?" Sam cut across Charlie, pushing past him into the room without waiting for an invitation. He barely took in the details of the small chamber—Emily sitting upon a small bed in the corner, the bustle of the market street drifting in through the open window—before he rounded on his friend.

"Tell me they made it to the ship. Tell me she's safe."

It was only then that Sam noticed the dark circles beneath his friend's eyes, how ragged and exhausted he looked, as if he had gone days without sleep.

"Raphael is aboard the ship and headed north," Charlie said, his voice hoarse. "I assume. He went on without us after..." he hesitated, looking suddenly afraid. "Sam...Annabelle has been taken."

At these words, Sam felt the ground vanish beneath his feet as he began to tumble into a bottomless void.

"Taken," he could not believe what he was hearing, what he was *saying*, "But she can't be...*how*? By whom? Charlie..."

"I know" Charlie looked wretched, and Emily seemed on the verge of tears. "We were ambushed by bandits in the forest near Rosewood Manor."

"You expect me to believe that *bandits* took the princess" Sam nearly laughed at the lunacy of the idea. "When you *and* the captain of the legendary Branai warriors were there to defend her?"

"They weren't there."

Sam turned to see Emily seated with her knees under her chin, eyes wide and watery. She looked dreadful, perhaps even more worn and sleep-deprived than her brother.

"They weren't there," Sam repeated, "But you were, weren't you." He couldn't keep the note of accusation from his tone.

"Sam, it's not her fault," Charlie interjected at once, but his sister gave him a stern look.

"Now isn't the time, Charlie" she said. "Yes. I was there when she was taken."

"What happened, Emily?" Sam asked more gently.

And Emily told him everything that had happened. Sam listened, his horror rising with every word. When Emily explained how Annabelle had used magic against the bandits, Sam swore and sat beside her on the bed, holding his head in his hands as she finished her story.

Bad. This was so, so bad.

"Where did they take her?" he asked when Emily stopped speaking. She looked pale and shaky as if reliving those events had left her physically drained. "I assume you attempted to follow them."

"We did," Charlie said. "I sent Raphael to meet the ship at once. He wanted to stay and help, of course, but I knew if we did manage to rescue the princess, it would do her little good if we didn't have a way to get her out of this Gods-forsaken kingdom."

"But obviously, you weren't able to rescue her," Sam pointed out.

"No," Charlie agreed. "By the time we caught up with the bandits, they had taken her to Rosewood Manor. The new Baron has the place crawling with guards. It's like a fortress."

"Gustav," Sam said and spat upon the floor. "The snake. Of course he would dress the manor up as his own private fortress. And now that he knows Annabelle is alive, it's only a matter of time before...before..."

Sam frowned at the dark spot where his spittle had struck the dusty floor, thinking. Something was wrong with this story.

"Why?" He asked, looking up into Charlie's face. "Why did the bandits take her to Rosewood Manor. They shouldn't want to be caught dead so close to a noble house."

Charlie and Emily exchanged a look. "We wondered the same thing," he said, reaching into his jacket pocket. "But then we saw this nailed to the temple door."

He produced a scroll of parchment, which he handed to Sam, who unrolled it with a sick sense of foreboding. The parchment was a notice printed in large black letters that read:

By order of HIS MAJESTY KING ALEXANDER,
Any person who has knowledge of any man, woman, or child who is possessing UNEARTHLY AND UNHOLY POWERS, and aids their Lord in the CAPTURE of said EVILDOING PERSON, shall

be rewarded with ONE SILVER COIN. May the GODS bless you.

"They're rounding up witches," Charlie said darkly. "These are posted to the temple door in every village we passed on our way here."

"The men who accosted us might have been bandits," Emily chimed in, "But a silver coin is a lot of money. They wouldn't have passed up the opportunity."

"Perhaps." Sam turned these new details over in his head, trying to see them from every angle. "Perhaps Gustav is working with the bandits in the south. Either way, it's impossible to know for certain. And now that Gustav has Annabelle, I'm certain he'll use it to his advantage. The Lord who saved the princess. It's just what he's been waiting for to win the crown's favor."

"That's the interesting bit," Charlie said. "Watching from the outside, it didn't look like he even knew who she was."

Sam blinked up at him. "What do you mean?"

"He had her thrown into the prison wagon with the other accused witches and carted north. That's why we're here. We followed long enough to be certain of their destination and rode ahead to warn you. They should be here by tomorrow."

"He did *what?*"

Sam was on his feet now, pacing. The more he learned, the less any of this made sense. He said as much, turning to his companions for assistance—desperate that they remember some detail, divulge some bit of information that would make the pieces of their story fit together sensibly.

"Maybe he didn't recognize her," Charlie suggested. "She was pretty filthy by the time the men dragged her into the manor."

"I don't think so," Emily said, shaking her head. "Gustav may be cruel, but he's no idiot. He knew exactly what he was doing. I think it more likely that he wanted to let Annabelle suffer the abuse of his pig guards for a while before telling anyone she's alive. Teach her a lesson. Bastard," she added for good measure.

"And risk the king's wrath when he discovered what had been done to his daughter? No, it's as you said," Sam murmured, chewing his lip. "Gustav's no idiot. Whatever the reason he had for doing what he did, it's a good one. I just wish I knew what it was."

The three of them sat there for a while in silence, Sam wishing he could return to the days when all he had to contend with was a nearly impossible plan to rescue the imprisoned prince. Now he had to figure out how to save the princess as well. He was going to need all the help he could muster.

"Right," he said suddenly, startling the other two. "There's obviously nothing more we can discover sitting here twiddling our thumbs. If what you say is true, and Annabelle will arrive tomorrow, I have work to do. But first," he turned to Emily. "I need you to leave the city immediately."

Emily looked taken aback. "But…I want to help, Sam."

"And that's what you'll be doing," he said. "I need you to ride to the rendezvous point as fast as you can. Meet the ship and tell them to move farther north—to the river delta. Make sure the captain knows to be ready to weigh anchor at a moment's notice."

"She's exhausted, Sam," Charlie cut in. "Let me go instead. She needs to rest."

"I'm fine," Emily retorted, getting to her feet. "And you're in no better shape than I am, Charlie. It's alright." She met Sam's gaze unflinchingly. "I'll do it. For Annabelle."

"For Annabelle," Sam replied.

Emily turned to Charlie. "I'll be fine, brother," she said.

Charlie sighed heavily and scrubbed a hand across his face.

"I hope you know what you're doing, Fisher," He said, eyes finding Sam's over his sister's head. "For all our sakes."

Sam nodded, for what could he say? He had only as much as his friends at that moment: hope, and the knowledge that to turn back was no longer an option. All illusions of king and country had been shattered. The veil had been pulled away, revealing shadows and death. He only prayed that they could escape before the shadows could swallow them whole.

)))●(((

Sam left Charlie and Emily to say their goodbyes. He had another errand to run in the city before returning to the castle—the final piece to the puzzle, the one part of the plan that must remain secret until the last possible moment, the difference between life and death.

Sam found Eddie napping in his longboat, which he had tied up under one of the bridges that stretched across the river. There were at least five other hiding places where Sam might have found him, but with the heat of the afternoon sun, he made a lucky guess.

"Ahoy there, pirate," he called as he approached the boat.

Eddie opened one lazy eye, spied Sam, and closed it again. "Go away, Fisher," he drawled. "Nothin' you've got to say is worth losing a bit o' well-earned shut-eye."

Sam snorted. "Well earned, my hat. I've never known smugglers to be the type for hard work."

Eddie sat up. "Smuggler? No, Sir. I've gone respectable. No more smuggler's life for me."

Sam raised an eyebrow. "Oh really? Is it considered respectable to make off with five…no, *six* casks of the king's favorite Petran wine during the midsummer festival without raising any alarms. Not to mention somehow managing to convince no fewer than ten of the city guard that the king himself intended that the wine be sent as a birthday gift to the queen of Dedriana—the fact that the island of Dedriana has been famously uninhabited for generations notwithstanding."

Eddie shrugged. "Can't say that I know what you're talkin' about," he said with a wink. "Though whosoever managed such a heist must be quite a skilled, charming, and handsome chap."

"Is that so?" He and Eddie stared each other down for a long moment before the other man sighed.

"Alright, you've got me. What is it you want, Fisher?"

"A job," Sam said without preamble.

"I assumed as much. What's it pay?"

"Ten silver," Sam said.

Eddie sighed and lay back again. "Bad luck, handsome," he drawled. "I don't get out of bed for less than thirty."

"Don't play games with me, Eddie," Sam said patiently. "We both know you'll take the job, no matter what it pays."

"Is that right?" Eddie shot Sam a wary look.

"That's right," Sam said, pausing for effect before adding, "You owe me a favor, smuggler—a big one."

Eddie groaned. "Oh, now. Why'd you have to go an' make this unpleasant, Fisher? I used to think you were all right."

"You'll get over it," Sam said. "So, do we have a deal?"

"Blackmail gets you shoddy work, you know," Eddie grumbled.

"If I wanted shoddy work, there are three other smugglers I could just as easily blackmail into doing this job for me, for free," Sam said. "But I need this done right, and so I came to you with the generous offer of ten silver and the added bonus of clearing your debt to me once and for all."

Eddie was not an unreasonable man, for a thief and a smuggler. Sam waited.

The smuggler sighed finally. "You drive a hard bargain, Fisher. But the price is indeed worth the effort, I find. What's the job?"

Though Eddie squirmed a bit when Sam explained he would be smuggling people, he eventually agreed—with a few suggested alterations of his own. Sam took his input without complaint. Eddie was the best smuggler in the kingdom, and the plan would be worthless without his help.

With matters settled with Eddie and half the silver paid upfront to retain his services and his silence, Sam headed back to the castle. He had one more piece to set upon the board before the game could begin.

Chapter Thirty-One

Despite the initial impression that Rengon City had made from a distance, Annabelle began to feel a sense of trepidation as they approached the city gate. Though she yearned to drink in her first glimpse of the place that was the seat of her father's power, Annabelle kept her head down, mimicking the other prisoners.

The contrast between Annabelle's arrival in Ellasport and this homecoming was stark in its brutality. Passerby did not stop to stare this time. If they paid the prison wagon any notice, it was to hurl insults and projectiles at the cowering passengers. One citizen threw a stone that struck one prisoner on the head, leaving a deep oozing gash. The man fell instantly, senseless, and did not stir again.

The guards paid no attention to these assaults, driving the wagon at a steady pace through the streets, snaking their way up the base of the mountain toward the castle's looming edifice. Annabelle cursed them silently as she and Phyllis huddled together against the onslaught that tailed them through the lower city.

Even after the attacks had stopped, Annabelle did not dare raise her head to inspect her surroundings until she felt a sudden chill crawling down her spine. Looking up, she saw that they had passed through the castle gates and into the shadow of the mountain.

Rengon Castle was nearly as layered and complex as the city below—comprised of four levels, each surrounded by its own high wall and protected by heavy iron gates. As they passed between the first and second gates, Annabelle spied long thatched guardhouses, stables, and training yards. The second wall enclosed the animal paddocks and food stores that catered to the castle inhabitants.

The wagon took a right turn inside the third gate, skirting the inner wall past more guardhouses, and came to a stop in a stone courtyard with wooden gallows erected at its center.

Annabelle began to shake at the sight of the noose, terror robbing her of any drive to fight as the guard removed her roughly from the back of the wagon. The women were chained together in one long line and the men in another.

The small boy began to scream when the guards removed him from his mother's arms. Tears sprang to Annabelle's eyes at the sight of his mother's face—so far beyond pain, whispering comfort to her son, even as he was dragged away from her.

Three of the guards led the women through a door and down a long flight of stairs that would have been treacherous to descend even if their ankles had not been chained. Progress was slow, and Annabelle stumbled on more than one occasion, earning a sharp slap from her captors.

At the bottom of the staircase was a long, windowless corridor. Cells, their iron bars running from floor to ceiling, ran along both sides of the corridor, each occupied with bodies that shifted and moaned in the dark.

The guards led Annabelle's group to the last cell on the right, where they were unchained and locked inside with the small huddle of women who already occupied the space.

Annabelle did not seek to become acquainted with her new cellmates, instead choosing an unoccupied corner of the damp floor where she might curl up against the wet cold that already penetrated the ratted remnants of her clothing.

The solitude was not long-lived, as Phyllis sat beside her and sidled up until their shoulders were touching. "It will be warmer if we sit together," she said.

"Are you alright?" Annabelle asked. "Did you get hit by anything on the ride in?"

Phyllis shook her head. "I was lucky. That man...I think he's dead. I heard one of the guards say as much while he chained me up."

Annabelle shuddered. "That's horrible."

"Well," Phyllis shrugged. "Better him than us, I suppose."

"You don't mean that," Annabelle said.

"No. I don't." Phyllis sighed. "From the sight of that gallows, I assume it will be us before long. It's enough to make anyone envy the man his quick and unexpected death. Funny, the things you always took for granted before that now seem a damned luxury."

Annabelle said nothing. The situation did seem hopeless, but as long as Annabelle was alive, she had time to figure out a way out of this mess. If that stone had struck her down, it would have been over.

But she did not say this to Phyllis. Phyllis was an old woman and an outcast. She was not a princess and had no knights sworn to protect her. There would be no rescue for Phyllis.

And so princess and crone sat together in the wet, freezing quiet of the dungeon, sharing a moment in time when there was nothing at all between them but the fear of not knowing how many breaths still remained left for them to breathe.

$$)))\bullet(((($$

It was late, and the fire had already been reduced to glowing embers on the hearth, but Ronan Barrick was still awake—sitting up in his study, staring down at a letter that lay unfolded upon the desk before him.

My Lord Barrick,
Check the dungeons. I have sent you a gift. Tell no one.
Your servant,
Lord Gustav Wallace, Baron of Rosewood Province

Ronan frowned down at the letter. Gustav Wallace was the eldest son of the late Lord Roger Wallace, Annabelle's former guardian. What little Ronan knew of the man he found distasteful—a history of gambling and investment in seedy business ventures, a habit of associating with criminals and surrounding himself with thugs.

Ronan could admire a man for wanting to lift himself from humble beginnings, but there was no loyalty and no principle in the life of Gustav Wallace. So why would such a man be writing to him now?

What was waiting for him, many floors below the tower where he now sat, in the castle dungeons?

A twinge of pain started at Ronan's temple, and he rubbed at it, closing his eyes. Usually, the weight of his responsibilities was a comfortable mantle, like a rich velvet cloak—heavy but so fine and soft that it made him feel tall and important. These days it was becoming harder to bear. With the king spending day and night on his knees in the temple, Countess Emilia Addalara on her way from Aelnìr, and a rebellion hanging in the balance, Ronan was beginning to feel a bit run-down.

And now a message from Gustav Wallace, of all people, telling him to go to the dungeons. Why? No doubt the Lord had captured some bandit or rebel and wished to take the credit to gain favor. He would do better to burn the letter and forget about it. There were more pressing matters that deserved his attention.

And yet, Ronan grew tired of mystery and intrigue. It was better to know what pieces stood on the board, no matter how insignificant.

The faint tolling of a bell signaled one hour past midnight. Ronan pushed to his feet and stretched his stiff limbs with a groan. Better to find out what gift Lord Gustav Wallace had sent him and then get some well-deserved rest.

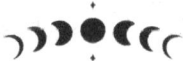

The dungeons were underground, and so Annabelle had no way to count the hours she spent huddled in the dark cell, the proximity of Phyllis and the other prisoners the only defense against the dank chill.

Every time a noise echoed down the staircase, the entire group of women shrank against the stone walls as one, afraid that the guards would return and they would begin that final walk to the gallows. It was worse than anything Annabelle had yet experienced, this interminable suspension between exhaustion and terror.

Exhaustion eventually won out, and Annabelle drifted into a fitful sleep filled with dreams of cages and haunting visions of corpses—their faces mutating from Annabelle's face to Emily's face to Sam's face to Charlie's face. Annabelle woke herself several times, rebelling against these horrible apparitions before she fell into a true sleep that finally delivered her into the sweet embrace of nothing at all.

She was awoken sometime later by the deafening clang of metal on metal. Dragged from sleep, Annabelle sat up straight and looked around, disoriented and confused. The other prisoners shifted nervously, and one woman began weeping quietly into her hands.

A door at the end of the corridor, just beside the cell where Annabelle and Phyllis huddled together, opened. Three men entered, the first carrying a torch and the last retrieving a set of keys from the lock.

One of the men—a royal guard, Annabelle realized, noting the crown and rose insignia stitched into his tunic—stepped forward. "This lot arrived only this morning, my Lord," he said, indicating Annabelle's cell.

The man holding the keys stepped forward to unlock the door and held it ajar for the third man to step inside. As he turned to take the torch from the guard, its light fell upon his face, and Annabelle's heart stopped beating.

Lord Ronan Barrick turned to face the prisoners, holding the torch aloft so the light fell upon their faces. The other women shrank from it as if it burned, but Annabelle did not cower. She gripped Phyllis's hands tightly, mind working furiously as she tried to figure out what to do.

She had seconds—seconds before he saw her and recognized her face. Should she try to hide? Should she shrink away like the others and hope he did not recognize her? Could she trust him? Could this be her way out—her one last desperate bid for freedom?

But before Annabelle could make up her mind, his gaze met her own, and she saw the color drain from his face as the eyes widened in shock and recognition.

The moments ticked by, but Barrick said nothing, did nothing. He just stared at Annabelle as if seeing a ghost. Which, Annabelle noted vaguely, he was.

Finally, one of the guards cleared his throat. "My Lord? Is everything…"

"This woman," Barrick said, seeming to return to his senses. "She'll need to be moved at once."

The guard looked taken aback. "But, my lord. These women are set to stand trial for—"

"I am aware of their fate," Barrick snapped. "I am the one who gives your orders, am I not?"

"Yes, my Lord," the guard said, bowing his head in contrition. "My apologies, my lord."

"She is a rebel spy," Barrick continued, "And must be moved to a more secure location."

Annabelle held on to Phyllis more tightly, suddenly afraid.

"It will be alright," the old woman whispered in her ear.

"I can't leave you," Annabelle said in a cracked whisper. "I…I can't…."

"You can," Phyllis assured her. "You are strong, my girl."

"No," Annabelle sobbed. "No, Phyllis, you don't understand...."

But one of the guards had seized Annabelle by the arm and was dragging her from the cell. Annabelle let him take her but could not take her eyes off of Phyllis's face—Phyllis, who had kept Annabelle alive and sane. Phyllis, who would be dead soon, hanged for the simple crime of keeping her people alive. Hot tears rolled down Annabelle's cheeks at the injustice of it, at the utter helplessness she felt not to be able to do a thing to stop it.

The guard dragged her after Barrick, who led the way deeper into the dungeons.

Annabelle was careful to remain quiet and meek as they passed through several more corridors lined with cells and up two flights of stairs. The air was milder here, and Annabelle could see tiny slivers of light through windows set high in the stone walls at intervals. She gulped down the fresh air, desperate to rid her body of the stifling filth.

At last, they reached a quiet corridor of cells that all appeared to be empty. Barrick turned to the guard, who was still holding fast to Annabelle's arm.

"I wish to interrogate the prisoner," he announced. "Alone."

The guard shifted nervously beside Annabelle. "Are you...are you quite sure, my lord?"

Barrick raised a slim eyebrow. "Do you think me incapable of handling myself against a weak, injured, and half-starved woman?"

"No, my Lord," the man replied hastily, shrinking under Barrick's cold stare. "Of course not, my lord."

And so the guard relinquished Annabelle into Barrick's custody, shutting the door behind him with a satisfyingly loud *clunk*.

When the guard had gone, Annabelle opened her mouth to speak, but Barrick lay a long finger to his lips, leading her by the arm to the farthest cell from the door.

"My lord Barrick" Annabelle breathed when he finally released her, "Thank y—"

"I have one question," he said, interrupting her. Annabelle saw that his expression when he turned to face her was suspicious, guarded. "And if you are who I believe you to be, you will have no trouble answering it."

Annabelle nodded, a bit wrong-footed by this request. She had not expected the need to prove her own identity when he was standing not two feet from her, but then again, she realized it should not have come as a surprise. After all, there was still someone, or several some-ones, at large who could create a copy convincing enough to trick the king himself into thinking his daughter had been murdered. How was Barrick to know that she was not the imposter?

"The day I placed your mother's crown atop your head, I said something to you. What was it?" Barrick asked, his tone betraying no emotion.

"You said I looked just like her," Annabelle answered confidently. "You said to see me wear her crown was a balm to those of you who loved her and miss her still." At the time, she had believed the words to be a gift; now, they seemed more like a prophecy of darker times to come.

"And so it was," Barrick said, eyes filling with tears and shoulders sagging with relief. "Princess...forgive me. I had to be sure."

"There's nothing to forgive," Annabelle assured him.

"But how?" He asked, disbelief painted across his thin face as he drank in the sight of her. "How is it that you are standing before me, alive? And *here*, of all places?"

"It is a long story," Annabelle said evasively. Though she was grateful to him for rescuing her from the cages, she still did not know if she could trust him.

Barrick frowned, but then his eyes brightened as if he finally understood something that had been bothering him for some time. "The knight—Sam Fisher helped you, didn't he? I should have guessed. Perhaps I underestimated the man after all."

"Please do not punish him," Annabelle begged, suddenly light-headed with fear for her friend's life. "He was only trying to protect me."

"No, I wouldn't dream of harming him," Barrick assured her, laying a warm hand upon her shoulder and squeezing it gently. "He did as I would have done. I only wish he had confided his plans to me. I might have been able to help. Now…" he sighed heavily. "Now things are more…complicated."

"My father's bride," Annabelle said with a nod. "I know. Lord Barrick, please. You have to help me. I have to get out of Dunea."

"I agree that it is not as safe for you here as it once was," Barrick said thoughtfully, "But, Princess…you are alive. The king must know. He can keep you safe from Aelnìr."

But Annabelle shook her head vehemently. "He mustn't know, Lord Barrick. Please trust me. My father cannot know that I am alive. The only way to keep me safe is to get me out. No, please listen to me," she pressed on because he looked like he was about to argue with her. "Find Sam. He has a plan to get me out. I'll stay here, I don't mind. Just…please don't tell anyone what you've seen. If you ever loved my mother as you claim, help me."

It was her last hope, she knew, and so she held his gaze as his mind turned over what she asked of him. This man was loyal to her father, his most trusted friend, but the way he had spoken of the late queen—she dared to hope that his loyalty to her would somehow prove a stronger force.

Finally, Barrick sighed. "I will speak with Sam Fisher," he said. "If I agree that his plan is a good one and will not cause you greater harm than returning you to your father's side…then yes, I will help you."

Annabelle felt her knees buckle with relief. "Thank you, Barrick," she said. "I owe you a great debt."

He smiled ruefully, then cast his eyes around the cell. It was cleaner than the one she had previously inhabited, its floor scattered with fresh straw. A bucket was provided for her use, and there was a pile of ragged blankets in one corner.

"I'll have the guards bring you some food," he said. "And more blankets. It's cold as ice down here."

"It's warmer than the cages," Annabelle said with a shrug. "And the wagon."

Barrick's kind smile did not wholly mask his horror that his princess should have endured such conditions. "I will not make you wait here long," he promised. "You have my word."

With that, he closed and locked the door and was gone. Annabelle was alone.

Or so she had believed. No sooner had Barrick's footsteps faded into silence than Annabelle heard movement in the cell that stood opposite her own and a hoarse voice rasped into the silence.

"Annabelle?"

A prisoner—a man with a beard and a mane of matted hair, dressed in rags that hung from his thin frame—moved into the dim light filtering through the high window of the cell and stared at her with wide, sapphire eyes.

Annabelle let out a gasp of shock.

It was Mica.

Chapter Thirty-Two

"Goddess…it really *is* you," Mica breathed, still staring at her as if he couldn't fully believe she was real.

Annabelle nodded, tears welling in her eyes. "It is me."

He was far too thin, and his hair and beard had grown long and tangled in the weeks that he had been held captive, but he was alive, and he was smiling at her. That smile—it still made her heart flip over in her chest. Perhaps she wasn't entirely broken after all.

"What happened?" He asked, still staring, drinking her in like her very presence meant his salvation. "How are you alive? How are you *here?*"

Annabelle took a deep breath in and then let it out again. What a question. She had no idea how to answer.

Fortunately—though fortune was becoming a somewhat relative term—she was saved from having to figure out what to say by the reappearance of the guards. This time they bore a basin of water, a pile of blankets, and a tray bearing a loaf of bread and a sizable block of cheese. They left these in front of Annabelle's cell and departed again without so much as looking at her.

Annabelle seized the bread at once, ripping a great mouthful off of the loaf and sighing with happiness.

"Go slowly," Mica cautioned her, eyeing the food. "I vomited up the first three meals they brought me; I was so desperate to eat."

Though it felt nearly impossible, Annabelle forced herself to chew each mouthful of bread. Eyes roving across Mica's skeletal frame, she ripped off half the loaf and a piece of cheese and held them out to him. "Have some," she said.

"I couldn't take your food," Mica said with a shake of the head.

"Don't be an idiot, Mica," Annabelle sighed, and tossed both bread and cheese so that they rolled up against the bars of his cell. "There's plenty, and from the looks of you, they aren't feeding you nearly enough."

Seeing that Annabelle was not about to take no for an answer, Mica thanked her and picked up the food. They ate together in silence. Though Annabelle could have eaten every crumb and more, she forced herself to tuck away a bit of bread and cheese in one of the blankets. Barrick would never let her starve, but she had no way to know if the guards would obey his commands to keep her well fed.

Next, she began to splash water on her filthy face, arms, and legs. Mica offered to turn his back so she could clean more of herself, but the water was freezing, and Annabelle was still cold. Nothing in the world could tempt her to remove a single scrap of clothing, no matter how filthy or ragged.

No longer aching with hunger, and reasonably refreshed, Annabelle wrapped a blanket around her shoulders and sat cross-legged before the bars of her cell.

They didn't speak for a long time, content to simply be in each others' presence, to be with a friend. But Annabelle knew Mica would want an explanation at some point, and he more than deserved one.

"Why are you so happy to see me?" She asked.

Mica looked a bit taken aback by this question. "Why shouldn't I be?"

"Well...my father attacked your people, burned your ships, and took you as a hostage," Annabelle said, feeling like this bit should have been obvious.

"Yes, he did," Mica said evenly. "But you did not do those things."

"How do you know?"

"Annabelle," Mica looked very serious. "There is much about that night that I still do not understand, but the one thing I always knew was that you had nothing to do with what happened."

"You had no way to know that." His faith in her burned like a brand.

But he was looking at her with the same confusion she felt. "It was fairly obvious," he said. "You never would have taken the time to get to know me, to be close to me, if you knew the king would betray us. No offense, Princess, but you are not *that* good a liar."

Annabelle sighed. "Painfully true. At least that particular shortcoming has finally worked out in my favor."

Mica laughed at that—actually *laughed*. It was so unexpected to hear laughter in such a place, so beautiful and welcome that Annabelle was momentarily dazed. But then he stopped, and his smile vanished so suddenly it was like the sun had been snuffed out.

"I also knew that you had nothing to do with what had happened when I heard you had died in the attack," Mica said. "The charge of your murder was formally leveled against my companions and me when we were imprisoned here."

"Where are they?" Annabelle asked, dreading the answer.

"Dead," Mica said flatly. "Executed, one week after we arrived."

Annabelle had not thought her heart had the capacity to feel even more anguish. "Oh, Mica," she said softly, "I am so sorry."

"I am too," he said, and Annabelle saw a firelight behind his eyes. "But the king made a grave mistake in executing members of the council. He let me live, thinking that I was the most valuable hostage. He will learn his error in time, and he will be the more sorry for it."

"I regret their deaths," Annabelle said. "But you cannot ask me to be sorry that you are alive. And," she added, realizing that she could give the prince one bit of good news to hold in his heart, "I wouldn't go talking like that in front of Raphael, not unless you want him to beat you to a pulp."

Mica's eyes snapped to hers. "What are you talking about?"

Annabelle grinned, her face tingling a bit from twisting into such a strange and unfamiliar expression. "Raphael is alive, Mica. He survived."

Mica inhaled sharply, and tears welled in his eyes. "And you've seen him?" he breathed.

"Yes," Annabelle nodded. "He was badly burned, but he made a full recovery. He is well and whole."

Mica chuckled, wiping his eyes. "Raphael was always a fast healer. Annabelle, thank you for telling me this."

"I…" Annabelle hesitated but forced herself to continue. He deserved more, so much more. "I would tell you the whole story if you would like to hear it."

"I would," he said. "But please, if it's too much…."

Annabelle shook her head. "No, you deserve to know. You need to know."

And so Annabelle told him everything.

It was nice in a way she did not anticipate, telling her story from beginning to end, omitting no details, and making no excuses. There was a power in owning this truth, this experience that was entirely her own and that no amount of torment or fear could steal from her.

Mica listened without interruption or comment, even when Annabelle paused to recall specific details or backtracked to provide more information where required. This made it easier to tell the story in its entirety.

"I don't know what will happen now," Annabelle said when she reached the end of her tale. "If Charlie and the others managed to get to Sam, he may have been able to come up with a new plan to get us out. And if Lord Barrick decides to help us, there may still be a chance that we will make it out of here alive."

Mica let out a low whistle. "That," he said, "is quite the story, Annabelle."

"I know," she said, feeling suddenly anxious that she had perhaps divulged too much. Suddenly she found it hard to look at him.

When Annabelle did finally manage to meet his gaze, she saw that he was smiling again.

"Thank you for telling me everything," he said.

Annabelle returned his smile shyly. "You're welcome."

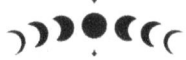

Barrick came for her the following night.

He shook Annabelle from a deep and dreamless sleep, and she rebelled against his entreaties—it had been so long since she had truly slept. But finally, her mind caught up to what was happening, and she pushed up to a seat, rubbing her eyes and blinking in the light from his torch.

Barrick crouched beside where she lay curled up in the pile of blankets. Her eyes took in his black cloak and his warm expression.

"We have to go," he said quietly. "Now."

"Have you spoken to Sam?" Annabelle asked, suddenly very awake and alert. "Have you decided to help us?"

"Yes," Barrick said. "But you have to come with me. Now. Quietly."

Annabelle scrambled to her feet, heart leaping with excitement. "Thank you, Barrick." She made to follow him up the corridor, then paused. Mica lay on the floor of his cell, one of her blankets draped across him, snoring gently. She hated to leave him here, but there was no way to know what Sam had chosen to relay to Barrick about his plan. Better to leave him and trust her friend.

"Annabelle?"

She looked to where Barrick stood in the open door, hand outstretched.

"I'm sorry," she said, hastening after him. "I'm coming."

Annabelle attempted to memorize their route—through the iron door, up one flight of stone steps, through another door, down a corridor lined with more cells, up a spiral staircase. The dungeons were dizzyingly massive, massive as the castle's reflection above in the waters of the river.

Still, she tried. If she could lead Sam to Mica's precise location, it would help. She would help. After everything that had gone so wrong, she would try to help.

Soon, Annabelle noticed a change in the quality of the stone floors, the walls, the ceilings now vaulted with wood. They were in the castle basement now, tracing the same pathways used by servants.

Up and up, they climbed through the walls of Rengon castle, ascending narrow spiral staircases. Annabelle gulped down lungfuls of air, trying to steady her nerves in the small spaces until they finally emerged onto a landing that faced a single door.

It wasn't until Barrick opened the door and Annabelle stepped into the room beyond that she realized what had happened. She had followed him unquestioningly, without fighting—why? Because she had trusted that he would protect her; because the moment Barrick had taken her hand, she had felt safe.

If she had known, if she'd had any inkling of what would be waiting for her at the top of that spiral staircase, she would have fought, kicked, screamed, bit, and thrashed against him. No man, no guards, no army would have stood against her fury.

But she had not fought. The wolf had not had to hunt her. She had allowed herself to be led to bare her own neck at its feet. And so she held her head high as she could manage and met those horrible eyes that were the same and yet not the same as her own.

"Hello, father," she said.

The king looked her up and down, drinking in the sight of her hair, her face, her living body. "I don't know how this is possible," he exclaimed, falling to his knees before her, "But I thank the Gods for delivering you to me—whole and living."

Annabelle cast a glare over her shoulder to where Barrick stood in the doorway. "The Gods had nothing to do with it, I'm sure."

Barrick winced as if she had struck him, but it was the king who spoke. "I do not expect you to be grateful now," he said quietly. "Barrick suggested you have been…corrupted. But you will see the blessing in time."

"Did he." Annabelle felt the bite of rage and the sting of his betrayal anew. He had no idea what he had done. It was too late to convince him of his mistake now.

The king was on his feet again. He looked dreadful, worse than she had last seen him. His face was too thin, accentuating the horrible burning of his red-rimmed eyes, and his hair was unkempt—though his clothing was still fine as ever, finer even. It was as if he believed that gold embroidery and velvety furs could mask the sight of his deteriorating body.

Annabelle was no healer, but even she could see that the king was dying.

"You do not look well, father," she said, emboldened by the knowledge that things could not possibly get any worse than they were already. There was no need to behave or to disguise her curiosity. "What has happened to you?"

This question seemed to momentarily wrong-foot the king. He blinked at her, and for a moment, she saw a spark of recognition flare in those heated, fevered eyes. But these moments held no more fascination for her now. She only waited, and that flash was gone.

"I weaken as my kingdom suffers," the king said, his voice a hollow rasp. "But all will be well. Soon our enemies will be dust, and Dunea will rise from the ashes, born anew."

"Because of your new wife?" Annabelle could not stop the question, nor could she disguise the bitterness in it.

The king cocked his head to one side, regarding her owlishly. "Do not be afraid of her, my dear," he said, misinterpreting the ire in her words. "I will keep you safe."

Annabelle took a step forward. "Please, father. You have to let me go. You think you can keep me safe here, but you cannot. If Aelnìr discovers that I live, if your queen finds out, you will not be able to protect me. Nobody will be able to protect me."

He didn't say anything, only looked at her. Encouraged, Annabelle took another step forward.

"Let me go to Eìrlan," she urged. "I can speak to King Leo on your behalf, convince him to send aid to your cause. You will have both Eìrlan's ships and Aelnìr's gold on your side, and the north will fall. When it is all over I will…I will abdicate my claim to the throne, I will return to live with you here at the castle, or I will go south to the palace in Ellasport and live the remainder of my days in safety. I'll do whatever you wish, just please let me go."

No more cages.

It would not work. Annabelle knew it would not work. Men like her father, like Gustav, delighted in bringing her to her knees. The king finally had her at his mercy. There was no reason that he should give her anything at all.

Expecting the blow did not make it less painful as it careened across her already bruised face, taking with it the last shred of Annabelle's hope, energy, and breath. She collapsed to her knees right there in the middle of the room. She did not even clutch the place along her cheekbone where fresh agony bloomed. She just knelt there, traitorous tears falling to the floor as the king, her father, stepped around her deflated and motionless body.

"I will keep you safe," was all he said before he left her to fall to pieces alone.

"Where is she?!"

Sam did not wait for permission to enter Barrick's study. The plan was crumbling to ash around him, he was losing control, and the force of his panic and anger was like a battering ram against his ribcage. The iron restraint he had held upon his own self dissolved the moment he discovered who exactly had removed Annabelle from the cages.

Sam had made haste to the castle dungeons, desperate to be confident that Annabelle was alive. When his search of the cages proved a dead end, he began questioning the guards. A piece of silver in the right hand had bought Sam the information he sought: Lord Barrick had come to the cages, late at night, and removed a female prisoner—a rebel spy, the guard said. Sam knew better.

Barrick stood behind his desk, holding sheaves of paper, poring over documents and maps. For the first time, this image struck Sam as deeply disturbing—this man who always seemed to be nearby, always witnessing events or manipulating them, but always standing just outside of the line of fire. Lord Barrick had once compared Sam to himself, and Sam had been flattered. That initial impression was fading rapidly.

"I do not know to whom you are referring," Barrick said, setting down his papers, not so much as flinching at the violent interruption.

Sam wanted to reach across the desk, grab the man by the collar, and throttle him until his face turned purple. He didn't care what the cost might be. "You know perfectly well of whom I speak," he growled. "The princess, my lord Barrick. Where is the princess?"

Barrick met Sam's eyes, and Sam saw nothing at all within them—not the shock that should have registered at his mention of the princess, not the flicker of anxiety over her fate and future—nothing but cold, flat, emptiness.

"Where is she?" Sam repeated.

"She is none of your concern," Barrick replied mildly. "She is safe."

"She is *not* safe," Sam pressed him. "My lord, please. If you are angry that I did not confide in you, that I did not tell you she was alive, you have every right—"

"Of course I have every right," Barrick snapped, losing grip on his self-control. "Gods above, Sam. How arrogant you are to think that I would trust you after what you have done."

"You told me to protect her," Sam countered at once, fueled by Barrick's anger. "That is what I did."

"That is what you *failed* to do." Barrick retorted. "Sam, I cannot deny that your instincts were good. If I had been in your shoes, I cannot say that I would have chosen differently. Even so, you made a mistake in not trusting me. Now it is too late."

"Too late," Sam repeated, horrified. The truth finally dawned on him. "You told him. You told him where she was, and now he's stashed her somewhere nobody will ever find her. *How* could you have done it?"

"I do not owe you an explanation," Barrick said dismissively.

"She isn't safe with him," Sam protested. "He *attacked* her!"

"*He* is the *king*," Barrick shouted, slamming both fists against the desk.

Sam knew he had gone too far. Barrick was panting, his eyes wide and wild. They simply stared each other down for a long moment. Then, appearing to regain a hold upon himself, Barrick straightened.

"Get out of my sight before I have you arrested for treason, Sam," he said quietly. "It would be a dreadful waste."

Sam said nothing.

"I hope you understand one day that, even if I wanted to help her, there is nothing I can do for her now."

There was nothing he *would* do for her now, Sam knew as he left the study. Barrick had betrayed his princess and had left Sam without options. The brilliant strategist, the man who was trusted to run the kingdom in the king's stead, believed Sam to be beaten. It was only because of this that he allowed Sam to leave with his freedom to seek out a quiet place to lick his wounds.

It was a very good thing, then, that Sam always had a backup plan. All was not lost. Not yet.

Chapter Thirty-Three

Annabelle did not rise from the floor until well after the sun had come up. There was no hurry. There was nothing she needed to do, nowhere she needed to be. This tower would be her final cage, and there would be no escaping it.

Good, Annabelle thought. She was tired of running. She was tired of being beaten and threatened, of being terrified for her friends. She was tired of falling in love, only to have that love ripped away. She was tired of loving anything, or anyone, at all.

And this was not such a terrible place to die. There were far worse. The prison wagon and those cells she had briefly inhabited were all fine examples. Although there were more pleasant places, she knew. The farm. The cliffs overlooking the sea at Rosewood Manor.

She had been too distracted by the king to notice her surroundings, but now, getting wobbly to her feet, she took stock of this place that would be her home. The room was large and circular, with skinny windows and a wooden trap door set into the ceiling. Annabelle imagined it must have served as a guardhouse for the soldiers keeping watch upon the crenelated tower above.

She was surprised, therefore, to find that the room was richly appointed. In fact, the decor reminded her very much of the tent she had occupied on the road to Ellasport, with everything set into sections of the one room: the sitting area to her right, the bed standing to the left, and even a little bathing corner behind a pretty wooden screen.

Investigating the bathing area first, Annabelle found a large empty tub set against the wall. There was a strange pipe protruding from the stones with a tiny knob atop it that, when turned, allowed clear water to flow through the pipe and into the tub.

Annabelle marveled at the contraption. There must be a cistern on the outside of the tower to collect rainwater. That made it unnecessary for maids to carry buckets of water all the way up the stairs. Her prison had been well designed indeed.

With nothing to do and with no compulsion to clean herself, Annabelle set about exploring the rest of the room.

Simple dresses and a few nightgowns were hanging in the wardrobe—all fresh and new and clearly intended for Annabelle's use. There was also a set of linens in the trunk sitting at the foot of the bed, and the writing desk was stocked with inks, pens, and a few blank leather-bound books. If she wanted to document the lonely days of her confinement, she would be well prepared.

Perhaps she would write her story on those pages. Maybe one day, these books would be found, and they would grace the shelves of a great library. A kindly librarian like Herbert would say how these were the unfulfilled hopes and dreams of a princess, lost and forgotten, more believable than the faeries, more real than stories of magic.

Absently, Annabelle opened the cover of one of the books, wondering how her story would begin. But she was startled and amazed to see that the book had already been written in. Was it possible that Annabelle was not this room's first inhabitant?

Intrigued, Annabelle carried the little book over to an armchair and flipped through its pages, hoping to distract herself with its contents.

Every inch of every page was covered in scratchings and markings that were unfamiliar to Annabelle. With a sinking heart, she realized that, whatever language this was, she could not read it. Still, she continued to scan the markings for something she could recognize. And then there it was, right at the bottom of the very last page, the only word in the entirety of the book that Annabelle could read:

Ilenna.

Ilenna. Annabelle's mother. The former Queen of Dunea. Annabelle's finger traced the ink that formed the name, hardly daring to believe that this book could have belonged to her mother. But then the memory returned to her—a bone-white face and feverish eyes. *I will protect you, Ilenna.*

Her dreams. Her mother's desperation to keep her safe. Was it possible that Ilenna knew what awaited her daughter within the walls of Rengon City? Could she have known what her husband would do to their daughter because she had experienced his cruelty firsthand?

Annabelle curled up in the chair and stared at that one little word. She stared and stared at it as if her attention alone could conjure its writer into flesh and bone before her. She stared at the word until nothing else existed, but those curving letters, the black ink like the tendrils of hair everyone told Annabelle was so like her mother's—the one link to prove that Ilenna had lived, the one spot of light in the growing darkness.

Eventually, the light in the room began to dim, and so Annabelle set about finding candles and a way to light them. She found what she needed at the bottom of the trunk, under the layers of folded linen.

The flicker of light from the newly illuminated candle reflected back to Annabelle from a corner of the room. She looked up to see her own gaunt reflection staring back at her from a full-length looking glass, cast into haunting light and shadow by the candle she held in her hand.

It had been a long while since she had seen her full reflection. There was something jarring about suddenly seeing her whole body after so long of only giving herself cursory glances to simply ensure that there was not a large smudge of dirt across her face.

There were yellowing bruises everywhere and inflamed red slashes where her skin had split. The days of near starvation had begun to show in her sunken cheeks and in the way her skin seemed taught against her bones and muscles.

And yet, despite the lean lines of her body, Annabelle could see the strength that her days of training had wrought. Annabelle had always felt slightly uncomfortable in her own body, but this woman reflected back in the mirror did not seem awkward in the slightest. Bruised and sore, perhaps, but tall and strong. This strange reflected woman stood evenly on her two bare feet, and she held her head high.

Annabelle had only considered what she would learn to do, how she would learn to fight, but not who she would become. It was as if she were now a book, and could read the steps she had taken laden with buckets of water, the screaming pain of her limbs, the countless times Charlie had sent her tumbling onto her backside, in each precious inch of skin, in the faint lines of new muscle, in the set of her shoulders.

Gratitude consumed Annabelle, for this body, for the gifts it had given her. It now seemed intolerable that it should be in such disrepair. She lunged for the bathing tub, stripping off the remnants of her ragged traveling clothes as she went.

The water was like ice, but Annabelle welcomed the sting of it as she scrubbed her body raw with the bit of soap and cloth she found beside the tub. Slowly the water turned dark with grime as Annabelle sloughed off the layers of pain and terror. When the water was black, she drained it through a hole in the floor and refilled the tub again.

It took four tubs of water for Annabelle to become acceptably clean. But once she managed to rid herself of every bit of grime and was wrapped warmly in the dressing gown, she felt more alive and more human than she had in a long time.

The dresses that had been procured for her use were all the same soft cotton that Annabelle preferred, which made her smile sadly. Months ago, she would have given anything to be allowed to wear only dresses like these. Now she would gladly don the most horrible and gaudy monstrosity that Lady Malisa could procure if it meant she could have her freedom from this place.

But she would not, not for anything in the world, return to those days of ignorance. Now that she had seen the world beyond the walls of the manor, beyond the gardens of the palace, she had expanded so much that she doubted she could stuff herself back into the smallness of the person she had been. To do so would require cutting off a limb, slicing off a toe just to squeeze it into a shoe that had never fit to begin with.

No, Annabelle thought as she once again inspected her reflection—scrubbed from head to toe, hair combed and braided, wearing one of those simple cotton gowns. *Better to be here, to be now, just as I am.*

Just then, Annabelle heard the oddest sound. It came from the other side of the door—muffled voices, and then a loud thud, a shout, and then another thud. Curious, Annabelle took a hesitant step forward, craning her ears to try to discover what had caused the disturbance.

Then she leaped back again as a key turned in the lock, and the door swung wide. Annabelle could see two guards who had been stationed on either side of her door, splayed unconscious across the landing. Sam stood in the doorway.

"Sam!" Annabelle gasped, running to him, hurtling into his chest with enough force that he let out a grunt of pain. Annabelle didn't care. She clung to him as if he would vanish into smoke at any moment.

"Annabelle," he murmured, kissing the top of her head. "Gods above, I'm so glad you're alright."

"It was Barrick," She mumbled into his shirt. "He found me in the dungeons and…Sam, I'm so sorry. I hoped I could trust him, and I told him to find you, but I don't think he did. And then he brought me here, and my father was here, and they locked me in."

"Shhh," he hushed her soothingly, pulling away so he could look down into her face. "It's alright. You're going to be alright."

"But, *how?*" Annabelle still couldn't believe that he was there, even though she could feel the solidness of him. "How did you find me?"

"Well…I had some help," Sam said, looking suddenly awkward.

He extricated himself from Annabelle's embrace and stepped aside, revealing the Duchess standing on the threshold.

"Aunt Penelope," Annabelle exclaimed, and, tears now rolling freely down her face, she rushed to embrace her aunt.

"Pull yourself together, child," the Duchess scolded her, though the hand that stroked her hair was gentle. "The night is not over, and you are not yet out of danger."

"But you helped him find me," Annabelle said, wiping her face. "Why?"

The Duchess's expression was forbidding as she said, "Because you are my great-niece and the princess of Dunea."

"I thought you wanted me to be queen," Annabelle protested, without knowing why she was doing so. "All those years, those lessons…if you help me escape, I'll never—"

"You listen to me," the Duchess cut across her, gripping her chin in one gnarled hand. "If you stay here, you will never be anything but a prisoner. I have wished many things for your future, Annabelle, but I love you too much to allow this to be all that you will become. As to what will happen if I help you escape…I have seen some fantastic things in my long life. I should caution you against using the word 'never.' Do you understand me?"

Annabelle nodded, too overcome to say anything at all.

"Good." The Duchess turned to Sam. "We need to make haste."

"Very good, Duchess," Sam said quickly and then held out a rucksack to Annabelle. "I need you to put this on."

Annabelle reached into the sack, producing a pair of trousers, boots, and a shirt. There was also a green cap and a white robe—the traditional garb of one of the court healers.

Annabelle took the clothing with a thrill of anticipation. She donned the trousers, boots, and shirt with haste. Carefully, she tucked her mother's journal into the inside of her jacket before shoving her hair under the cap and slipping the robe over her head.

Sam took her trembling hands in his. "It's going to be alright, Annabelle," he said. "I'm sorry that I failed you before, but I will not do so again."

"You didn't fail me," Annabelle protested, but Sam shook his head.

"We can argue that point later," he said, setting about tying the fastenings himself. "But right now, I need you to trust me. I will get you out of here."

"I trust you," Annabelle said. "I've always trusted you."

"If you're quite finished," The Duchess said impatiently from the doorway, "It's time to go."

They followed the Duchess down from the tower, keeping to the shadowed, deserted corridors of the castle.

$$ \text{)}\text{)}\text{)}\text{)}\bullet\text{(}\text{(}\text{(} $$

Nerves made Annabelle jumpy, and she twitched so badly at every sound, every distant echo, every creak, that Sam took her hand in his. "Nearly there," he assured her, squeezing it gently.

Annabelle needn't have worried. It was late, and the Duchess had planned their route well. Before long, they were descending the long twisting staircase that led to the dungeons.

When they reached a heavy iron door, the Duchess paused.

"This is as far as I go," She explained in a hushed voice. "The guard changes every hour, on the hour, which should be any moment now. Once you're inside, you won't have long to find the prince and get out."

Annabelle threw her arms around her aunt's neck and held on tight. "Thank you," she whispered. "Thank you for everything you've done for me. I'll never be able to repay you."

"Stay alive," the Duchess said as Annabelle released her. "And be well. That is the only payment I require."

Annabelle nodded, wiping tears from her eyes.

The Duchess gently extricated herself from Annabelle's embrace, then turned to Sam. "All our hopes rest on you now."

"Duchess," Sam replied, bowing respectfully.

The old woman gave him an approving nod and smiled warmly at Annabelle, drinking in the sight of her. And then she turned and was gone.

"The guard will change soon," Sam said quietly, turning to look Annabelle in the eye. "And when it does, we will need to move quickly. I need you to be silent, to follow my lead, and to do exactly what I tell you to do."

Annabelle nodded her understanding, but Sam shook his head. "I need you to promise me you'll follow me without question."

"I promise," Annabelle murmured and then jumped as a bell tolled somewhere on the castle grounds. It was faint, but in the silence that surrounded them, Annabelle felt like it was ringing inside her very bones. She followed Sam down into the dark of the dungeons.

They met with two guards on the other side of the door. "Your business, sir...?" Asked one in a bored voice.

"My name is Sir Roger Wallace," Sam said when they approached. "This is the healer, Mysa. She has come to see to one of the prisoners in the cages."

Annabelle thought her heart would explode as she felt the guards' eyes upon her, but she kept her gaze lowered.

The guards waved them on without further inquiry. This happened two more times, and after the third time they were able to pass without objection, Annabelle began to relax. This was a good plan. This was Sam's plan. This would work.

This was also where their good fortune ran out.

The guards who stood before the final door separating them from the corridor where Mica was being held were not so easily swayed by their story.

"That may be," said one of the guards when Sam explained the reason for their presence, "But this is a closed level. You'll have to go back and use the courtyard entrance."

Sam opened his mouth to argue, but the second guard cut in. "Hang on," he said, peering up at Sam's face. "I've seen you before."

"I don't believe so…" Sam said with a frown.

"No, I have," the man objected. "You were the one who came down to the cages, asking questions about a prisoner."

"That's right," said the second guard, recognition dawning on his face. "What did you say your name was again?"

His companion had begun eyeing Annabelle with interest. She kept her eyes trained on the floor, clasping her hands before her to keep them from shaking.

It happened so fast that Annabelle nearly missed it. Sam reached out with the speed of a viper, driving a dagger through the throat of one guard, who dropped to the ground, sputtering. Before the second guard could so much as shout his surprise, Sam had the man by the neck. There was a sickening crack, and he dropped like a stone beside his dying companion.

Annabelle stared down at the men, at the blood spreading across the floor, frozen with shock. Sam slid a hand under her chin and forced her eyes upward into his own.

"You promised me," he said.

And so Annabelle took some steadying breaths and pulled herself together while Sam retrieved a set of keys from one of the guards and unlocked the door.

Mica was sitting up in his cell with his hands clutching the bars when they arrived.

"Thank the goddess," he breathed when he saw Annabelle. "When I woke to find you gone, I feared the worst."

"I'm alright," Annabelle assured him as Sam unlocked the cell. "Just very, very lucky to have Sam on my side."

"We both are," Mica agreed as he pulled himself to stand. "They told me this afternoon that I'm meant to hang in the morning."

Annabelle suddenly felt dizzy. They had been so close, so close to missing their chance.

"Hang?" Sam frowned. "But why?"

Mica shrugged. "I suppose I've finally outlived my usefulness."

"Even so," Sam continued, "holding you prisoner was the only conceivable way to keep Eìrlan from retaliating for the king's actions. If they execute you—"

"Sam," Annabelle cut across him. "We don't have time for this."

"Right, of course," Sam said, eyes widening in panic as he came to his senses. "Can you walk on your own?" he asked Mica.

Mica nodded. "Yes, but not much else I'm afraid."

"Take this anyway," said Sam, wiping the bloody dagger on his trousers and handing it to the prince, hilt first. "Just in case."

Sam led them down the row of cells to the other door, using the keys he had taken from the dead guards. Annabelle followed him, and Mica took up the rear, brandishing Sam's knife.

It was slower going with Mica in tow. Their cover was useless now, and so Sam was forced to incapacitate six more guards as they progressed deeper into the dungeons.

Four of them he rendered simply unconscious. They guarded mostly empty levels and were dozing at their posts, which made it easier for Sam to sneak up behind them and knock them out.

Two guards were not so lucky. One of them nearly managed to escape and raise the alarm, but before he could run more than five paces, he cried out and fell to the ground, the dagger protruding from his back.

"Good throw," said Sam as he retrieved the dagger and slit the man's throat for good measure. Annabelle felt her stomach roll in response.

Mica shrugged. "It had to be done, but I took no pleasure in it."

"No," Sam agreed. "But it will be over soon. We're nearly there."

He led them down a long stone corridor that was lined with several wooden doors that stood ajar. Peering into the chambers as they passed, Annabelle saw not cells but rooms with metal instruments of torture hanging on the walls, complicated contraptions designed to maim and mutilate, and in the last chamber, a stack of linen-wrapped corpses piled against the wall.

When Annabelle had first glimpsed the city, she had been struck by its glory and majesty. Now that she knew such horrors lay behind its proud walls, she saw the lie for what it was. This was not a proud kingdom. This was a kingdom built from bones and blood.

"In here," Sam called out from ahead.

Annabelle tore her eyes from the horrors of the torture chambers and followed Mica around the corner to where Sam stood in a small alcove.

"We need to jump," he explained, pointing to the floor.

A large round hole was carved out of the stones, big enough for a large man to slide through.

Annabelle gave Sam a reproachful look. "You want me to just jump down there?" She peered over the edge and quickly withdrew, retching. The stench was unbearable. "What is that smell?"

"Bodies," Sam said bluntly. "Thieves and bandits, men and women who do not deserve the crown's mercy, or the dignity of a burial. Now, unless you would like to join them Princess, I suggest you jump."

There were no other options, and Annabelle had agreed to do whatever he said without question. Thinking that she ought to consider her promises more carefully in the future, Annabelle held her breath and approached the edge of the hole. She couldn't see the ground in the dark. How far was it? Would she be able to land without injuring herself?

"We'll lower you down as much as we can," Mica offered. "Then just make sure to let your body go limp when you hit the ground."

"The ground?" Annabelle raised an eyebrow, highly doubtful that she would be so lucky.

"Don't think about it," Mica urged her. "You've got to do it either way. Best to get it over with quickly."

Sam and Mica each took hold of Annabelle's arms and lowered her beneath the edge of the hole. On the count of three, they released her. The fall was shorter than Annabelle was expecting, and so it came as a shock when her feet struck something that was definitely not the ground.

Trying to do what Mica had said and not think too hard about what was happening, Annabelle let her body go limp as she rolled down a lumpy pile that reeked and buzzed with flies. She felt the impact in her entire body, and the crunch of it made her stomach roll. As soon as she hit grassy earth, Annabelle scrambled away from the dark, hulking mound and vomited.

First, Mica and then Sam made the jump from the hole as Annabelle cleaned herself up and discarded her healer's disguise. In the dim light of the moon, she could see that they were standing in a shallow, grassy ravine. From the outside, the hole appeared to lead up into the dark solid mass of the mountain. Though Annabelle craned her neck, she could not see the castle that loomed somewhere above them. How far down into the mountain did the dungeons go?

"Wait here," Sam said, striding off down the ravine. "I'll give a signal when it's safe to follow." And then he was gone.

"I'm sorry."

Annabelle turned to see Mica looking at her sheepishly.

She frowned, confused. "Whatever for?"

He hesitated. "I know this is hardly the time or the place, but…the last time we were together, in Ellasport, we fought. I was horrible to you. You were only ever open and kind and willing to make the best of a situation that was beyond your control…and I treated you cruelly. I am more sorry for it than you can know, and I hope…I hope we make it through this, and I have the opportunity to explain and to have a second chance to be your friend."

He said all of this in a rush as if he was afraid that he might lose his opportunity or his nerve. The fear in his wide eyes was so genuine and so endearing.

Annabelle reached out and took his hand, squeezing it reassuringly. "We *are* friends, Mica" she said. "It's alright."

Mica's face relaxed. "Good," he said with a shy smile. "I've wanted to apologize to you from the first moment I saw you in the dungeons, but I wanted to do it when I was free."

"I understand" Annabelle said. And she did understand. Some truths were best shared in the open air, where the stars and the moon could bear witness.

A low whistle echoed up the ravine, and Annabelle and Mica turned in unison to peer into the darkness.

"Sam's signal," Mica said quietly. "Let's go."

Just around a bend in the ravine, a great stone wall stretched from one steep, rocky hillside to the other, its sizeable wooden gate standing slightly ajar. As they approached, Sam poked his head through the opening. He motioned for them to hurry.

Annabelle and Mica crept toward him as quickly and quietly as they could manage. Annabelle did not see or hear any guards. As she slipped through the gate after Mica, she realized that it was best if she did not know what had happened to them.

Standing on the other side of the wall, Annabelle looked around. It was hard to know for sure in the dark, but they appeared to be standing at the edge of a forest. She remembered seeing the trees that pressed up against one side of the mountain, like a wave breaking against the shore. If they had traveled this far underground, it couldn't be long before someone raised the alarm.

She turned to Sam. "What now?"

Sam didn't answer her. He was scanning the trees, looking agitated. "He should be here by now," he murmured under his breath.

"Who should—"Mica began to ask but then fell silent. Annabelle heard it too; hoofbeats thundering in the dark.

"Get behind me," Sam ordered them, drawing his sword.

The rider came into view then—just one man riding at full-tilt, a second horse tied to the first by a long rope. Sam lowered his sword as the man pulled the horses to a halt before them and swung down from the saddle.

Annabelle let out a sob of joy and relief when he removed his hood, and she threw herself into his arms.

Charlie held her tight for a moment before letting her slide to the ground. He grinned down at her. "Happy to see me?"

She giggled wetly, drinking in the sight of his face. She thought he looked strangely pale, but it was difficult to tell with the moon casting everything in its silvery light.

"We need to go now," Charlie said to Sam, keeping a grip on Annabelle's hand. "My story didn't convince the guards at the gate. I had to fight my way through, but one of them got away from me and—*damn*."

Alarm bells crashed through the quiet of the night, their horrible pealing rolling down the mountainside.

"It doesn't matter," Sam shouted over the bells, swinging onto his mount as Mica scrambled up behind him and Charlie lifted Annabelle onto the back of his horse. "If we ride hard, we can still make it in time."

Sam urged his horse forward, and they took off into the forest, riding with such speed that Annabelle had to shield behind Charlie to keep from being slashed by passing branches.

Charlie and Sam steered their mounts between trees and over massive roots that broke the surface of the earth. Annabelle could only cling to Charlie as they made their way deeper into the forest, wondering where they could go that the king's men could not follow.

Soon, Annabelle heard a sound over the pounding of hoofs and the hammering of her heartbeat—deep and constant as rolling thunder. Water. They were headed for the river.

Sam and Charlie pulled the horses to a stop on the riverbank. While Charlie helped Annabelle down from the saddle, she heard Sam call into the dark.

"Eddie? Eddie!"

"I'm here, mate."

Annabelle looked around to see a boat creeping up the shoreline toward where they stood. It was long, narrow, and shallow—propelled through the water by a tall, reedy man gripping a long pole. She eyed the boat skeptically as Sam moved forward to help the man hold it steady against the riverbank.

"Annabelle," Sam called over his shoulder, "get in."

Annabelle didn't hear him. Something had caught her attention—a dark stain running down the inside of her arm from the wrist all the way up to the elbow. Frowning, Annabelle lifted the stain to her nose and sniffed. The scent was far too familiar; blood.

But when had she been injured? She felt no pain. A frantic moment passed when Annabelle pulled her shirt sleeve up, searching for any sign of a wound. Her skin was smooth and whole.

She whirled on the spot. Charlie stood a few feet away, leaning against the side of his horse. No, holding onto the saddle—holding onto it to keep himself upright.

"Annabelle, get in the damn boat!" Sam was yelling behind her.

The words were drowned out by an odd ringing sound in her ears, as if the alarm bells from the distant castle tolled inside her head. She crossed the distance between herself and Charlie and seized the front of his jacket. Ignoring his protests, she ripped the jacket open and let out a cry of horror. The entire left side of Charlie's body was soaked with blood.

"You're injured," she said unnecessarily.

"Annabelle," he said weakly, "You have to go."

"Why didn't you say anything?" She demanded, tears springing to her eyes. There was so much blood. "Charlie—"

"Annabelle, please" Sam's voice was frantic now. "We need to *go*."

"Charlie is hurt," Annabelle shot back at him. "He needs help."

"Listen to me, Annabelle," Charlie said, wincing as he gripped his side. "There is no help for me."

She looked up into his face. Pale, too pale. And not because of the moon. Because he had already been bleeding to death by the time he reached them at the gate.

"There has to be something I can do," she whispered, clutching his blood-soaked shirt, wishing she could heal him, wishing she knew how.

"You have to go," he said. Those eyes, those golden eyes were steady and clear. "Please, Annabelle. Go. Be safe. Find friends. Learn to fight. And then come back and save this place. Save our home."

Annabelle shook her head, tears blurring the sight of his beautiful face, his precious face. "I c—can't," she moaned, crying in earnest now. "I can't d—do it without you."

Charlie smiled, cupping her face in one hand. "You can, and you will," he said, and then he kissed her.

She drank in his kiss, clinging to him, holding him upright, willing her power to rise up and fix this, fix him. But there was no response, no fire, no flicker of life. Everything inside of her was empty and cold.

Then strong arms looped around her waist, dragging her away. "*No!*" she screamed. "Charlie!"

Sam deposited Annabelle into the boat, where Mica wrapped his arms around her and held her as she tried to get free, tried to claw her way back to the riverbank, back to Charlie. She would die with him; she didn't care.

And then she heard it—what they all must have heard while she was too distracted by her entire world falling to pieces: the sound of horns, the barking of dogs, and the shouts of men.

"I'll lead them away from you," Charlie said to Sam. "It's the least I can do. You would have had time if I hadn't been so sloppy."

"Don't say that friend," Sam said, gripping Charlie's arm. "We would not have made it without you."

"Get her to safety," Charlie said, and released Sam's grip. "I'll do the rest."

"It has been an honor soldier" Sam said after he'd helped Charlie into his saddle and handed him the lead to the other horse.

"The honor has been mine Sir," Charlie said, inclining his head respectfully.

This was too horrible. Annabelle thought she would shatter into a thousand tiny pieces from pain and terror. Sam clambered into the boat, exchanging words with Eddie, but Annabelle could not have dragged her gaze from Charlie if every life in her kingdom depended on it. His golden eyes met hers, and he stared as if he could drink the sight of her like a tonic.

As Eddie steered the boat into the river's current, Annabelle let Mica pass her off to Sam without protest. He clasped her trembling hands in his, rubbing them. Odd. When had she begun to shake? Annabelle hardly cared. There was nothing else in the entire world except for Charlie—the softness of his face and mouth, the glint of starlight in his eyes, the way his hair fell in waves to his neck, swinging in the breeze as he tipped his face toward the heavens.

He let loose a battle cry, and Annabelle saw the façade of the kind and handsome farmer's son fall to the ground like an unclasped cloak, as Charlie Rabbold, soldier of his majesty's army, gave his horse a swift kick and galloped off into the night.

Chapter Thirty-Four

There was no time to grieve—to lay down and give herself to the darkness that had already sunk its talons deep into her heart. The hoofbeats and the city bells faded, replaced by a low thundering rumble growing ever closer.

Sam released his grip on Annabelle's hands only long enough to unroll a blanket and hold it out to her.

"I don't need it," she said, waving him off. "Give it to Mica. His clothes are barely more than rags."

"There are plenty of blankets for everyone," Sam said, stone-faced as he forced the heavy material around her shoulders. "This boat ride is about to get very wet, and you need to keep warm."

Annabelle did not inform him that she would likely never feel warm or alive again, but she accepted the blanket without further protest. The roaring sound was growing louder with each moment, and Annabelle remembered that her ordeal was not over.

The first rapids were small. Eddie maneuvered the slender boat between the clusters of rocks with little visible effort or concern. Even so, a considerable amount of icy river water splashed over the edge of the boat and onto its passengers, and Annabelle was grateful for the blanket that Sam had foisted upon her.

The second rapids looked like a pot boiling over with water, and Annabelle gripped Sam so tightly as they rolled and crashed between the rocks that her arms burned with the effort by the time their little boat was once again gliding across smooth water.

This break between rapids was so long that Annabelle believed for a moment that the worst might be behind them. Then they rounded a bend in the river, and she cried out, leaning back in her seat as if she could reverse the very flow of the river by sheer will alone.

"It's alright," Sam said soothingly. "Eddie has navigated these rapids countless times and never once wrecked."

"Yet," Eddie chimed in unhelpfully. But he grinned, and Annabelle decided to keep her eyes on him instead of the water around her. She would not give herself permission to panic before he did. Charlie had given his life to get them this far, and she would be brave now, for him.

The thought pained her like a knife in the gut, but she held onto it all the same. The pain drove away the fear as the nose of the boat plunged into the angry foaming river, toward the towers of rocks that jutted up from the water like the jagged jaws of a monster just waiting to bite down and crush them all to bits.

But Sam had not lied. Eddie maneuvered the vessel with nimble skill, finding the pockets of safe water and easing the narrow boat between rocks at the last minute, just when Annabelle had decided they were done for. Watching Eddie, Annabelle was reminded of the musicians at the palace, the conductor moving and waving his baton in time to the music—shaping the flow of the river even as he was carried away upon its waters.

"Annabelle…Annabelle!"

The urgency in Sam's voice brought her screaming back to the moment, looking around the boat, frantic. What now? What else could possibly have gone wrong?

Her gaze fell on Mica, who was gripping the sodden blanket around his thin shoulders and shaking violently, his teeth chattering and clacking so loudly she was afraid they would crack.

The water was too cold. She had known it was too cold, and yet she had allowed Sam to hold her close and to keep her warm even though Mica was the one who was too thin, too weak. Mica was the one who was skin wrapped loosely around bones. She had been loved, cared for, admired, adored. He had been alone, and now he would die.

Annabelle sat next to Mica and wrapped her blanket around them both, pressing her body close against his.

"I'm f—fine princess," he stammered, hardly able to form the words he was shaking so badly.

"You are not fine," she said evenly, "and I will help you. Let me help you."

Sam joined her on Mica's other side, and they clung to each other as the little boat crashed and bucked in the rapids, new waves of water hurling and splattering across their faces, slapping painfully against their freezing skin. But they held on, to each other, to the edges of the boat, and soon there was no roaring. There was no heaving and tipping of the boat. There was only the soft lapping of the water against the hull and the sound of creaking wood as Eddie steered them down the river and to safety at last.

༄༄●𝄔𝄔𝄔

The little boat had made it through the rapids with all passengers still aboard, and it now glided smoothly out into a wide bay. The delta had nearly claimed them, but they had made it to the ocean. Sam was more relieved than he would ever admit to his companions.

Nobody but Eddie could have seen them through those rapids in one piece. Though Eddie didn't generally trade in living cargo. The extra weight alone had put them at significant risk, Sam knew. Sam knew the risks, but he also knew the risk of playing it safe. It would be days before any search would think to follow the river to the delta. By then, they would be long gone.

There had always been the chance that, even if they survived the rapids, Emily wouldn't make it to the ship in time, that they would sail into the bay to find it empty.

When the rigging and tall masts came into view, Sam nearly cried aloud with happiness. So many pieces to the puzzle, so many things could have gone wrong—and they did go wrong, so very, very wrong—and yet the mission had been a success. He had gotten Annabelle and Mica to the ship alive. But the cost had been too steep.

This way of thinking would not serve. It was over. Charlie was a grown man who had chosen his death. How many soldiers could say the same? Sam would not give in to the temptation to play the game of what might have been. There was no winning that game, only losing, painfully, each time.

They were pulling close to the ship now, and Sam could see distant smudges running back and forth across the deck, making preparations for their departure. A group huddled by the rail, gesturing. Sam squinted to try to make them out.

There. The small figure, hair blowing in the breeze, had to be Emily. And that broad shadow beside her…could that be Raphael? Sam's traitorous heartbeat quickened.

The ship itself was small and simple but well-maintained. Crisp lines of red paint declared her name: *Featherdancer.*

Eddie let out a low whistle. "Well, I'll be the Gods' fool. Ye didn't tell me the ship belonged to Neal Featherer."

Sam turned to him and lifted an eyebrow. "Is that a problem?"

"No," Eddie chuckled. "Only I'm impressed, Fisher. That man's harder to pin down than the wind these days."

Sam was well aware. Ilya had made Sam trade away everything short of his soul in exchange for this most valuable of her connections. "Yes, he is," was all he said.

When Eddie pulled the boat up broadside against the side of the ship, Annabelle scrambled up the ladder first, leaning over the side to bring Mica up after her. As they both vanished over the edge, he could hear the princess already barking commands.

"He needs a change of clothes, warm ones." Her words carried to him on the breeze. "Food, too. And fresh water."

Smiling to himself, Sam turned to Eddie, holding out a purse bulging with coin. The smuggler's eyes widened at the sight of it, but he did not take it.

"To buy my silence?" he asked.

"No," Sam replied. "To pay you for services rendered."

Eddie took the purse and weighed it in his hand. "If you say so, Fisher. Either way, I thank you."

"Take care of yourself, Eddie," Sam said and took hold of the ladder.

"Always do." Eddie waited for Sam to clamber onto the deck before tipping his hat and pushing his little boat back toward the shore.

Sam scanned the deck. His friends were nowhere to be seen—probably gone below deck to see to the prince. And Annabelle would be telling Emily about Charlie, he realized. Best to leave them to it. He went in search of the captain.

He found Neal Featherer on the aft deck by the helm, overseeing his men as they made preparations to take sail. In the flesh, the legendary Captain Featherer was a bit of a surprise—younger than Sam had imagined, perhaps only forty, forty-five years of age. He wore a belt of knives, and his dark hair and beard were cropped short.

"Sir Sam Fisher, I presume," the captain said, extending a weathered and calloused hand.

"I don't know if I've a right to call myself 'Sir' anymore," Sam said, shaking the man's hand. "Sam will do well enough."

The captain gave him an appraising look. "Ilya mentioned you were an unusual sort of fellow," he said.

Sam grinned. "Coming from her, I'll consider that a compliment. She is an unusual sort of lady."

"Aye, that she is." The captain said, grinning wolfishly. When Sam did not return his smile, he asked, "I trust that your companions are settling in below?"

"I believe they are," Sam replied. "I will join them in a moment. I thought it best that you and I meet properly first."

"I appreciate the gesture," the captain said. "But you need not worry. Miss Emily and the commander have filled me in on everything I need to know. The rest is your business. As long as you let my men do their work and trust me to read the wind and the sea, we will drop anchor at our final destination without incident."

"Good," Sam nodded. "Then we agree."

"Sail's up soon," Featherer said before taking his leave. "If I were you, I'd pop below and warn your friends they're about to miss one hell of a show."

Sam highly doubted that his friends would care, not with reunions to be made and tears of grief to be shed. But he bowed his acknowledgment all the same.

Sam did not go below, not just yet. Instead, he walked to the rail at the back of the stern and looked out toward land. Dunea had not been a home to him—not the way a home was supposed to be. It had been a place to survive, a place to strive and to sweat and to earn every last scrap of anything he had to his name.

But in all that time, in all those years training and begging and fighting, what had he really achieved? Could it have been all that important if it was so easy to leave it all behind now? Could it have mattered all that much if those titles and accomplishments would not follow him where he was bound? And did it make him the most horrible person in the world that, even despite the hardships he had faced there, and despite everything this place had tried to take from him, from Raphael and Mica, from Annabelle, he was sad to leave?

A massive hand closed around Sam's upper arm, and he tensed on instinct, ready to strike. But there was no attacker, nobody to be feared here upon the *Featherdancer*. Sam was finally among friends. He relaxed, allowing Raphael to pull him into a rib-cracking embrace.

"Thank you," Raphael's voice was hoarse with emotion. "Thank you for saving him; for saving them both."

Sam tried to shrug but couldn't. Raphael was pinning his arms to his sides. "It was the only thing to do," he said instead.

Raphael's laughed wetly, pulling away to wipe his streaming eyes. "I won't argue because I know you see it that way. So I will only say this: my cousin owes you his life, Annabelle owes you her life, and I owe you my life. These are facts, Sam."

"Charlie…" It was painful to say his name. Sam tried again. "Charlie…"

"Annabelle told us what happened to him," Raphael cut in gently. "But Charlie was a grown man. You knew that back at the riverbank, and you know it now. You will never be able to save everyone, and if you start keeping a tally of the ones you lose now, it will drown you."

"I know," Sam replied after a moment, deflating a bit. "You're right. It's just…now is the hard part."

"It's all the hard part."

That was undoubtedly true. "How is Emily?" Sam asked.

Raphael's expression was grave as he said, "Grieving. Annabelle is with her now."

As long as he lived, Sam doubted he would ever know how Annabelle found the bravery to be such a good friend.

"The lass will be alright," Raphael said soothingly when Sam continued to look miserable.

"How can she be?" Sam asked, staring at Raphael in disbelief. "She has lost the last family she had left."

"She may feel that way now," Raphael acquiesced, leaning against the railing and sighing deeply. "She may feel that way for a long while yet. But she will discover that she has not lost the last of her family. She has Annabelle and you and me." He paused. "But I wasn't speaking about Emily."

Sam loosed a long breath. "Annabelle…Gods, I pray she will be alright, eventually."

"She will be."

"How do you know?"

"I don't know. It's just a feeling." Raphael's grin was slow and lazy, his eyes sparkling in the dawn light as he said, "But I'm definitely going to stick around, just to find out how this all turns out."

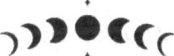

Annabelle didn't leave the tiny cabin that she shared with Emily for two days. She heard the sounds of the sailors shouting, the cries of "Anchors aweigh" and "raise the mainsail," and felt the movement as the wind began to propel the ship through the water. Some deep piece of her soul yearned to be above, to see the vessel under full sail, to watch as land finally vanished into the mist behind them. But she could not move.

Telling Emily that her brother, the last living member of her family, was likely dead—fallen in the rescue attempt that saved hers and Mica's lives—was the single hardest thing Annabelle had ever had to do. But she knew she had to be the one to do it. Those words should never be heard in a stranger's voice.

Emily had borne it well, all things considered. She and Annabelle held each other and cried until they fell asleep together on Annabelle's bunk. There they had remained, huddled in that small cabin with their enormous grief and pain, leaning against each other in order to survive.

Sam brought them meals, which Annabelle forced herself to eat, but otherwise, the others left the two women alone.

The next day, Emily had ventured above deck, feeling the need for some fresh air to combat a slight case of seasickness. She urged Annabelle to accompany her, but Annabelle refused.

Hopelessness pinned her to her bunk, weighing her limbs down. It had been her final surge of strength, leaving Charlie behind, keeping Mica alive, being there for Emily. Now her work was done, the others were safe, and Annabelle was free to fade away into nothing.

On the second day, the door to the cabin opened, and Annabelle cringed away from the sudden flood of light.

"Emily shut the door," she muttered into the blankets, her voice muffled.

"Get up, Annabelle."

It was not Emily who had spoken. This voice was deeper. It struck something, some memory inside her heart, tracing along the grooves that love had once carved there. She brought the blankets away from her face.

Mica stood in the doorway, sunlight casting his too-thin frame in shadow.

"Mica?" Annabelle blinked. "What—"

"Get up, Annabelle," he repeated pleasantly. "It's a lovely afternoon. Get dressed and meet me at the bow of the ship. Now."

And he closed the door to the cabin with a snap.

Annabelle should have ignored him. She should have rolled over and gone back to sleep. Instead, she hurled herself groggily from bed and set about searching for something to wear.

She found clothes in a trunk that was shoved under her bunk—her things from the farm, she realized. Raphael must have brought them in his saddlebags. Annabelle selected one of her soft cotton dresses and slipped into it, trying not to think about how much Charlie had liked it. She needed to get up, get dressed, and go above deck into the rest of the world. She must not think of Charlie.

Minutes later, Annabelle stood upon the deck of the ship, blinking in the warm afternoon sunlight. The deck was a maze of ropes, winches, and people. She wound her way up the worn wooden planks, trying to return the pleasant greetings of the crew. It felt strange to smile. It felt strange to exchange words with people. It felt strange to walk and to breathe.

She found Mica, as he had promised, at the bow. The crashing sound of the ship carving its path through the waves was loudest here. Annabelle could feel the sound battering against her, wearing her down, urging her to bend, to soften, to break.

"You made it," Mica said cheerily when she came to stand beside him.

He looked…he didn't look *better*, really. It would take time for him to regain his full weight and muscle. But there was color in his face, which was shaven once again, and someone had furnished him with a clean shirt, trousers, and boots.

"You look well," Annabelle observed. Her voice sounded harsh and flat in her ears.

Mica's smile did not falter. "I feel well—well and lucky to be alive."

Annabelle snorted derisively and then instantly felt ashamed.

"I'm sorry," she said quickly. "I just…I don't feel lucky. I don't feel much of anything at the moment except tired."

He nodded understandingly. "Come stand by the rail with me."

Annabelle did as he asked. The setting sun gleamed blue and silver and gold upon the water. It hurt to look at. Annabelle lowered her gaze to her hands, gripping the rail.

"Look up, please, Annabelle," Mica said softly.

"Why?"

Tears pricked Annabelle's eyes. She couldn't do what he asked.

"We do not know each other very well," Mica said. "Not like you know Sam, or I know Raphael. But there is one thing that I understand about you, Annabelle."

Annabelle kept her eyes down toward her hands, but she wasn't really seeing them anymore. She was listening to Mica's voice. It was a pleasant sound, and it didn't hurt.

"I don't pretend to be an expert on people," Mica continued, "Raphael will be the first to tell you that. But I know the sea. I know what it is to love the sea. You love the sea. This water—the depth and the power, the wind and the salt air—has magic, and you feel that magic. It reaches down into the core of your body and brings you to life. You are drawn to it as I am. You are not whole unless you can taste the tang of brine on your tongue."

Annabelle could no longer see her hands at all. Tears were gathering in her eyes, falling upon the wood of the railing. She said nothing about this, and neither did Mica. He continued.

"I don't know the first thing about your power or about how you feel right now. But I do know one thing: if you turn away from the sea, you turn away from her ability to heal you—to bring you back to life. Let her. Please."

"I can't," Annabelle whispered, tears rolling down her cheeks now. "It hurts too much to look."

"Then don't look," Mica suggested. "The ocean is not out there; she is all around you. She is on the air you breathe and the sounds you hear. If you cannot look, then feel."

And even though she feared she might burst through the fragile boundary of her skin, exploding into nothing but fire and pain and grief and fear, Annabelle took one, deep breath.

The ocean came rushing in, borne on the wave of her breath. It poured down into her chest, filling her aching heart, traveling down her tired and heavy limbs, cleansing and cooling where it touched the sore spots, the darkest places. Annabelle sobbed, letting her tears run free, expelling the numbness along to the rhythm of the waves crashing against the bow of the ship.

She felt it all, everything she had been hiding from, trapped in that tiny cabin below—the loss of her mother, her father's betrayal, the hope she had felt when she looked into Charlie's eyes, the yawning chasm of grief when that hope was ripped away. She felt a yearning for a place that wanted her, a place to belong, a yearning for home.

The crashing of the waves, the heavy depths of the ocean, and the salt on the air all swept through Annabelle, dislodging the festering black sores that had become her insides, leaving raw flesh in its wake, soothing the angry wounds, falling away just as suddenly as it had come.

But something had changed. The grief and pain were still there, still horribly real, but they had not drowned her. She was alive and standing. And she could bear them now, these wounds. They would eventually heal, and maybe they would scar. That was, Annabelle knew now, the cost of loving.

When she opened her eyes at last, she was startled to see that Mica was no longer standing beside her. He had pushed her to feel and had left her to be alone with her pain. She was grateful to him for it.

Annabelle turned her gaze to the horizon, her eyes once again dazzled by the intensity of the sun and sea but no longer burned by it. Healing would take time, but there were miles of sea still to cross. The waves would carry her away from the past that had gnawed on her body and heart until she was nothing but shards and broken pieces. The waves would carry her across the horizon to her future.

A future, Annabelle prayed, where she might once again become whole.

Acknowledgments

Even as I'm typing these words, I cannot believe that I am. Writing this book has been a dream of mine for as long as I can remember. Now that it is a reality, I am swamped with gratitude for every person who has helped bring this dream to life.

First and foremost, I have to thank my parents for their undying faith that I can do anything I set my mind to. Thank you for giving me life; thank you for giving me your strength and humor; thank you for giving me the gift of stories and the freedom to tell them.

To my husband, my partner in crime, and my partner in outlining: none of this beautiful life of ours happens without you. You are my leading man. I love you so deeply.

To Kyle & Jake — your support and encouragement mean the world to me. I cannot do any of this without knowing that you've got my back. Know that I always have yours.

Suzanne Bellavista, my fairy godmother. Thank you for being so patient and so kind, and sitting with me in my darkest moments when this dream did not seem possible. Thank you for always knowing that it was not only possible, but inevitable. I don't have any of this without your support and guidance.

To David Rich. Thank you for teaching me how langauge works, lives, and breathes. I endeavored to infuse my work with the sublime. I hope to have done you proud in the end.

Sue Nestor, thank you for your encouragement and support. I love you so much. Thank you.

David Dell. If I am the Queen, then you must be the Sage. I bow to you, sir.

Steve Treat & Josh Levine — this book is the kind of magic that happens as a direct result of the work we all do together. You're the best. Thank you for your steadfast guidance.

To my sisters (in-law is just a detail at this point) Kailey Shuhan & Kristina Endler. Thank you for being my unofficial reading & marketing team. Also thank you for putting up with me fishing for compliments any time I'm feeling a little fearful & fragile (which is often). I love you!

A big, big thank you to Thérèse Plummer, Marisa Calin, and everyone at CDM Studios. You guys put together a wonderful production. Thank you from the bottom of my heart. You cannot know what this means to me to have such a rockin audiobook!

Thena Lindhorst — thank you for championing my book, and being such a wonderful friend and professional resource! I cherish you.

Kelsey Phariss...there are no words. You have become an irreplaceable partner-in-crime. I cannot wait to see where our work together goes. I know it will be magical. Thank you for believing in me.

To Susan Taylor: your thoughtful critiques and profound encouragement saw me across the finish line, and I cannot thank you enough.

Last but never, ever least—to my grandfather, who appears in this book in the form of the friendly librarian with the clear blue eyes. Thank you for passing down your poet's heart to me. I love you.

Writing can often feel like such a solitary activity, and it can be— especially when working on a first novel that often spends years existing only in one head and heart before the first words are put to paper. Sharing this book with the world has been the most wonderful and humbling experience. And so I thank you, dearest reader, for going on this adventure with me and with Annabelle. A book is not a book without someone to read it. You are precious.

To all the countless others—my family, friends, and teachers—this book belongs to all of you; this book does not exist without *all* of you. Thank you. We friggin did it!!!

$\mathcal{A}$nnie Westphal is an author, award-winning translator, and fairy tale scholar. Annabelle is her debut novel (and COVID baby). Book two in the series, *The Lost Princess*, is slated for release Summer 2024.